Best Laid Plans

Pineview University Series

DB Jacobson

ISBN-13: 9798994214817
ISBN-10: 1477123456

Cover design by: DB Jacobson
Character art: DB Jacobson
Library of Congress Control Number: 2018675309
Printed in the United States of America

Table of Contents

Welcome to

Pineview University

Congratulations on your acceptance to Boulder's own D1 school. We are so pleased you have decided to join us in furthering your studies and education!

As a student at Pineview, you may enjoy the firsthand account experiences from several of our best and brightest.

We hope you enjoy your time spent at Pineview and with all her students.

The Best Laid Plans focuses on two Pineview's favorite students: Ava Reiser and Henry Foust.

Henry is the secret dominant who is recovering from a violent attack that ended his cousin's career before it even started. He's been busy trying to cope with the guilt of the attack and healing from a concussion. He refuses to do anything that would jeopardize his friendships with the very people that saved his life.

Ava is Will's half-sister and wants to escape the abusive shadow of her mother and sister. A little white lie to her parents about what school she is attending, and she can live her own life and be closer to Will.

Being only eighteen and doing everything on her own means she didn't know she needed to sign up for student housing. Luckily Will and Lily would never allow Ava to be homeless, so they set her up with a place to stay.

The problem? Her roommate is Henry, and he is without a doubt the most gorgeous man she has ever met. It makes matters worse she's 'off limits' but that doesn't stop her from crushing on her brother's friend.

Best Laid Plans is a steamy college romance. Tropes: brother's friend, roommates, forced proximity, dom/sub, first time.

Trigger Warnings:

Contains sexual content, mentions of narcissistic abuse (off scene), parental neglect (off scene), drug and alcohol use, infidelity (off scene), and depression and anxiety.

No spoilers, but if slang terms for penises and vaginas trigger you, this book may not be for you. It's plot forward, but it's an open-door romance. Sex happens, especially when one of the main characters has serious dom tendencies.

Lastly, Ava is eighteen. She makes the same mistakes that any older teen would make. She is a little more mature than your average eighteen-year-old, but still has her whole life to live and learn from her mistakes.

Prologue

Ava

Age 7 ½

"I've got bad news, Ava Darling," my mom cooed to me.

That was how she started every conversation whenever she was trying to let me down gently. Discarding my favorite book, I looked up to my beautiful mom.

Her makeup made her brown eyes look like caramel. Her shiny dark hair was straight down her back. In comparison to all to my friends' moms, she was the prettiest mom in my entire school, maybe the world.

My dad could barely keep his hands to himself. He was always kissing my mom and telling her how beautiful she was. It was gross. But I would never say that out loud. My mom would get mad when I pointed out how uncomfortable it made me that they kissed all the time.

My lumpy throat swallowed thickly. Christmas was next week, and her bad news must have been tied to that. All I wanted for Christmas was to spend the day with my dad. But it was on Saturday this year, so he had to work. I didn't know what he did, but every Friday morning he would leave and not come home until Monday night.

"Well, it's double bad news, really," my mom amended. Her warm brown eyes flashed at me.

"What?" I braced for disappointment.

"It turns out that your father cannot spend Christmas with you this year. Your birthday is also on a Saturday, so you won't get to spend the day with him then either, unfortunately."

My chin quivered. "But I don't understand. If he knows now maybe he can ask to stay home from work."

She huffed and gripped my cheeks hard with her thumb and pointer. Her nails pinched the skin as my lips puckered together.

"If you want him home Christmas morning and for your birthday then you are going to have to ask him yourself."

My eyes pricked from how hard she was pinching my face. I nodded. She smiled at me, showing too many of her straight white teeth. "Get your dress on, or we are going to be late."

I ran to my bedroom that I shared with my sister Daphne. She had pushed my twin bed into our shared closet, wanting the room to herself. I was scared of sleeping in my new space because it was too dark in there.

Daphne was at her friend's house, so I was able to turn all the lights on in our room and flung the closet door wide open. I stood on my bed and reached for the red and black checkered dress my mom had bought for me.

We were going to my dad's annual holiday party that his company hosted. It was one of my favorite days of the year. All the families at his company would come and every child would get to select a present from the Christmas tree. My brother Jacob had selected a Nintendo DS last year. It was so cool, but he wouldn't let me play with it. Daphne had selected a Vera Bradley backpack that she had wanted. I wasn't able to go last year because I was sick, so I was extra excited about being able to go this year.

With my dress on Daph's bed, I attempted to comb my long hair. My brush tangled and stuck to the hairs at the nape of my neck. Tears pricked my eyes. My mom was never gentle when brushing my hair. She made sure my ballerina buns were slicked back and so tight it hurt. I pulled my dress on and hoped that the brush that was dangling down my shoulders was hidden.

Tiptoeing across the hall, I glanced towards my parents' bedroom and knocked on Jacob's door. He was much older than me, having just turned fourteen. He scowled as he opened his door but softened his expression on me. "Thought you were Daph. What do you want, Ava Bear?"

My teeth gnashed my lip, and I stared behind at our parent's room again in our three-bedroom apartment.

"I need help," I whispered.

Jacob sighed and looked down the hall before letting me in his room. I turned around and showed him the brush that was pulling my head back.

He chuckled. "Ava, mom is going to be pissed."

Emotions burned my nose. "Can you please help me and get it out?"

He groaned and walked over to his television and gaming system to turn them both off. "Sit." He pointed to the floor at the foot of his bed.

Moving my hair this way and that, a few sharp tugs made me wince and whimper.

"Sorry, it's really stuck. Hold on, okay?" he whispered.

Another five minutes passed before he was able to free the brush. Gathering the long ends, he started rhythmically brushing through the tangles. It was something he had learned from our mom. For as long as I could remember he would brush our mom's hair. She said that Jacob was the reason why her hair was so shiny.

He flicked my ear when he was done. "Okay, all done, now go away."

I turned around and scowled at him. "You're so mean."

"And you're a pest."

My nose wrinkled as I stuck my tongue out at him and made my way back to my room to look for my shoes.

"Why aren't you dressed?" my mom said from the hallway.

Oh, no.

I held my breath, she sounded annoyed. My heart started beating hard. An annoyed mom could mean she wouldn't take us to the party. And I needed to go to this party. It was the only way I had a hope of getting the American Girl Doll I had been wanting for months.

"I'm not going," Jacob said. His voice cracked and settled into a deeper tone. It was weird that he was taller than our Mom and Dad. He looked more and more like our dad every day. He was the only one in the family with blond hair, just like him.

"When did you make this decision?" My mom's voice was full of warning. It was the same tone she used with me when I refused to eat my smashed peas. I couldn't get past the texture and she forced me to sit at the dinner table until bed time. Smashed peas served as my breakfast the next day.

"When I discovered that I have a brother, and Dad has a whole other life. I don't want to go."

"Who told you?" my mom hissed.

My heart pounded frantically.

I had another brother?

I hoped he was as nice as Jacob. I wondered where he had been hiding my whole life. Was he older than me or younger?

"We go to school together, mom. We have PE during the same period. Did you not think I wouldn't wonder why a kid with my last name looks exactly like me? I asked him if we were related, and he said his parents didn't have any brothers or sisters. I asked him what his dad's name is."

"Did you tell him you had the same father?" She was calm and happy. I didn't hear my brother say anything. She hummed in response.

"It's probably for the best that you found out anyway. I have a feeling things are going to change, and everything will be out in the open soon."

The front door to our apartment slammed shut. My shoulders touched my ears.

"Mom, I'm home. Lucy wants to spend the night tonight."

A soft whimper escaped my throat. Daphne's best friend Lucy was mean. Last time she spent the night, she locked me in the closet and didn't let me out until morning. I was so scared I wet the bed. Mom yelled at me for an hour and taught me how to do the laundry.

My pulse hummed in my ears. Maybe Jacob would let me hide in his room tonight.

"Of course, dear. How are you today, Lucy?"

My heart was beating too loud to hear Lucy's response.

Maybe my new brother would help protect me from Lucy. If he went to school with Jacob, it meant he was older than me. I could use another protector. I hoped he liked me.

"Well, your brother decided at the last minute that he didn't want to go to the party today. Are you planning on attending?"

"Do I have to? It's so boring and I'm getting too old for the childish toys they give away," Daphne whined.

My mom scoffed. "I personally shopped for the majority of those presents. I know for a fact that the purse you want is under that tree with your name on it."

"Why didn't you say so? Yes, I'll go." Daphne sighed.

Her footsteps slapped against the tile as she walked down the hallway towards our room. My breaths were coming in stuttering pants. The last thing I needed was for Daphne and Lucy to corner me.

I stepped into the hallway. "I'm ready, mom." I said as calmly as I could.

Daphne tilted her head and crossed her arms as Lucy gave me her mean-spirited smile.

"Were you spying?" Daphne hissed. Her lip curled showing off her silver braces. I shook my head as my knees clacked together.

My mom poked her head in the hallway from her bedroom. "Ava Darling, I need your help."

A sigh of relief pulled my cheeks, and I followed my mom's voice into her bedroom. She held up two dresses. "Which one do you like better?"

Heart still racing, I breathed slowly. "I like the red one."

My mom preened and nodded. "Your father bought that for me last week."

My small fingers pulled the delicate zipper of her dress, and I bent over to clasp the buckle of her high heels. They were the same ones that I got in trouble for trying on and walking around the house in.

Jacob didn't go, leaving me to fend for myself. His attendance meant he would protect me from Lucy and Daphne. He always did. Without him, I was on my own.

As soon as we pulled up to the building my dad owned, Daphne and Lucy got out giggling about some cute boy that they could see by the entrance. He had blond hair and looked too much like Jacob for my liking. He was Lucy's age, a year younger than Daphne, and had a few classes with him.

My mom helped me out of the car and smoothed my hair. Her nails scraped against my scalp as she finger-combed my tresses. I was grateful that Jacob had already taken care of all the tangles.

She knelt to be eye level with me. "Listen to me, Ava Darling. If you want your father home for Christmas and your birthday then you must ask him yourself. But it will only work if he is talking to a tall, brown-haired woman. What you will need to do is run up to him and hug him really big."

I shook my head. "But Daddy said he doesn't want the other kids to treat us differently and they would if they knew he was my daddy. I'm not supposed to hug him while he's at work." I tried to explain it like Dad had explained it to me. I didn't want to disappoint my dad by not listening.

My mom's smile widened, and she gripped my cheeks again. "Ava, you are his daughter. He won't be upset with you for giving him a big Christmas hug. Besides, I promise you, if you ask him to spend Christmas with you and you ask him right in front of the tall woman you will get your dad for Christmas. Actually, I'll make sure you get him every day of the week."

My eyes widened. "No more traveling?"

She shook her head. "No more traveling. He won't miss another weekend away again. And then he'll buy us a big house, and you'll get your own room."

Tingles spread in my stomach at the thought of not sharing a room with Daphne. "I'm so excited to surprise him with a big Christmas hug."

Spoiler alert, he wasn't happy with my Christmas hug. That little action crumbled his carefully crafted double life. It wasn't until I was 15 that I realized my mom had set me up. She denied telling me to go and hug him in front of his wife, Charlotte, and call him daddy. She denies it to this day calling it a child's illusion, but I know the truth. I, Ava Marie Reiser, was Kimaya Sofia Gentilozzi's pawn in a fourteen-year-old game of chess. She won with a simple move of sacrificing me to put the king in checkmate. She was right about one thing though; he was home every weekend after that.

Henry

Age 14

"How was swim practice, mon canard?"

It was a question my mom asked me every single day. I was a competitive swimmer, so I had practice five days a week. And when I wasn't practicing, I was in our pool at home. We lived in Colorado Springs, so it wasn't practical to swim daily, but that didn't stop my dad from building an indoor pool on our property.

My parents had Olympic hopes for me. I wanted the same, but the constant practices were starting to make me dislike the sport. Most of the time it was a much-needed release of energy for my ADHD. But when I had a competition coming up, it was a burden. My parents cared too much whether I won or lost.

She combed her fingers through my wet hair. I loved it when she scratched my head, but I didn't want her to know that.

I shrugged with all the boredom of any fourteen-year-old boy. "It was fine. Coach Jasmine was a little tough on me, but Dad straightened her out."

My mom scowled. She had been away for the past week visiting my aunt in Seattle. "How was she a little tough on you?"

"I was slow off the block. She made me swim extra laps while she and Dad disappeared in her office. She told me to swim until they were done. I think they fought pretty hard about it because I swam for an extra thirty minutes."

My mom's fingers were frozen in my hair. "Your père disappeared in Jasmine's office for thirty minutes while you swam today?"

A yawn vibrated my ears and I nodded, walking over to the kitchen pantry to look for some food. Hunger was a constant but especially after swim practice.

"Yeah, I think she hit him in the mouth because his lips were all red when he came out. But they worked out their differences because Coach Jasmine was smiling and told me I did a good job today."

I grabbed a box of cereal and stuck my hand inside to fish out the marshmallows. My mom didn't notice to me spoiling my appetite. She looked like she was going to be sick to her stomach, looking down to the table with a furrowed brow and cupping her mouth.

"You okay, Maman?" I set down the box.

She nodded stiffly. "Does your père have to talk to Jasmine often?"

My head wagged from side to side, and I stuck my hand in for another grab of cereal before she stopped me. "Yeah, basically every practice."

She let out a slow choppy breath. "Can you do me a favor?"

I shoved my contraband into my mouth and nodded.

"Don't tell your père you told me that, oui?"

"Okay. How's Aunt Genevieve?"

She blinked rapidly and gave me a forced smile. "She's good. She missed you, and your cousin Weston wished you had come too."

My lip curled. West was sort of weird. He was into reading books and science to the point of being a nerd. I couldn't have a normal conversation with him because he only wanted to talk about Star Trek.

I much preferred my cousin Matt who lived in Tempe. His dad and my dad are brothers, and I see him more often. He was also normal. We could talk about baseball and play around. He was a little older than me, but I didn't care. He was like the brother I always wanted.

"Don't make that face. You wait til you are older, and you'll appreciate that Weston is a little different than you."

"If you say so."

The buzzing need to move gripped my brain. The hour and a half of swimming didn't take the urge to climb the walls away. My fingers tapped my thigh.

My mom tracked the movements and scoffed when she finally saw the cereal. "Henry Cole Foust, did you shovel sugar directly into your mouth?" She cursed in French and shook her head at me.

I snickered and nodded.

"Ugh, it would be faster if you main lined it. You, of all people, do not need anything to give yourself more energy."

I bounced on the balls of my feet as she pulled the box of cereal away with a huff. "I swear to God, mon canard, you aren't going to be able to sleep tonight. I don't want you to swim to burn this energy off. Why don't you go ride your bike. Dinner will be ready in an hour."

I nodded too fast and bounced from the kitchen into the living room. My dad was sitting at his desk when I passed by his office.

"You look like you're still amped up."

I thumbed towards the garage. "I'm going to get on my mountain bike."

He chuckled and went back to his work.

We lived on the top of a hill. The cold breeze on my face made me grin as I went down the road as fast as I could. It calmed my brain down from the buzzing as I pedaled my legs faster. I took a small goat trail that led to the back of a neighborhood. My legs pumped faster as the valley approached. I loved the weightless feeling I would get from the divot.

My friend Dan was up ahead, sitting on a swing. I slowed my bike down. Dan was two years older than me, but he knew me from the swim team. I had always been fast and tall, so I competed in his heat.

"Sup Fousty," he said when I stopped in front of him.

My breathing was barely elevated as I shrugged. "Nothing, feeling too hyper my maman made me bike it off before dinner."

He grinned at me. "You're like the Energizer Bunny, bro."

I shrugged again. "Can't help it. My maman says it's how I'm wired."

Dan lifted his hands. "I get it, my brother was the same way."

His brother, Kyle, was the coolest guy in school. He was a senior in high school, captain of the football team, and had the prettiest girlfriend I had ever seen in my life. She had long black hair, brown eyes, and the face of a doll. Her name was Olivia Gracen, and she held the standard of beauty in my mind.

My lip curled. "He doesn't seem like he bounces off the walls to me."

Dan laughed. "My parents made him take medicine to help. He hated how it made him feel, but he found something that works for him."

"Yeah, my dad tried to medicate me too. I hated it. What does your brother take?"

Dan pulled a little baggie of gummy bears out of his pocket. "He eats one of these a day. He says it helps him sleep and calms his brain down."

I curled my lip. "Candy has the opposite effect on me."

Dan chuckled. "It's not candy. They're edibles. Try one." He opened the bag.

My fingers pinched one out. A shudder of disgust vibrated my shoulders. "I think the sugar went bad." My face cringed at the bitter aftertaste.

Dan shook his head. "Nope, that's how it's supposed to taste. Anyway, sit down, it'll chill you out if you are feeling hyper."

With my bike propped up against the slide, I sat on the swing next to him. My legs pumped until I had good momentum. Dan stayed still next to me, grinning as I swung higher and higher.

"Let me know when it hits," he said on the downswing.

"When what hits?" My swing was cresting to be as high as the bar, and then my brain down shifted. I don't know how else to describe it. The buzzing energy that told me to go and never stop slowed down. My shoulders relaxed, I hadn't realized how much I was flexing my body. My legs pumped slower.

"There it is." Dan watched as my momentum brought me to a leisurely swing.

My feet dragged grooves into the bark that lined the park. "Whoa, it's quiet."

Dan chuckled and nodded. "Welcome to what everyone else experiences."

I gaped at him. "But it's quiet in my head."

Dan's smile stretched across his face. "Changed my brother's life too. He was a jerk before he tried this strain of cannabis."

My eyes bulged. "You drugged me?"

Dan threw his head back and laughed. "Calm down, bro. I had one, too. And it's not like the hard-core shit. Besides, this is Colorado. It's legal here. It's a small edible. Tell me honestly, how do you feel?"

A smile cracked my face. "Calm. Is it quiet in everyone's head all the time?"

Dan laughed again and nodded. "Yeah, bro, it is." He stood up from his swing and wiped his hands on his jeans. "I gotta head home. Let me know if that helps you sleep." He walked over to the monkey bars where his bike was.

He knew sleep had never been a friend of mine. We had traveled and shared hotel rooms at a few meets. He knew my brain didn't turn off until close to 3am every night.

I pumped my legs harder again and closed my eyes as the cool breeze rushed against my face. It was so peaceful. The distant buzzing of the streetlight popped loudly as the light switched on for the night. Slowing the swing down, the wooshing air in my ears lessened enough for me to hear the cicadas screech and the errant baseball being hit by a metal bat on the baseball field a block over. Everything seemed to be slowed down, but I knew it was me that was matching the world's pace.

My trip back up my hill was lazy. It took twice as long as it normally did.

Dinner was odd. My parents were quiet, but I didn't know if it was always like that or if they were fighting. They had been fighting on and off for a few years.

Their fights were always weird. Either my dad worked too much, or my mom was putting too much pressure on me. Once they fought because my dad bought my mom a car that she didn't want. He rebutted that she was overreacting that it was the wrong color, but it wasn't about the color. She had been specific and gave him a picture, but he ignored it and gave her what he wanted because it was a nicer car.

"It seems like the extra swimming and bike ride calmed you down. We need to write down the exact recipe that has made you this quiet," my dad joked.

My mom glared at him and cleared her throat. "How's your chicken, Hen?"

With my thumb up I said, "I had an edible today. It calmed me right down. I think you should look into getting me some because everything is so quiet."

My mom's fork clattered to her plate. "What?"

"I had an edible. It was sort of gross, like a cherry gummy bear that went bad, but Maman, the world slowed down. Hey, is it quiet in your head all the time?"

She blinked calmly at me and flicked her gaze over to my dad. His face had turned bright red.

"It is."

My knife scraped against the stoneware plate as I cut off another piece of chicken. "This is so good. I know you make it every week, but Maman, this is the most delicious chicken I have ever had."

She rolled her lips in like she was hiding her smile. I grinned over to her.

My dad cleared his throat. "Who gave you drugs?"

There was a warning in his tone. I knew I had to protect Dan. "Friend of a friend of a friend of a friend." My grin towards my dad didn't ease the severe slant of his eyebrows.

He wasn't amused. I cringed at his expression and held my hands up. "Look, I think you guys should look into getting more. Especially if it helps me sleep."

"Absolutely not." My dad pushed his chair away from the table. "I will not have a drug addict as a son."

My mom sat back. "Whoa, Roger, that is taking quite a leap. If this helps him, why would we keep it from him? Look at him, he is calm, happy, eating without fidgeting. When was the last time we ate dinner while he stayed seated the whole time?"

My dad flung his arm in my direction. "It's a gateway drug."

My mom scoffed. "Only if we allow it to be. If we get it for him, he'll never be introduced to anything else. We can easily get him a prescription..."

"He's already been compromised, Juliette. How do we know this is all he has done?" my dad raged. My lip curled at the two of them. With my chicken finished, I pushed away from the table.

"I should have known you'd be so liberal about this," my dad continued.

"And why is that?" she snapped.

"Because you're French, you don't have the same values as me. I was raised knowing drugs were bad. God knows what you were taught in school."

"Values? You want to talk to me about values? The man fucking our son's swimming coach!"

I paused at the top of the stairs and listened to them rage at each other. Turns out my little observation of my dad disappearing into Jasmine's office wasn't as innocent as I thought it was.

I took a long shower, enjoying how the water rushed against my skin. *How had I taken the soothing flow for granted for so long?* I begrudgingly turned the water off when someone knocked on the door. My maman was waiting for me on my bed.

"Mon canard, we are going to sleep somewhere else tonight." She had already packed my bag.

I nodded and slipped on a pair of boxers under my towel. "Okay."

I had no idea why I was so calm. I was pretty positive my parents were going to get a divorce, and it was going to be all my fault, but at that moment, I couldn't muster an ounce of anxiety.

It's odd knowing the exact moment you went from being your dad's favorite person to a thorn in his side. For me it was that day when I was high as a kite at the age of fourteen.

My parents did get divorced; it lasted way too long. I lived with my maman and got a new swim coach. She also looked into medicinal marijuana use for me. It was fortunate we lived in Colorado because she was able to microdose me until she decided to move back to Paris when I was seventeen.

I was forced to live with my dad who didn't allow me to microdose, which did drive me to finding a dealer.

He was sort of right in calling weed a gateway, but so was my mom. Had my dad continued to get my medicine from the legal dispensary I'd never have met my dealer, who introduced me to harder things. Cocaine was amazing but messed up my taste buds and made me make bad decisions.

My mom helped me detox the summer after my junior year of high school. I had gotten kicked out of school from a prank gone wrong and I was too high to correct anything. I promised her to stay away from the hard stuff. It was an easy decision to make after seeing how wrecked she was as I retched in the toilet for a few days straight. She felt responsible for leaving me to deal with my father.

Chapter 1

Ava

Age 18
Present Day

"Do you really think you are going to be able to pull this off?"

Jacob and I were packing my car up for me to make the long drive to Boulder, Colorado. I had gotten into Pineview University, the same school as my half-brother Will, who was my best friend. His girlfriend, Lily, was also attending Pineview which made the allure to spend my next four years there that much more appealing. She was awesome, and I loved her.

My parents were under the impression I was going to Baylor which was my mom's alma mater. It was also where my siblings Jacob and Daphne went. I had less than zero interest living in Daphne's shadow any longer. I hated her and now that she was married, she was finally out of my too short hair.

I had chopped it all off as a form of resistance when she named me as her flower girl. If she was going to give me a child's job, then I decided I'd look the part and ruin her wedding photos in the process. She hated it, which brought me more joy than it should have. I had maintained the chin length bob for nearly nine months and only after her nuptials, I was allowing my hair to grow again.

I beamed at him and blew my short dark hair from my face. "Of course I can pull this off. I'm resourceful and have two parents that are so wrapped up in themselves that they won't notice I'm gone." I shoved my bedding into the trunk and heaved it down.

"How are you going to feed yourself?"

I rolled my lips in and leaned against my trunk. "I opened a bank account in my name only when I turned eighteen and transferred all my graduation money in it. Mom and Dad don't know about it. And Dad is still sending allowance money in my shared bank account every month. I have been transferring money over for two months now and he hasn't said a thing."

Jacob scowled at me, not fully done with arguing with me why this was a bad idea. "You don't think they'll try to visit you?"

My hip popped out. "Did either of them attempt to visit you or Will?"

He shook his head. "That's different. I went to Baylor when our parents lived in Dallas. I was less than two hours away from home. And you know mom would never allow Dad to visit Will in Boulder."

I shrugged.

"But mom visited Daphne at Baylor," he warned.

My lip curled. "Daphne was in mom's sorority. I have already told her that I was not going to pledge, she has no reason to visit."

Jacob rubbed his temples and looked at the sky. "I think you need to tell someone though."

My smirk tipped one cheek higher than the other. "Both you and Will know. Also, Charlotte knows, that counts for something."

Jacob groaned. "Charlotte knowing is not going to stop mom from killing you. She hates Charlotte. Mom is going to freak out when she finds out."

Charlotte was Will's mom. She was one of my favorite people alive. She never held it against me that I ran up to my dad that day. She made sure that Will was a part of our lives and I was all the better for it. Will was amazing, so much so that I wanted to go to his alma mater. I was risking a lot so that I could have a little bit of a bigger piece of his life.

My eyes rolled dramatically. "And then what is she going to do exactly? Come to Pineview and drag me out?" I snorted. "She wouldn't set foot in that place. She knows that Will loves it too much and she wants nothing to do with anything that makes Will happy."

"She could refuse to pay for your tuition." He crossed his arms.

That was a huge possibility especially considering my dad tried to pull that card on Will a few weeks ago. Will told our dad he had decided he wasn't going to join the family business but become a lawyer like his mom. It was more nuanced than that. They also wanted Will to break up with Lily. It was misguided and stupid.

"Speaking of tuition, how are you going to pull that off? Dad will pay attention to being double charged from Pineview."

A grin spread as I walked back into the house to get another load of clothes. My mom was out shopping, and my dad was at work.

I passed two heavy trash bags of my belongings to Jacob and heaved my two bags over my shoulder. The weight made me grunt, and I let one slip down back onto the floor.

"That's the beauty of dad saying he was going to cut Will off, Will found alternative funding. I've already talked to Charlotte to confirm she is paying for his schooling. I'm going to use the family credit card to charge my tuition. Dad will think that Will is falling back into his good graces."

Jacob stared at me with a slack jaw. "That's actually smart." He shook his head. "But what about in February when Dad asks for your tuition receipt so he can file his taxes?"

"I'll email Ted Hurst directly. I already had to do that this past year since Mom and Dad insisted I went to the private high school. What a waste of money, by the way." Sweat dripped down my temple as I pushed the three bags into my back seat. I frowned at how little space I had.

Jacob chuckled. "I told you; you didn't need all the books you packed."

I rounded on him and huffed a breath. "I'm telling you this in confidence. I don't plan on ever living here again. I'm getting everything that means anything to me out of here. You and I both know that as soon as mom realizes what I did she will give everything away."

Jacob blanched. "You aren't coming back?"

I shook my head. "I'll come visit you, but living here has not been a good experience for me."

Jacob blinked rapidly. "Where are you going to go during the summer? Dallas?"

I curled my lip and shook my head. "I hate Dallas more than I hate it here. I don't want to share a zip code with either Daphne or mom."

He rolled his lips in and nodded. "You can always stay in my guest house. We won't tell Mom or Dad you are here, I promise."

My shoulders dropped away from my ears and my lips twisted to the side. Jacob may have been my older brother and enjoyed being a pest, but I knew he loved that I was only ever a short drive away.

"I'll think about that. I can't live with mom anymore. Daphne's wedding showed me how toxic she is. I can't allow myself to be her victim again. Daphne too, I realized when I spent so much time with Lily and Monroe that how Daphne and mom treat me is not normal."

Monroe was Lily's older sister and amazing. She was like the older sister I had always wanted. She was so kind and funny. She was patient and never allowed me to talk bad about myself.

My self-esteem wasn't exactly stellar considering Daphne, Lucy, and my mom were quick to point out every flaw I had. I was short, 5'1" with my shoes on. I looked younger than I was because of my height and build.

My boobs never came in, barely one of my handfuls, which doesn't mean much. Daphne accused me of having Carnie hands. Like a freak show carnival worker because my hands are so small, but they are proportional to my body.

Petite in stature, great for ballet, but it has been weaponized against me. My mom, sister, and Lucy were all over 5'5", which isn't that tall, but in comparison, they towered over me. Daphne still makes fun of me for barely being tall enough to ride roller coasters, not that I've ever had the opportunity to.

From the moment I met Monroe and Lily, they never once treated me like I was a little freak. And both are taller than average, Lily at 5'6" and Monroe at 5'9". They treated me with respect and respected my opinions on things. They thought I was funny and fun to be around. I wasn't the butt of all jokes. I could let my guard down around them.

Jacob swallowed thickly and nodded. "They are pretty awesome, and I am happy you have them in your life now. Don't forget about me, okay?"

My arms slung around his stomach. My pest of a brother was over a foot taller than me and refused to slump down so I could hug his shoulders. "I could never forget about you. Besides, who do you think I am going to need as my spy here?"

He snorted into my hair and kissed the top of my head. "You got everything?"

"Almost."

We went back in for the last bag. Jacob shoved it in the footwell of my front seat and pulled me into another hug. "And you're cool with leaving without saying goodbye to Mom and Dad?"

"I told mom I was going to leave today at noon. She told me she wasn't going to be home, and she'll be shopping until four. She is deliberately not being here. As far as Dad, I said bye to him last night."

Jacob huffed a breath. "I can't believe they are okay with you driving. They think you are going all the way to Texas on your own."

A guilty cringe lifted my lips away from my teeth. "They think I'm flying there and having my car shipped."

Jacob groaned. "What a confusing web of lies."

I giggled and gave him another hug. "Give my niece an extra squeeze for me and tell your wife I said bye."

Jacob nodded and roughly rubbed the top of my head with his knuckle. "Text me every time you get gas."

Finger guns wagged in his direction. "You got it. Oh, if Dad asks, you drove me to the airport."

Jacob gave me an annoyed look and nodded. "I love being the alibi of my eighteen-year-old sister while she disappears on a solo road trip. It's the beginning of a horror story."

"Or an epic adventure."

My chin wobbled as I backed out the driveway of my parent's Pasadena home. I hadn't lived there long, so I wasn't going to miss the house. But leaving was symbolic. I was taking control of my life. Jacob waved to me as he walked over to his SUV. I gave him a quick wave back and began my journey.

"Fucknuggets," I hissed as I glanced down at my phone.

Mommy Dearest: You didn't wait for me?
I told you I'd be home at 4!

It was 5:30, which made her point moot. She expected me to wait, but I had a message to send by leaving on time. Technically, I was supposed to be in the air, so I was careful to not click on the preview of her message. I would respond in a few hours when I "landed".

My legs were feeling jittery as I filled up my tank in St. George, Utah. I looked around the town and pulled up my GPS. Will had booked me a hotel a few miles away from where I was pumping gas. I sent Jacob a quick message.

> *Me: Made it to St. George. Getting*
> *gas and then I'm going to check*
> *into my hotel.*

Jacob: I know you're in St. George because your FindMe is activated. And as much as I want to be able to track you, it means mom and dad can too.

I cursed, turned off my GPS tracking, and crossed my fingers that my parents hadn't noticed their youngest daughter was way off course for Texas. What a rookie mistake. I should have paid better attention to my father when he lived a double life for fourteen years straight. Although GPS and FindMe apps were not prevalent at the time, which led to his success.

It took him a long time to forgive me. It didn't help that my mom labeled me an attention seeking liar or that Daphne corroborated her story that I took it upon myself to out my father. It's laughable now over a decade later that my dad didn't see through my mother's thinly veiled attempts to get him to leave Charlotte.

Charlotte was his soulmate. Anyone who had ever seen them together would know that, and I completely understood. She was special and deserved better than my father. But he was obsessed with my mother. I had started to believe that my mother drugged my father and kept him on a steady supply of meds to keep him compliant to her whims. But I think Will's theory has more merit. My mother *was* a drug for my dad. Will said that our dad had gotten dopamine mixed up with love and he was addicted to my mom choosing him. Whatever it was, it was toxic and a terrible example of what a healthy relationship may look like.

My stomach clenched when I got to the hotel. Being a novice solo traveler, I had never tried to check into a hotel room on my own. I felt like I had eyes watching me everywhere.

Because of my height I was often underestimated as being young and stupid. I was also physically limited. I could easily be tossed into someone's trunk and disappear.

My head was on a swivel as I made my way to the front desk. An older woman smiled warmly at me. A skeezy looking guy sitting in the lobby with a ragged backpack at his feet gave me a creepy smile. I whispered my name to the clerk.

Her smile dropped as she leaned closer to me. I repeated myself a little louder, not wanting the stranger danger in the corner to hear my name. My mom made me watch enough kidnapped documentaries for me to know the real trouble I could be in. A quick glance over my shoulder to see the guy not paying the slightest bit of attention to us eased my paranoia. I leaned in and repeated my name a little louder again.

The older woman nodded and began typing on her computer. "Are you in danger?" she whispered.

I rolled my lips in and shook my head. "I don't want anyone to know that I'm alone," I whispered back.

"Smart girl." She passed me my room key and whispered the instructions on how to get to my room. My breath puffed my cheeks until the elevator door shut. I had never felt so paranoid in my life, but I had also never been this alone.

Even when I drove down to San Diego to crash Lily's solo vacation, I wasn't this nervous because I was going to be meeting her. I had heard way too many amazing things about Lily to be worried about being alone. But Lily wasn't waiting for me in a hotel room in Utah.

My fingers tugged my backpack closer, and I made quick steps down the hotel hall. A little tool I had bought online helped secure the door, and I latched it. I breathed out a deep breath and looked around the average hotel room.

The past few weeks had spoiled me. The hotel I crashed in with Lily was a five-star resort and then the room I stayed in while in Barbados for Daphne's wedding was in Lily's family's beach mansion.

This room was average with two beds and smelled faintly like bleach. I ordered room service and sent my mom a message back.

Me: Sorry, you knew when I had to go, I didn't want to miss my flight.

Mommy Dearest: You could have rescheduled. Now I didn't get to give you a proper goodbye.

Me: Sorry. Tell me what I missed.

Mommy Dearest: Don't take that tone with me.

I rolled my eyes. There was no tone over text. She was assuming I was mad at her and guessing I was getting snippy. And had I not realized what a terrible person my mom was, I might have actually been upset that she wasn't there to see me off. I also would have missed my flight waiting for her. Which is what she expected.

Me: No tone. Sorry if it came out that way.

Mommy Dearest: Well, if you

would have stayed I would have
told you the good news.

That she was getting a lobotomy? That she wasn't my
biological mother? Another pipe dream because we had the same
face. The same everything except for height. She was taller than
me and her boobs were gigantic, but I was 110% positive that
they were fake.

Me: What good news?

Mommy Dearest: Daphne's
Little is the president of the
Phi Mu chapter. You are expected
to meet Krystal in two days in
the main house.

My lip curled. I would barely be in Boulder in two days.

Me: I'm not pledging. I already
told you that.

Mommy Dearest: You have
to. You are a legacy. Do you
know how bad it will look for
my own daughter to not
pledge?

Me: Sorry. I'm not interested.
I don't want to be compared
to you or Daph. You are both
so beautiful and I don't want to
sully all your accomplishments.

I grinned at the message. My mother wasn't going to be able to deny her own beauty or what a disappointment I was to not be like her. Rule number one of placating a narcissist: stroke their enormous egos.

Mommy Dearest: Don't worry about sullying anything. I already knew you'd never be a president. Meet with Krystal, you may love it.

I rolled my eyes at the dig.

Me: I'll see if I have time. I have a lot I have to do.

Mommy Dearest: Make time.

A whimper vibrated my throat, and I cautiously answered the room service call. Leaving the room alone was a no-go, and I didn't want to talk to anyone else. The silence was nice. When I was home, my mom had me doing chores or helping her with projects just for her to abandon them five minutes in.

Rest assured that no one is better at polishing our silver than me. I'd like to compare myself to Cinderella, but the reality is, Kim isn't my evil stepmother. She's my full-blooded entitled mother who is a complete narcissist.

"Helping her with dinner" had been the expectation since I was nine and by the time I was twelve I was making it completely on my own. My mom would then take the credit when my dad made it home to eat.

I wonder how she's going to explain her lack of culinary skills now that I'm gone.

Will was next to know that I had made it to the hotel. We text messaged each other back and forth for a little bit while I ate dinner.

The rest of my long drive took another two days. The hotel room in Grand Junction was much the same without the skeezy guy in the lobby. The drive was absolutely beautiful and probably took me an additional two hours because I kept stopping to take pictures. I had never actually seen the Rocky Mountains before. I wasn't expecting them to be so… big.

The views were mesmerizing, and I was getting more and more excited that this was going to be my home for the next four years. Errr, at least one year. I could get away with one year of school in Pineview. I doubted my parents would come to visit before add/drop of the second semester.

Things had the potential of being a little hairy around Thanksgiving, but I had already planted the seed for my mom to suggest going to some exotic place for the holiday since she was officially an empty nester. She seemed taken by the idea, so fingers crossed she was going to follow suit.

I played the card that Daphne's wedding had been so stressful that she deserved to have a vacation and not worry about cooking for the holiday. I didn't want to bring up that Jacob, his wife Stephanie, and their one-year-old, Taylor, were definitely not planning on joining her for dinner. Not after the shenanigans they pulled with Will and Lily. Jacob basically told my parents to take a long walk off a short pier and that their relationship with Taylor was put on hold because my parents were *that* unreasonable about Lily.

Christmas break was still up in the air and unplanned. I didn't want to go home for that either, but I wasn't sure what excuse I was going to give. I'd hedge my bets that my parents wouldn't get suspicious until February and by then add/drop would be over so I could justify staying because the semester would already be paid for, and it would mess up my GPA to leave school.

After that? I had no idea what I was going to do. I had considered asking Lily to help me out. Her family's wealth made mine look like child's play. She would happily pay for my schooling, but that wasn't the route I wanted to take.

Signing up for student loans had merit, but I would need a cosigner, and my parents would definitely not support that. *Let's not borrow tomorrow's problems.*

I squealed as I drove through the beautiful campus of Pineview University. The views and the thick forest of trees felt magical. There was no available parking, but Will shared that parking was nearly impossible on campus. I parked in his apartment complex and walked the mile to the administration building so I could get my housing assignment and pay my tuition.

Chapter 2

Ava

"**W**hat do you mean I was supposed to sign up for housing? I thought all freshmen had to live on campus." I tried to keep my voice low, but I was panicking. I had driven a total of fifteen hours with my car packed to the gills with all my belongings, and I was officially homeless.

"Only student athletes on scholarship are required to live on campus freshman year." The woman behind the glass partition in the bursar's building tried to look sympathetic.

My teeth pinned my lip. "Okay, let's sign me up for a dorm." I nodded vigorously.

The lady gave me another sad smile. "There's a waitlist, hun. I can give you a few recommendations for student housing off campus."

Swallowing was becoming an impossible feat to get past the growing lump. "Okay, yeah." Blinking rapidly, I refused to let the stress tears to fall. "That would be great. Um, can I pay my tuition now?" I pulled out my dad's metal credit card he had added my name to use for school.

She tilted her head and reached her hand out palm up towards the glass partition. "Sure, Ava Reiser, correct?"

I nodded. Words were stuck behind the lump.

"It says here you are taking fifteen credits, that's full time, does that sound correct?"

I cleared my throat. "Yes, I signed up for my classes a few weeks ago."

She gave me the total, and my eyes bulged. College was expensive. My hands shook as I passed over the card. Fingers crossed that the card would go through.

"Okay Ms. Reiser, there is freshman orientation starting in about an hour. You'll get a full tour of campus and student ID. Here is your class schedule as well as the booklist required for the classes. You may want to pick them up now before classes start in a few days. A part of the tour will be the bookstore."

"Great."

She passed me my schedule as well as the list of affordable student housing options. My lips rubbed together.

"Thanks," I squeaked.

Panic didn't fully set in until I was back to my car. Stress burned the back of my eyes before I bucked up and pulled the housing list out.

There was a total of ten places near campus. I didn't know how I was going to pay for it, but I had a good amount in my bank account and depending on rent, my allowance would cover it. Only two places had vacancies. I made my appointments and called Will to let him know I had made it to campus. I wasn't going to freak him out by telling him about the housing situation. I was going to figure it out. This was an adventure.

Orientation started minutes after I made it back to campus. My legs were tired and heavy. I was strangely exhausted like I couldn't take a full breath of air. I didn't consider myself out of shape, but I sure felt like it. My cheeks were a little too red in my ID photo.

My lungs stung as I tried to keep pace with the energetic tour guide, and I groaned at the easily twenty pounds of books I had to buy. It was another eye-watering amount that Dad was going to pay for. Using his card for essential campus purchases would fly under the radar, but anything other than that was going to throw up a red flag.

Heaving breaths dried out my parched lips and sweat poured down my back as someone honked their horn at me. I was firmly on the sidewalk, so I ignored it until they changed their speed to keep pace with me. My fingers gripped my bag tighter.

"Look at that gorgeous girl," Lily called to me.

My shoulders dropped from my ears as I turned to see her beaming at me.

"Get in." She motioned with her head. There was another beautiful girl in the car with her. She had brunette hair and light eyes.

"This is my best friend, Nicole. Nicole, this is Will's sister and my favorite person in his family, Ava."

Nicole's smile was wide. "I've heard so much about you."

I shuffled into the back seat of Lily's luxury SUV and dropped my heavy books against the seat. "When did you get in and why didn't you call me?" Lily chastised.

"I got in a few hours ago, but I had to go directly to the bursary building."

"Were they actually helpful?" Nicole asked.

My cheeks flushed as I made an uncertain waggle with my head because they weren't really *that* helpful.

Lily nodded and made the turn into her neighborhood. "I thought I saw your car parked in our parking lot. When do you move into your dorm?"

My lower lip rolled beneath my teeth. "Uh, well, it turns out you have to sign up for those."

Lily's head whipped around as she parked. "Ava, you didn't sign up for housing?"

My brow furrowed. "I'm eighteen and I've never done this before. It's not like I could ask my parents for help. They don't know I'm here. But it's okay. I have two appointments for housing options. Which reminds me, I need to head to those now."

"Uh, are you serious?"

I nodded and scooted down from her SUV. "Yep, so anyway. Have either of you heard of Frasier Avenue apartments?" I read off from the notes I wrote down on my phone.

Lily blanched as Nicole's lip curled. "You can't live there."

I shrugged. "I may not have a choice. I can afford the rent with my allowance. If you want to come, I'd appreciate a second and third opinion."

"Let's unload the groceries and I'll take you," Lily said.

"Sure. You want help?"

Lily shook her head. "It's probably for the best that Will doesn't know I'm taking you to Frasier Ave."

My stomach knotted again as I sat in the backseat. Nothing good was shared on the complex's online reviews. One review was all about the bedbugs. My skin was already crawling, but I refused to give up now. Housing was an oversight, but I was fixing it.

Lily gave me a flat smile when a man offered to watch her car while we were inside the leasing office. She passed over a twenty and looped her arm into mine. I was hopeful when I saw the leasing office was clean and bright. The agent was nice, but he kept asking us if we were sure we wanted to see the apartment.

There was a warning in his tone that didn't make sense until we stepped inside the basement studio. The single room smelled like mildew. There was a bare bulb in the center of the room. The little kitchen had two burners and a mini fridge. My nose wrinkled at the lack of furnishings. Mold crawled up the wall of the bathroom and a few dead cockroaches were in the tub.

Lily tugged my arm. "We will let you know," she said diplomatically to the agent who was still standing in the doorway.

The guy watching her car was leaning against the hood. "Ain't nobody tried for the rims, miss."

She smiled at him and passed him another twenty.

There was no way I was going to be able to afford forty dollars a day for a parking attendant.

"I didn't think parking would be so expensive."

Lily drove away and shook her head. "That wasn't a parking fee. He was insuring no one would steal my car. Ava, you can't live there."

My lips twisted to one side. "It wasn't that bad. Lots of potential really. I could get a decent futon and desk that could double as a dining table."

She shook her head slowly. "Where to next?"

I pulled out my phone. "Uhh, The Views?"

She tilted her head. "That's my neighborhood's townhouse side. Okay, I can get on board with that. Let's go."

We knocked on the door. A man in his forties answered in a silk robe. "Ava, right?"

Lily blinked at him and shook her head. "So sorry. This *is* Ava, but unfortunately, she is going to have to pass. We wanted to tell you in person."

My jaw clicked shut as he slammed the door in our face.

"What the hell?" I hissed.

She grabbed my arm and tugged me two buildings over. She pulled out her key and shoved it in the door. "Under no circumstances can you live with Creeper Peeper."

"Do you know that guy?" I thumbed over my shoulder towards his building.

Lily gave out an exasperated sigh. "Only by nickname and reputation. In case the silk robe wasn't a big enough clue, he's a pedo. Literally he is on the sex offender registry. My dad made me check the list before moving in here. He was arrested for jerkin his gerkin outside of a middle school."

"Oh." Blush creeped up my cheeks.

She nodded to me. "So, unless you want all your panties to disappear and wake up with him jerking off over your body, he's not an option."

My lip curled, and then the emotions started to take over as tears stung my eyes. "I'll make do with the Frasier apartment."

Lily gave me an unamused glare. "Peach?" she called out.

I shook my head at her rapidly. She ignored me. A bedroom door opened up and my awesome half-brother walked out.

"Ava!" Will came up to me quickly and yanked me into a hug, pulling me from my feet. "What dorm are you in? How was orientation?"

Anxiety dried my mouth. "Uh, orientation went well. I have all my books; tuition is paid for. I know where all my classes are."

"Tell him," Lily said.

"Tell me what?" A pucker formed in his brow as he stared at the both of us. Nicole was sitting on the couch eating popcorn. Her legs were draped over Will's best friend, Matt's legs. I had met him over the disastrous Thanksgiving that mom essentially locked Will out of.

I waved over to Matt. "Hey Matty." I ignored Will's stare. "You look good." He really, *really* did.

His good looks had rendered me speechless when I met him ten months prior. He looked like Brad Pitt when he starred in Thelma and Louise, in other words, gorgeous. I'd always had a thing for Brad Pitt….

"Ava!" Lily warned. My shoulders creeped back up to my ears.

"I don't want to tell him," I whined.

"Tell me what?" Will said again with a little more annoyance.

Lily was tapping her foot, looking at me. I twisted my lips to the side. "Well, it turns out that you have to sign up for dorms, which I didn't know. But it's fine, Lily and I looked at two apartment options, both viable places to live."

Lily scoffed. "No, they aren't." She turned to Will. "Basement Frasier Ave studio and Creeper Peeper's townhouse."

Will's lip curled as he shook his head. "Absolutely not. In no circumstances can I allow you to live in either place."

That made my hackles rise. I hated the insinuation that he thought he had authority over me to *allow* anything. "I'm not asking permission. I'm eighteen. I can live where I want and considering those are the only two places available near campus, I don't exactly have a choice."

Will tipped his head back and cursed. He pulled out his phone and started texting someone.

"Are you telling Mom and Dad?" Panic made my heart pound.

He gave me the get-real look and continued with his message, giving me the give-me-a-minute finger motion.

My cheeks puffed dramatically out, and I winced at Matt and Nicole who were watching me with a weird smile on their faces. Will rolled his eyes as Lily read over his shoulder. She giggled to herself and winked at me. It didn't make me feel any better about the situation.

He dug into his pocket. "Ava, I want you to go next door. This is the key to my apartment. Stay in there. We are going to have a roommate discussion. Give us like an hour. Use the tv, take a nap. You'll know which room is mine. I will come get you when we are done with our talk."

My teeth pinned my lip. "Am I in trouble?" My voice was quiet.

Will's furrowed brows softened. "No. We will figure this out, okay? Go relax. Are you tired from the trip?"

"I've never felt so tired in my life."

"It's the altitude. Go lay down. We are waiting for my other roommate, Henry. He's out and not responding, so go and relax. There may be a short blonde in the apartment. That's Tama or Prairie as I call her, introduce yourself, but don't be alarmed if she doesn't say much. She's shy and she'll be heading over here momentarily. Go." He passed me the key to his apartment.

Feeling overwhelmed with exhaustion, I nodded gratefully. The sweat from all the walking was gritty on my skin and the altitude, apparently, was wreaking havoc on my ability to stay upright.

A short girl, no taller than me squeaked when she saw me in the hallway. She had long blonde hair and huge boobs. I was instantly envious of her. She gave me a tight smile and scooted into Lily's apartment.

I take it that was Tama.

I slipped my key in the lock and eased inside. This apartment looked the same but was less homey. A large leather sofa looked comfortable. I wanted to nap, but I wanted to shower more. I wondered if Will would let me crash on the couch until we figured out my housing situation.

The room closest to the kitchen was definitely not Will's room unless he got really into quilting. I went into the room closest to the living room and shrugged.

It was masculine. There was a picture of Matty, Will, and some guy that looked like Matty but with a reddish tint to his hair. Matty was a gorgeous man, so the fact that there were two of them… Yowzers.

Will's bathroom was decently clean, not that I would judge him if it were dirty, considering he had only gotten back to his apartment a week ago after being gone all summer. I turned the water on and stripped out of my sweaty clothes. It wasn't until I was in the shower that I realized all my clean clothes were still in trash bags in my car.

I guess I'm going to have to borrow a shirt and boxers. Better to ask for forgiveness than permission. The shampoo had a masculine scent. It was expensive, which I credited to Lily for upping my brother's grooming tastes.

My mom and Daphne made me get laser hair removal when I was fifteen. It was like a rite of passage amongst the women in my family. Dark hair and Italian blood meant copious amounts of body hair. My petite face wasn't pulling off the mustache look or unibrow. My mom had taken me to monthly waxing appointments from the age of ten on. When I refused to go because it hurt, she compromised with me.

I had to endure twenty laser sessions for everything from my eyebrows down. Arguing with my mom that I might want armpit hair one day was pointless. She scoffed at me and told the esthetician to remove everything. It was a confusing demand. What woman wanted to be like a Barbie doll?

I was already accused of being a child, my lady hair was my one bit of proof otherwise. Appreciation didn't percolate until I was in Barbados and didn't have to worry about my bikini line. All the bridesmaids complained about waxing and ingrown hairs during that trip.

There wasn't a loofa in Will's shower, not that I was surprised. The bar of soap reminded me of the expensive stuff my mom used from Paris. I had never noticed that Will smelled like that, but I didn't exactly sniff him.

By the time I turned the shower off, I felt like a new woman. Excess water streamed from my hair as I rung it out and I knotted the towel around my chest.

Stealing my brother's t-shirt and a pair of boxers wasn't on my Bingo card. I had to fold the waist multiple times, but beggars couldn't be choosers. There was a small comb on the vanity. I ran it through my short tresses. Grateful for the first time in months that my hair took so little to maintain.

Will's bed looked big and cozy. I fell backwards on it and made bedding angels with my limbs. I wasn't expecting the apartment to have a queen bed, but I wasn't going to complain. I scooted my body up to the pillows and checked my phone. My lip curled.

Mommy Dearest: Krystal said you missed your appointment. I told you to make time. Fix it.

Me: Sorry, I totally forgot. I was taking a campus tour. I'll reach

*out to her on social media.
What's her last name?*

Mommy Dearest: Krystal Quinn.

*Me: Got it. I'll see when she is
available to meet with me. But
mom, I am not planning on
rushing. I'm sorry if that is a
disappointment. It's not my
thing.*

*Mommy Dearest: Make it your
thing. We have a reputation to
uphold.*

Me: I'll see what I can do.

I sighed and went onto Daphne's social media to find Krystal. She was tagged in a few pictures. I sent her a message.

Krystal,

Hey, I'm Ava, Daphne's little sister. Here is the thing, I'm not planning on rushing. I know the standards of your sorority, and I know that I don't meet them. I know you'd only let me in because I am a legacy, and I don't want to bring your group of amazing women down. But my mom really wants me to rush. Can you do me a favor, if she asks, tell her we met. That way she gets off my back.

*Thanks
Ava*

I thought it was self-deprecating enough to make Krystal pause and possibly agree to help me out. My eyelids grew heavier and heavier as I fell to sleep.

Henry

You know the feeling you get when you walk into your home, and you know something is wrong? My ADHD superpowers flared heavily. I was supposed to head straight over to Lily, Matt, and Nicole's apartment, but I needed to stop into my room and change from the gym.

The pool was too heavily chlorinated. Ever since I was mugged and my skull cracked open three months ago the chemical gave me a headache. I needed to wash it off before the light tension in my temples turned into a debilitating migraine.

One of the worst side effects of a concussion are the headaches. Stupid shit triggers them too. Sneezing too hard, bright lights, overly strong smells. Things I never worried about were making my life a little more difficult. My skull was as healed as it was going to get and the headaches were getting better, now I only got one a week. My edibles helped. I was told to stop smoking or taking edibles for the first few months after the injury, but I was able to resume over the past few weeks.

Going through the summer without a way to keep the buzzing sensation to move constantly was exhausting. I started swimming a few hours a day, the result was I was ripped again. It was the only way I was able to get a few hours of sleep at night.

My other vice was sex, but the girls I had dated had either graduated or I was no longer interested in them. I had one girl that enjoyed our time together a little too much.

Raven was stunning, but sort of damaged. She enjoyed pain in a way I no longer felt comfortable providing. I love a good submissive scene. I love being a dominating fucker, but she wanted me to cut her, hit her, strangle her to the point of blacking out. I wouldn't do it. Intentionally hurting someone innocent made me feel queasy.

We parted ways a little before I was mugged. I missed her but there was no way we could get back together again. She burned that bridge when she wouldn't respect my decision to end things.

The kitchen was empty as the ticklish feeling crawled up my spine. Something was different. Maybe it was that I wasn't used to Tama's things being in the apartment.

When my cousin Matt told us that he and Nicole were back together and planning on sharing a room, it left us with a few different roommate options between the six of us that shared the two apartments.

Matt mentioned wanting to keep one room and pay rent so he could have an office for his work. He was recently hired on as a baseball scout and pitching coach for the Pineview baseball team. Pretty sweet gig considering he lost his dreams when he stopped the muggers from killing me. He sacrificed his career when his arm was dislocated and broken by the three guys trying to murder me in a side alley.

When Will told us that he and Lily were officially together it put a different dynamic on the group. Tama had been on the fence about living with me. She was like the sister I never had, and she treated me like the annoying brother she never wanted. It worked for us. Plus, she was an amazing cook and one of the nicest girls I had ever met. Never said a mean thing about anyone in her life.

The urgent meeting at Lily's was probably about new rules since four out of the six of us were a couple. It didn't matter to me who lived where as long as no one fucked with my shit, I'd be content.

My bedroom door quietly creaked, and I tilted my head when my soap was heavy in the air as if I had gotten out of the shower. I glanced over to my bed and squinted at the gorgeous doll lying in the center. She looked like a tan Snow White. Her dark hair was short, just below her chin. Her pink lips were deeply hued closer to a purple red. Dark lashes fanned across her cheeks.

She was wearing my shirt, and it looked like my boxers too. My stubble was rough under my fingertips as I observed her sleeping. I didn't want to wake her yet. Was she a gift from a previous lover? It wasn't unheard of for one of my former subs to offer me someone to get into my good graces again.

I took very good care of my subs. Everything was consensual and pushed boundaries to ensure ultimate pleasure. Spoiling them with time, devotion, and words of praise was a pleasure for me. You'd be amazed with how many girls had daddy issues, and all they wanted was someone to tell them they were good enough.

The girl's brows furrowed as her plump lips parted like she was mumbling in her sleep. She snored loudly, and the trance was broken. I chuckled to myself and walked over to get a better view of her beautiful face. She looked like Olivia Gracen, but more delicate. She resembled a mix between Christina Ricci and Nicki Reed, stunning.

It was tempting to tie her to my bed so I could play with her later but decided that she could wait until after the meeting was finished. I stepped into my wet shower and rinsed the chlorine off quickly. The last thing I wanted was a headache while I explored the doll in my bed.

It had been months since I had been with someone. Anticipation shivered down my spine as I jerked myself off so I could last as long as possible. She was still sound asleep when I got out of the shower. I walked around naked in my room and slipped on a pair of sweatpants and a t-shirt.

Chapter 3

Henry

Will was pacing Lily's apartment when I slipped in. His eyes bulged. "Bro, what took you so long?"

I shrugged. "I needed to shower after my swim.

What's the big deal? We all know what you are about to say."

Lily giggled and shook her head. Will rolled his eyes and turned to Tama. "As you are all aware Matty and Billie are officially together. Sunshine and I are also officially together."

Will had a habit of only calling people by nicknames he made up. Nicole was Billie, I was Hank, Lily was Sunshine, Tama was Prairie, and Matt was Matty.

Tama nodded and curled her thin legs under her butt.

"Matty is still going to pay normal rent so he can use one of the bedrooms as an office space. I was going to do something similar, but things changed today."

I tilted my head. Lily was looking at Will like he was her next meal, so I had no doubt that they were still going strong and happy.

Will blew out a breath. "My half-sister, Ava, moved here today and didn't realize she had to sign up for student housing. She and Sunshine checked out a few places that are available."

Huh, not where I thought he was going with this.

"Frasier Ave and living with Creeper Peeper."

My lip curled. "Frasier Ave gave someone bed bugs. If your sis lives there, she can't hang out with us."

Matt cleared his throat. "I thought it was scabies."

I shivered and stifled a gag.

Will rolled his eyes. "Regardless, neither are ideal for my little sister."

Tama raised her hand. "Who is Creeper Peeper?"

I chuckled. "You know that weirdo that hangs out by the mailboxes. He walks around in a long trench coat and flip flops during the summer. I'm pretty sure he's a flasher."

Tama's big eyes bulged as she nodded sagely. "He was the second penis I saw in real life."

"What the fuck?" Matt's eyes bulged.

She shrugged. "I didn't ask him to do it; he walked up to me and opened his coat." She turned to Will. "Yours is bigger, if that matters."

Lily snickered as Will's brow furrowed. "Was he flaccid?"

"Does it matter? Jesus, Tama, did you call the police?" Matt asked.

She shook her head. "No to both. My uncle-dad would have found the police report in an instant with my name attached."

"Don't call him your uncle-dad, Tama. It makes a beautiful situation sound creepy." Nicole grimaced.

Tama shrugged. "But he is my uncle and now my stepdad."

Her dead dad's brother married her mom over the summer. Not a connection most people would make when you learned that she was homeschooled and the first guy she met that she wasn't related to or in his seventies was Will last year.

She led a sheltered life. Tama waited until she was twenty before she and her uncle were able to convince her mom to let her go to college. She was old for a sophomore, but you'd never know it by looking at her.

Will sighed. "We are off topic. Ava can't live in either place. I am calling this meeting to see if you, Prairie, and you, Hank are okay if she stays in my room? I'll pay the portion of the rent she can't cover with her allowance."

I shrugged. "Can she cook?"

Nicole threw a pillow at me. "Does your stomach rule your brain?"

I smirked and nodded. "A million percent."

Will huffed a breath. "Yeah, she made my entire family's Thanksgiving dinner last year."

"Oh shit, that food was good." Matt rubbed his hands together.

Will chuckled. "Yeah, she's basically been my evil stepmother's child slave, but she's free now. Which reminds me, my dad and her mom don't know she's here. She told them she is going to Baylor. I doubt it will ever come up with anyone, but you know in case you need to cover for her."

"Cool, when do we meet her?"

Tama nodded again. "I think I saw her earlier today. She's short, like my height. Dark bob. Really pretty face?"

Lily nodded. "That's her."

I rolled my lips in and chuckled. I guess she wasn't a present from a former submissive after all. My bad luck that she looks like the girl of my dreams.

I had to laugh at the fucked-up thoughts that had been running through my head since I saw her. I'm glad I didn't straddle her chest and fuck her mouth now. That would have been awkward to apologize for after the fact. Would she have screamed if she saw me walking around my own room naked? I wasn't fond of screamers, especially now that my headaches were on a hairpin trigger.

Will narrowed his eyes to me. "Don't get any funny ideas, Hank. She's my baby sister."

I held my hands up.

"Don't call her a baby. You know she hates that." Lily turned to the group. "She's petite, but her physical attributes have been weaponized her whole life. Please don't call her cute or little or anything like that. It's not a compliment to her."

Intriguing. That meant she was going to have a certain amount of sass. I liked a little bit of a brat. As long as she was standing up for herself, I'd find it sexy as fuck.

Just my luck she's Will's sister.

Tama rolled her lips in. "I know what that's like."

Will waved his hands in the air. "Right, yes, fine. But my point remains," he turned back to me, "she's off limits."

Yep, called that one. At least I had already tugged one out. Thinking more rationally and finding the humor in the situation, I decided to mess with Will a little bit.

A smile curled my lips. "So, I shouldn't tie her to my bed?"

Will took a step towards me. "That shit's not funny."

I shrugged. "I mean, she *is* passed out in my bed, in my clothes after taking a shower in my bathroom. It's a fair question."

Will lost all the color in his face as Lily giggled next to him. "She didn't."

My head bobbed in a single nod. "She did. Unless there is another girl with a bob wandering around the hallway, then yeah, she's sound asleep in my bed like a little Goldilocks."

Will rubbed his forehead and cursed. "I should have been more specific. I wasn't thinking clearly when I told her to go take a nap in my room. Why did I think she'd pick my room out correctly?"

He turned to me. "I'll take care of it."

"No worries, man. It's a big bed."

Will's eyes widened as he shook his head at me. "There will be zero bed sharing."

Lily groaned. "Peach, he's messing with you, calm down."

I perked my brow. "Since when do we call him Peach?"

Will glared at me. "That's only for Sunshine to call me."

Matt chuckled. "Apparently it's an inside joke from Barbados because he has a peachy ass."

I tipped my head back and laughed. "You do have a peachy ass. I love that you finally have a nickname, too."

Lily giggled. "You can also call him Button."

"No, they cannot."

"Oh, Button, don't deprive us of a good nickname," Matt joked.

Will flipped us all the bird. "If I had to choose, I like Peach more, but anyway. Is that Ava's?" He pointed to a backpack by the door. Lily shrugged with a nod.

"Process of elimination, I'd say yes," Tama said.

Will sighed heavily. "I live with a bunch of sarcastic dicks."

"Hey! I wasn't being sarcastic, I was being observational," Tama said.

She was being sarcastic.

Will walked over, unzipped the black backpack, and fished out keys. "Who wants to help me unpack her car? If she's in nothing but a t-shirt and boxers, I don't want to give Creeper Peeper any ammo to flash her. I'm pretty positive she's never seen a penis and his will not be the first."

Of fucking course she's a virgin.

I raised my hand. "I'll help."

Matt's lip curled. "Bro, you didn't help move yourself in."

I hadn't. I hired movers and swapped out half the furniture because I had zero intention of moving back to my dad's for the summer.

I chuckled and shrugged. "The faster I get this girl her clothes, the faster I can get her out of mine."

Will scowled at me.

"I didn't mean it like that." My hands were up. *I did mean it like that.* But it was so much fun to push Will's buttons.

We all trooped downstairs and grabbed a bag each from the little hunter green Mini. If I had to guess what car the doll in my bed would drive this was close to what I'd assume.

"Good god, why so many books?" Matt asked as he kneed a box higher into his arms.

Will sighed. "She's a reader. It's the one type of escape she's had for years. My half-sister, Daphne, is an asshole and my stepmom is a psychopath."

I frowned, not liking that someone had treated her like anything other than a jewel. It took us all one and a half trips to get all of her belongings out of her car. Lily locked up as Will marched towards my bedroom. I was glad I had cleaned a few days ago before Tama moved in otherwise I would have gotten an earful from Will about my pigsty.

My shoulder eased against the wall of my room as Will delicately shook Ava awake. Her eyes fluttered open and then she gasped and sat straight up.

"Oh, fucknuggets I fell asleep. It's dark out. Shitty shit shit. I still need to unpack my car. Hey, I'm going to need you to make a little room in your closet so I can at least store my stuff. Oh! Can I sleep on the couch? I won't be a burden. Tomorrow I'm going to expand my housing search. There has to be something. I refuse to be homeless at eighteen."

Will tried to interrupt her as I chuckled against the wall. Her eyes turned to me. "Shit balls, it's your hot friend from the photo," she said from the side of her mouth.

I rolled off the wall. "Henry, and you're in my bed."

Will growled. "Don't call him hot. He's off limits, Ava."

Her eyes flicked back and forth between me and Will. "Oh no you don't, William James Reiser. We discussed this in Barbados; you don't get to dictate my love life. I didn't say shit when I heard you railing Lily every night."

"Jesus Ava, calm down and get out of Hank's bed."

She pulled the comforter back and slid underneath. She slapped her hands on either side of her body and glared at Will. "I'm not leaving this bed until you tell me you aren't going to interfere in my love life."

I chuckled and looked over to the bathroom, so I wasn't facing them. She *was* a little brat.

Will let out an exasperated sigh. "First of all, get out of his bed so we can discuss things like adults."

She snuggled down further. "No." She fluffed the pillow and smacked her hands back down. "These are nice sheets," she muttered.

"Fuck my life. Ava, we have figured out a great place for you to stay. Nice, safe, and not with Creeper Peeper or in a bug infested room."

She perked up. "I'm listening. Is the rent affordable?"

Will nodded. "Very, but before I tell you about it. Get. Out. Of. Hank's. Bed."

She kicked the covers down and stood up. I wasn't expecting her to be so petite. She was the perfect size to toss around. I stood over a foot taller than her. She stopped in front of me.

"Am I wearing your clothes?" she whispered.

I smirked and nodded. A red flush crawled across her cheeks. "I'll wash them as soon as I can." She turned on her heel and faced Will.

"I'm starving, can you tell me about this place over dinner?" *Woman after my own heart.*

"Prairie, meet Ava, officially." Will motioned to Tama as Ava walked into the kitchen. Tama gave her an awkward wave and introduced herself with her actual name. Ava didn't wave back; she leaned forward and poked Tama's tit.

"Whoa, those babies are real."

"Ava, what the hell," Will groaned.

Lily giggled and covered her mouth with her hand. "Sorry Tam it's kind of her version of a handshake she did the same to me when we first met."

"Please tell me you are joking," Will muttered. Lily grinned and shook her head.

"Well, now I feel left out," Nicole said. Ava wagged her brows and walked over to Nicole and poked her boob.

"Wow, look at us, a bunch of natural nellies with our body-made fat bags." She turned back to Tama. "I heard big boobies make for achy backs. Asking for advice, my mom and sister want me to get my boobs done. Sunshine Lily thinks mine are fine as is. What are your thoughts?"

She pulled the overly large shirt tight across her body, showing off her tiny hourglass figure. My mouth watered and I wanted to shout to her to not change a fucking thing. Yeah, her chest was small, but I only needed a mouthful.

Tama blushed as Will pulled Ava's arm to get her to release the shirt.

"Is this the first-time meeting people?" he hissed. "You've gotta chill."

Ava twisted her lips to the side. "Sorry for the boob pokes."

Tama cleared her throat. "Yes, my chest does give me back issues occasionally. I vote no to an enhancement, but you should do what makes you happy. Not someone else."

Ava grinned at her. "I heard you're an amazing cook. What are you making? Do you want some help? What's your cooking genre specialty? Mine is Italian, but that's because my nonna is from the old country."

"Ava, take a breath. Sit down and let Will finish talking to you," Lily said calmly.

Ava huffed. "I babble when I get nervous and everyone here is staring at me. I mean I get it. I'm a little freak who fell asleep in the wrong bed and I'm wearing a stranger's underwear."

"Hey, Ava, no one is thinking that." Will's tone had softened.

She rolled her lips in. "Okay, did you say something about finding me a place to live?"

Will let out a breath. I looked over to my cousin who looked entirely too amused by the situation. His arm was slung around Nicole's shoulder who was grinning at Ava. I had to admit she was pretty entertaining.

"We all discussed it and agreed that you can stay in my room. It's furnished and realistically I wasn't going to stay in there. There are roommate rules that I want to lay out."

Ava pulled her cheeks in and stood up straight. There was something elegant about her as she rolled her shoulders back and tipped her chin a little to show off the delicate lines of her throat.

When Will felt confident that she was listening he continued. "Stay out of people's rooms. We rotate who cooks and we make meals for all of us. Clean up after yourself, meaning don't leave your dishes in the sink for more than a day and don't leave your trash in the living room, period. We go grocery shopping on Mondays and since the parking situation is a beast we pool our schedules together and make a carpool schedule."

His list of roommate rules was interesting considering he was guilty of every single one. Not that I was completely innocent. Matty mostly took care of our messes last year. It wasn't until the past month when I was the only one contributing to the growing mess that I realized I had to work on being less of a slob.

She wrinkled her nose. "I'm not going to be homeless?"

Will and Lily laughed and shook their heads. "I'd never let that happen. Monroe would probably buy you a house here to keep that from happening," Lily said. I had no idea who Monroe was, but whatever. Must be another inside joke from Barbados.

Tama cleared her throat again. "To answer your question, I'm making fried chicken. I guess I specialized in classic American. Nicole makes Tex/Mex or California Fresh depending on who you ask, so Italian is a good genre to round us out."

Ava nodded. "Cool, cool, cool, cool. Welp, I'm going to get my things so I can get out of Henry's underwear."

"Please stop mentioning that," Will said. "And we already brought all your shit inside. It's in my actual room and I already mostly emptied my closet out when I moved back here. Last door on the right."

She took a step towards the hallway. "Do you want me to wash these tonight?" She looked over to me as she pulled the shirt away from her body. I couldn't stop my eyes from doing another once over.

I shook my head. "Don't worry about it. I'm doing my laundry tomorrow. Toss them on my bed."

She chewed on one side of her lip and nodded. "I'm really sorry," she whispered. "Apparently altitude makes you tired, who knew?" She giggled. "Well, you guys all did because you live here. Okay, I'm so awkward, let me just." She made a weird noise with her mouth and pointed to the hallway.

I watched her disappear into her new room. Will was scowling at me when I turned back to the group.

"Abso-fucking-lutely not."

My eyes went wide and innocent. "I didn't say a thing, bro."

And while I enjoyed riling him up, I wasn't interested in actually pissing him off or betraying him. He came to my and Matt's rescue when the three guys jumped me. I only remembered glimpses of that night, but I do recall him swinging the bat and hearing a crunching noise. When the guys were arrested one of them had a double fracture in his arm, three broken ribs, and bruised kidneys. The reality was, I owed everyone in the kitchen my life.

Matt interrupted the assault. Will and Lily attacked when we were losing. Will with his bat, Lily with a taser. Nicole called the police and Tama detailed everything out, so the police were able to find the fuckers. A skill she learned from her uncle-dad who was a cop in Hemet. Will also pretended to be my brother so he could give everyone information on me and called my dad.

"You didn't have to." His eyes were squinted in annoyance.

Lily sighed and tugged on his arm. "Give it a rest, Peach. Now you're sounding like Kim, and Henry hasn't said or done anything."

Will blanched. "I can't believe you compared me to that evil bitch."

Lily giggled. "If the shoe fits. Besides, you told me to remind you to call Jacob. Why don't you do that now before we eat dinner."

Ava

Oh my god. Ohmygod. Oh. My. God. What is happening to me? Could I be any more cringe? And holy shitballs Henry is gorgeous, like what the literal fuck. The way his brow perked when I asked him if I were wearing his clothes. He seemed more at ease with me than I would feel if some weirdo was in my bed wearing my clothes.

At least I have a bed.

I sighed and leaned against the shuttered door of my actual bedroom. I looked around, yeah, had I checked this room I would have known it was Will's. Catcher's gear was in the corner of the room, and it smelled faintly of sweat and his cologne. *I can't believe I took a nap in Henry's bed.*

Why was I so embarrassing? And why did Henry have to smell so fucking good? I sniffed my shoulder as my eyes rolled to the back of my head. Had I not been delirious with exhaustion I would have known that Will didn't smell this good.

My whole body was surrounded by how amazing Henry smelled. *This is bad, like so bad.* I know I made a huge show about telling Will I could sleep with whoever I wanted, but I wasn't expecting to *want* to within a few hours of getting to Boulder. Maybe that was also a side effect of the altitude, you got stupid horny.

My lip curled at the trash bags full of clothes. I needed to focus on something besides the dark look that flashed in Henry's eyes when I asked him if he wanted me to wash his clothes. The way his dark green gaze slid down my body and paused at the apex of my thighs before swooping back up and shaking his head.

I had made the same assessment and good lord in heaven I finally understood the world's obsession with gray sweatpants. I may not have ever seen a penis in real life, but his pants left little to the imagination.

I wasn't completely inexperienced. I had touched a dick before, I almost finished a hand job, but I didn't get to see what I was doing.

My parents wanted me to go to some expensive private school once we moved to Pasadena. You know the difference between private and public education? Access to drugs and a bunch of horny rich teenagers that will literally fuck anything that moves.

And maybe if I hadn't joined that school my senior year as the odd man out with a million cliques, I would have lost my V-card a year ago. And maybe had the earthquake drill lasted a little longer I could have actually seen Craig's dick, but I definitely felt it. And wow, warm, smooth, silky skin.

That's what the goal should be in skin care commercials. You should want your face to feel like a warm smooth penis. I admit, there are some definite flaws with the marketing. Anyway, I jerked off Craig as he fingered me under the bleachers while the earthquake drill droned on.

He was sweet, sort of, until he got back together with his ex the following week. I didn't blame him. We had met during my first week of school while I was hiding out under those bleachers during lunch. I had never fit in anywhere and the last thing I wanted to do was sit alone in the school cafeteria. So, I grabbed my lunch and headed to the quietest spot I could find.

Craig found me there and didn't say anything as he pulled out his Indica vape pen and inhaled deeply. He offered me a hit. I had never done any sort of drugs before. Being a good Southern girl, marijuana was the devil's lettuce and the path to being a strung-out whore, according to my mother.

But I didn't want to sully the first interaction I had with someone at the school, so I accepted. It tasted weird but the nervous chatter in my head died down. We became friends and when I told him I was completely inexperienced, he offered to teach me whatever I wanted.

He taught me how to kiss and what it felt like to be fingered. We had moved on to hand jobs. He had promised me we would start his lessons in blowjobs and then his ex told him what he had been waiting a year to hear, and he said our time was over. I wasn't crushed, but I was a little bummed. And horny.

Ugh, why does Henry have to look the way he does, and I acted like a Class A weirdo? I needed to get my mind off his face and perfect body. I could tell from the cut of his t-shirt that he was fit. It was wrong to lust over my new roommate, right?

I heaved the bag on top of all the others and dumped the contents on the bed. My underwear and socks littered the mattress as well as the little vibrator Monroe recommended when we were talking about sex. I snatched it up and hid it in the nightstand. God forbid Will walk in and offer to help me unpack. I'd die of embarrassment.

I pulled open the dresser drawer and sighed that it was empty. I dumped my panties inside and shoved them to the side to make room for my socks and bras. One drawer down, one bag down. The next bag was of my dresses and things that needed to be hung up. The closet was only a quarter full, so it was easy to push Will's dress clothes to the side and use the rest of the hanging bar.

I snatched a pair of pajama shorts and tank top from the next bag and set them aside to change into. Lily knocked on the door to let me know that dinner was ready. I was starving and nervous to share a real meal with my new roommates. I nearly left my room without changing. It would make me look like a true psycho to still be in Henry's clothes.

I inhaled deeply as I pulled the shirt over my head. My tank top was a little cool compared to the oversized t-shirt. It pebbled my nipples. I whimpered at the idea of putting on a bra after the day I had. I slipped nipple covers into my tight tank top. It was what I did often when I didn't want to wear a bra. I slid his boxers down my thighs and cringed.

Please, no, no, no. All my horny little thoughts about Henry's fucking face and clear dick outline had made a little bit of a mess in the crotch of his boxers. I stepped into the bathroom and snagged some toilet paper to remove as much of my snail trail as possible.

He's going to wash these tomorrow.

I let out a breath and folded the boxers and t-shirt neatly. The AC kicked on and my crotch felt distinctly cool. I gaped at my naked bottom half. I was about to leave this room like Winnie fucking Pooh only wearing a red crop top. I calmed down, my brain was messy, thoughts were running too fast, and I was tired. I slipped my shorts on and took a deep breath.

No one will know what I almost did.

Henry's door was propped open. I stepped inside to leave his borrowed clothes. His bed was still unmade because I went crazy and staged a lie-in in protest of Will cramping my dating life.

I stepped over to the twisted sheets, tugged them back into place, and folded them around the pillow like they were. Hooks and cuffs that were tucked between the headboard and the pillows. *Oh my.*

I had read a long book series about bondage, and it definitely had piqued my interest. Gripping the comforter, I finished making the bed.

"That's really not necessary."

My head whipped around to see Henry leaning against the wall where he had watched my protest against Will. His eyes were boring into my ass before he flicked his gaze back to my eyes. I was bent forward, butt high in the air, and my shorts had pulled into a wedgie when I had reached to tuck his sheets under his pillow.

My body snapped upright, and I spun around to face him. I swatted my hand to my butt and felt nothing but a bare cheek. Wiggling until the fabric fell away, my face cheeks were on fire. "Sorry, I made the mess, I wanted to fix it."

His eyes raked up and down. He licked his bottom lip a few passes before meeting my eyes again. "Ava?"

The way he said my name made me squeeze my thighs together. My eyes stared at the bulge in his pants, and I swear to God it twitched.

A choppy breath stuttered out. "Yeah?" Still unable to pull my eyes away from the outline of his dickhead against his thigh. He hung to the right and good lord I needed to stop staring at this man.

"Get the fuck out of my room." His tone was even, not angry or amused, like he was telling me the time of day. Which was apparently time to *get the fuck out of his room.*

Air deflated from my lungs. I mean I got it; I invaded his space again. I was breaking rule number one, again. I was already the worst roommate to this man. I was also practically assaulting him with my eyes. I slammed them shut and took a step back, walking into his nightstand. The lamp swayed, but I was quick to grab it before it hit the ground.

"Phew, okay, Henry, or do you prefer Hank?"

He blinked at me and looked behind me towards his nightstand. A picture had also fallen over. I reached behind me to right it. "Wow, she's so beautiful. Is this your girlfriend?"

He let out a patient sigh. "No."

I nodded rapidly. "Right, sorry Hank Henry. Anyway, I left the clothes I stole right there." I motioned towards the foot of the bed. "You're going to do laundry tomorrow, right?" I shook my head. "Of course, you are. You already said that. Okay, well," I clicked my tongue and pointed to the hallway. "I'll get out of your hair."

And not imagine running my fingers through it. His hair looked thick, brown with a red tinge to it. The top was long enough to grip; the sides were faded up. I rolled my lips in and scooted past him and into the hallway where I let out a breath.

"Ava?"

I whipped around. He was standing in the doorway with a slight smirk on his gorgeous face. "I prefer Henry."

I nodded a little manically and walked backwards towards the living room. Lily was giggling at something that Nicole was saying. They grinned at me as I waved.

"I think Henry hates me." I sat down next to Lily and cringed.

She frowned and shook her head. "I doubt that. He's very chill and sweet. He's just quiet."

Nicole leaned forward. "And if he seems grumpy, he probably has a headache," she whispered. I rolled my lips in and nodded. "He has gotten those a lot since the incident."

Lily elbowed Nicole and shook her head. I gave them a questioning glance. Lily sighed and leaned forward. "Will didn't want you to know because he didn't want anyone to worry, but last May Henry was jumped by three guys. They tried to kill him, cracked his skull. He was in a coma while he healed. Matt and Will stopped the attack." She gave Nicole a meaningful look when Nicole opened her mouth to add something.

My mouth parted as my brows furrowed. The idea of something like that happening to Henry made me sick to my stomach. I nodded. "I won't say anything."

We all leaned away from each other when Will sat down on the sofa with a heaping plate of fried chicken, mashed potatoes, and biscuits.

"Go get a plate before Henry gets out here," Tama said from the kitchen. "He's been insatiable since I moved in. He apparently spent his summer working out and swimming."

Nicole nodded with wide eyes. "I noticed." She mimed flexing her biceps. Matt grunted and leaned over the couch to whisper in her ear.

I ate dinner and finally with a full belly my nerves from the day started to calm down. Until I got back in my room and couldn't stop thinking about what a freak I had been around Henry.

Chapter 4

Henry

I stepped out of my bathroom and stared at the folded clothes on my bed. They were taunting me. I didn't like that I couldn't get Ava out of my thoughts and worse that I wasn't going to be able to work her out of my system like I would have in the past.

She's off limits.

My stomach was painfully full of dinner. I hadn't eaten this well all summer and my brain was reminding me by refusing to tell me when to stop eating.

My mind was the betrayer of all things good. I couldn't have a little energy; I had so much I needed to medicate. I couldn't eat a regular amount of food; I ate until I hurt. My thoughts couldn't flow at an easy pace; they had to whip from my head from idea to idea. I couldn't find a girl attractive; I had to own her body.

My closet held more evidence of Ava's intrusion. I groaned at the tiny white panties wadded in the corner with a matching bralette, jean shorts, and tank top. Her little sandals were in two separate corners of the closet as if she kicked them off in a hurry to get naked. I scooped up her clothes and tossed them in my laundry basket.

I shucked my t-shirt and sweatpants off. It was too hot to sleep in clothes, not that I slept in anything in the winter either. The worn and folded clothes sat at the foot of my bed.

The shirt was still warm. I lifted it up to press it to my nose. It only smelled like my soap; the expensive stuff my mom sent me from Paris. I scooped up the boxers but stopped myself from tossing them into my laundry basket. They were too cool to the touch. I pulled my fingers away from the damp crotch. My eyes rolled to the back of my head when I caught the intoxicating smell of her pussy.

She was wet when she wore these. *Maybe the thought of wearing my clothes got her all hot and bothered.* I gripped the shorts in my fist and stared at my bed. I shouldn't do this, but if this was the only way I was going to know what her pussy smelled like, then I was going to take advantage. And because I'm a sick fuck I grabbed her white panties from my basket and brought them to my nose.

I groaned as the blood rushed to my cock. I leaned back against the pillows of my bed and draped the wet fabric over my dick, letting her wetness smear against my head. I started making long slow passes up and down, twisting at my head until my tip leaked and dripped down my shaft. I set her panties on my chest, close enough for me to smell her. If she ever left her panties in here again, I'd gag her with them.

What I wouldn't give to tie her to my bed and suck her clit into my mouth. I'd edge her all night long. She'd be punished for making anything more than a gasp. I'd make her pussy drip all over my sheets and then I'd make her clean up the mess with her tongue while I pounded into her from behind. She'd bleed all over my cock, guaranteed.

My hand gripped my shaft in a chokehold like I imagined her tight pussy would feel like. My orgasm rolled up my spine as

I spilled into the boxers she wore. I shuddered a few breaths and let my eyes focus back to the ceiling.

What the fuck was wrong with me?

I needed to get laid.

I kicked the sheets off that were twisted around my legs. The clock read 2am. I hated having insomnia. I hated that the world around me was able to sleep while my brain hummed constantly.

I looked over to the photo of my maman on my nightstand. She was my favorite person in the world and lived in Paris. She was probably getting ready for her day.

Me: Bonjour Maman

Maman: Mon canard, why are you awake?

Me: A lot on my mind. School starts in a few days. I have a new roommate.

Maman: Are you worried about school? I thought your grades were good last year. Boulder seems to agree with you.

Me: I'm not worried about school. Despite my reservations, Pineview is great.

*Maman: Is it your head? Is this why
you can't sleep? Or perhaps you
don't like your new roommate. Tell
me about him.*

> *Me: It's not the concussion. My
> brain is busy. And my new
> roommate is a woman.*

*Maman: Oui, that brilliant brain of
yours doesn't like to calm. Are you
talking about Tama? Are you having
feelings for her? Or fighting?*

My lip curled at the idea of being with Tama in that way. I
loved her like a sister and that was it.

> *Me: Not Tama, and I told you that
> nothing is going on with her. Will's
> half-sister, Ava, moved in.*

*Maman: Ah. Is she a beauty? I
have never met an Ava that wasn't.*

I chewed my lip. My mom knew me better than anyone in
the entire world, so there was no point lying to her.

> *Me: Very. And Will is very
> protective of her.*

*Maman: I see. Well mon
canard, you can be her friend,
oui? Perhaps you will see her
like Tama soon.*

She sent her love and well wishes for my head to calm down. It wouldn't, not on its own. I walked over to my closet and grabbed the shoe box I kept on the top shelf. I sighed that I had forgotten to refill my edibles again. I pulled the papers and baggie out to roll a joint. My sweatpants from earlier eased up my thighs. I didn't want to get dressed, but that was no reason to flash the neighborhood since we already had one of those.

The living room was blissfully quiet. Only the dishwasher was whirring in the kitchen. My small balcony had two small chairs set up. I preferred the one in the corner that you couldn't see from the living room. It was dark on the balcony, exactly how I liked it. The overhang of the trees completely blocked out the streetlights and the moon was hardly a sliver in the sky.

I lit my joint and took a deep inhale, resisting the urge to sputter and cough. It had been a while since I smoked. I was too paranoid to mess up my lung capacity, and I didn't like the lingering skunk smell that permeated my skin and fingers for hours after. I was going to need to shower after this, but that would only aid in my desire to relax. The warm water against my skin when I was high was heavenly.

The smoke unfurled from my mouth in lazy curls.

Ava

I stared at the ceiling too wound up to sleep. I hated that my anxiety wasn't allowing me to stop thinking about the million ways I embarrassed myself today. I was still reeling from the knowledge I hadn't signed up for student housing.

What a stupid oversight! And then the whole blunder with Henry, God kill me now.

I replayed every interaction and conversation I had, and I came up with one conclusion, everyone either hated me or felt sorry for me.

That's not true, Lily and Will love you.

Maybe, but I was still staying in his room as a pity handout. I still needed to be rescued because I was a dumb baby. I whimpered to myself. My anxiety was taking on a mean edge.

My hand slipped into the nightstand. I was tempted to use the vibrator to help me sleep, but after embarrassing myself and reliving it for the past three hours I couldn't muster the ability to do that.

I gripped my vape between two fingers and tiptoed out of my room. No one in my family knew of my little habit I had picked up from Craig a year ago. It had taken a lot of experimentation to find the right blend that worked to tame down my anxiety as well as a decent fake ID compliments of Craig.

After I got back from Barbados, I got a doctor's note that prescribed medical grade marijuana for my anxiety. I had already confirmed with a few places near campus that they'd take my prescription, so I was going to be set for the year.

That didn't stop me from getting a year's supply before I left. It was one of the biggest reasons why I needed to drive. There was no way I was going to be able to fly with that much cannabis and I was positive the amount I had on me could be considered trafficking.

I paused outside Henry's door. When I didn't hear anything, I made my way to the patio. The kitchen light was bright compared to my room and hallway. I blinked the brightness from my eyes and slowly opened the sliding door. I kept my ears open for anyone getting out of bed. The last thing I wanted was for Will to find out.

The door quietly rolled down the track. It was too dark to see anything. It didn't help that my eyes were adjusting from the brightness of the kitchen. I fell ungracefully into the chair that was in front of the door.

My first hit was heavenly. I closed my eyes to the familiar burn in the back of my throat and coughed out my exhale. Like a lightweight blanket falling over my head I calmed down with a sigh.

My head tipped back, and I looked at the sliver of moon that I could barely make out from the tree's overhang.

In the corner of my eye, I caught an amber glow. I lazily turned my head to the corner of the patio and squeezed my eyes shut. *There is no way a shirtless Henry is three feet away from me.*

Smoke curled from his lips. His head was tilted, assessing me. He didn't say anything, so I kept quiet too.

Nerves fluttered my stomach. When my dad tilted his head, it meant he was pissed. But Henry looked curious. I licked my lips and took one more hit from my vape and rested it on the table between the chairs so it could cool down.

My eyes turned back to Henry as his cherry glowed bright. It illuminated his handsome face. He stared at me through the entire inhale, making my insides squirm. *I need to stop staring back at him.*

I watched in fascination as he licked his fingers and put the end of the joint out. He set it next to my pen and leaned back in his chair. His head tilted again.

I rolled my lips in and finally gathered the strength to break the eye contact that was holding me hostage. "It's a nice night, huh?"

The wind blew and shifted the branches enough for the streetlight to shine. I watched his eyes drag from my chest back to my eyes. "It's a little cold."

Two very pointy nipples saluted my roommate. I hunched my chest and crossed my arms to cover the evidence. A bead of sweat dripped down my back as I licked my dry lips. "I was feeling warm actually."

He hummed. "Ava?"

It was like his lips were moving in slow motion and he was savoring how my name tasted. My toes curled and I clasped my hands into fists.

My teeth pinned the corner of my lip. "Yeah?"

"Why are you out here?"

I huffed and looked away from his beautiful face. "Couldn't sleep. I have anxiety and today was a big day. I've been reliving every interaction in my head for hours."

He hummed again. "How long have you smoked?"

My throat was bone dry, I wished I had an ounce of saliva to help the cotton mouth I was experiencing. "About a year. No one in my family knows." I flicked my gaze over to him. He was rubbing his chin with his thumb and pointer. "You can't tell anyone."

He nodded slowly. "Your secrets are safe with me, Babydoll."

A shiver ran up my spine when he called me that. I normally hated anyone referring to me as a baby or anything childish like a doll. But the way he said it, he wasn't trying to put me down. He was calling me a term of endearment. It almost made me feel sexy, and there was literally nothing sexy about me.

"I'm really sorry about earlier." I was glad it was dark so he couldn't see my cheeks were burning red.

He dragged his eyes away from me and tipped his head back in his chair. "Don't worry about it."

A humorless laugh slipped from my lips. "That's the thing, Henry, all I'll do is worry about it."

He nodded slowly. I wasn't sure if it were the mutual high or exhaustion or what, but everything seemed to have slowed down. "Why are you out here?"

"Couldn't sleep, but to be fair I rarely can."

I twisted my lips to the side. "Insomnia?"

He nodded. "I have ADHD, meds don't help with the lack of sleep, and I don't want to take anything that I could get heavily addicted to. I promised my maman a long time ago that I would keep my drug use to cannabis only. I'm recovering from a brain injury, so I've recently been cleared to use THC again. I'm out of my edibles, so as a last resort I am out here."

"Oh, yeah. Nicole mentioned something about an attack. Are you okay?"

He blinked at me a few times and shrugged. "I don't remember the attack. I get glimpses, but my memories from that day until I woke up from my coma are murky at best."

I had bitten into my lip hard enough to draw blood. I relaxed my mouth and let my tongue glide along the bloody gash. "I'm sorry that happened to you."

"You apologize a lot."

I gave him a half smile. "Hazard of having an unstable parent at home. Both my mom and sister are narcissists. I've spent my life walking on eggshells, so I don't incur their wrath."

He leaned forward; tension bracketed his mouth. "They hit you?"

I shook my head. "No, they aren't physically abusive."

He looked over to the swaying trees. "Just emotionally and verbally then," he said as another statement of fact.

I nodded. "My brothers protected me from a lot. My dad doesn't know. Well, he didn't know until a few weeks ago. I let it slip that my sister and her best friend have been tormenting me for years. He didn't take it well."

Henry leaned back and turned his gaze to me again. "Your dad is the one that led a double life, right?"

I giggled and nodded. "That would be correct. And I am the one that ruined it for him. I hugged him when he was talking to Will's mom at a holiday party. The jig was up after that. My mom put me up to it but denied it after the fact."

We were quiet for a moment while he absorbed what I had said.

"It's cool that you are so close with Will considering how you started out your relationship. I doubt my mother would have been so gracious."

I sighed wistfully. "That's because Charlotte is one of the best moms alive. She didn't punish me or my siblings for something my Mom and Dad did. She accepted me and encouraged Will to have a relationship with all of us.

"The house my dad bought for us to live in when Charlotte divorced him was only a short bike ride over to her house. I would sneak over to Will's place when I was old enough to ride a bike on my own. My dad knew, but he never told my mom."

There were another few beats of silence. His eyes were boring into the side of my face, but I refused to look over to him. It was too mesmerizing and tempting to get into another staring contest with him. It would make my crush too obvious. I didn't want to make him feel uncomfortable by my gawking.

Movement caught my eye as he rose from his chair. I turned to face him as his crotch stopped six inches from my face. I had never been so close to a dick before, and I could see the outline of him in perfect clarity. My eyes quickly tore away from his cock, and I looked up to him from my lashes. He was looking down his nose at me with a blank expression on his face.

"Ava?" I loved how my name sounded when he whispered.

"Hmm." Words had escaped me. I wanted him to cup my cheek and kiss me or drop his pants and let me kiss him in other places.

"I need to get by you."

His words didn't register at first. I was still staring into his dark eyes. And then my brain caught up. "Oh, uh, yeah. Sorry."

I scooted my chair away from the door. He moved his body around mine and disappeared inside. I whimpered and cupped my flaming cheeks. *What the hell was wrong with me?*

Chapter 5

Ava

"How was your first day?" Tama asked me as I made my way to Lily's car. She had a coveted parking spot. Will also had a parking spot because he was in the law school and they had their own lot, but his schedule didn't mesh with mine at all.

"It was fine. Pretty standard day. I only got turned around once, but I was able to get to my class on time. Where is everyone?" I looked around the parking lot.

"They'll be here soon. Nicole and Lily have weight training with their volleyball team that should be over in like fifteen minutes. And I think Henry is swimming."

I wish I would have known. My classes ended an hour ago. I went to the library to wait for the time Lily said she'd be ready to go.

"So, we wait?"

Tama nodded. "We could walk. It's a nice day."

I leaned against the SUV and shook my head. "I'm still getting used to the altitude. I don't want to admonish myself for being so out of shape that I'll get winded by a walk home."

Tama gave me a single, knowing nod. "I'm not one for exercise so it took me a while to get used to the thinner air. Do you work out at all?"

My lips twisted to the side. "I was into ballet for a long time, but I stopped when I moved to California." My tone dipped at the mention of the move that had disrupted my senior year and took me away from the two people I had considered a friend. Though neither had ever reached out or responded to my text message when I wished them separately happy birthday.

Tama hummed. "You don't like California?"

I sucked my cheek into my molars and shrugged. "Nothing wrong with the state. I was forced to move there last year."

"Ahh, well, that was all I knew until last year. My mom didn't let me leave the house until I was twenty. I was homeschooled and finally my uncle, who married my mom this past summer, convinced her it was time for me to experience the world."

My lip curled. "Do you feel mad about that?"

She shook her head. "My mom loves me. She wanted to protect me. My dad was a teacher and died protecting his classroom in a school shooting. I was young. Instead of starting traditional school, my mom home schooled me. She was depressed and didn't want to lose me, so she kept me to herself. She wasn't trying to hurt me. It was always to keep me safe.

"Where I grew up is not exactly safe. My neighborhood was great but outside of it wasn't. There's a lot of drug trafficking and stuff like that. My uncle-dad is a police officer, so he would share with me all the things that could hurt me. I didn't want to leave, you know?"

"I guess. I honestly can't relate though because as long as I can remember I've wanted to get away from my mom and sister."

Tama grinned at me. She was very pretty in the way she could be a model for how striking her features were. She didn't need makeup to enhance her clear brown eyes, they were wide set and big, her chin narrow. She looked elfin or anime-like. Her skin was a creamy white with a natural pink hue to her cheeks.

"I heard all about your mom and sister."

I smiled. "They are notorious."

"Have you thought about what you want to cook for dinner tonight?"

We had all drawn a night of the week. My night was Monday, which was okay because it meant I would be able to use fresh groceries for whatever I was making. I had already put aside my dough for fresh pasta and it was resting in the fridge. Sunday night I guess once upon a time was leftover night, but since there were never any leftovers Lily ordered dinner.

"Chicken parm with fresh pasta. I'm not sure if anyone has any food allergies, so it's a basic recipe that can be modified."

Tama chuckled. "No one has any food allergies that I've been made aware of. Henry doesn't love cilantro, but that's easy enough to avoid since it's mostly a garnish."

My cheeks blushed at the mention of Henry. We hadn't spoken since the night on the patio. I also hadn't seen him on the patio since then. "Are there any likes or dislikes that I should know about?"

"I haven't heard of anyone's dislikes, but likes are mostly sweets. Henry and Lily are suckers for lemon desserts. Nicole is a chocoholic. Will loves any sort of sweet and Matt loves coffee-based desserts."

"Will has a sweet tooth, doesn't he?"

Tama snickered and nodded. "He does. I once watched him plow through a dozen chocolate chip cookies in one sitting. He was so *excited* to eat them he got crumbs everywhere."

"I make a good lemon curd. My nonna has lemon trees in her backyard in Italy so she makes all sorts with her fruit. She taught me how to make a few different things."

Tama hummed. "You want Henry to fall in love with you, make him lemon bars. He begged me for months to make him some. I don't have a good recipe for them. He ate them, said he liked them, but I know that I've had better."

I rolled my lips in before I let them pop out. "Well, I don't want him to fall for me, but I will settle for him to not hate me. I don't think he likes me since the whole sleeping in his bed and wearing his clothes situation."

Tama frowned. "I haven't heard him say one way or another about you. It's probably in your head. He's private. He's been very quiet since the attack. Don't get me wrong, when he wants to be annoying, he will find out what needles you and poke, poke, poke." She mimed a stabbing motion.

A forced smile hitched one cheek higher. I would take him being a pest to me if it meant he was giving me any sort of attention.

"Shotgun!" Nicole yelled from twenty feet away.

She was speed walking with Henry elbowing her with a huge smile on his face. It was unfair how gorgeous he was.

I had never seen him smile before. It made me want to turn and stare at him. He had smile lines that bordered on dimples that bracketed his straight white teeth. His eyes were squinted in mirth.

"Not the middle seat!" Henry yelled at the same time as Tama.

My head bounced between the two and it dawned on me that we were staking our spot in the car. Lily was a few paces behind Nicole and Henry who were still elbowing each other in a weird foot race where neither were running. They were speed walking and looked ridiculous.

The trunk beeped and clicked from the tailgate Tama and I were leaning against. She gently pulled me away so the trunk could float open. She tossed her bag inside and headed for the back seat. Since I hadn't said anything, I was getting the bitch seat. I was used to it. It was my designated seat growing up.

I slid to the middle and waited for everyone else to join me. Tama sat next to me and passed me my seat belt. Henry was the last to climb in. He gave me a quick nod and leaned forward.

"How was your day? Do you have any classes with Rhys?"

She chewed her lip and nodded. "It was fine, and I do."

Intrigue. His lip curled as he huffed a breath. I didn't know what his reaction meant. His back hit the seat a little harder than I was expecting it to.

The smell of chlorine clung to him. His hair was wet and dripping down the collar of his t-shirt. With little space in the backseat his whole leg pressed against mine, but he didn't look at me. After the question to Tama he turned to look out the window.

I wonder if he's into Tama.

I wanted to know who Rhys was but based on Henry's reaction I decided to ask her in private.

Heat was radiating off Henry's leg. He looked tense for the entire short drive home. Lily and Nicole were making small talk in the front seat. When we got home Lily turned around. "Who all is going shopping?"

Tama and I raised our hands. I was a little disappointed that Henry wasn't going with us, but he doesn't cook, so I shouldn't have been surprised. Lily nodded and then looked at me.

"If I give you a list and some money, can you pick up a few things for me?"

I nodded. "Absolutely."

She grinned at me. "Do you mind driving to the store? If you do mind, I can drop you two off and pick you up in an hour. I need to shower, and I already have homework I need to tackle."

"No problem." I turned to look over to Nicole. "Do you need anything?"

She sighed and nodded. "I feel bad though, but I'm in the same boat as Lil. Plus, I was up way too late last night with Matt. He's traveling all week scouting some high schools for players."

"It's no bother. Just give me a list and some money. I can make it happen. It's nothing short of what I've been doing for the past two years since I got my driver's license."

Henry's jaw clicked as his temple bounced. My brow furrowed as he was getting out of the car. I turned back to Lily and Nicole. "Text me what you need and Venmo me money."

Tama and I dropped our bags off in our respective rooms. I started simmering the canned tomatoes and spices from the pantry to get the marinara started while we were out. She stopped in the kitchen to get a stash of reusable bags. Will walked in as I was scooping up my car keys.

"Ava Bear, how was your first day?"

"Fine, nothing crazy happened. Tama and I are going grocery shopping. Do you need anything?"

"A fuck ton, but that's why I'm going with you. Ready?"

A sigh of relief slipped out that Will was coming along. It was a lot of pressure to buy people their groceries. What if I selected the wrong brand? I didn't want to waste food or money in that sort of blunder. "Yeah, are you driving, or am I?"

"You are. There isn't a backseat in my truck."

The three of us made our way to the grocery store. It was weird not seeing the same brands for things I had been using for a year. I had already gone through the culture shock of not being able to get the same creature comforts after we moved from Dallas to Pasadena. Honestly, that was probably the worst part, not being able to get my favorites that felt like home when I was feeling homesick.

Tama sighed heavily next to me as we each grabbed a cart. I looked over to her as she rapidly text messaged someone back. She rolled her eyes. "I don't understand Henry sometimes. He sent me a huge list of things he needs. I asked him why he didn't come with us, and he answered by Venmo-ing me $200. That's not an answer."

My teeth pressed into my inner lip. "Does he normally go grocery shopping?"

She nodded with raised brows. "He loves it. He's like a child. His cart is always busting with impulse items and candy."

I swallowed thickly. "Maybe he has homework like Lily and Nicole."

She scoffed. "Doubt it. Henry is crazy smart and spends very little time actually doing homework. Last year I think I only saw him doing schoolwork twice and that was leading into finals before Christmas break."

"Oh." My stomach pitted with anxiety. I was probably the reason why he didn't want to go to the store. He must know I have a crush on him, and he thinks I'm some annoying little kid. My nose burned, and I shook my head to stop the thoughts from making me spiral. I needed to focus on each aisle, so I didn't forget anything.

"Am I grabbing Nicole and Lily's things?"

Will shook his head. "Nah, I got it. Tama, you have two different color bags, right?"

She nodded. "Learned from last year." She turned to me. "We color code the bags to what goes in what apartment."

A fresh loaf of bread was added to my cart. Our varied shopping list had us going to aisle by aisle. I needed basics like toilet paper and bathing products that everyone else had already. I was eager to swap out Will's crappy single ply toilet paper that looked like he stole it from the bathroom at school.

We filled the trunk and half the back seat up with our groceries. Will promised me that most trips weren't that robust. Everyone was out of a lot of things because it was the beginning of the semester.

My sauce needed a pinch of salt, and I some stock to loosen everything up. The red wine I had Will buy for the marinara splashed unceremoniously in. It took me way too long to figure out how to uncork it. All the wine I'd cook with at home was always already opened.

As soon as the groceries were put away, I started making my lemon curd for lemon bars. My headphones and my favorite music helped me get in the groove and stop fixating on the fact that Henry wanted nothing to do with me. The sugar cookie crust was partially baked, and then I added the curd and finished baking it while letting the chicken marinate.

While still in the marinade bag I pounded the meat into thin, equal pieces and dredged them in egg and breadcrumbs with parmesan cheese. The oil popped against a drop of water. With it at temperature, I added the first piece. I slid the headphone off my ear to listen to the sizzle and pop of the oil and turned my music up. My shoulders shimmied as I swapped out the raw chicken for cooked. With half the poultry cooked I started the pasta. My marinara was nearly ready. It only needed some fresh herbs.

While the chicken was resting and the pasta was draining, I chopped up fresh basil for the sauce and pulled the lemon bars from the oven. I sprinkled powdered sugar across the top and sighed at the delicious smell.

No one was in the living room or had inquired when dinner was going to be ready. I took a moment to throw together a salad and made a balsamic vinaigrette from scratch.

I chewed my lip when no one had arrived and decided to wash the pots and pans while waiting for someone to come eat. When everything was cleaned and still no one had come out I felt the prickle of being pranked. What if no one was planning on eating? What if it was all a big joke?

A knot of anxiety thickened in my throat, and I breathed out to calm down. Will and Lily wouldn't do that to me. Tama didn't seem like the type either. I washed my hands and knocked lightly on her door. She didn't answer. The same for Henry's door. My chin quivered as I went next door. No one answered there either.

I went back to my apartment and sent Will and Lily a message that dinner was ready, but they didn't respond. I made myself a plate and brought it to my room to eat alone.

You're so stupid for thinking that people would want to eat with you because you made dinner. You aren't a part of the group. You are a pity resident. You aren't wanted here.

Eating dinner alone, I wiped the tears from my cheeks. It was stupid to cry. It was honestly everyone's loss because this dinner was delicious. I set my plate in the sink, covered all the food, and grabbed my keys. Facing anyone when I felt so vulnerable was out.

Target was my favorite place to go when I was feeling down. The home goods section was my first stop, and I grabbed a few pillows for my bed. I bought a new lamp for the desk because the one Will had was ugly. New curtains and towels were added to the cart. I was splurging and probably buying my emotions away, but it was the only way I was able to cope with the overwhelming feeling that no one actually wanted me around.

My phone pinged with a message, and I held my breath that it was all a misunderstanding. But it wasn't from my roommates. It was Krystal Quinn's response to my email. Finally, only a week later.

Ava,

I appreciate your level of self-awareness to know when you aren't the right caliber candidate for our tremendous group of women. I can tell by your request that I withhold the truth for you that we would not have seen eye to eye from the beginning.

Unfortunately, I am going to have to decline your request to purposefully deceive two former presidents of my sorority. Legacy or not, that sort of behavior and request is completely unacceptable.

Krystal Quinn
President Phi Mu
Baylor Chapter

My lip curled at the message. What a cunt. I can honestly say I wouldn't want to be around her either. At least I can tell my mom that Krystal and I did not see eye to eye. That's assuming my mom remembered to message me again about it.

My phone buzzed again.

Jacob: How was your first day?

> *Me: It was okay. School was fine.*
> *I made dinner for everyone and*
> *they stood me up, so I feel sort of*
> *stupid.*

*Jacob: WTF! What do you mean
they stood you up?*

I chewed my lip and regretted mentioning anything to
Jacob. There was no way he wouldn't tell Will immediately what
he thought about the situation.

*Me: It's fine. I probably misunderstood
everyone yesterday when they said
they were available for dinner. I'm
being dramatic. How's work? Steph?
Taylor?*

*Jacob: Everyone is fine here. Well
mostly. I think mom and dad are
fighting. I don't know. He's just
been quiet at work. Maybe he's
taking my threat about not seeing
Taylor seriously.*

*Jacob: So, if you aren't eating dinner
what are you doing?*

*Me: I did eat dinner. And now I'm
at my favorite place.*

*Jacob: Yeah, Steph loves the bargain
section at the front of the store. Are
you sure you are okay?*

*Me: Yeah. I found a turquoise lamp
and matching curtains. I'm great.*

*Jacob: :D Love you Ava Bear. Let
me know if you need anything, ok?*

94

Jacob: Will do.

I dropped my phone into my purse and went down the aisle with the books. A few novels for a series I was interested in starting were added to the cart. The patio needed a nice plant, too. I had been out there every night and decided it needed a little something to spruce it up.

After I had wandered around for an hour, I finally checked out. I parked around the back of the apartment building because there weren't any spots in the front. Creeper Peeper hanging out near the mailboxes, making me slump my body behind the steering wheel so he couldn't see me. He was wearing flip flops and a trench coat. His posture looked relaxed as he flipped through the coupon savers.

The living room light was on in my apartment, so someone was at least aware there was food. It also meant that I was going to face them when I went inside. I wasn't ready to do that.

I grabbed the first book of the new series I bought and made myself comfortable in my car. I kept an eye on the living room light, waiting for it to go out. After another hour my butt was starting to hurt. I desperately wanted to go inside, but the light was still glowing.

Finally, the light flicked off. I braved a look up the steps. When it was nice and quiet I scooped my purse up and clutched the ficus in my arms. I paused every few steps to make sure no one was around. I rushed over to the door and slid the key in the lock. My apartment was too quiet. Dishes were piled in the sink.

At least everyone ate.

The plant looked good outside between the two chairs. I grabbed the last few bags from my Target haul. My new towels and curtains were thrown in the washer. And then I washed all the dishes that were left in the sink. I spent some time setting up the new accessories in my room. My shower was short as I waited for the towels to be ready to rotate.

I was settling into bed when I remembered I needed to plug in my phone. I dug around the bottom of my purse and cringed. Seventy-five missed text messages and twenty-five missed calls. All from Will, Lily, Jacob, and a few California numbers I did not recognize.

Will: Sorry, we just got this message. We were in the shower. Coming over now.

Will: Where are you?

Lily: I am so sorry. Where are you?

Will: We are going to eat, I'm assuming you are in the shower. I saw your plate in the sink.

Lily: Where are you?!

Will: I just checked your room, where the fuck are you?

Will: I just got off the phone with Jacob. We would never stand you up! I know it looks like that, but Ava no! Where the hell are you?

*Lily: We are so sorry and getting
really worried about you.*

And on and on.

The two California numbers I didn't recognize were from Tama and Nicole. It was good for me to have their numbers, so I saved them on my phone. The messages were sounding desperate, and the last ones were apparently heading to Target to find me since I wasn't responding. I took a deep breath and created a group chat with the numbers.

> *Me: Hey, didn't mean to make
> anyone worry. I was at Target
> because I needed to get a few
> things. Sorry, my phone was in
> my purse and I didn't hear it. I'm
> home now and going to bed.
> Sorry.*

A cringe lifted my shoulders at the messages from Will as he yelled through his texts about how I scared the hell out of him. I felt terrible. I wasn't trying to make anyone worry, I wanted to be alone.

> *Me: I'm really sorry. I knocked on
> your door and messaged you. I
> also knocked on Tama and Henry's
> door. No one answered. And no one
> came out when the food was ready.
> And by the time I was done eating
> and still no one had joined me, I*

The front door to the apartment slammed shut, and I braced when hurried footsteps ran down the hallway. I threw the covers over my head, hiding from whatever wrath I was about to face.

My door opened, followed by Will's heavy sigh. Then he climbed on the bed and hugged me over the covers. Tears breached my lids. I was so relieved my head was covered because the last thing I wanted anyone to see was me crying.

"Ava, of course we want you here. Don't think that for one second. I am so excited that you are here. So is Lily. And no one was trying to prank you," Will murmured against the covers.

My weight shifted on the bed as another person surrounded my other side.

"We messed up. We should have added you to the dinner chat last week, but we forgot. We were in the shower, Nicole was in her room and didn't hear your knock, and Tama was on the phone with her mom," Lily said quietly.

I nodded against Will's chest to let them know I had heard them. "It's fine. I overreacted when I left, and I didn't keep my phone on me."

Will hummed.

I could tell he was still peeved that I didn't respond to any of his messages as they got more and more frantic.

Lily clicked her tongue. "You didn't overreact, Ava. We under-reacted when we ate and didn't go try to figure out why you weren't joining us. We saw your plate and figured you were working on your homework. It wasn't until we were done eating

98

and wanted to compliment you that we saw you were nowhere to be found."

I let out a slow breath, still controlling the emotions whipping through my brain as they placated me.

"No one blames you for taking a moment to yourself. It's good that you went somewhere that made you feel good. You came back when you were calm, and that's good," Lily crooned. "No one is mad at you," she started.

Will scoffed. "I'm a little mad at you, but only because you scared the shit out of me. You were just gone and not answering your phone. You have your location turned off and no one knows you are here but a few people."

He let out a deep breath. "We let everyone know that you needed some things from Target and I overreacted."

I nodded again, feeling relieved that not everyone thought I had run away like a child.

"We were walking around the store looking for you when you responded. Henry and Tama had to buy the stuff in their carts," Lily added, "otherwise we would have been here sooner."

Will's head rocked against me in a nod. "Can you come out of there?"

I sighed and slowly released my grip on the hem of the comforter. The cool air hitting my warm cheeks was a welcome relief.

"There she is," Lily said. She gave me a soft smile. "Don't do that again. We would never prank you. Do you believe us?"

I rolled my lips in and nodded.

Lily leaned forward and hugged me. "Everyone loved your food."

I twisted my lips to the side. "Thanks for saying that."

Will scoffed. "We are not just saying that. That shit was good as hell. I had seconds. Hank had thirds. There is none left. Matty FaceTimed Billie while we were eating and bitched about how there wasn't going to be any left over for him to try."

"I'm glad you guys liked it."

Will rolled to his feet first. "I love you, Ava Bear. But I swear to God if you run away again, I will kill you."

Lily swatted his stomach. "No, he won't, and she didn't run away. She took a moment for herself in a safe space where she could collect her thoughts."

Will rolled his eyes and gripped Lily's arm, tugging her into him and wrapping his arms around her front. He kissed her temple and whispered in her ear.

"Okay, we are heading to bed. See you in the morning, yeah?"

They shut my door behind them. I waited a few quiet minutes until I padded to the laundry room and rotated my new linens to the dryer. Tama's door was shut, and her light was off. Henry's door was shut, and his light was on. I tiptoed past it and back into my room. I didn't want to see anyone until I had a good night's sleep.

I fluffed and refluffed my pillow, tossed and turned, and sighed when I realized it was going to be a long night.

Chapter 6

Henry

I'm a fucking asshole. I've been actively avoiding Ava since we shared the patio together. She has no idea that we share so many commonalities that it's driving me insane. I had never met another person that had the ability to understand what I had been through as a child until her. And she didn't know that we could have bonded over the fact that we were blamed for an adult's actions.

My dad treated me like a disappointment and a waste of space after that fateful dinner. He blamed me for outing his affair, and it took a long time to realize that I wasn't to blame. He was the one that made the mistake. I had an innocent conversation with my maman. I wasn't the reason why my maman divorced him. His actions did that. It wasn't his first affair on her, but his anger towards me hardly bated at that knowledge.

I was a disappointment for not wanting to try out for the National swim team when I was seventeen. He didn't ask me why I wasn't interested any more. I was depressed my mom moved to Europe and left me behind; swimming wasn't a priority when I was struggling to get out of bed. He chalked it up to me being a drug addict.

I wasn't, not at that point in my life. I hadn't tried anything harder than marijuana until my mom moved away and I had to figure out shit on my own. My dad certainly didn't help, but he had no issues sending all the blame in my direction.

Ava had no idea when she shared the brief story about her family that I related on a level that impacted me deeply. I knew by how she held her shoulders that someone had abused her and when she ruled out physical, I knew we shared the same abuse. Hers from her mom and sister, mine from my father: verbal abuse and emotional neglect.

Tama's knock on my door was a distinct triple tap. I had memorized all the knocks of all the people that used my door. I rolled up from my bed to answer. She glared at me and walked right in and sat at my desk.

"Sit." She pointed to the bed. I crossed my arms as one brow shot high into my hairline.

"I don't take orders well, Tama."

She mimicked my stance. "We need to talk."

The least favorite words any person hears. I rolled my eyes on a sigh and sat across from her. She crossed her thin legs as her slipper flopped onto the floor. She scowled at it and then straightened back up to glare at me.

"Why are you avoiding Ava?"

Not what I thought she was going to say. "I'm not."

She rolled her eyes. "I have known you for a year now. I am an observant person. I notice patterns and behavioral changes. And do you want to know some interesting things I have noticed lately?"

I rubbed the back of my neck, not liking where she was going with this. She continued taking my nonverbal as an answer. She held up one finger to start her count of all the ways I have changed in the past week.

"One, you no longer are waiting in the kitchen or living room like a hyena when someone is cooking dinner. You've been quiet as a mouse until we get the message that dinner is ready.

Last year, heck two weeks ago, I had to swat your hand away from the prepped food while I was cooking. Two, you don't acknowledge her when she is in the room."

"That's not true." *When we were in the same room, I had to fight myself from staring at her.*

She glared harder at me. "Today was her first day of school. She moved to a strange town in an area that she has never been to. She has no friends except for Will and Lily, and you didn't even ask her how her day was. You literally leaned past her to ask me how my day was, but you didn't ask the most vulnerable person in the car."

My teeth bit the inside of my cheek.

"Three, you didn't go grocery shopping today. You love grocery shopping. I made the mistake of mentioning how much you loved to fill your cart with candy, and she looked crushed. So, whether you are avoiding her or not, she thinks you are. Four, you were the only one that didn't explain what you were doing when Ava was trying to get our attention that dinner was ready. What were you doing?"

"Jerking off." A waved a dismissive hand.

She rolled her eyes. "No, you weren't. You prefer to do that in the shower or right before bed in hopes it'll help you sleep. And I know that you took a shower as soon as we got home from school because chlorine gives you a headache now, so you weren't jerking off."

My lip curled. "What the fuck?"

She shrugged. "We've shared a hotel room and bed before. I told you I am observant."

I rolled my eyes and shook my head. "Be less observant of my dick habits."

She tilted her head. "What were you doing?"

I looked away from her and shrugged.

"Did you hear her knock?"

I scratched my cheek and nodded.

"And you ignored it because you are avoiding her. Why, Henry? She's so sweet and kind. I know she's a little much and sort of word vomits, but we've all been there."

A breath huffed out. "I don't know. I think she has a crush on me, and I don't want her to."

Tama rolled her eyes. "Get over yourself. So, what if she has a crush. It doesn't give you the right to be a jerk to her. Has she done anything to make you feel uncomfortable?"

My chin tipped towards my pillows.

She scoffed. "She had no idea it was your bed she was napping in. That was made incredibly clear to me, and she apologized to you several times."

Ava's door quietly squeaked open. Tama held one finger up to silence both of us. She walked over to the door and listened. It looked like she was holding her breath. After a few minutes she came and sat back down at my desk.

"I suspect we gave her an anxiety attack today. She has shared a little bit about her life, and I did some research on rejection sensitivity. Based on what I read and how she left and didn't communicate with anyone, I've concluded that when no one ate dinner with her, she panicked. She probably spiraled for the nearly three hours she was gone. I feel terrible."

Tama wanted to be a psychologist, so she was taking a ton of classes on human behavior. It didn't surprise me in the least that she was trying to diagnose what happened tonight. Even I could admit that eating alone after making an amazing dinner would have fucked me up. My stomach knotted. I hated the idea that something I did hurt Ava.

I chewed on my cheek. My fingers started to tap along the side of my thigh. I needed to move, the buzzing in my brain told me to do something. I needed a fresh dose of my edibles, or I was not going to be able to sleep tonight. "What should we do?"

She sighed. "Lily sent me a text that said not to mention anything about her disappearing and to compliment the food. I think Ava feels bad, so we shouldn't add to it. Let sleeping dogs lie and tell her dinner was good."

My head bobbed in agreement. "It was fucking good."

She smirked at me. "She made those lemon bars for you."

I rolled my eyes. "No, she didn't."

Tama shrugged and nodded. "She did. She asked me if anyone had any likes or dislikes. I mentioned you were a sucker for lemon bars. I guess she has a bunch of lemon recipes because her nonna is from Italy and has a bunch of citrus trees in her backyard."

My shoulders slumped. I was such a fucking asshole. She made something special for me, and I've been avoiding her.

Tama hummed at my posture change. "Don't beat yourself up. She's young, she'll get over her crush on you. But you've got to stop being a jerk to her. She doesn't deserve it, and by the sounds of it, she's had enough people in her life treat her like dirt."

After I was properly chastised, she left quietly and snuck back over to her room. I sighed and looked up to my ceiling. I needed to say something to Ava.

The issue wasn't that I disliked her or was annoyed by her crush. I liked her a little too much. Not only was she absolutely gorgeous, but she *was* sweet and kind. And after eating her food I was positive she was made for me. It's a fucking twist of fate she's Will's sister.

Guilt pitted in my stomach that she noticed I was avoiding her, and I hurt her feelings. I was still reeling from Tama's insistence that Ava made the lemon bars for me.

I had always had a sucker for that dessert. It reminded me of my grandma. She was my favorite person behind my maman growing up. She was funny and never made me feel bad for being a hyper kid.

She took advantage of my hyperactivity. When I would visit my grandma, we would go bike riding. Well, she would ride, I'd pedal my ass off as she rode in the attached bucket seat. We looked ridiculous in our homemade pedicab, but I loved it. She would cackle and direct me to the grocery store. We'd grab ingredients for dinner and then I'd bike us home.

She made the most delicious lemon bars. She tried to teach me how to make them, but there was no way my brain absorbed all the information needed to make them successfully.

I had been chasing a duplicate of those bars since she passed away three years ago, and Ava's were a near match. I would never admit this to my gran, but Ava's were slightly better. There was something about the crust that gave it an edge. The lemon curd in the center was a dead ringer though.

While everyone was eating, I snuck back into the kitchen and cut out a huge piece and hid it in the back of the fridge because there wouldn't be any leftovers otherwise. Tama insisted on us leaving one piece for Ava since she didn't cut into the dessert at all before she left.

My fingers danced across my thigh as I thought about what to say to Ava. At this point taking an edible would be pointless because my brain was spiraling with worry. I wanted to apologize, but I also wanted verification that what Tama said was true.

When two o'clock hit, I slipped out of bed. My window sat next to the patio, so I was more than aware of Ava's nightly 2:15 outing to vape for fifteen minutes. I wondered why she always waited so long. Did she fall asleep fast and then wake up at 2am every night? Was she optimistic that she would be able to fall asleep unassisted until her brain proved otherwise?

A fucking ficus tree smacked into my face. It had been added to the patio since last week when I had been out there. Adjusting it to further hide my spot in the corner, I slanted my head back and listened for signs of Ava coming out to the patio.

Like clockwork she slid the patio door open at 2:15am and eased into the chair closest to the door after slowly and silently shutting the door. I watched her quietly. Her brow was furrowed; her mouth was twisted to the side. It looked like she was having an argument in her head. It was fascinating.

She huffed out a breath and tipped her head back, rolling her eyes as if she were annoyed. She shook her head and sighed before grabbing her vape from her pocket. The end of her vape glowed as she took a deep hit. Her shoulders eased away from her ears.

It was interesting seeing her tense expression slowly morph into a relaxed state. She took another hit and laughed to herself as if whatever was going on in her head was funny. Her head slumped back, and she let out a deep breath. She was staring at the treetops with a small smile on her face. *God, she's so beautiful.*

"I shouldn't have done that," she muttered to herself.

My interest was piqued. "Shouldn't have done what?"

Her body jerked forward as she slapped her hand to her chest. Wide eyes stared over to me as she swatted at the ficus tree. "Oh my god, you scared me half to death," she hissed.

I chuckled and leaned forward, pushing the tree away so we had a clear view of each other.

"Sorry."

She rolled her eyes. "Don't be, I shouldn't have assumed I was out here alone."

I tilted my head. "I'm not apologizing for being out here, Ava. I'm apologizing about dinner."

Her brows furrowed, her shoulders creeped up towards her ears. "Don't be. Nothing happened."

My tongue swiped against my bottom lip. "So, your body *didn't* go into fight or flight at the perceived rejection that we didn't want to have dinner with you?"

She huffed out a breath and stood up quickly. "Fuck you."

Grabbing her arm, I stopped her from going inside. Her skin was warm and smooth against my palm. Her gaze was boring into my hand that was clasped around her bicep. I yanked her closer to me, so she was standing between my spread thighs. It was a dangerous position to be in, but it didn't stop me.

She looked down at me. She was barely taller than I was while sitting, but it was enough for her to have a slight height advantage. My thumb rubbed in circles against her skin. "Don't leave yet, Babydoll. I'm trying to talk to you."

She swallowed thickly. Saying the pet name I had given her was an impulse. She looked too much like a perfect doll, and I called all my subs baby. *Not that she was my sub.* Or that she could be.

She flexed her fist a few times. "You've been ignoring me for almost a week. What changed tonight?"

I ignored the question. "How was your first day at Pineview?"

She bit hard into her lip. The moon illuminated her face enough to show all color had leached where her lip was pressed into her teeth. My free hand gently tugged her lip loose. "How was your first day?" I repeated.

My thumb was still on her mouth. Her little breaths against the tip of my finger made me hold back a groan.

"It was fine," she finally answered.

I hummed. "Why did you run away?"

She looked up and huffed another breath. "I didn't run away. I needed to get a few things at Target."

A chuckle rumbled my chest. "Like a tree?"

"And other things. I needed a new lamp and towels." She was still looking down at me.

My thumb rhythmically swiped back across her pillowy bottom lip because I'm a masochist. "Earlier was an accident. Tama was talking to her mom. Will and Lily were fucking, which you are going to need to get used to. They both have very high sex drives."

Ava's upper lip curled, and her nose wrinkled in disgust.

I fought my smile at her revulsion of Will's sex life and continued. "Nicole was doing her homework. None of them were trying to reject you."

Her nostrils flared. "What about you?"

I hummed again. "I was avoiding you."

A confused furrow in her forehead replaced her look of disgust. She swallowed again and tipped her face away from my grasp. I let my hand fall to her hip and slid the hand grasping her arm down. Her waist was so tiny my fingers were touching against her back. I let my pinkies rest right at the top of her ass. My thumbs continued to make smooth glides. One had made its way under the hem of her tank top.

I looked into her eyes from my lashes and let my gaze drag back down her body. Her hard nipples were inches away from my face.

"Why were you avoiding me?" she whispered.

Both thumbs had worked under the hem of her shirt and caressed her silky warm skin. "Because you are off limits."

She made a little noise in the back of her throat that sounded like a muffled whimper. "No, I'm not," she said barely above a whisper.

I chuckled and tipped my head to look at her beautiful face. "Dinner was delicious."

She rolled her lips in before popping them out again. "Thanks."

My tongue slid across my bottom lip. "Thank you for making me the lemon bars, they're my favorite."

Her gaze shifted to the left. "I didn't make them for you. Lily loves lemon desserts."

My thumbs stopped their rhythmic glides. I released my hold on her stomach. She was lying to me, but I wasn't going to call her out on it. Telling people their tics was detrimental in always getting a read on them.

"My mistake."

I was secretly thrilled that she didn't move once my hold on her was gone. Her thighs lightly pressed against my knees. She tipped her head down, no longer looking down her nose at me. "I'm glad you liked them, though."

My grin hitched one cheek higher.

Her bottom lip disappeared between her teeth to hide her return smile. "Can we be friends now?"

My head shook. In no world would it work for us to be friends. I would want more. She frowned at me.

"But I'll stop avoiding you."

"Promise?"

She looked so fucking hopeful. "Promise."

I stood up slowly, she didn't move from between my knees so when I was upright our bodies were flush against each other. She tilted her head up to look at me. I settled my hands on her waist again and bent down so our cheeks were touching.

Her breaths were choppy in my ear as I lightly kissed her cheek and dragged my lips to hers. I didn't kiss her mouth. I let my lips brush against hers. "Good night, Babydoll."

Picking her up from her waist, I moved her aside so I could leave the patio. I left the door open and didn't turn around to see her reaction, but I heard it loud and clear from my partially opened window.

"Holy shit," she breathed.

Ava

"I think he kissed me," I muttered to myself. I was still frozen on the patio, the door was open, AC lightly breezed towards me. My hot skin welcomed the chill.

"Well, he definitely kissed my cheek."

I giggled to myself in a delighted way. "I can't feel my knees. Work legs."

My palms smacked my thighs a few times to test to see if I could at least feel those. I could. My legs were trembling and felt heavy. I twisted my body around, snatched my vape and walked woodenly to my room.

I went over some facts once I was back in bed. Number one, Henry *had* been avoiding me. That made my stomach twist at the thought. Number two, he'd been avoiding me because I'm "off limits". Did that mean he wanted me *in limits*? Number three, I felt an undeniable chemistry between us. Maybe it was one sided, but why would he avoid me if it were? Number four, he picked me up like it was nothing. A fact I found sexy and rife with possibilities that made me squeeze my thighs together.

I put away my vape and grabbed my little vibe. My back arched when it buzzed against my clit. I imagined what I wanted to do on the patio. I wanted to straddle his lap and kiss him until I was breathless.

He'd guide my hips to rub up and down his huge dick. I squeezed my eyes shut as a little gasp escaped my mouth. He'd like my tiny breasts, praise them, bite them. My chest heaved as the fluttering started, and I couldn't complete a coherent thought as I rode the wave of my orgasm.

I clicked off the vibe and caught my breath. *That was fast.* Even the thought of Henry had me cumming quickly. It normally took me at least thirty minutes to get myself there. I knew why of course. I was drawn to him.

This wasn't only an attraction. I had been around attractive men before. I wasn't mooning over him because he was ridiculously hot. It was more than that. I didn't know *what* it was exactly, but I missed him when I didn't see him for the day. I would seek him out and try to slyly watch him eat his dinner. I would listen intently to whatever he said and pay attention to his facial expressions as he reacted to what was said around him. It hurt when he wouldn't look in my direction. It felt like winning the lottery when he did. There was a strong probability I spiraled so quickly about dinner because I was embarrassed that Henry would see me be a victim of a prank.

This was an obsession, which was a first for me. Normally, I forgot people existed, but not Henry. I'd been aware of him since the first moment we made eye contact while I was staging a protest in his bed.

My breathing settled and a wave of exhaustion hit. I let my vibrator clatter in my nightstand as my eyes got heavier. My one thought before I went to bed: I'm not going to allow us *not* to be friends.

<h1 style="text-align:center">Chapter 7</h1>

Ava

Dad: I haven't been charged for
your tuition yet. Did you forget?

My lip pulled into a cringe. I was hoping that would fly under the radar. I looped my bag higher on my shoulder and continued the one mile walk to the apartment. I had started using the gym and going through my recorded ballet routines from two years ago. My whole body hurt as I realized how much I had let my muscles fade from disuse.

There weren't any dance studios that I could use, but the racquet ball courts worked in a pinch. It was the suggestion of the front desk girl at the gym. I had booked a court a few times and allowed my body to attempt to make the moves that were easy over a year ago. I hadn't let anyone know that I was dancing again. I didn't want Will to make a big deal about it, so I had made sure to schedule my time when no one else was working out.

Most days all my roommates, sans Tama, would work out after school between four and five. When Matt was in town, Will would work out with him in the afternoon if he had a break in his class schedule, which was intense.

I had started taking the early ride to school with Will since his classes started two hours before ours and I would dance in the morning. I'd shower at the gym and then go about my day like normal. I told Will I was going to the library every morning. It was a silly lie, but I didn't want him to worry about me or worse, slip and tell dad or Jacob I was dancing again. That would inevitably get to mom and then she'd call the dance instructors that we knew near Dallas, and I would have more excuses I'd need to make regarding why I couldn't go to the lessons. I was still waiting for mom to react to my refusal to rush.

My legs were a little rubbery when I took the flight of stairs up to my apartment. It had been five days since Henry promised to not avoid me anymore. And he hadn't been avoiding me, per se. He hadn't been seeking me out either. I would start a conversation with him, but he would keep his answers simple and allow other conversations to begin before ours was over.

It was early enough Saturday morning that I wasn't expecting anyone to be awake. Lily and Will preferred to sleep in as long as possible. They both needed the rest. If Will's first week of school is any indication on how the semester is going to go, I doubted I would see much of him. He already had hours' worth of homework. Lily and Nicole did too as well as practice for their volleyball team.

Tama was in the kitchen. She whirled around with her big eyes blinking at me, "I thought you were sleeping." She slapped her hand over her heart. I shook my head and slid my gym bag down my arm. It wasn't heavy, it had my water bottle, headphones, ballet flats, and a towel in it.

Tama squinted at me. "Where were you at 8am on a Saturday?" She leaned her narrow hips against the counter. She was making cinnamon rolls by the looks of it.

I chewed on my bottom lip. "Gym."

Her nose wrinkled like a bunny as she shook her head at me. "You couldn't work out with the rest of the health freaks yesterday?"

I snickered and went into the living room to sit on the floor. My legs needed a stretch, and I didn't like doing it at the gym. The court I was in faced the weights, and I caught a few guys staring at me while I danced.

"Can I tell you something without it getting back to Will?" I pulled myself into a slow split. At least my flexibility was still mostly intact. My hamstrings protested when my butt hit the floor.

"Sure." Tama turned back to her rolls. She had already spread a cinnamon mixture across the dough and was rolling it up to cut into equal pieces.

"I'm dancing again. Nothing official or with anyone insuring I'm doing everything right. I'm using old recordings my dance instructor gave me before I moved."

Tama tilted her head. "Why can't Will know that?"

My chest touched the ground. The burn through the back of my thighs and into my glutes made me hiss. "Because he'd worry. And I don't want it to get back to my dad and mom that I'm dancing again. My mom put way too much pressure on me. I'll never be a prima, but that didn't stop her from pushing me to the point of hating it."

"Do you hate it?"

I rolled up, still in my split, and pushed my chest over my right leg. "I hate the pressure. I hate the idea that I know I will disappoint my mom when I don't make parts I wasn't interested in trying out for. I hate the competition and the ugly side of it. But I don't hate ballet. Actually, some of my most calm moments were on the ballet floor. I was able to get through my dad's divorce to Will's mom by focusing on dance. It was hard when Jacob moved away for school, but dancing brought me a certain peace."

Tama hummed as she placed the last roll in the pan. She washed her hands as I moved my stretch to the left leg. "Did your mom pressure you a lot with ballet?"

I nodded and adjusted myself into a side split and pulled my chest back to the floor. "She had illusions that I would be the prima ballerina in New York one day. I was forced to try out for leading roles in ballets from the age of ten on."

"Did you get them?"

I nodded with a sigh. "But not by my talents. Daphne told me that mom paid off the instructors to select me to lead a few times. There were girls better than me. Actually, I was told constantly that there were talented girls in the school. It wasn't realistic for a ten-year-old to get the lead role in Swan Lake against dancers that were as old as fifteen."

Tama squinted at me. "Do you believe your sister told you the truth?"

My chin tilted up so I could look at her. I had never thought Daphne had lied about it, which was naïve. She hated anything that made me happy or put the spotlight on me, and she was a pathological liar.

"I honestly don't know. Lifts are easier for the male dancers when the ballerina is small and light. I'm also lighter on my feet and have a lower center of gravity so I can keep my balance better. But my lines and limbs are too short to be as elegant as other dancers. It doesn't matter anyway because I'll never be a prima. I'm too short."

I adjusted my split to face the other direction and saw that Henry was leaning against the wall watching me. His expression was thoughtful.

How much of the conversation had he heard?

My face flushed as I bent forward to complete my stretch sequence.

"How many times did you get the lead?"

I kept my face down, resting my cheek against the carpet by my knee. "I got every lead role until I was seventeen and moved to California. But that isn't saying much. There were only two major productions my school would put on a year. And like I said, I'm easy to pick up, so it made the male lead look good and tall."

I rolled up and grinned. "Kipler was my male counterpart. Our moms were friends. He was a decent friend and one of a few that I miss, but he's never reached out to me. I'm pretty sure our friendship was one-sided. He's a true talent, but only 5'7" so against me he looked huge and strong. I was cast with him as the lead because it made him look good, not because of my talent."

Henry grunted, pushed off the wall, and walked over to the coffee maker.

"Is this your assessment or what you were told?" Tama prompted.

I licked my lips and adjusted my back leg up to curl into my back. "My assessment and what other dancers in the school told me."

Tama hummed. "And do you think that maybe the other ballerinas had a reason to lie to you like Daphne?"

My leg dropped as I thought about it. I shrugged. "It doesn't matter one way or the other. Performative dance is no longer in my future. I want to dance because it brings me joy, not because it's a status symbol for my mom."

"Did your mom try to get you involved in ballet when you moved?"

I laughed. "Of course she did, but she didn't have the pull like she did in Texas. She got pissed when the companies she wanted me to join required me to try out. She knows I get nervous and would screw up. She was right by the way; I hate auditioning and would always throw up before I had to go on stage. A year ago, I told her that I didn't want to dance anymore anyway. It was easier than failing in front of her."

Henry let out a loud sigh and flicked the coffee maker on harshly.

Tama scowled at him. "Calm down, the rolls will be ready in an hour and a half. They have to rise. I wasn't expecting everyone to be awake before ten anyway."

I rolled to my feet and stretched my arms overhead. "I'm going to take a shower. Remember, please don't tell Will about this."

Henry squinted. "About what?"

"I'll explain it to him. Go take your shower." Tama turned to stare up at Henry. He gave her a little smirk that made my stomach twist. He had never looked at me like that. Maybe I needed to take a hint and try to start dating someone, get Henry out of my head for a little bit.

That had potential. A guy from my English Lit 101 class did ask for my phone number the second day of class. He was attractive, not Henry attractive, but nice to look at. He had text messaged me late last night, and I still hadn't responded. I pulled my phone out and saw another message from my dad.

Dad: The Bursar's Office is closed

today. I can call on Monday and
pay over the phone.

Panic crawled up my throat at the thought of my dad calling the school. They would inform him that there was no Ava Reiser as a member of the student body and then my dad would start asking questions.

> *Me: Sorry, I was sleeping. No,*
> *don't worry about it. I'll head*
> *down there first thing Monday*
> *morning.*

Dad: How have your first two weeks
gone? Sorry I didn't ask sooner, a lot
is going on at home.

> *Me: No worries. They've gone*
> *great. I really like my dorm mate.*
> *Her name is Tama and she's from*
> *Southern California too. I think*
> *that's why we were put together.*
> *Classes are fine, but I really don't*
> *want to rush for mom's sorority.*
> *I spoke with the president and I*
> *don't think I'm going to get along*
> *with her. I just want to be my own*
> *person without living in Daphne's*
> *shadow, but mom is insistent.*

Maybe it was dumb to use Tama's real name. It's not a common name at all, but I doubted Will ever mentioned her to my dad. Or if he did, the likelihood of our dad remembering is next to nothing.

Dad: I'm still good friends with the man
I lived with my freshman year too. If you
are already getting along, she'll probably
be a friend for life. As far as the sorority
goes, I know it means a lot to your mother
to try.

> *Me: And it means more to me to*
> *be my own person. Dad, mom and*
> *Daphne have been just as verbally*
> *abusive to me as Lucy was. I don't*
> *want to do it.*

Dad: Let's not get parenting confused
with verbal abuse. She wants what
is best for you.

I rolled my eyes. My dad never believed me, I don't know why I thought saying that would be any different. He always took my mom's side of things.

> *Me: What's best for me is not living*
> *in someone else's shadow. I'm not*
> *rushing. You can either support*
> *this decision or not, but either way*
> *I'm not doing it.*

Dad: When did my children decide to
hate me so much that they think it's
okay to lash out at me?

I sighed and softened my tone.

*Me: I don't hate you dad. I love
you so much. I just don't like to
be forced to do something
against my will.*

*Dad: I'll talk to your mother about the
sorority thing. Please let me know
when you pay your tuition. Love
you Ava Bear.*

I turned the water on and tried to calm down. I hated the idea of starting a fight with my dad. It was hard enough to stand up to him at Daphne's wedding. I had a bit of a panic spiral after that, and Monroe had to calm me down the whole next day. *I miss Monroe.* I needed to text her soon to see how she was doing.

The apartment was full by the time I wandered out of my room. Matt and Nicole were wrapped around each other on the sofa. Lily was sitting on Will's lap in Henry's gaming chair. Tama was talking to Henry in the kitchen.

Lily grinned at me when she saw me. "What took you so long?" Will griped next to Lily.

She elbowed him in the stomach. "Calm down, Peach."

He pushed his bottom lip out in a pout. "But I'm so hungry."

She perked a brow. "You ate for an hour straight this morning."

He grinned at her. "And it was delicious, but not very filling."

My lip curled in a cringe. "What the hell is wrong with you two? I'm right here and your coded conversation isn't hard to crack."

Nicole giggled as Matty whispered something in her ear. "Ugh, you four are gross. I'm heading into the kitchen where the sane singles are."

Tama laughed at something Henry had whispered to her, apparently not hearing a word I had spoken. I chewed my lip and realized I was the odd man out. I clutched my phone and answered the message from my classmate.

Josh: Hey this is Josh from EL 101. There's a welcome back party at the Kappa house Saturday night. You should come.

Me: I'd love to. Just give me the address and I'll be there.

There, if everyone else was going to buddy up, then so was I.

Tama looked up to me innocently. "Okay, Ava gets first pick in cinnamon rolls because she made the best dinner this week."

I twisted my lips to the side. It was an absolute reach in explanation why they waited for me. Tama felt terrible about Monday.

She pushed a pan of ooey gooey rolls in my direction. My fingers wiggled in thought, and I went for the one in the middle of the pan. Henry whimpered at my choice. The noise would have been enough for me to choose a different piece, but I was still feeling indignant over the conversation with my dad and the overwhelming feeling of being the fifth wheel in this coupled out dynamic.

I scooped a slice of quiche on my plate and poured myself a coffee. The dining room table had been cleaned off, no doubt by Tama, so I was able to scoot into my usual seat. I was starving after my workout. Everyone else had shuffled into the kitchen. Tama went next and grabbed a corner piece and sat down next to me at the table.

Her smile was contagious. It lit up her whole beautiful face. "I hope you like them." She pointed to my plate that I hadn't started on yet.

I kept my head down while I was eating. Henry didn't eat at the table but instead ate in the living room next to Matty and Nicole.

"I saw you walking pretty early this morning, what were you doing out at 8am?" Will asked me as he dug into his food.

Fucknuggets. "Are you stalking me?"

He chuckled and scooped another huge bite. "Nope, but my window looks out onto the main road that leads to campus. You didn't have your backpack on you, so that rules out the library. Also, you were wearing your ballet leotard with your sweats, and your hair was clipped back."

I focused on my plate. *So much for not wanting Will to know.* "I don't think it was me you saw."

Will chuckled and shook his head. "I think I'd know my own sister." His eyes flashed over to the front door where I had discarded my gym bag. I rolled my lips in pretending to act nonplussed about the whole scenario.

He picked the last ribbon of his cinnamon roll from his plate and shoved it into his mouth. His cheeks bulged.

"Are you worried someone is going to steal your food?" I curled my lip.

He nodded and tipped his chin in Henry's direction. "Hank is a garbage disposal. If I leave my plate unattended, he'll think it's free rein." He sounded muffled as he spoke with a full mouth.

My brow furrowed as Will pushed away from the table. My bag was in his possession within two long strides. I cupped my cheeks as he unzipped my tote. One brow rose high and then he zipped my bag back up. He stayed silent as he settled back into his seat and scooped up another bite of quiche.

Tama was frozen next to me. Her wide eyes were bouncing between the two of us.

Lily wrinkled her nose in confusion. "Is this like a head in the bag situation?" She slowly rose to her feet. My heart was pounding as my chest started to rise too quickly. My face was on fire. Lily looked in the bag. "I'm confused."

Will shrugged. "I'm not. Come eat, Sunshine, or I'll steal your cinnamon roll."

I chewed my lip and kept my head down. Lily guarded her plate and pretended to growl at Will.

"But is there a head in her bag?" Nicole asked. "I know she's Italian, but like, she's not mafia, right? Is there a big mafia syndicate out of Dallas that the world doesn't know about?" she continued. I snorted.

"There's no head in the bag." Will chuckled and stood up to get another helping of breakfast. "So, what's new with you, Ava?" He didn't look up from the pan of rolls. I chewed on my lip and decided to play along.

"Nothing new. Oh, I do need advice though. Obviously, I haven't paid tuition at Baylor because you know, I'm not there. Dad texted me this morning asking me why I haven't paid. So how do I get around this?"

Will huffed and sat. "Yeah, I know you paid the tuition here because Dad text messaged me saying he was glad I had forgiven him." He sighed again and cut a ribbon of roll. "You're lucky I love you so much because I haven't forgiven him, not in the least."

I nodded and bit into my lip. I didn't consider that aspect of the lie. Our dad would think he was back in Will's life, and he wasn't.

Lily hummed next to him. "You could donate to the alumni association. He'd see a charge to Baylor. It wouldn't be until February when the tax man would need the receipt."

I winced. "That's a hell of a donation, it's like $55k a year plus housing."

Will chuckled. "So? He has the money. Fuck him."

I shook my head. "I cannot, in good conscience, donate that amount. It's so deceitful."

Tama smiled. "To be fair, what you are doing is deceitful."

"Tell your dad you got a scholarship," Henry said.

Lily tilted her head with a nod. "Has merit."

"Would the scholarship include housing? I know mine didn't. A lot of academic scholarships don't completely fund housing," Nicole said. I sat back in my chair.

"So, say you got a scholarship for tuition and fees and only had to pay for housing, I'm sure that's a much more reasonable amount to donate," Will said.

Henry chuckled and shrugged. "Sure, but who is this donation going to go under? It can't go under Daphne or her mom's name. They'll get a letter in the mail thanking them for their donation," Henry said.

The fact that he paid attention to me mentioning that my mom and sister were alums shocked me.

"Donate under Jacob's name. He knows what's going on," Lily suggested.

"You need to look up housing costs and you're good to go." Tama pulled out her phone and typed away. "Let's see, are you living in your own room?"

I shook my head. "I told Dad I was living with a girl named Tama."

She preened. "So, a double. Do we have a bathroom, or do we have to use the community toilets?"

I curled my lip. "We share a bathroom. The idea of community toilets freaks me out."

"As it should," Lily said.

"Okay, roomie. Double room with a private bathroom is $4660 a semester. You have to pay for a meal plan if you are a freshman living on campus, the cheapest one is $900, but they go all the way up to $3400." Tama looked up to me.

I nodded. "Okay."

"You gotta make sure it's an odd amount you are donating otherwise it'll look suspicious. You can't donate a flat $7000. It would need to be $6659.12. That would be a realistic amount for room and meals," Matt said.

I chewed on my lip. "Okay. Looks like I am donating that weird amount in Jacob's name and telling Dad I got a scholarship to cover tuition and fees."

Will grinned at me. "Great! Now that we got that cleared up. What. Else. Is. New. Ava?"

I swallowed hard, still not wanting to tell him about wanting to dabble in ballet again. Will always supported me, but he knew it impacted my mental health. I never told him why it impacted it. I'm sure he associated me dancing again with my obsession with my weight and nearly burning myself out with practices. The obsession to be perfect for my mom and to prove Daphne wrong. But that wasn't what I was doing by getting back into it.

"Uh, I have a date tonight." I tried for misdirection.

"The fuck you do." Will dropped his fork with a clatter.

I squinted at him and held my head high. "I'm going to repeat myself again because I don't think you believed me the first time. You don't have a say on who I date. I could decide to screw around with Tama, and you have zero right to say a word about it. I put up with you dating the literal antichrist. I supported you. I kept my mouth shut about what a terrible person she was because she made you happy."

"Lily is right there. Does she know you hate her this much?" Matty joked. I glared over at him. He cringed a little and shrugged. "Lucy fucking sucked. I'm just bringing some levity. We love you, Lil," he said.

I looked back over to my brother who had a clenched jaw. "Lily you're amazing. Point remains." I stood up and leaned over the table to get a little closer to Will. I was now eye level with him. He didn't look amused. "I supported you and didn't say a word when you were with the wrong person. I deserve the same respect."

"But had you told me, I wouldn't have been with the wrong person. I would have listened to you and broken it off."

I rolled my eyes. It wasn't the time to express to him how delusional that statement was. I *had* told him how Lucy treated me, and he waved it off as me not understanding what she meant.

"Where's your date?" Lily asked in an amused tone. She was grinning widely from me to Will who looked very put out.

"Welcome party at Kappa house." I sat back in my chair and cut a piece of my quiche.

"Abso-fucking-lutely not," Will said. "That was my frat. I know exactly what goes on at that party and you aren't going."

His face was morphed in disbelief that I would deign the idea of going to a frat party.

I looked down at my nails, acting nonchalant about the entire interaction. I didn't want him to think he was pissing me off more than he was. Besides I was still trying to misdirect him from the ballet bag.

"I was actually planning on going to that, too," Tama said.

I turned to face her with a wide grin. "Perfect. Maybe you can help me get dressed."

"Fashion is not my thing." Tama folded her hands on the table. "But I am happy to go with you to the party. I have learned a lot over the past year, and I'd love to share some tips."

"I'll help you get dressed," Lily said.

I gave her a grateful nod. Nicole giggled. I looked over to her and caught sight of a stony-faced Henry. He looked about as amused as Will. I didn't know why he was acting so affronted. He said it himself, *"I'm off limits"*. Whatever.

"Kappa welcome party is fun. A few girls from the volleyball team were planning on going," Nicole said. "I can have them look out for you tonight."

"Can anyone hear me?" Will said.

I continued to ignore him.

Matt sighed. "I'm not going to any frat party. I'm a coach now, so it wouldn't be right."

I nodded and gave him a sympathetic smile. "I understand your reservation about going."

"Well, I can maybe go, too." Lily looked unsure. Will's cheeks were flushed red with anger. "Or maybe not. I think maybe I should spend the evening with Peach."

"Boo hiss." I turned to look at Henry.

"Don't bother asking. Henry doesn't like frat parties," Tama whispered. Henry's eyes narrowed on Tama and flicked over to me.

He sighed heavily. "I'll go to keep an eye on the girls."

Will blew out a breath. "Seriously, are words coming out of my mouth? Because I definitely said Ava's not going."

"Great Henry, I appreciate the sacrifice."

He rolled his eyes over to Will before flicking them back to me. He gave me a little nod and then went back to eating.

"Fine, I guess if no one can hear me. Then it doesn't matter what I say. For instance, my sister has a bag of her ballet gear, and I have concerns. For one, the last time she danced she became so obsessed with her weight I was worried we were going to have to ship her off to a clinic."

"William James Reiser, that is not dirty laundry to share," Lily hissed.

"Oh, so you can hear me. Ava, why are you dancing again?" Will asked me.

My gaze went back to my hands.

"You do ballet? That's so cool. I didn't know that. I always wanted to be a ballerina, turns out I'm a little too tall," Nicole said.

I laughed. "I'm a little too short."

"Ava, I swear to God if you don't acknowledge me, I'm going to lose my shit," Will said. I sighed.

"Why are you dancing again? Are you looking to join a company here?"

I lifted my gaze to Will's. His forehead was furrowed in concern, and his eyes had a pleading pinch that made my posture soften.

"I'm not planning on joining a company here. I wanted to dance and get back into shape again. I don't have to worry about my weight because I'm not dancing with a partner. I don't have to worry about lifts."

He rolled his lips in; his nostrils were flared. "If you start obsessing about your weight again, I'm pulling the plug on this whole experiment. I will not allow you to become unhealthy on my watch."

I nodded. "That's fair. But I also want to point out a big part of the pressure I had was from mom and Daphne, so without them around I should be fine."

He blew out a breath. "I still don't want you to go to the party tonight."

I shrugged. "And I still don't give a shit about what you want in terms of my love life. The bar where you get to intervene is literally in hell. I don't want to hear shit about my choice in a partner unless he is cheating on me or hurting me or others. And you can get off your high horse, I *did* tell you that Lucy was a bully and you brushed it off. She tormented me for years after you two were broken up. She would come over and needle me."

Will's face screwed into a frown. "I'm sorry. I should have listened, so if I have an opinion because I feel like whatever fuckface you are dating is like Lucy, I'm going to share it. You deserve better than what someone like her can give."

I rolled my eyes. Will grinned at me and leaned forward. "But don't forget, dear sister, I know a lot of jocks on his campus. I say the word, and you are off limits."

"You wouldn't," I hissed.

"I. Already. Did." His grin was wide with a challenging glint.

"You motherfucker," I hissed.

Lily giggled and patted my arm. "Don't worry, Ava. He doesn't know all the new students. Tell me about this guy you are meeting tonight."

I shrugged. "He's okay. I met him in my English Lit class. He asked for my number on the second day, and text messaged me last night to see if I wanted to meet him at the party."

"Is he cute?" Tama asked.

I waved my head around. "Yeah. He's attractive."

"I'm not convinced you are actually interested in this guy," Lily said.

I gave her a sad smile. "Beggars can't be choosers. Literally no one finds me attractive so if this guy does, I am going to give him a chance."

Lily frowned hard, her brows furrowed. She began to shake her head at me.

"Let's change the topic because I don't need forced compliments to placate my ego."

Chapter 8

Henry

I hate frat parties. Everyone is trying so hard, it's inauthentic and annoying. But I was going to this stupid thing because I said I'd keep an eye on the girls. It was a simple enough excuse. God knows Tama is so innocent and keeps getting pulled in Rhys Goodman's web that she alone could use the protection. But that wasn't why I agreed to go. No, I'm going because my Babydoll has a fucking date. And it's not with me.

I understood, at a level, that Ava was entitled to date whoever she wanted to because she was off-limits to me. But at a deeper level she was mine and I wasn't going to sit by and watch some unworthy fuckwad strip her innocence from her.

"Rule number one, never accept a drink from someone you don't know. And if you do have a drink, always keep your eye on it," Tama said. We were still a few blocks over to the Kappa house.

"Got it. Stranger danger with the drinks. What else?"

"If a guy asks you to find someplace quiet it's code for having sex. If that's what you want to do, fine, but ask yourself if you really want to hook up with a guy while in a stranger's bed."

Ava's lip curled. "Probably not. I don't know when they changed the sheets. That can be a real biohazard situation."

Tama giggled. "Yeah, exactly. It's one of the hurdles I can't get over. Well, that and no one asks me out either."

"But you're so pretty and have fantastic boobs," Ava whispered.

I cleared my throat. "It's because some douche claims her at every party but as opposed to bringing her up to a room and finally sealing the deal and popping her cherry, he brings other girls up and then hangs all over her when he's done."

Ava's nose wrinkled and turned to Tama to confirm.

"It's more nuanced than that. Rhys is my friend. He's going to help me find a date this year. He admitted that he might have been accidentally cockblocking me, but he is going to be better."

"Oh, is this the Rhys Henry asked you about on the first day of school?"

Tama hummed a yes. "We are friends. He's very attractive, but nothing has happened between us. And as Henry has stated, Rhys tends to hang all over me, but that's because he tells me I'm his best friend."

I scoffed. "I'm your best friend."

She giggled and nudged me with her arm. "Yes, you are, but apparently, I am his. So anyway, rule number three, don't leave the house without telling us. It is not safe for you to try to walk home alone. When one of us wants to go home, we all go home."

"Sound rule, I like it. Okay, so backing up a smidge." Ava paused and chewed her lip as she leaned closer to Tama and said something that was too quiet for me to hear.

"Yes, I'm a virgin. I've never been kissed either. It comes with the territory of living such a sheltered life."

"But you're so pretty," Ava hissed again.

Tama chuckled. "And picky apparently. It'll change this year. With Rhys helping me instead of hindering me, I should get lucky this school year."

Ava giggled. "Well, I'm not quite that inexperienced, but most of my dirty deeds were accomplished under the bleachers during an earthquake drill."

"Scandalous."

I grit my teeth. I didn't want to know about any other guy that had his hands all over Ava. The thought made my skin crawl.

"Any other rules?" Ava asked.

Tama shook her head. "If you don't feel safe grab Henry, it's why he tagged along."

I rolled my eyes, already feeling a headache coming on from the music that was pounding from the speakers of the house.

"You want to be my beer pong partner?" Tama asked me.

The beer pong tables were always in the center of the house with views of everything. As long as Ava didn't go upstairs, I could keep an eye on her.

"Of course."

Tama clapped and looped her arm into mine. "I'm so excited you decided to come out tonight. Don't get me wrong I feel confident that I could have made sure Ava was safe, but it's nice to hang out with you outside of our apartment. Vegas was so much fun." She rested her cheek against my bicep.

I chuckled and tucked her into my chest and kissed the top of her head. "Vegas *was* fun."

Ava was watching us with a confused expression on her face. Then she rolled her shoulders back and walked up the house steps.

The smell of old beer, sweat, and too much cologne hit my nose. I was going to have to take an edible early to stave off the headache I felt coming on. I reached into my pocket and tore my gummy in half. I chewed through it as Tama tugged me into the center of the house.

Lydia Carmichael launched herself at me as soon as she saw me. She almost elbowed Tama in the face while cupping mine and pulling me down to kiss her. Lydia and I had hooked up a few times last year. She wasn't quite submissive material, but she gave decent head.

I caught Ava's eye as Lydia released my face. A flash of hurt followed by a blank expression filled her face. I looked down at Lydia who already looked wasted. "What's up Lydia?"

"I want to suck your cock, Henry. May I please? It's been so long."

The indifferent expression was gone as Ava's mouth twisted to the side. She closed her eyes and walked away from me, not turning around as I stared after her.

The button of my jeans pulled. I gripped Lydia's wrists. "Not tonight, I'm going to play a few games with my friend Tama. Apologize for pushing her out of the way."

"Oh, that's not necessary," Tama began.

"It is." I turned back to Lydia.

She rolled her eyes like a bitch. "Sorry didn't see you." She turned back to me. "I'll call you." She tried to kiss me again. I gave her my cheek.

I looked around the party for Ava as Tama set up our cups. She was talking to some preppy looking fucker. He was about 5'9", average looking. His eyes kept dragging up and down her figure. Lily dressed Ava in a short dress that showed off her legs and tiny waist.

He leaned into her ear. I watched blush creep up her chest to her cheeks. Tama pushed the ping pong ball into my hand.

"Your turn," she yelled over the crowd. I was too distracted to make a good shot. Tama groaned at my side.

My eyes kept flicking over to Ava. She was talking animatedly to this kid. Her smile was wide as she nodded at whatever he had said to her. She tipped her head back in a laugh.

"Drink." Tama handed me a cup from where the ball had landed. I shot the beer back and looked over to the other side of the table. Tama had apparently been running the table because there were only two cups left on their side. We still had five.

With the ball back in possession I chanced a glance back over to Ava. The guy had handed her a drink. I turned to Tama. "Go check on Ava," I whispered.

She gave me a concerned look. "We just got here."

I nodded. "And she broke rule number one."

She nodded and marched over to Ava with a determined gait. I rolled my shoulders back and took aim at the cups and sunk my shot. "Ball back."

My opponents were equally annoyed, one tipped his head back and the other yelled a curse. I shrugged and wiped the wet ball on my jeans. My last shot sailed right into the last cup. A few cheers erupted. I glanced over to Ava and Tama. Tama was talking to Ava's date. She had the cup of beer that Ava had been handed in her hand, and her free arm was wrapped around Ava.

"Next game." Some bros with backwards hats and football jerseys muscled up to the table.

"Tama!" I yelled over the music.

She turned towards me with Ava wrapped under her arm and whispered something in her ear. Ava's cheeks flushed as she nodded again. Tama walked up to me and set the full beer down on the window ledge.

"Good call, Henry. She didn't know how to tell him no about the drink."

I nodded and set up the cups.

"There's my girl." Tama was picked up in a bear hug next to me.

I gave Rhys an amused smile. He hated me because he thought I had stolen Lydia away from him. What they had was a casual friends-with-benefits situation that she wanted more from. Rhys was adamant that it was my fault she wasn't interested in what he was offering any more. It wasn't my business to correct him and let him know not all women are okay with an indefinite friend with benefits situation. Lydia wanted a relationship, he didn't.

"Henry," he said with a tight smile.

"Rhys, how was your summer?"

"Fine. Missed my best friend." He buried his face into Tama's neck. It wasn't something I would do to Tama, but that was because I wasn't using her as a backup plan like I suspected he was.

Tama squealed that he was tickling her and elbowed him playfully. "Don't try to distract me. Henry and I are trying to run the table."

Rhys chuckled and looped his arms around her waist, pulling her back to his front. "I can't believe I didn't get to see you all summer. Tell me about your road trip you've been mentioning for weeks."

"It was an epic road trip with Henry. We hit up a bunch of national parks and Vegas," she said.

Which was true, but she was playing with fire by not disclosing that literally four other people were on the trip with us.

Rhys's jaw clicked shut. I rolled my lips in to keep my smile at bay and turned to look for Ava again.

"That sounds like fun. Why wasn't I invited?" His tone was playful, but I could hear the thinly veiled annoyance.

I don't know why he treated me like I was his competition. If he wanted Tama and was going to treat her with the respect she deserves, I wasn't going to stand in his way. The issue was, he wanted her on his arm, not in his bed.

It was too noisy to hear Tama's response. I was too distracted to focus because my Babydoll wasn't where I had last seen her. My eyes darted around the party and passed the ball over to Tama.

"I'm going to grab a drink."

"Get me one too," she called after me. Rhys saddled up to where I had been standing like he was her partner.

I checked the kitchen. No Ava. I stepped outside, no Ava. I walked back in the living room, still not around. And neither was the fucker she had met. I looped back into the kitchen and grabbed a beer and a bottle of water for myself. I needed to keep my head. I walked back over to Tama.

"Ava's not around. Can you check the bathrooms?" She squinted at me and nodded.

"Be right back. Henry, Rhys, play nice." She floated the ball across the table and into the last cup. The little crowd around us erupted at the ease in which Tama made the shot.

"Fuck, she's awesome," Rhys said.

I gave him a tight smile and nodded. "She is."

"What's going on with the two of you?" Rhys was trying to act casual as he set our cups up, but his shoulders were by his ears, and his nostrils were flared.

"She's my roommate and friend. What's going on with the two of *you*?"

Rhys lifted one brow. "She's my *friend* too."

I looked distractedly to where Tama had disappeared. I was starting to feel uneasy about the situation.

"So, there's nothing romantic going on between the two of you?"

I rolled my eyes and shook my head. "No, there isn't. And if you want something to happen between the two of you, you better piss or get off the pot. You're stringing her along and it's fucking shitty."

He held his hands up. "I'm not stringing her along. She's my friend, nothing more. I told her I was going to help her find someone suitable for her this year."

My chuckle was closer to a scoff. "You know that requires you not hanging all over her like some prize, while you are warning off all the other cavemen."

Rhys scoffed. "That is not what I'm doing. She's my friend."

My smile was patronizing. "Right, my mistake. Your shot." I passed him the ball.

Tama came back with an annoyed look.

"Where's Ava?"

"You aren't going to like it."

My jaw clenched. "Is she in a room?" Tama gave me a single head nod.

"Which room?"

"First one on the left of the stairs. The door was open when I walked past."

I was marching away before she finished talking and took the stairs two at a time. The door was still cracked. I pushed it open. Ava was sitting on a bed looking at her shoes. Her gaze jerked up to mine.

"It's not what it looks like."

"Get up."

She bit her lip and looked over to the bathroom door. "I think he's sick," she whispered.

I rolled my eyes and pushed the bathroom door open. Ava's date was curled over the toilet puking his guts up. "Too much alcohol?"

He shook his head. "Bad sushi, I think."

I chuckled and passed him my unopened water bottle I had shoved in my back pocket. "What's your name?"

"Josh," he wretched.

I nodded. "I'm going to take Ava off your hands, okay? Feel better." I tapped his back a little harder than I would have if it were one of my girls. Josh nodded and wretched again.

"Let's go." My chin tipped towards the open door.

"Is he going to be okay?" she whispered back.

I shrugged. "Not my monkey, not my circus, Babydoll. But you broke two rules within an hour of being here. Do you know what that means?"

"No," she squeaked.

I turned on her and pushed her back against the wall. It was loud in the house so I bent down so she could hear me clearly.

"It means you don't get to leave my side the rest of the night." My lips brushed against hers as I spoke harshly to her. "Got it?"

She sucked in a breath and licked her lips. The tip of her tongue flicked against my mouth. We were too close. Anyone could see us. I backed away a fraction.

"Got it?"

She nodded. I grabbed her hand, laced our fingers together, and tugged her back to the beer pong table. Tama's eyes were wide when she saw us. She gawked for a moment at the clasped hands and then turned to Rhys as he tossed the ball across the table.

"Ava's in time-out."

She scoffed in my ear. "I'm not a baby. I don't need to be in time-out."

I leaned back into her and whispered against her ear. "You broke the rules, Babydoll. You get punished. You're lucky I don't spank your ass for acting like a brat."

Her cheeks flamed as she swallowed thickly. "Yes, sir."

My cock started to thicken at the term. I didn't want to know why she said what she said, but it was exactly what I expected my subs to call me in the bedroom. "Careful Babydoll. You call me that, it means something."

She licked her lower lip and flicked her eyes over to Tama who was watching us with a furrowed brow. Rhys passed her the ball seemingly not paying one ounce of attention.

"How do you play this game?"

Tama turned to her with a smile and started to explain the rules and concept to her. Ava kept her fingers laced with mine for the rest of the time we were at the party.

My unruly desire to keep her close was broken as soon as the crisp wind hit my cheeks. Ava turned her body into my chest, like I was going to shield her from the weather. On instinct, I untangled our fingers and walked forward to lead, putting much needed distance between us. My head was messy.

As soon as we got to the apartment I walked straight to my room and into my shower. I chewed through the other half of my edible and turned my face into the hot water. Annoyance still pricked my brain that Ava had a date. It didn't matter that it ended up being a total dud, she still went. She still entertained the kid and had he not eaten bad sushi he would have entertained her, too. Which pissed me off.

I stared at my ceiling and grit my teeth when Ava opened the patio door. My bedroom window was still cracked open. She sighed heavily. I knew when she was taking her hit and exhaling. Joining her on the patio was tempting, but that could lead to putting myself in a bad situation. Teasing her lips with mine had been a mistake. It didn't matter that we shared similar childhood trauma and coped in the same way. It was a twisted knife of fate that she revealed another aspect of her life that wove together with mine.

We both were driven to compete until the sports we loved were weaponized against us. I didn't tell either of my parents when I started swimming again because I didn't want them to get their hopes up that I wanted to compete again. Just like she didn't want her mom to know because the pressure to perform was too great and made her hate something that brought her happiness.

She whimpered. "Why do I have to want him? It's clear he doesn't want me back."

She often talked to herself while she thought she was alone. It was one of the reasons why I kept my window cracked open. I liked the unfiltered view into her head as she talked through whatever was plaguing her that night.

Tonight, it sounded like she was worried about me.

Same, Babydoll.

"But why kiss me if he didn't want me?" she hissed.

My jaw clenched, maybe she isn't talking about me after all. I wondered if Josh the puker kissed her before he started barfing. What if he brought her up to that room, was making out with her, and then his lunch betrayed him? I clenched my fists. I didn't want anyone to kiss her.

I wanted her for myself, but that wasn't going to happen. Ava's rhetoric about Will not getting involved in her love life was inconsequential to reality. The fact of the matter remained, he was my friend first, and that meant something. If the roles were reversed, I wouldn't want someone like me dating their innocent sister either. I'd pull her into my depravity. I'd own her body in every way, and she'd like it. The beautiful light she emitted would be absorbed into my darkness. And when we were done with each other she would be a little dimmer and a shadow of herself.

I listened when she went back inside and let out a deep breath. I had resisted the temptation to join her. My fingers tapped along my thigh. The buzzing in my brain was dull, but still there. What I wanted to do was ride my bike around Boulder at this late hour. I wanted to feel the breeze on my face and clear my head of every thought of Ava.

At about 3am I did just that. The apartment complex was on a slight incline so the initial push down the hill got good speed. I pedaled around the area and stopped at a 24-hour diner. My stomach was growling so I ordered pancakes.

I watched the other patrons coming in. It was a weird mix at 4am. Some people were starting their day; some were ending it. You could tell by how crisply the person was dressed to determine which category they belonged to.

The waitress slid my bill towards me as someone sat down in front of me. I looked up from the table. Raven was sitting opposite of me. She had a gentle smile on her face. Her once creamy complexion looked a little sallow. "You look good."

"So do you." I lied, but it wouldn't be polite to point out the fact that she looked strung out. "What have you been up to?"

Raven licked her pale lips and shrugged. "This and that. What about you?"

"This and that."

She chewed her lip. "I heard about the attack. I'm sorry that happened."

I nodded slowly. "Me too. I don't remember much of it, but thanks. What brings you here at 4am?"

She gave me an empty smile. "Just got off work. You?"

"Couldn't sleep."

"Ah, yes. I could help you with that. If I remember correctly you slept like a baby after an evening with me."

I gave her an unamused look. When I had broken it off with her initially, she didn't take it well. She would show up at my apartment at all hours. She'd be a drunk or high mess, and I'd bring her inside and nurse her back to sober. Then the morning after, I would have to rebreak it off with her. This went on until she saw me out with Lydia. The meltdown she had was so severe I had to cut her off completely.

"You know that's not a good idea, Raven."

Her chin quivered as she nodded. "I thought I would offer."

The waitress came to pick up the bill. I gave her a brief nod in acknowledgment and turned back to Raven.

"I don't understand why we can't try again. I know your hard limit. I can live with it."

"It stopped being about hard limits when you stalked Lydia," I answered calmly.

She scoffed. "That was a misunderstanding."

"So, it was a coincidence that you waited for her outside her classes for a week after you saw her with me, and then at some party that you both happen to be at, she ended up being drugged."

Lydia was fine. I wasn't at the party, but I heard about it after the fact from Matt when she kissed him mistaking him for me. He told me about it the next day. I was not amused when I confronted her. She told me point blank she didn't remember half the night and was positive she had been drugged. She went to the clinic and tested positive for Rohypnol. I wouldn't have connected the dots, but Tama mentioned talking to Raven at that party.

Her brow furrowed as she looked to the left out the window. "I had nothing to do with that." *Another lie.* "It doesn't matter anyway. I'm with someone new." She looked at me through her lashes.

I didn't think she was lying, but she was testing me to see my reaction. I gave her a warm smile. "Good. I hope he's able to give you what you need. Is he treating you well? Making sure you eat?" *By the looks of it, no.*

"He prefers me a certain size, but yes he treats me well."

I nodded, hating that he clearly isn't taking care of her, but knew if I showed real concern she'd latch onto me again. "I'm happy as long as you're happy." I stood up. "I'm going to go. Take care." I walked away without waiting for her to get up. She'd follow me and I didn't want to drag out the goodbye any longer than necessary.

By the time my head hit the pillow I truly had worked myself into an exhausted stupor.

Chapter 9

Ava

"Wait, so you fly places to play volleyball?" I asked Lily.

She grinned at me and nodded. "We do indeed. And they offered to pay for all my education too," she quipped. "But I asked for the scholarship to go to someone in need instead."

"Yeah, me." Nicole grinned as she collapsed down on her sofa.

I was over at their place avoiding Henry. I didn't know what to think about him. He was so hot and cold. One minute he's practically claiming me in front of half the student body, the next he's speed-walking away from me leaving me and Tama to jog in his wake. Then he didn't leave his room all day Sunday except for meals. He said he was up late, but I doubted that because normally when he couldn't sleep, he would be on the patio with me. But it was bereft of him.

Two days post-party and he was still avoiding me. Lily, Nicole, and I were waiting on Will to finish his reading so we could go to the grocery store. Which Henry has opted out of again.

"And you start traveling when?"

Nicole yawned. "Two weeks. We have a Wednesday game at Iowa State and then the following Saturday is at Baylor."

"You're going to be at Baylor in three weeks?" I hissed. My mind whirled with the possibilities.

Lily nodded. "We are indeed. Why? Do you want me to pick up Baylor shirts so you can Tama can pretend to be there and have school spirit?"

I shook my head. "No, I want to go to your game."

Lily's lip curled. "I'm all for your support, but that's a long way to travel for me."

I grinned. "It would be a double win. I could support you, take pictures around campus. Oh," I sat forward, "I could bring different outfits and have a little photoshoot all over campus. I could post the images on my socials along with my hair growth journey. It's perfect," I squealed.

"I'm not going to point out the flaws in your plan and focus on the fact that your hair has gotten longer since the summer," Lily said.

I nodded. "I was cutting my hair every four weeks to maintain the bob of resistance. My hair grows pretty fast at about half inch to a full inch a month depending. So, it's grown, what?" I tucked my chin and looked at the ends of my hair. "A full two inches. I can almost fit it all back in a ponytail again."

Nicole giggled and muttered, "The bob of resistance."

"Ready," Will said from the hallway. "Is Matt coming?"

Nicole shook her head. "Not this week, but at least he'll be home for another week before he goes back out for a week. He's trying to match some of his travel schedule to where our games are going to be, so we won't go too long without seeing each other."

"Let's take two cars so we know we have enough room in the trunks," Will said.

Lily shrugged. "Suit yourself." She looked over to me and then to Nicole. "Which of you wants to be the second driver?"

"I vote for Ava so I can spend some quality time with her." Will slung his arm over my shoulder.

"That's fine, but I don't know how quality a five-minute drive can be."

I popped my head into my apartment to grab my keys and Tama. She looked like she was having a serious conversation with Henry.

She smiled at me. "Are we headed out?"

My eyes flicked over to Henry before returning to her. His gaze remained stoically on Tama. "Yes, we are taking two cars, so we have enough space in the trunk."

She turned to Henry. "We will continue this later."

"Continue what?" The vibe in the apartment was weird.

Tama stared at Henry for a moment before turning to me with a mischievous grin. "Henry is going to teach me how to perform a blowjob."

I blanched. "Oh, like on him?" My voice hitched at the end.

Tama shook her head rapidly. "No, like on cucumbers, which reminds me I need to add that to my list."

I nodded and felt my shoulders inch down from my ears. "I had a friend in high school that was going to teach me how to perform a blowjob, but we weren't going to use cucumbers. Oh well, ready?"

Will sat next to me in the car. As soon as I turned the car on, he turned to me. "You get everything figured out with Dad?"

I nodded. "Yeah, I told him about my scholarship. He was surprised it was so robust for it being an academic scholarship.

He chuckled. "Did he ask which scholarship?"

"No, but I sort of over-explained it. I told him that I had written a few different essays and applied for every scholarship I was eligible for."

He grinned and then sighed as his smile slipped from his face. "How was your date?" A smidge of annoyance laced his tone.

I shrugged as my lip curled. "A dud. He got sick to his stomach."

He hummed. "What time did you make it home?"

I shrugged. "Midnight-ish. Tama and Henry were running the beer pong table and Tama's friend Rhys was there too."

He nodded. "I like Rhys, he's a good guy. Well, except for the fact he keeps stringing Tama along."

I lifted a finger. "Tama said that they are friends. So, I don't think he's actually stringing her along. I got the vibe that she is friends with him the same way that she is friends with Henry."

"Whatever you say." He paused for a moment. "Look, I want to apologize again about how I acted on Saturday morning. It wasn't okay for me to out you about your pseudo eating disorder. I'm just really worried about you."

I licked my teeth and shot him an unamused look. "That was shitty, especially considering I didn't have an eating disorder. I didn't control what I ate. Mom had me on a strict diet and daily weigh-ins. I was complying to her demands."

"That's so fucked up. Why didn't you tell me?"

I twisted my lips to the side. "Because I didn't know it was weird until she stopped doing it when we moved. Also, I can admit her obsession became my obsession, but it was more about making her happy than looking thin."

"I fucking hate that she did that to you."

I followed Lily through the yellow light. "You don't want to apologize for trying to control my love life?"

Will grunted. "Nope, as your older brother I will always worry about you and the decisions you make regarding men. I know they are garbage at this age, and you've already dealt with enough."

"Well, garbage or not, I need to deal with them on my own. It's a rite of passage that I want to go through. I want to kiss some frogs because that means someone may find me pretty." It was more vulnerable than I wanted to get but sometimes I word vomit.

"You are very pretty, Ava. You look exactly like your mother who is so beautiful it makes Dad insane. I think she may be some sort of succubus or siren."

I rolled my eyes. "I appreciate the compliment, but it's not that meaningful coming from you. I want the ability to feel pretty because people, not blood related and bound to me, think so. And on the siren front, it's a possibility. I wouldn't be surprised if mom was into some sort of witchcraft, blood magic, dark shit. She's probably killed kittens to maintain her beauty."

Will chuckled. "And she shared her secrets with Daphne. They sacrifice their personality for a pretty face."

I grinned at him. "Well, there you go. I still have a personality, that must be why I've only been asked out once in my life."

Will sighed and looked at the sunroof. "Well, I heard a rumor at Daphne's wedding that you were a lesbian."

I scoffed. "That's Daphne's go-to."

He nodded. "Yeah, but it was from Bob Carlyle, your old neighbors. You remember his son, Jay?"

I nodded. Jay was popular, handsome, and wanted nothing to do with me. "Of course, I lived next to Jay from the age of eight until seventeen. What about him?"

"Well, Bob heard it from Jay. So, I think it's possible that you were never asked out in Texas because Daphne poisoned those waters for you."

I rolled my eyes. "What a cunt. It doesn't surprise me in the least. And can I say, I hate that she says it like it's a bad thing. I was serious when I told Lily I would worship her lady garden if that's what did it for me."

Will's lip curled as he made a disgusted look on his face. "Less talk about you hooking up with my girlfriend, yeah?"

I snickered and parked next to Lily. "Anything else you want to talk to me about?"

He tilted his head. "Yeah, Henry mentioned that you accepted a drink from a stranger and went into a bedroom at the party." One eyebrow was high into his hairline.

I shrank into my shoulders. "Accurate, but in my defense, I didn't know how to tell Josh no about the drink. I wasn't going to drink it. Tama was an expert in taking it off my hands. As far as the bedroom, Josh told me that he wasn't feeling well and to wait in the hall for him. He left the door open, so I went and sat on the bed when he took longer than five minutes. I could hear him throwing up. I felt bad."

Will rolled his eyes and bit back a smile. "Only you. You have to be careful, Ava. Shit happens at those parties all the time. Girls get drugged, fights break out. I want you to have a normal college experience, but you need to be safer about it. I am not going to be the one to tell Dad that something happened to you while you were here."

I nodded. Lily, Tama, and Nicole had already started walking towards the entrance. I opened the door when Will reached for his handle.

"How do you like living with Tama and Henry?"

I smiled. "Tama is great. She's really sweet and smart."

"What about Henry?" He looked over to me with his eyes cut to the side.

I shrugged. "He keeps to himself mostly. I know that he and Tama are friends, so I try to not interfere or impose on their friendship. He's nice, cordial."

He nodded. "Has he had any friends come over?"

"No, why?"

Will blew out a breath. "He has a few girlfriends that he rotates through. He's into some bondage type shit. Lily confirmed he's a pseudo dom and into dom/sub relationships. He likes to have extreme control in the bedroom. Like the girls aren't even allowed to talk. Tama has met a few of them, but I wanted to make sure you were okay with that. If you feel uncomfortable, I can ask him to keep his door shut. I lived with him for months before finding out that he regularly had someone over, they were just tied to the bed."

My eyes widened as I nodded. "It took you months to notice? Wouldn't you have, I dunno, heard her?"

He chuckled and nodded. "Yeah, you are right when you said he keeps to himself. He's a private guy. We only know about the bondage thing because he mentioned it in jest, and Tama confirmed that he did in fact have a girl tied to his bed. As far as hearing anything, he told me he's into silent play. Which I guess makes sense because I had no clue someone was in the apartment with us. When he was in a coma, I had to go check out his room to make sure he didn't leave someone in there while we went out for drinks. He didn't, in case you were wondering."

Confusion, disappointment, curiosity all mingled into one spiral of thoughts at the information. It was quite possible Henry had a person in his room every night. Maybe that was why he didn't join me on the patio.

"Honestly, the reason why he hasn't been grocery shopping is probably because he brings his girls over when the apartment is empty and then lets them leave when everyone is in bed."

My stomach twisted as I nodded. "Maybe, like I said, he keeps to himself."

Of course he's with someone. I knew he was into bondage because I saw the cuffs tucked between his mattress and headboard. And he did prefer to be in his room a lot. He got so annoyed both times I went in uninvited.

I needed to work my crush out of my system because if he was with someone it was a nonstarter for me. I could give Josh another chance. He seemed a little distant in class, but I also didn't exactly start any conversation with him. Maybe he was embarrassed and was gauging how I reacted to him.

Tama and I went aisle by aisle as Will walked ahead with Lily. It was sweet watching them together. He was so tender with her, stealing kisses, casual touches, and whispered conversations. I had no doubt in my mind that he was madly in love with her and she was equally in love with him.

I want that.

Dinner was pan-seared fish with cannellini beans and a fresh tomato salsa fresca. I also made some bruschetta for everyone to snack on while the beans were cooking. This Monday couldn't have been more different than the last. Everyone was waiting in the living room and kitchen as I cooked.

They were hanging out and talking about the loads of schoolwork they had accumulated so far. I reduced a balsamic glaze for the top of the toast and drizzled it on the salsa.

"Holy shit." Matty snagged another piece of bruschetta. I gave him a quick grin and went back to flipping the fish as they came to temperature. I set the beans to simmer and added spinach and whole garlic cloves to the broth.

"Yeah, you missed out last week," Will said with a full mouth.

"Wait til you try the tiramisu. The custard is spot on," I said to Matt.

"Careful, Ava, or I might think you're trying to steal my man away," Nicole said playfully.

I snickered and shook my head. "I'd never be so brazen and bold to think I could compete. How was practice?"

"My body is sore. I wasn't as diligent this summer with my workouts," Nicole said.

"Ugh, neither was I," Lily said. "Turns out sex and swimming will keep your figure, but it's not helpful on the court."

I made a gagging face.

Lily giggled. "Sorry, I forgot you are siblings. I see you as my friend first and his sister second."

I tilted my head and touched my chest. "Thank you. I think it's the first time I have managed to pull myself from beneath one of my siblings' shadows."

Will tousled my hair. "Oh, Ava Bear, you and I both know we are the pariahs. My shadow is nonexistent in the household."

"This is true. My mom truly hates you."

He snickered. "I'd say the feeling is mutual, but I've managed to move on to cool indifference."

"Very mature." I flipped the last piece of fish from the pan and set it onto a platter. "Dinner is ready."

I grabbed a plate first and scooped the beans and spinach, nestled my piece of fish over, and then liberally scooped the fresca onto the dish. I squirted a little lemon and walked into the dining room.

"That's how it's done." Tama followed my lead and plated hers the same way.

"Oh my god, Ava, what do you want to do for a living? Because straight up, I will pay you to make me meals. I know Monroe can get on board with it, too." Lily sat across from me and scooped another bite. She had begun eating as she was walking.

I shrugged. "I honestly don't know what I want to do. I have no clue what my major should be. I'm in school because I was told I must get a degree to be included in my dad's will."

"Don't pressure yourself. I declared last semester. Take a variety of classes and see what makes you happy," Nicole said from the kitchen.

We all ate together, talking about classes and homework. It was exactly what I was hoping last Monday would have been like. It was nice to feel like I belonged. At least they liked my cooking. I kept subtly trying to catch Henry's eye as he ate. He was busy talking to Nicole and Matt for most of the dinner. I wondered if he had someone in his room while we all ate dinner.

I should have finely chopped the garlic so at least he'd have killer garlic breath. But I was nice and left them whole in case anyone wanted to pick them out.

Matt rubbed his hands together when I took the dessert from the fridge. He wagged his brows at me. "I heard you made

Henry's favorite last week. I was bummed I didn't get one. This makes up for it though."

My lips rolled together. "I didn't make it for Henry. I know Lily loves lemon desserts, and it was the fastest lemon sweet in my arsenal."

The last thing I needed was for Henry to think I made them for him like some pining child. Especially while he had some sexed-up woman in his bed waiting to satisfy his every whim.

Will had drawn the short straw and was doing the dishes when I excused myself to my room. I paced, letting the anxious thoughts race. If Henry was with someone, then I needed to get over him.

Me: How are you feeling? You didn't seem very chatty in class or I would have asked you then.

Josh: Yeah, I'm fine.

Me: Well, I had fun the other night up until you got sick. Sorry that happened.

Josh: It's cool.

I didn't know what to make of the monosyllabic answers. It felt like a brush off, but I hadn't done anything wrong. Ignoring the voice in my head that said he was mad at me, I kept going.

Me: Do you think we should try again?

Josh: It's best we don't. You seem nice, but you aren't my type.

My chin quivered at the rejection. I didn't like him, but it still stung. Apparently, I wasn't anyone's type. Even if what Will had told me was true about my experience in Dallas, it didn't mean Daphne had the same reach in LA. I mean, right, I had Craig, but that was not serious. And he got back together with his girlfriend and didn't talk to me again.

Josh: I'm not going to be in class
on Wednesday. Do you mind if
I use your notes from the day?

Me: Sure.

Well, I was good for something at least. There was a little knock on the door and Will popped his head in. "I'm heading home. Dinner was awesome."

"Thanks." I attempted a fake smile that fooled no one.

He frowned at me. "Something wrong?"

"Just tired." My teeth dug into my lower lip.

He nodded and sighed. "Ava, if you want to dance, don't hide it. I put it together that you aren't going to the library in the mornings, so if you are waking up early for it, don't. Just work out with Lily and Nicole after class."

"Sure, yeah, you're right. Good night."

I settled down at my desk in thought. I didn't have any homework because I spent my time this afternoon in the library while everyone was working out. I was restless and all I wanted to do was sneak into Henry's room and confirm whether he had a guest.

There was another light triple tap on my door. I could tell by the knock that it wasn't Will. I told whoever was knocking to come in.

Tama grinned at me and poked her head in. "Henry is giving a blowjob lesson in a few minutes if you want to join us."

I sucked my cheek between my molars. It would be beneficial to have a vague understanding of the skillset. And I could casually see if he had someone tied to his bed. "You don't think he'll be annoyed that I'm joining?"

She shrugged. "I know he won't, so ignore him if he acts all bullish. Come on, it'll be fun."

Henry

Tama knew I was into Ava. She didn't suspect, she knew.

"It's not Ava's crush on you that has you concerned. It's the other way around, isn't it?" she hissed at me when she finally cornered me after school today. I told her that she didn't know what she was talking about which she replied with all the evidence that said the contrary. She repeated how I had been avoiding Ava, but then at the party I was keenly aware of her every move. She was already confused that I had agreed to go to the party in the first place, but she told me it clicked with her the moment I wouldn't let go of Ava's hand.

And I knew she didn't panic when she told Ava I was going to give her a lesson in blowjobs because it was something she had been asking me to do for months. I had refused on the premise that she was my friend, and I didn't want to encourage her to do sexual acts near me.

When I asked her not to say anything to anyone, she strongarmed me. The moment I saw the flash of an idea come across her face when Ava asked what we were talking about I knew it wasn't going to bode well for me. And now, my best friend was blackmailing me to give her a lesson in blowjobs to keep the fact that I am very much into our other roommate a secret.

I grit my teeth when Ava came out of her room. She had already changed into her pajamas. Her little nipples peaked in excitement. Tama passed her a cucumber and grinned. "The floor is yours."

I cursed under my breath and tried to subtly adjust my semi in my pants. Ava had no idea what she did to me daily. And it was going to test every ounce of willpower when I saw her wrap her lips around the vegetable. I rubbed the back of my neck and decided to make it as clinical as possible. I needed to focus on Tama because my imagination would go wild if I paid attention to Ava.

"First things first, every guy is different. These are basics that are in general crowd pleasers."

"I'm not planning on a gang bang any time soon, so I am not sure if pleasing a crowd is in my future." Tama was joking, but her deadpan delivery made her sound serious. It was something that took me time to realize that she was a sarcastic brat but played it off as rigid or inexperienced when someone didn't think her sarcasm was funny. I ignored her.

"Go ahead and take your cucumbers in hand and position them near your mouth. I want to see how you are holding your hand."

Tama was gripping the vegetable so hard her knuckles were turning white in an underhand grip.

"Jesus, Tam, did the guy offend you? Loosen the grip a smidge and roll your hand to the top."

I grabbed her hand and adjusted it for her. "This gives you the most range of motion. Any decent blowjob will include a hand. A dry hand is not friendly to your cucumber, so you need to either spit into your palm or on the cucumber directly. Most blowjobs start with a little hand action."

Ava remained in my periphery, but she was mirroring my every motion. "Go ahead and pick whether you want to lube it directly with your tongue or spit in your palm." Tama loudly hawked the saliva from the back of her throat and forcefully spit into her palm.

My laugh vibrated my chest. "This is supposed to be a sexy act, Tam, maybe work on quietly gathering your saliva." She nodded. Ava had chosen to lick the cucumber directly. I clenched my fist when I saw she was staring at me. Her innocent brown eyes looked up through her sooty lashes as she ran her tongue up and down the length.

"Oh, that looks hot. Henry, should I do what Ava is doing?"

I cleared my throat, so my voice didn't crack. "Yeah, until you can figure out how to not hawk a loogie while blowing the guys, start like that." I waved a hand dismissively towards Ava.

I started to walk the girls through the different things they could do: flick the tip, lick the balls, lavish the shaft. Clenching my jaw so hard it hurt. "Now that you've teased him you can start the blowjob."

"We haven't started yet? My jaw already hurts," Tama complained.

I chuckled to myself. "Surround your lips around the headfirst."

Tama wrinkled her nose. "We both have small mouths, is it necessary?"

"If you want him to remember who you are, then yeah, it's necessary. Make sure you wear lip balm, nothing with menthol in it because that shit stings like hell."

"Oh, that's a hot tip. Okay, I'm going to have to invest in a menthol-free lip balm, got it. Okay, here goes nothing." Tama unhinged her jaw like she was trying to eat a huge bite of food.

I rolled my lips in to hide my smile. I wasn't sure if she was trying to be funny or if she was graceless. "Don't make that face. Make something like this."

It was awkward for me to drop my jaw and make an O shape while trying to look seductive.

Tama giggled and nodded. "Got it. How's this?" Her eyes looked less manic, but there was a trace of humor still in her big eyes.

My nostrils flared as I gave her a flat smile.

She was trolling me.

"Better. Once your mouth is around the tip, slowly work yourself down the shaft, watch out for teeth. If you have to, roll your lips over your teeth to protect the sensitive skin, then do that. Take it as far into your mouth as you can go."

Tama's gag reflex was garbage. "You are going to have to work on that, Tam. Breathe through your nose." I chanced a glance over to Ava and regretted it. She was staring up at me with her doe eyes, lips stretched wide, and more than half of the cucumber was down her throat.

"Go until you feel like you need to gag and then back off a little."

I couldn't tear my eyes away from Ava. She blinked innocently at me and nudged the vegetable further down her throat. "Do you have a gag reflex?"

She shrugged.

Motherfucker.

"Is it at the back of your throat?"

She nodded.

My nostrils flared at the possibilities. "Swallow."

She did and a little more the cucumber sucked into her mouth. I looked over to Tama who had her cucumber in her hand and was watching Ava with an impressed smirk.

"I can't do that." She pointed to Ava lazily with the vegetable.

I huffed. "Not many can. Ava's deep throating it. Okay, Ava, pull it out and create suction with your cheeks. Suck as hard as you want." She nodded and followed my instruction. My semi twitched so I sat down in my gaming chair like I was bored.

"Okay, Tama, your turn. Do what you can and when you gag pull back with your cheeks sucked in."

I instructed them how to use their hand in conjunction with their mouth. Tama was not coordinated, but she was getting better. I almost felt glad I had taken the time to teach her because she had a high probability of embarrassing herself otherwise.

"Great. You can also play with the balls with your free hand. Don't handle them roughly, lightly fondle them. If the guy is into it, he'll tell you to keep going."

"Great." Tama snapped her teeth into the cucumber with a loud crunch. "These are good," she said with her mouth full.

My eye bounced at the violence she inserted on the vegetable. "Any questions?"

Tama nodded. "Will a guy expect a finger in the butt before or after?"

Ava dropped her cucumber and stared at me with wide eyes.

I shook my head. "Don't do that on your own. Get a feel for the situation. Most guys do not want you to do that to them."

"But I've done a decent amount of research on milking prostates and perineum massages. I think if men could get past the idea of something going in, they may enjoy it."

I chuckled, unsurprised that my best friend had researched the p-spot. "Most men can't get past it. Let your guy know you are open to anal play whether to give or receive."

Tama took another loud ass bite of her cucumber. "Good advice, communication is key to every relationship. Welp, thanks Hen, I appreciate the lesson. I'm going to go to bed now."

She walked over to the fridge and set her freshly wrapped cucumber inside. Ava looked over to me with wide innocent eyes. "How did I do?"

I shrugged. "Passable. I'm sure Josh will be pleased." The words tasted bitter on my tongue. I stood up, my semi was tucked into my pocket. "I'm going to head to bed, too."

She chewed her lip and nodded. "Okay, yeah. Don't want to keep her waiting, huh?"

I tilted my head to her, unsure what she was talking about. And if I weren't fighting with my dick I would have questioned her.

"Night, Ava."

Chapter 10

Ava

"Can you explain to me how to buy a plane ticket and then book a hotel room?" I asked Monroe.

Her face looked pinched through the video phone call. "Why? I thought you were already incognito, why do you need to go somewhere else?"

"Well, actually, it's so I can go where I am supposed to be. Lily's game is at Baylor in two weeks, and I have decided that it's the perfect time for me to go."

Monroe smiled at me. She was looking a little tired, so the smile made me feel better about waking her up from her Saturday nap. "And you didn't ask Lily this because?" Monroe prompted.

I stuck my lip out. "She'll tell Will, and I don't want him to talk me out of it. The more I think about it, the more I realize it's a great idea. I want to fly down, take a bunch of pictures in different outfits throughout campus, and then post them periodically on socials. It reinforces my alibi."

Monroe snorted. "I love it. Have you considered what you are going to do about your hair?"

I tugged on the ends. "It's growing fine, why does it look weird?"

She shook her head. "No, if you are planning on taking pictures and posting them periodically it needs to match up with your hair length. Love the journey you are on, by the way. You should do a timelapse when you get it to the length you want it at."

I stuck my lower lip out. "I haven't thought about that. What do you suggest?"

She hummed and tapped her chin. "You could go the wig route, but they can be expensive if you are buying multiple wigs. You can also take pictures with your hair pulled back. When are you planning on going anyway?"

I settled against my pillows. "Saturday the 26th. She has an evening game, so her team is flying in the morning and then spending the night. I figured I could do the same thing and spend my afternoon on campus setting up my alibi."

Monroe was walking around her penthouse apartment in New York. Some papers shuffled around in the background. Then she wagged her brows at me. "You're in luck. I'm flying out of LA on the 25th, I'll push it a day. I can pick you up on my way and we can spend the day in Waco. I'll be your photoshoot assistant."

"I'd love it if you came, but you don't have to." My teeth dug into my lip.

She waved her hand dismissively at me. "I need to talk face to face with Lily about something anyway. This is the perfect excuse. Plus, I haven't been to one of Lily's matches in ages. She'll be thrilled."

"Perfect! What do you need to talk to Lily about?"

Monroe sighed. "I'll tell you after I talk to her, okay? Anyway, how's school going? Have you found any guy that tickles your fancy?"

I rolled my eyes up to the ceiling and thought of Henry. It had been another five days since the blowjob lesson and he's pretty much steered clear of me. Though when he all but confirmed he had a girl in his room, I understood why he stayed holed up.

"I have a small crush on someone. But he's not single. What about you?"

Monroe chewed on her lip. "I'm sorry and I'm taking a break from dating for a while. So, no news from me in that regard."

A whimper slipped past my lips. "It's so confusing because he does these things that makes me think he likes me, but then he avoids me. Last week we were at a party together and he got annoyed with me because I ended up in a bedroom. It was innocent, like my date was puking his brains up and I was worried about him.

"Anyway, he grabbed my hand and didn't let go of me until we were walking home. Then he avoided me until Monday evening. He told me once that he was avoiding me because Will told him that I'm off limits. But we have these intense moments where he is really close to me. He's semi kissed me a few times, like he'll speak against my lips when he's telling me good night."

Monroe tilted her head. "Like he's taking you on a date and that is how he is saying goodbye?"

My face pinched in a guilty grimace. "You cannot tell Lily this."

She hummed. "I won't mention it to her directly, but I won't lie to her either."

I nodded. "Good enough because it won't come up organically. I have a crush on my roommate Henry. He's Matt's cousin."

"Oh intrigue, yeah Lily told me all about him last year before she and Will got together. She thought he was super-hot and sort of mysterious, and Will was sort of stringing her along because he was still stuck on Lucy."

I curled my lip at the mention of the antichrist. "I feel like I have this intense chemistry with him, but nothing is coming from it. I found out earlier this week it's because he has a girlfriend. But he's so private he keeps her in his room and doesn't let her leave until we are all sleeping."

Monroe made a face. I held my hand up. "Before you ask or think it's weird, he's a dom and she's his sub. Tama has confirmed all his relationships are consensual and he's in his room all the time anyway, so I think he leaves her there because he doesn't like people in his business."

Monroe rolled her lips in before rubbing them back and forth. "Got it, okay. He's a dom daddy. Okay, well, if he's in a relationship the only thing you *can* do is get over your crush on him because it is unfair and unrealistic to expect him to dump someone for you. Also, he has already told you you're off limits, which is so caveman and antiquated. I'm honestly disappointed that Will is trying that bullshit, but I'd want to protect you too if I were there." She sighed and looked at her watch. "I have a doctor's appointment I need to get to, but I will text you the flight details, okay?"

I nodded and slumped further into my pillows as I got off the phone with her. My relief eased some of the tension in my shoulders. I figured out how to get to Waco and I got to vent about Henry to someone. When I muttered to myself in the middle of the night only my twisted thoughts answer back.

How do I get over Henry?

I was way too amped up to take a nap, though I had been sleeping poorly all week. It was at the weird time on a Saturday where it was too late to start anything or make afternoon plans and too early to begin your evening plans.

My closet was a mess. Two piles of clothes littered the floor, one clean, one dirty. I pulled on my ballet leotard and my hair into a low ponytail. It was exciting that I was able to fit it all in one bundle at the nape of my neck. I was looking forward to being able to put my hair in a high bun again.

My sweatpants eased up my legs, and I grabbed my gym bag. The living room was empty. Tama was hanging out with Rhys, and I assumed Henry was in his room entertaining his guest.

The walk to the gym was quick. I grimaced when the only court available for me to use was the one with windows that looked out onto the entire gym. Every time I danced there, I felt eyes on me.

With my portable speaker set up, I began with some light stretches as the music played loud enough to drown out the gym's music selection but not so loud to disturb other patrons. A few guys watched me from their weight benches when I was in my deep split stretch. I rolled my eyes closed to concentrate on warming my muscles up.

When I was finally feeling limber, I went through the workout routine. Then with fifteen minutes left of my reserved time I started to dance what I was feeling. The room wasn't huge, but it was big enough for me to do spins, twirls, and jumps. I switched my music selection to Hozier; he always made me want to move my body.

The lyrics were so passionate that I poured myself into the leaps. My form was perfect; I could feel it when I landed. My spins had good momentum and then I went a little more contemporary in dance style and incorporated some tumbling leaps. By the time the last chord of the song played my chest was heaving, but it was a beautiful performance. It was one of those that I wished I had saved the choreography or recorded it to show other people.

My eyes closed as I caught my breath.

"Holy shit."

I jerked my face from my knee to see a man I didn't recognize staring at me in awe.

Henry

My attention was intensely focused on the racquet ball court as I watched Ava from the pool wall. She had a quiet gracefulness about her, but watching her pour her entire soul into a performance that was for only herself… I was speechless.

The song she had decided to dance to was irrelevant. Whatever it was, she felt every chord and beat of the song. The soft lines of her face spoke her passion. It was sexy as hell.

I had been passively watching her since she walked into the court. Catching glimpses of her as she stretched and went through basic moves as I swam my laps. I'd pause to drink some water or take a breath and watch her for a moment before continuing with trying to wear my body out in hopes that I might be able to sleep tonight.

My brain had been too buzzy since Sunday. I was staying up till 2:15 to listen to her breathe outside my window. Looking at her for more than a few moments made memories of the seductive look she had when she was mock sucking off the cucumber rear forward. I had worked through many fantasies where I replaced the vegetable. It was unsustainable. I needed a new sub or at least someone to fuck around with again.

170

My jaw clicked shut as some gym bro stepped into her court space. He startled her. Her wide eyes were open, and her chest heaved beneath her hand. I tried to look at him with an unbiased eye. He was more attractive than that Josh kid, but he looked like a grade-A douche nozzle.

Ava laughed at something he had said and stood up to shake his hand. I pulled myself from the pool and started drying off, wrapping the towel around my waist. My eyes remained glued to the situation happening from across the gym. I don't know what the fuck I would do if she left with him. I had to prevent that from happening at all costs.

My wet jammers slapped against the tile floor, and I tugged my sweatpants on while on the pool deck. It probably wasn't allowed, but no one was in the pool except me. I tossed my towel in my bag and shuffled towards the exit while kicking my sandals on.

My hoodie went on next as I hit the gym floor. For some reason guys weren't allowed to work out without a shirt on, which I thought was weird considering all the women were only in sports bras.

Gym goers scoffed as I brushed past a group, in a hurry to get to the court Ava was still standing in. The gym bro had invited himself further in. Her eyes flashed when she saw me.

"You ready to go, Babydoll?"

She blinked rapidly at me and then turned to the other guy in the room who gave me an amused once over.

"Grant, this is my roommate Henry."

He gave me a nod as she gave me a tight smile. "I'll be ready to go in a moment; I need to collect my things."

I nodded and pretended to not take the hint that she wanted me to leave the room so she could finish whatever conversation she was having with the meathead. An innocent smile spread across my face as I walked over to her bag, slipped her shoes out for her to change back into, and pushed her towel into her bag. Her little speaker was set on the top of the tote.

"Such a courteous friend." She emphasized the last word. I perked an eyebrow at her, stood up, and passed her the shoes. She gave me a little glare, slipped her flats off, and tugged her shoes back on.

"Anyway, Grant, I would love to have dinner with you some time."

"Cool, yeah, let me get your number." Grant flashed his eyes over to me. He pulled his phone out and handed it to her. I watched her text message herself with his phone and rolled my eyes.

Grant grinned at her and tucked his phone back in his pocket. "Well, I guess I'll see you later." He nodded in my direction and tipped his chin at Ava.

I was not amused. Ava let out an annoyed huff, which I found funny because it was my sentiments exactly.

She marched out of the gym without looking back at me. I chuckled to myself at how mad she seemed to be. I mean I understood; I was cockblocking her. But I felt justified in blocking all cocks swinging in her direction until I could figure out what to do about my obsession with her.

As soon as we were cleared of the parking lot she turned on me. "What the hell, Henry?"

With my chin tipped down, I stared at her from my lashes. "What do you mean? I saw we were at the gym at the same time and offered to escort you home."

Her face twisted into a scowl. "No, you didn't. You peed on my leg in front of a very attractive man."

My jaw clenched but I forced a smile on my face. "I'm not into waterplay Babydoll, but I'm willing to try anything once so you can experience it."

She growled at me. She reminded me of a little kitten. "That's not what I meant, and you know it. What was that about back there?"

I squinted at her and shrugged. "I thought women hated it when men hit on them while they were working out."

She rolled her eyes. "They do, but don't pretend for one moment that what you were doing was some altruistic action to save me from some perv. That was about your own self-interest."

My eyes narrowed on her, not liking for one second that she was so close to the mark in what prompted me to stake my claim on her. "What self-interest would that be?"

She threw her hands out. "If you can't have me then no one can."

I couldn't stop the grin from splitting my cheeks. "Oh, Babydoll, that's where you are wrong. I can have you whenever I want. I just shouldn't."

"Ugh, you are so frustrating." She turned on her heel and started walking quickly away. My strides were longer than hers so while she was speed walking, I was enjoying a leisurely stroll on a beautiful day.

"You know what's the biggest piece of bullshit about this entire situation?"

"Tell me." I rolled my lips in to stop myself from laughing.

"You think that you can have a girl tied up in your room and fuck with her all night and then turn around and fuck with my mind all day. It's bullshit and I'm fucking sick of it."

My brow furrowed as I kept pace with her. "I don't know what you're talking about."

She huffed. "I'm talking about the fact that you tie girls up in your bed and leave them in there for hours at a time. And how last year it took months before your roommates knew you had *guests* over."

I chuckled. "Is my Babydoll jealous?"

"Fuck you." She started walking double time.

I had to increase my pace. "I'd love to, but as we have established you are off-limits."

She whirled around. "What do you expect from me, Henry? Because it sort of feels like you expect me to stay your virginal sacrifice until you grow the fucking balls to stand up to Will. In the meantime, you get to fuck everything that walks, but if I *look* at another guy you are running him off."

My eyes widened. "I am not fucking everything that walks. As you have pointed out, I preferred them tied to the bed." She shook her fist at me and stalked off. I grinned at her as she stomped her feet.

"Hey Ava."

She whipped around. If looks could kill, I'd at least be in some pain. Her face was way too beautiful to kill anyone with it.

"I'm not fucking anyone, and I haven't for months. Honestly, since my coma."

She huffed out another breath and her shoulders inched down from her ears. Her fists unclenched, but her nostrils were still flared. "So, what do you expect from me?"

My head tilted as I assessed her. "I expect you to turn down every advancement that Grant sends your way."

She whimpered. "Why though?"

I didn't answer directly, I simply shrugged and let her lead the way back home.

She didn't disappoint me with the quiet rant she had when she sat alone on the patio at 2am. She let me have it. I had to muffle my laughter, so she didn't hear me. She was so fucking cute in that bratty sort of way. She had no idea that she had me by the balls.

The next week was spent watching her dance while I swam my laps. She was so beautiful as she moved her body around the floor. She never noticed the small group of people that would stop what they were doing as she danced her final song every day. She was so graceful with every leap and turn. None of the technical terms were in my knowledge base, but I knew fucking beauty when I saw it.

When she told Tama that her mom bought her lead roles, I thought it was probably bullshit and something terrible her cunt of a sister made up. After seeing her dance, I had no doubt Daphne was jealous of her sister's extreme talent. It pissed me off that the waters had been so tainted that she didn't want to attempt to dance professionally because of how her mother and sister treated her.

I never told her directly that I was watching her, but I did see her squint at the one-way glass that enclosed the pool area and shielded the swimmers from the prying eyes of gym goers.

"Hey Will, before Lily gets here can I talk to you about something?" Ava asked.

Lily had left to go pick up dinner for everyone. The diner we wanted didn't deliver and since it was her night she had to go get it. We were all hanging out in my apartment because I had the more comfortable couch and seating that fit everyone.

"What's going on?" Will had been a ghost. I had heard that the first year of law school was tough. If the tension bracketing his mouth and across his forehead was any indication it appears those rumors were true. The only time I saw him was during dinner. And the longest time period was on Wednesday when we were watching the girls' volleyball game on ESPN+, and he still had his computer in his lap as he watched.

"I am flying to Baylor next Saturday morning so I can go to Lily's game and while I am there, I am going to take pictures all around campus. I'll post those pictures occasionally on social media to make it really look like I'm there."

Will sighed and rubbed his eyes. "I hate it. Are you going by yourself?"

She winced. "Yes and no. So, the reason why I needed to wait for Lily to be gone is because Monroe is going to pick me up on her way home from LA. She wants to surprise Lily and I guess she needs to talk to her about something. So, after the game she is planning on spending the evening with her."

"About what? Is she okay?" He looked a little concerned.

She shrugged. "I don't think it's serious. She said she'd tell me once she told Lily. Anyway, I wanted to let you know that I will not be here Saturday, but I am flying back Sunday morning. I didn't want you to worry."

He groaned. "I don't want you alone on the Baylor campus, Ava."

"But I won't be. And I also think it needs to be said that I'm not asking permission."

Nicole giggled as Tama made an uncomfortable face. I fucking loved that Ava was so quick to stand up for herself.

Will cursed. "I'm so fucking swamped with homework, and I already know I can't go with you because I have a paper due the following Monday."

"I don't need an escort," she began to argue.

He gave her a deadpan look. "You accepted a drink from a stranger and ending up in a bedroom at the first party you went to."

"Oh damn, I missed a good one, huh?" Nicole said. She laughed to herself as Matt squeezed her thigh. "I'm joking. Ava, come on man, those are like the first two rules of surviving a frat party."

Ava groaned. "I didn't drink it, and the guy was puking, I was worried. Regardless, I don't need an escort."

Matt grunted. "I was supposed to fly to that game, but Coach Daniels wants me to check out some kid in Orlando, so I can't go."

Tama raised her hand. "I might be able to go."

Will squinted. "Don't take this the wrong way, but do you think you can stop someone from tossing Ava in a trunk?"

Ava scoffed. "You act like Waco is dangerous."

"I can't. I'd probably end up in the trunk with her in solidarity," Tama admitted.

I chuckled at the thought of Tama panicking and throwing her body into a trunk to keep Ava company. Tama's eyes turned to me. I let out a withering sigh. "When is this game?"

"The 26th," Nicole answered.

I looked up to the ceiling and then over to Will who was squinting at me. "I can go if it makes you feel better. And I can stop someone from tossing them in a trunk."

Will grunted and nodded before he turned back to Ava. "I'll go along with it. Thanks for letting me know."

She gave us all a satisfied nod and turned to me. "Thank you," she mouthed to me.

Chapter 11

Henry

"What do you mean you can't go?" I hissed to Tama as I placed my overnight bag by the door.

She faked a cough. "I'm sick."

I shook my head at her. "What are you doing?"

She shrugged. "I'm not doing anything but being responsible. It's not a fair decision to possibly get you and Ava sick."

I squinted at her. She mocked me with her expression and then a little smug smile ticked her cheek. Ava's door snicked shut, and Tama's entire demeanor changed from normal to hunched over and looking pathetic.

"I'm so sorry you aren't feeling well." Ava pulled her little bag behind her.

Tama gave her a sad smile. It would have been more convincing if she hadn't been telling me for two weeks now to admit how I felt about Ava. I suspected this was a setup from the beginning, but I didn't say anything.

"It's okay. I'm sorry I can't help with the photoshoot to trick your family, but I would feel terrible if I got you sick."

"You don't sound sick," I said.

Tama sighed. "It's diarrhea, so I wouldn't sound much different."

My lip curled at the same time as Ava's. "Well, get some rest. Stay hydrated. I'll text you when we get in. Oh! I am going to get us matching Baylor shirts so we can take pictures together here in the apartment."

Tama gave a quick thumbs up. Ava turned to me. "If you don't want to go, you don't have to. I know you only said you'd go because Will was freaking out."

Grateful for the out I started to accept, but Tama spoke over me.

"Of course he's still going to go. What sort of friend would bail at the last minute? It's not like *he's* sick. Besides, Will may worry if you are alone and that will not help him concentrate on his studies."

My jaw clicked shut. Ava chewed her lip and turned to me. "Are you sure?"

I shot a glance over to Tama who was staring daggers at me. I nodded. "Yeah, let's go."

It wasn't that I didn't *want* to go. I didn't want the temptation that would follow if I went. Every day was getting harder and harder to resist her. She was so beautiful and funny. I loved that she was a little bratty when she was standing up for herself. And watching her dance had mesmerized me time after time.

Ava was unusually quiet as she drove out of the neighborhood. I figured we were headed to Denver, so she surprised me when she put in the address to Boulder Municipal Airport. I hadn't asked her for any information about our flights, just figuring that she had my basic information. My brows rose when we went through to the private hangars.

"What is going on?" I whispered to myself.

A tall auburn-haired beauty was waiting at the base of the steps to a private jet. She was on her phone and pacing. There was something familiar about her, but I couldn't place it. Ava threw her car into park in the small, attached lot and took off running towards the redhead.

She pocketed her phone and spread her arms out to catch Ava in a hug. I got out slowly from the car. Ava was leading the way back towards me with the redhead on her heels.

"Henry this is Monroe, Monroe this is Henry." Her smile was so big it had to hurt her cheeks.

Monroe stuck her hand out at me after flashing a questioning look at Ava. "Pleasure to meet you. Are you Matt's cousin?"

I nodded and understood why I recognized her. She looked like Lily. "Yeah, you must be Lily's sister. I've heard a lot about you."

Her wide grin made her twin dimples sink deeply in her cheeks. "Same." She turned back to Ava. "Are you ready to get this show on the road?"

Ava nodded quickly. "Thank you so much for doing this. It means so much to me."

Monroe chuckled. "From everything I've heard about your mom and Daphne, I don't blame you one bit for not wanting to live in their shadow. I bought a decent wig for you to wear."

"Oh fun! It'll be like I'm in a movie."

She looped back to her trunk and grabbed her bag. I followed suit as Monroe led the way up the private jet steps.

A lot of things were making sense. For one, it had been clear to me for a while that Lily grew up wealthy. It was how she carried herself and never seemed to worry about money. Her clothes were expensive and high quality, but she never wore a label. And last spring break she refused to accept any money for the resort stay that she treated us all to. I tried multiple times to foot the bill for everyone since they let me tag along, but she said it was covered by her dad. She tried to lie about some bullshit regarding frequent customer points, but I never believed her. I guess my friend Lily was a secret millionaire by the looks of the private jet.

"So, Henry, tell me about yourself." Monroe passed us each a bottle of water.

I took a sip. "I grew up in Colorado Springs. I'm a computer science major and swim for fun?" I said it like a question because I wasn't sure what she wanted to hear.

She nodded. "I love swimming, do you surf at all?"

I shook my head. "Not a lot of waves in Colorado. I do mountain bike and snowboard though."

"Do you like video games?"

I looked over to Ava who was looking out the window like she wasn't paying attention, but I could tell from how tense her shoulders were that she was hardly breathing.

I nodded. "I do. It chills me out after a long week."

Monroe grinned at me. "Same! I actually just got back from LA. I work for the company my dad owns, and I tagged along to learn from a deal with a door and window manufacturer. It was sort of my lead because Ava and Will's brother, Jacob, is the VP of sales for their dad's company and they make doors and windows. We acquired a new resort in San Diego so I thought it would be a perfect test to have Jacob's company provide that service for us."

Ava's head turned to us. "I didn't know that's what you were doing! Did you see Jacob?"

Monroe nodded. "Oh yeah, and Stephanie and Taylor too. Jacob was insistent on a rematch with Fifa after I demolished him at Daphne's wedding."

Ava chuckled. "He had a minor meltdown and talked shit about it for a week after."

"Jacob sends his love and wanted me to thank you for making the generous donation in his name. He said you'd know what he was talking about." Ava snickered. I caught myself smiling because it was clear he had gotten some sort of confirmation about Ava's alumni donation.

"What's your dad's company?"

Monroe looked over to Ava and then back to me, like she was surprised I didn't know. "ML Properties."

My brows shot up. Michael Lauren Properties owned over 400 luxury resorts, including the one we stayed at in Mexico last year. My friend Lily wasn't a secret millionaire; she was a secret billionaire.

"So, what do you want to do with your computer science degree?"

I licked my lips. No one ever asked me this question. "I've made a prediction algorithm. My test used major sporting events. I tested it out last year and made a pretty penny from it. I was able to take a control group, also known as my obsessed cousin, Matt. I compared his predictions and his data with those my code collected. He was right almost as often as my program was. He's limited to baseball and football. My AI engine considers all major sporting events. It collects keyword data about performances, interviews given by competitors and creates an output on their level of success based on everything from mental health to physical health, to weather conditions."

Ava's mouth was dropped open. "I had no idea that's what you did."

I chuckled. "It's a prototype. What I plan to do with it is utilize the algorithm and expand it away from sports gambling."

Monroe gave me an appreciative nod. "That sounds time consuming. Do you find it hard to balance your girlfriend with your project and school?"

My lips twitched to hold back my smile, and I looked over to Ava. She was staring out the window again, her shoulders were by her ears. I turned back to Monroe and gave her a charming smile.

"I don't have a girlfriend at the moment. Interested?" I was needling Ava, who did not disappoint by sucking in a breath and rolling her eyes.

Monroe chuckled and shook her head. "Don't get me wrong, you are a very attractive guy, but I've sworn off all men for at least the next year. I need to concentrate on myself."

I nodded. "Respect. So, what do you do with ML?"

She preened a little. "I'm basically a finance lackey. Last year I spent half the year working in service level positions, so I got a sense of what it was like. I think it was a humility test my father put me up to. Whatever the reason, it worked. So much of finance is about cutting the bottom line and that normally happens with cutting staff or hours of the service people. Even though I only spent a week in each position I got to know a lot of the staff, and I understand how hard the job is and how much the staff relies on hours.

"Then I was a finance intern. I've just finished up my round with accounts payable where I worked for the majority of the past nine months. It was only in the last two months that my dad wanted me to tag along to observe negotiations. I was in Cannes on and off for a few weeks after Barbados."

I nodded. "Cool. I dabbled a little in finance. I plugged my AI code into the stock market trends over the summer. It's a lot of information so it took like two months for it to gather baseline information, but I've gotten some decent recs on what to invest in. I've been dabbling in that, which will make my dad happy because he hates that I like to gamble."

Monroe's eyes widened. "You're working on predicting stock outcomes?"

I shrugged. "Sort of, like I said, it's a lot of data that changes daily. I'm getting to the point where I may need an investor to help me pay for the data storage fees, but I'm not quite there. Right now, it's funding itself. I make money from sporting events and stocks to invest in data storage for my stock program."

"Okay, I could literally talk about this all day, but that would not be fair to Ava. What's new with you?" she asked over to Ava.

She shrugged. "Nothing much. School is easy. I have no idea what I want to do with my life."

Monroe nodded. "Don't worry about that. Honestly, if my dad didn't have me and Lily slated to take over for him in twenty years, I would have zero clue what I would want to do. I'd probably be some day trader too stressed to date and eventually be hospitalized for high blood pressure."

Ava's lip curled. "That's weirdly specific."

Monroe's giggle filled the cabin. "You need to think about what you feel passionate about and figure out a way to make money on that."

Ava moaned. "That's the problem, I'm not good at anything and there is nothing I feel passionate about."

I scoffed. "That's a lie," I said before I could stop myself. Monroe looked over to me with a raised brow. I licked my lips and looked directly at Ava. "I've seen you dance. Are you really going to tell me that you don't feel passionate about ballet?"

"You're a ballerina?" Monroe looked like someone dumped a bunch of puppies in her lap.

Ava glared over to me before looking on to Monroe. "I've dabbled."

I scoffed again but didn't add any more to it.

"Changing the subject. When we get there, we need to head straight to Baylor. I brought a few different outfits to change into. I want to get a bunch of shots all over campus. I was thinking we are going to have to eat in one of the cafeterias so I can get some pictures in there."

My lip curled. University food was normally crap. At least it was where I went my freshman year.

"The match starts at 5pm so we will have plenty of time to look around and stuff," she continued.

Monroe nodded. "Sounds good." She yawned widely. "Sorry, if we are going to be walking around most of the day, I'm going to try to catch a quick nap."

Ava

*Dad: Checking in, Ava Bear. How's
school?*

I chewed on my lip and sent him a picture of me outside the library that Henry had taken of me. I was sweating like crazy with my wig and hoodie on, pretending it was wintertime, not an uncomfortable 90 degrees.

*Me: School's fine. I've been at the
library to get ahead. Oh! Lily is in*

town, so I'm going to her match tonight.

Dad: Lily Young?

I rolled my eyes. He knew exactly which Lily I was talking about. I'm sure he was feigning like he didn't know because he and my mom treated her so poorly at Daphne's wedding.

Me: the one and the only.

Dad: Did Will fly out too?

Me: No. I asked him if he wanted to but he said he had too much homework I guess he has a big paper due Monday.

Dad: You talk to Will often.

Just every night at dinner. I guiltily chewed my lip.

Me: Not often, like I said, he's really busy with homework.

Dad: Well, tell him I said hi since he still won't take my calls.

Me: Will do.

I shoved my phone back in my pocket. "I'm starving and hot. Who wants to eat some lunch?"

Monroe looked a little green. She said she gets vertigo from flying.

"Cold water would be good."

Henry pulled the campus map out and led the way to one of the dining areas. He turned around and snapped a picture of me walking past the sign for the building. As soon as we were in the air conditioning, I pulled the wig off my head and shoved it into my bookbag. The hoodie came off next as I fanned my armpits.

Henry and I ate lunch while Monroe slowly drank her ice water.

"Are you okay?"

She nodded and slipped her hand into her bag. "I need to take something." I recognized the little pill pack from what Daphne would take when she would get car sick.

"Maybe we should head to the hotel after this so you can lie down," I suggested. "I think we have enough pictures, and I want to shower before the match tonight."

Monroe gave a grateful smile. "That would be great, actually. After this medicine kicks in and a nap, I'll be right as rain."

We were opening the door to the rental car when my sister's unmistakable whiney voice stopped me in my tracks.

"Ava Bear, I was hoping to run into you today," she spoke loudly from across the way.

Monroe had parked along the street, not in a parking lot. I was too shocked to pay attention to anything other than my sister walking towards me. So, I didn't grab the door in time when the wind blew it closed on my thumb.

A blinding pain shot through me as the door bounced away innocently. I swallowed a curse and took a step towards Daphne. Monroe's eyes were wide on mine. Henry's eyes were squinted in Daphne's direction.

I closed the distance to my sister. My thumb tucked protectively into my fist as it throbbed menacingly.

"What are you doing here?" I forced a smile to my face. I hadn't seen my sister in over two months.

She gave me a weak one arm hug where she leaned into me. "Ugh, why are you so sweaty," she complained in my ear. Her hands dramatically wiped on her pretty dress.

"I'm here for a sorority luncheon and to welcome the newest members to Phi Mu. It was a good thing you didn't rush; I really didn't want people to associate me with you."

I grit my teeth together at the dig as pain radiated up my arm. She tilted her head. "Your hair is longer. You still look like a dyke, but if the shoe fits. Is that your girlfriend?" She pointed behind me where Monroe was sitting in the car. Henry had already started walking towards us.

I shook my head as Henry slid his hand to my lower back. He tipped my chin up and kissed me right in front of Daphne. It was a quick, nothing kiss, but my whole body lit on fire.

"Babydoll, who's this?" He cupped my cheek and gave me another quick peck.

"This is my sister, Daphne," I squeaked out.

"Henry, nice to meet you."

Henry slipped his arm around my waist and pulled me against his chest. His palm reached out to shake my stunned looking sister's.

Daphne stared at his hand a little too long before taking it and batting her lashes at him. "I could have sworn my sister was gay. Anyway, how long have you and my baby sister been dating?"

"A little over a month," he answered coolly.

Daphne made a noise of confusion in the back of her throat. "Who's the other woman then?" She pointed an accusatory finger towards Monroe. Her lip was as curled as the Botox injections allowed it to be. She looked like she smelled something rotten.

"That's my sister. She wanted to meet Ava since she had heard so much about her."

Daphne rolled her eyes. "Well, I've heard nothing about you."

"I've also haven't spoken to you since the day after your wedding, so that tracks," I quipped back.

Daphne huffed and turned away from Henry. His fingertips were running up and down my ribcage. If I wasn't so stressed about my sister saying something shitty, I would have enjoyed the contact.

"Mom is pissed you told Dad you didn't want to rush. I told her all about the email you sent to Krystal, and I told her that I agreed with everything that Krystal said. I also agree with everything you said." She gave me a cruel smile and leaned into me to give me another fake hug. Henry released me.

"Don't get comfortable with Henry, a man like him would never want someone like you long term."

I bit hard into my cheek and smiled at my sister. "Good to see you Daph."

Henry looped his arm over my shoulder and guided me towards the car.

"Is that the infamous Daphne?" Monroe asked.

I nodded and let out a pained groan. I unclenched my fist and looked at my thumb. It was already swelling. A bruise had formed under the nail.

Henry looked back at me and frowned. "What happened?" he asked when he saw my finger.

I winced. "The wind blew the door shut on it. I was too shocked from seeing Daphne to react in time."

Henry turned his body from the front seat towards me and pulled my hand closer to his face. His fingers were gentle as he tried to move my thumb. I hissed in pain.

He grunted. "Can you bend it?"

I shook my head. "Not without extreme discomfort."

He licked his lips. "Do you think you broke it?"

I shrugged. "I have no idea. It hurts a lot." He glanced over to Monroe who had also turned to look at my thumb.

She winced. "Okay, new plan, you need to go to the doctor."

I whimpered. "But you're not feeling well. I'll be fine. It's probably a little bruise."

Henry cleared his throat. "Let's drop Monroe off so she can rest and I'll take you. We should have enough time to get back for the match," he suggested.

Monroe went to protest but I nodded. "Yeah, we can do that."

Monroe looked over to Henry with a grateful smile. "I'll check us in and leave your name at the front desk for your room keys."

She drove us to the hotel where Henry took over driving after Monroe pulled her bag from the trunk. "Text me if you think you won't make it in time for the match."

I nodded and made my way to the front seat. Henry was already on his phone looking up directions for Dallas General. He called a few hospitals to see who had an orthopedist available.

He drove the forty-five minutes to the hospital complex and grabbed the door for me when we went into the building. The waiting area was an open space for a few different doctors' offices. I cringed when Lucy's voice interrupted my thoughts and turned my face into Henry.

"What's wrong?" he whispered.

"I can hear the antichrist," I hissed back.

He cupped the back of my head before he slipped his fingers into my hair and finger combed through my tresses in a soothing way. "Stay there as long as you need. I'll tell you when she's gone."

I nodded against his chest. He smelled so freaking good. His arm around me felt even better. I couldn't believe he had kissed me. It was all a ruse, but he definitely did, twice. And it wasn't a maybe kiss, it was intentional lip to lip action.

"Ava Reiser?" a nurse called.

Lucy's confused glare made my stomach clench. My eyes concentrated on my toes, and I let Henry guide me into the doctor's office. Two hours later and a bill that my parents were going to have to pay we were free to go.

"I can't believe you cracked the tip of your thumb. At least the healing time is only three weeks, and you can still dance," Henry said.

He had sat next to me through everything except the x-rays. He was the one that asked the doctor if I could still practice ballet. And since it's a non-contact sport he told me I could after five days.

When we got out to the lobby, I wiggled a little. "I need to pee."

He chuckled and nodded towards the hallway where there was a restroom sign. There were two small stalls. My flow had started when Lucy's husky voice made me clamp back up again.

"Last night was crazy. I can't believe how trashed you got." She cackled on the phone. She took the stall next to mine. I stayed put, frozen and waiting for her to finish.

"Are you ready for tonight?" Another pause. "Twist it all around and blame him. Don't think I didn't hear you do the same thing to Thomas last month. I need that same energy."

She cackled again. "Because Botox and Juvéderm doesn't pay for itself, and the sex is incredible." She made another little laugh. "Doesn't mean I don't like a lot of variety. You didn't seem to complain when we were trashed last week."

She flushed and washed her hands. When the door closed again, I slipped out of the stall. I was attempting to wash my hands around the weird plastic brace when the bathroom door opened again. I ducked my head down.

Henry chuckled. "Coast is clear, Babydoll. Let's go. It's almost an hour drive back to the hotel and we still need to stop by the pharmacy to pick up your pain meds."

I nodded into the mirror and dried my hands.

Monroe was waiting for us, looking a million times better. "What's the diagnosis?"

"Fractured thumb, three weeks to heal. We didn't have time to pick up my pain medicine because traffic sucked, but the doctor gave me some before we left. We need to get it before we go back to the hotel."

Chapter 12

Henry

I had never considered myself a guy that got into volleyball. But after watching several matches over the past year, I could see the appeal. There wasn't a large gambling pull, but it was still entertaining as hell. It was especially cool knowing my two friends were playing their asses off and we were there to support them.

We were invited to go out drinking with Nicole and Lily after the game, but I had declined because Ava couldn't go. I didn't want her to have to sit alone in her hotel room while we were out having a good time.

"I'll meet you guys there, but first we have to pick up Ava's medicine and apparently the only pharmacy still open is like thirty minutes away." Monroe hugged her sister. When they were side by side you could clearly see the family resemblance.

Lily nodded. "No worries, we still have the post-match meeting and late-night team dinner. You have plenty of time before we are ready to go out." Lily leaned over to hug Ava.

I gave both girls a fist bump. I had spent the match trying to not touch Ava. It was so fucking tempting when I had essentially spent the four hours prior touching her constantly. Kissing her was a mistake but I was so pissed at how Daphne had been treating her sister. The first kiss was to get Daphne to back off.

The second was because I couldn't help myself. Her lips were so soft and warm.

"I have to pee so bad." Monroe threw the rental in park and hustled into the pharmacy. Ava chuckled and slipped out of the car after her. I wanted to sit with my thoughts, but I didn't want to be away from Ava any longer than necessary.

Ava stopped short in front of me. "Holden?" She pulled a tall Ken look alike into a hug. He patted her back and asked her what she was doing in his neck of the woods. He was a charming motherfucker. From his smile to his green eyes, I didn't like him. I took the few extra steps that separated us and slipped my hand onto the small of Ava's back.

Holden squinted at me in surprise.

Yeah, fucker, she's mine.

"Holden, this is my boyfriend, Henry. Henry, Holden." Ava waved her hands between us. His hands were full of two pints of ice cream, one was mint chocolate, and the other was chocolate chip cookie dough.

I nodded at him, and he returned the gesture.

"Your hair looks longer, but it hasn't been that long since I saw you, has it?"

Ava giggled, she fucking giggled and twirled a lock of hair into her finger. "About two months. Which you would know if you followed me back on social media. I'm documenting the whole growth journey." She pointed down to the ice cream in his hands. "Big night?"

He chuckled and looked at the labels in his hand. "Just got finished with a couple's therapy session where I was blamed for Lucy being a cheating bitch. I'm trying to disassociate to happier times."

Oh shit, I have heard of this guy.

He's the one that Lucy was cheating on Will with and then he found out it was the other way around.

Ava's lip curled. "I thought you two broke up."

He sighed. "We did and we are, but apparently condoms and birth control aren't enough to prevent a pregnancy."

Ava winced. "Oh shit. Do you think she's lying?"

He shook his head. "I saw the positive pregnancy test."

She twisted her lips to the side. "Do you think she lied about taking birth control? Because I've been on it since I was fifteen and my doctors have assured me that if I take it at the same time every night there is like half a percent chance of getting pregnant."

That's good information to have. Wait, what am I thinking? I can't fuck her.

Holden shrugged. "She wasn't that consistent in Barbados. I don't know. But listen, my dessert is melting. I'm going to go."

Ava gave him another hug and walked to the back of the pharmacy to pick up her medicine. Monroe came out of the bathroom as Ava was called up.

"You okay?"

She gave me an unsure smile. "Yeah, there was a small line. I almost wet myself, but yeah." She turned to look at me and leaned in. "Between you, me, and the lamp post, you like her right? Because you kissed her twice, you came on this trip, and you watch her constantly."

I rolled my lips in and looked away from her.

She hummed. "I'm not a gossip like my sister and Will. I'm looking out for Ava. I feel like she's my little sister and she likes you. She'll kill me for telling you, but she does. So, if you like her, do something about it."

I bit the inside of my cheek and nodded. "Yeah, I do."

She patted my arm. "Yeah, you do."

"Ready?" Ava said while looking through the contents of her bag. She held up a fridge magnet that was shaped like Texas with a grin. It was going to be added to the small collection on our fridge of California, Nevada, Utah, Colorado, and Barbados magnets that appeared when Ava moved in.

Monroe drove us back to the hotel. "Are you sure you don't want to at least have dinner?"

My girl shook her head. "I don't want you to feel obligated to leave to get me back here. Besides, I'm sort of tired and really want to take a shower."

Monroe nodded and turned to me. "I left the room keys at the front desk in your name."

"Sounds good."

She popped the trunk so Ava and I could grab our bags. I made my way to the front desk and gave them my name. I was a little surprised when it was to only one room, but then again Monroe acted surprised to see me on the trip. I'm sure Ava forgot to mention that I was going, and the single room was meant for her and Tama. Which meant there was at least going to be two beds.

I had no doubt Ava heard all about what a terrible bed partner Tama was. I had joked and complained about it enough from our road trip earlier in the year. She'd steal all the covers every single night. Plus, she talked in her sleep.

I could behave myself for one fucking night. I'd do what Tama did, I'd cocoon myself in the covers like a burrito and steer clear of Ava's side of the room. I held onto that hope until we stepped inside the room. My jaw clenched at the king bed. I wasn't going to be able to sleep a wink tonight.

I stared at the large king bed and glanced over to Henry. He looked pissed. I winced and turned on my heel. "I'm going to take a quick shower. Do you mind ordering room service? You know what I like." I slipped into the bathroom.

I snatched my phone from my pocket.

> *Me: You definitely told me that there were going to be two beds.*

Monroe: Did I? I don't remember that.

> *Me: How many beds are in your room?*

Monroe: I don't know if that's relevant.

> *Me: It is, if this is your way of meddling. Lily told me you liked to meddle, but I didn't believe her.*

Monroe: Meddling is such an odd term. I don't think I'm doing that.

Monroe: In a completely unrelated statement, I asked Henry point

Her message made me blanch. My whole body felt like it was on fire. There was too much I was trying to process. *Henry liked me.* Weird mention about condoms, but Henry liked me.

I turned the water on and sat on the edge of the shower ledge in thought. If the attraction was mutual, then my brother's threat *had* to be what was holding him back. It was silly because I'd deal with Will. It would be dramatic and annoying. It also had the high probability of being awkward for Henry. And I didn't want that. Regardless, we still liked each other. It meant that I would need to force Henry's hand, a little bit.

When the water was hot, I delicately peeled off the bandage that was holding the brace against my thumb and stripped out of my clothes.

I think I need to seduce him.

It had a chance of failure, but I'd always wonder if I didn't do everything I could. I wasn't going to have another chance like this again.

The literal stars aligned that I was even in Waco, Tama was sick, Monroe was out, and Henry was in the room with me. Monroe wasn't going to disturb us either, her last message guaranteed that. And if my seduction was a huge backfire, then I could go lick my wounds in Monroe's room. Which I was pretty positive had two beds.

The gritty sweat rinsed away as I lathered my hair in shampoo. By the time I had gotten out of the shower, my nerves had settled a little bit. I used the complimentary mouthwash to gargle and finger combed my hair.

Anxiety paralyzed me. My plan was bold, and leaving the bathroom had become a monumental task in my head. I was stalling when I turned the hair dryer on. The room service cart clanked into the room, and Henry had the polite conversation while I was quickly drying my hair. I stared at my body in the mirror. Not much to write home about, but there was nothing I could do to change it.

My cheeks still looked flushed as I let out a shaky breath. I hung my towel and rewrapped my finger. It was a real bummer that I had the weird flesh colored hard plastic on my thumb. It made it look fake, but at least it didn't hurt.

I gave myself one more look into the mirror and opened the bathroom door.

Henry

I was sitting in one of the club chairs on my phone. My chin leaning into my fist as I scrolled through the hundreds of pictures I had taken of Ava. She's so fucking beautiful. It was insane to me that she had never had a boyfriend.

Monroe's words had been playing on repeat in my head. The need to do something about the growing attraction consumed my thoughts. Dealing with the consequences of Will throwing a tantrum about it was the only thing making me pause. I knew that Ava loved her brother way too much, and I didn't want to be the reason for any rift between them. After meeting her sister and feeling Ava cower and shake against me at the sound of Lucy's voice, she needed Will in her life.

The club sandwiches had come fifteen minutes ago, but I wasn't overly hungry since I ate popcorn at the match. I was happy to wait for Ava to come out of the bathroom. I'd never make the mistake again of making her eat alone if I were near her.

The hair dryer turned off and a few minutes later she opened the bathroom door. My eyes flicked up in her direction. My face relaxed to cool indifference so she couldn't read my expression as she stepped into view. She was completely naked. Her little pink nipples were hard and pointed right at me. Her pussy was bare. She stopped a few feet from me, shoulders rolled back.

Her cheek was sucked in on one side, she was probably biting it. I slowly put my phone down, letting my eyes drag away from Ava's perfect fucking tits and body. My gaze slowly perused her. My cock thickened in my pants. It was pushing painfully against a seam. I wanted to adjust myself, but I didn't want her to think she affected me. Not yet.

"What are you doing?" My voice had deepened.

She let out a shaky breath. "What does it look like I'm doing?"

"Being a brat."

She licked her lips. "Don't brats get punished… sir?"

Motherfucker.

My eyes dragged up her body again. She was rubbing her thighs together. I tapped my knee and leaned my body back, giving a little space to my dick that was starting to throb in my pants. "Bend over and take your punishment, Babydoll."

She was trembling as she took the last two steps towards me. My knees spread wide as she draped her body over my lap. She looked back at me with innocent eyes. Her pupils were blown wide. Her teeth were digging into her pillowy bottom lip.

My palm glided up her warm leg and cupped her pert ass in my palm. She jumped a little when I first made contact. "I am going to spank your ass five times. I want you to count it out. That's the only sound you are allowed to make." She nodded and let out a choppy breath.

I swung my hand down hard, but not hard enough to hurt her. Watching the light ripple of her ass against my palm made me smile. She moaned when I smoothed my hand over the pink print.

"One," she breathed.

My other arm to ran up and down her back as my fingers dipped between her cheeks, she jumped again. I grinned to myself and continued to dip my finger down. I rubbed her clit in one circle and dragged my hand back up. She was already drenched.

I reared back and gave her another smack. She gasped. "Two."

My fingers explored a little more, dipping into her impossibly tight channel. She was going to choke the fuck out of my cock when the time came. I made it to my second knuckle, and her hymen stopped my progress. She was going to bleed. At least she was already on pain meds, it would keep most of the stinging at bay.

Her chest was heaving against my thighs as I delivered the next three smacks. I continued to reward her between spanks by fingering her clit, pussy, and ass. I was surprised she didn't fight me on the last one. She seemed eager to please me and do whatever I wanted.

Two fingers worked into her tight channel and gently tapped against her hymen. It had to go unless I wanted to play just the tip tonight.

"Stand up." She followed my direction and got to her shaky legs. She was flushed from the tips of her rosy nipples and up to her cheeks.

I held my fingers to her mouth. "Clean up the mess you made." She parted her lips and greedily lapped as her tongue lolled around them. I was going to go down on her first, but the eagerness in how she was moaning against my fingers made me change my mind.

"You're going to suck my cock, Babydoll. Do you remember what I taught you?"

She bit her lip and stared at my lap. My erection had made its way to my pocket. She nodded.

"Have you practiced on anyone else?"

She let out a shaky breath and shook her head.

"That's my good girl. Only my cock goes in your mouth. Get on your knees and take me out of my pants.

Her hands were trembling hard as she worked my zipper down. I lifted my ass a little and helped her tug my pants down enough for her to have full access to me. The relief of not having my throbbing dick pushed into the seam of my pocket was immense. I lifted again to help her slide my boxer briefs down. My cock sprung forward and slapped against my stomach.

She made a little whimper and licked her lips. I cupped her cheek. Her eyes were slow to leave my dick; she looked so good on her knees staring up to me with eyes full of desire. "Show me how much you paid attention, Babydoll."

She nodded and delicately gripped my cock in her hand and pointed it to her mouth. Her pink tongue flicked out and lapped up at the leaking precum. I grit my teeth. Then with a broad stroke of her tongue she lavished the underside of my head. Her tongue glided down the vein that led to my balls.

My hands fisted as I fought to control myself. She flicked at the seam before dragging her tongue back up. She swirled it around the head and then licked the top of my shaft. When I was decently lubed up with her saliva, she tightened her grip on my cock and slipped my head in her hot mouth. My jaw clenched so hard it hurt.

She worked herself down my shaft. The back of her throat gripped me as she paused and swallowed. *Fuck.* All I wanted to do was grab her head and fuck her face. Her eyes opened and she watched me as she hollowed out her cheeks, sucking hard as she slid back up my dick.

And then, like I taught her, she worked her hand in sync with her sinfully talented mouth. I wanted to cum down her throat at how she looked with her mouth stretched wide, innocent brown eyes gazing at me through her lashes. She deep throated me again as her other hand cupped my balls.

"You're doing so great, Babydoll. I want you to do it faster. Can you do that for me?"

She hummed her response which made me curl my toes. Her pace was perfect as the beginning of my orgasm rolled up my spine. "Suck as hard as you can and grip me harder, you aren't going to hurt me."

My eyes rolled to the back of my head as she sped up with her eager movements. "I'm going to cum down your throat. Don't stop sucking," I gritted out.

She hummed again, sucked me down, and flexed her throat around my head. I grunted as my release coated her mouth. Every time she swallowed, she squeezed around my head.

When the last tremors of my orgasm ceased, I eased my hips back. She chased me with her mouth. I chuckled and cupped her cheek.

"You did so good," I praised her. "Now stand up and get something to eat and drink. I want you to take another dose of your medicine, okay?" Her knees were wobbly as she followed my instructions.

"Are you going to eat?" she asked after she had finished half of her sandwich.

I nodded. "I want you to eat whatever you want first. Then I'll eat."

She chewed her lip but nodded, taking the second half of her sandwich in hand. When there was only a quarter of her sandwich left, she set it down. "I'm done."

My mouth watered. "Sit on the table."

Her cheeks flushed again as she stood up and awkwardly sat on top of the table. Her legs were hanging down. She had braced her hands on the edge. I stood up from my club chair, pulled my shirt off, kicked my pants down, but adjusted my boxers back up to cover my ass.

I pulled the chair she had been sitting on in front of her. "What are you doing?" she whispered.

"Eating." I gripped her knees and spread them far apart. My hands hooked under her thighs and tugged her to make her ass hang off the edge. She dropped back to her elbows. With each leg over a shoulder, I dove in.

My tongue made a long swipe through her slit. I hummed lightly, loving how she tasted, and I knew after one lick I was going to be addicted. She gasped and whimpered. My lips teased her clit. She was staring down at me, chest rising and falling rapidly.

"Be as quiet as you can. Nothing above a whisper." She bit into her lip and nodded.

My body covered hers, and I pulled one of her nipples into my mouth. She was a perfect mouthful. My teeth dragged to her other, and I praised her with my tongue and teeth. She was a writhing mess by the time I kissed my way back to her clit. She let out a needy little moan as I twirled my tongue around her bundle.

I tested to see which she responded to the most between licks, flicks, and sucks. Her thigh bounced against my cheek as I rapidly flicked my tongue against her swollen clit. I teased her opening with one finger before slipping a second in. Her back arched as the fluttering began against my tongue. She was a whimpering mess, letting out breathy moans, sighs, and gasps. I reveled in the fact that she was trying so hard to keep quiet. She had potential to be a perfect sub for me.

When her breathing calmed down, I lightly kissed her clit and eased her thighs around my waist as I stood up. I kissed a trail to her mouth and devoured her lips against mine.

"Taste how good your cum is, Babydoll." Her thighs gripped my waist as I rolled my tongue into her mouth.

It was the first real kiss we had shared. I ate her pussy before I felt her tongue against mine. She clutched against my shoulders as her nails scratched against my scalp. I moaned at the sensation. I fucking loved getting my head scratched.

I kissed her until we were both breathless and pulled away.

"Are we going to have sex now?"

She was wobblily as I helped her off the table. "Is that what you want?"

She licked her lips and nodded.

My head tilted. "It's going to hurt."

She shrugged. "I can handle pain."

I assessed her for a moment. "I don't have any condoms." I didn't pack any because I didn't want to be tempted. Never in a million years would I have thought Ava would be brazen enough to seduce me by walking naked into my lap.

She licked her lips and then rubbed them together. She did that when she was nervous. "I'm on birth control."

My gaze squinted at her. "You know I'm not a virgin. I've had many partners. Are you saying that doesn't matter to you?"

She chewed her bottom lip. "When was the last time you were tested?"

My brow rose. "That's a forward question, but after the road trip this summer."

She nodded at that. "And you haven't been with anyone since?"

"No."

I knew what she was giving me permission to do. It wouldn't be the first time I had done it bare. I was a little too reckless in high school. You only need to get the clap once before you wrap your shit up every single time. But Ava was different, and I wasn't thinking with the right head.

She let out a shaky breath. "Well, as you may remember I've been on a form of birth control since I was fifteen to help with my periods. Last year my doctor recommended an implant which essentially stopped them altogether.

Her cheek was hot against my palm. "Do you want me to fuck you bare, Babydoll?

"Please," she whimpered. "I want to feel everything my first…" Her lip hitched and her nose wrinkled in embarrassment, "time."

I reached down and stroked myself through my boxers. "Since you asked so nicely." My lips grazed hers. "Go get a few towels."

She nodded rapidly, and her stomach flexed. You'd think with how hard she had cum she would have relaxed a little bit. She came back a moment later and passed me two towels.

I folded one in half and placed it in the center of the bed. "Lie down, Babydoll."

She was taking quick shallow breaths by the time she had settled down in the center of the bed. I kicked my boxers off and leaned forward to kiss her ankles. Her legs were tightly pressed together.

She sucked in a shaky breath as I took her calf in one hand and massaged into the muscle. Her eyes rolled back as my thumb found a knot. I sat with her legs in my lap and gently massaged her muscles. I wanted her to relax and enjoy as much of the experience as she could. And there was no way she would enjoy it if she were clenching every muscle in her body.

By the time I reached her upper thigh, her pussy was glistening again. My finger softly circled her clit as my mouth licked up her stomach to her incredibly hard nipples. She shuddered at the first scrape of my teeth and dripped against my palm when I took her mouth again.

I rolled into the cradle of her hips and held myself up by one elbow as I continued to finger her. She was whimpering and gasping as we kissed. She sucked my tongue into her mouth, and I knew she was as ready.

Her legs to hooked around my waist as my cock replaced my fingers. My shaft ran up and down her dripping pussy. She let out a little moan every time the ridge of my head hit her clit. My head barely pushed in.

She whimpered and gripped my shoulders. I reached between us and circled her clit with the tip of my finger.

"I need you to relax, Babydoll."

She let out a slow breath as I gently pushed in. The thin wall of her hymen made me pause. "Are you ready?"

She gave me a shaky nod.

I adjusted her knee higher and slid my hand back against her clit. I swiped at where we were connected before easing back. She let out a gasp of pain as I quickly pushed in. I paused, gritting my teeth by how fucking tight she was. My elbow bared my weight as I licked a tear that was tracking down her cheek. Her thighs were shaking against my waist.

"I'm going to start moving, okay?"

She gave me a shaky nod. My hips pulled back and eased forward. A rush of warm liquid let me know she was bleeding all over both of us. I didn't fucking care. It was inevitable. She wasn't my first virgin. I kept circling her clit until the grip she had on my waist relaxed.

Then I started to move. My gentle rocks into her were replaced with faster sharper thrusts I started to hit her g-spot, and she tossed her head back in a gasp. Needing a different angle, I pulled her to the edge of the bed with the bloody towel. I was going to have to remove that before she saw it.

With both feet on the ground, I pulled her legs up and hooked her ankles around my neck and pushed back into her. She pushed her chest high in the air and let out a keening whimper. I leaned forward and sucked a nipple into my mouth. She was flexible enough that me folding her in half wasn't a discomfort.

Chasing my own orgasm, I rutted into her as my fingers were quickly flicked her clit. Her breaths were quick and shallow again. I didn't expect her to be able to cum while in pain, but she proved me wrong. Her pussy squeezed my cock so hard my eyes rolled to the back of my head. She milked my climax right out of me. I grunted and let out my own silent gasp when I collapsed on top of her. One knee had worked itself onto the bed and both of her legs around my neck.

My lips brushed her throat and jaw as I pulled her legs back down around my waist. "Are you okay?" I murmured. She hummed a yes. I kissed down her neck again before pushing up on my arms.

"Hook your ankles behind my back."

She adjusted around me. My hands slipped behind her shoulders, and I stood up, taking her with me. She giggled. I was still buried deep inside her. I kissed her smiling lips.

"Where are you taking me?" she laughed lightly. Her hands were back in my hair. She was making scratching passes along my scalp, goosebumps spread up my neck.

"Tub. Sex is messy without a condom."

She clung to me as I leaned forward and turned the shower on. The water warmed quickly. She gasped as I pushed her against the cold tile wall. "I'm going to pull out, now." She licked her lips and nodded. I shuddered at the final squeeze she gave me before releasing me. Our cum and blood rush down the drain. I kissed her mouth and eased her down to her feet.

The smell of eucalyptus filled the space as I washed her legs before quickly washing my whole body. She stood in the water's stream, so I was partially freezing my own ass off, but I was a romantic like that. Everything tonight was about her comfort. I kissed her again like a greedy motherfucker, I couldn't get enough of her.

A fresh towel draped around her shoulders, and I slung the wet one she had used earlier around my waist.

"Get ready for bed." I slipped out of the bathroom. The bloody towel made me grimace. I was going to have to attempt to rinse it tonight or housekeeping will think I murdered someone.

Ava was going through her toiletry bag and brushing her teeth. I tossed the bloody towel directly in the shower, adjusted the shower head to soak it, and grabbed my bag for the bathroom. She shot me a shy grin as I brushed my own teeth. Once the towel was no longer bright red, I turned the water off.

"Are we going to have sex again?" A blush creeped up her chest.

"No, your body needs to heal and rest for a few days. Speaking of which, are you still bleeding?"

She chewed her lip and ducked her head. "It's not a big deal," she whispered. Her cheeks were crimson.

I chuckled at her embarrassment and tipped her face up with a finger under her chin. "I know it's not a big deal. I want to know if you have anything for it."

She rolled her lips in and shook her head. I leaned forward and kissed her burning cheek. "Okay. Stay in the towel. I'll be back in a few minutes." I hung my towel up, slipped my sweatpants on, and tugged a t-shirt on over my head.

"You know people can see like your entire dick when you wear those."

My brows wagged. "You staring at my dick, Babydoll?"

She bit the corner of her lip. "It's hard to miss." I chuckled and kissed her forehead.

The little shop by check-in had a menstrual pad that was going to work for the night. I bought her the travel pack and headed back to the room. I felt lighter, happy. The indecision of what I was going to do about my attraction to Ava was gone. There was no going back now. I wasn't eager to tell Will, but I was willing to figure that out.

Ava was standing awkwardly in the room when I came back in. I passed her the bag and walked back over to the table to eat my dinner. She disappeared into the bathroom as I scarfed down my sandwich, what was left of hers, and all the fries.

Ava sat at the end of the bed with her knee tucked under her chin. "I don't think we should tell Will about this."

Disappointed that this was a one-time thing, I looked up at her slowly and pushed the empty plate away. "Why is that?"

She cleared her throat. "Well, because he'd freak out and I want to stave off on the drama for a little longer. Also, I don't know a lot about you. You've spent the better part of two months avoiding me, so I think we should get to know each other better before we tell anyone."

I shrugged. "That's fair." I bit the inside of my lip to keep myself from giving her a relieved smile.

She rubbed her lips together. "I would prefer it if you didn't sleep with other people while we are getting to know each other."

I perked one brow high. "What about you, Ava?"

Her brown eyes widened. "Oh, yeah, that's not an issue. I have zero plans or prospects."

My legs ate up the distance between us and I cupped her cheek. She had no idea how beautiful she really was. And she had less of a clue at how many men wanted her. The locker room chatter was always about her after she would dance.

"Are we together?" I knew what she was going to say, having heard her rant about me too often to have any actual doubts.

She nodded. "Just in secret."

My lips devoured hers. "I'll keep all your secrets." She shivered against me. I pulled my shirt off by my collar and pushed my sweatpants off. "Let's go to bed."

"I thought you said we weren't having sex again."

A chuckle vibrated my chest. "We aren't. I sleep in the nude." Her mouth opened in a little 'o'. I got into the bed first and Ava stretched next to me like a little satisfied cat. She slung her leg over my hip and nestled her face into my chest. I can honestly say it was the best night's sleep of my life.

Chapter 13

Ava

I woke up to Henry lightly stroking my back with his hand. I didn't think he was trying to wake me, I think he liked how my skin felt. He had commented on how smooth and soft my skin was right before he fell asleep. I watched him sleep for only a little while before my lids were too heavy to hold up.

He truly was a beautiful man. I wanted to trace the swoop of his nose with my finger or feel his lashes that looked so full against his cheeks. His pink lips had relaxed a smidge. He was no longer smirking or scowling which were his two normal expressions.

I snuggled closer to his chest and kissed his warm skin.

"How'd you sleep?" His voice was husky in the morning.

"Pretty great. My neck is a little sore, but I liked treating you like my personal pillow."

His chest rumbled with a chuckle. "How else are you feeling?"

My vagina and thumb were both throbbing and burning in the same way. Clearly my body was busy repairing all injuries sustained yesterday. "I'm okay. I need to take some more medicine."

He hummed and kissed the top of my head. "Get on top of me."

I looked up at his face. His eyes were still closed.

"I don't know what I'm doing if I'm on top."

A grin spread across his face. His eyes opened as he looked at me. "We aren't having sex. I told you; you need to heal. I want to massage your back and you being on top is the best angle."

I adjusted my leg that was draped over his thigh around to his other side and straddled him. He was still grinning at me. His hands settled on my hips and squeezed before he slid his hands up my back and pulled me down to rest my head back against his chest. He used both hands to knead into my shoulders and neck. I groaned at the knots he was working through.

By the time he was done, I felt like putty and the little crick in my neck was gone. "Are you hungry?" I whispered.

He shrugged, but his stomach growled loudly. He laughed quietly. "I wasn't, but my stomach has a mind of its own. He must have heard you ask about food."

I sat up and looked down on him. He looped his hands behind his head, smiling softly at me. The morning light had filtered through the curtains giving him a golden glow. Normally the auburn in his hair looked muted, but in the sun, it was highlighted to its natural hue.

"You're so beautiful," he murmured.

My cheeks flushed as I looked away from him. I had never heard that compliment from someone not blood-related. He reached up and guided my face to look at him again.

"You are. I've thought that since the moment I saw you sleeping in my bed. Anyone who has ever said otherwise is a liar."

I sucked in a breath.

"Come on, let's take a shower." He sat up with me in his lap and carried me over to the bathroom like I weighed nothing. I giggled in his ear as he sat me down. He turned the water on and brushed his teeth while the water was warming up. I had to pee so bad, but I didn't want him to see me remove my pad. It was like he knew what I was thinking.

He winked at me and walked out of the bathroom while brushing his teeth. He didn't shut the door behind him, but he gave me enough privacy to do what I had to do. He walked back in as I was sticking my own toothbrush in my mouth. He was still completely naked, and I had done amazingly well not looking at every perfect inch of his body. But it became more difficult when he came behind me and kissed my shoulder then my neck. His erection was digging into my back, hot and rigid. I squeezed my thighs together and winced in pain.

He stepped into the shower and stroked his huge dick a few times. "Get in here, Babydoll." I nodded nervously and pulled my tank top over my head. Thankfully I had stopped bleeding and had already thrown away all the evidence of that in the trash.

"Don't get in the water yet. I want to admire you." He motioned to the corner as I stepped into the shower. I stood and licked my lips as he slowly jerked himself off in front of me.

"You're getting a pass today because you need to heal, but next time I need to cum you're going to need to help me."

I chewed my lip. "I can help right now."

He shook his head. "Not when I can't reciprocate. I may be in charge in the bedroom, but that doesn't mean I'm a selfish asshole. Your needs come before mine, always. And you need to heal." His eyes raked up and down my naked body as he started to stroke himself faster. "Play with your tits."

I cupped my breasts before pulling gently on both my nipples. His nostrils flared. He was standing in the center of the shower, so the water's flow was cascading down his muscled stomach and straight down to his balls which were drawn up tight.

He reached his hand out to me, grabbing my throat lightly and pulling me to him. His lips crashed down on mine as he continued to get himself off. I rolled my tongue around his and then sucked his into my mouth. He moaned lightly. I let my hand travel from his chest down. His grip on my throat tightened a little when I bypassed his rapidly moving hand and went straight to his balls. He grunted when I cupped them and let my thumb run up and down the seam. His kiss was getting sloppy until he pulled his face away and tipped his head back into the streaming water. His hot cum hit my stomach as he groaned out his release.

When he turned his face down to look at me his smile was back. His kiss was less urgent, gentler. He chuckled and pulled away. A hot stream hit my thigh, and I looked down. My jaw dropped when I realized he was peeing on me.

He laughed at my expression. "What the hell?"

He leaned forward and kissed me again. "You accused me of peeing on your leg before. I figured you'd be into it, no?" he joked.

I shook my head. "You're so gross."

He chuckled and nodded. "That's what every boyfriend wants to hear his girlfriend say."

I couldn't hold back my smile at his casual use of the terms. "I'm marking my territory," he joked. His laugh was almost contagious. He kissed me again before he pulled away and grabbed the soap. He washed my stomach and thighs, laughing occasionally. He grinned at me. "I've never done that before, but I think the joke landed."

"Consider me marked." I rolled my eyes as he chuckled. Someone knocked on the hotel room door. We had the 'do not disturb' sign out, so I thought maybe it was Monroe. I slipped out of the shower and twisted a towel around my torso. Monroe was standing a few feet back in the hallway.

I unlatched and pulled the door open with me behind it so no one passing by could see that I was only in a towel.

"Am I interrupting something?" Monroe perked her brow when I shut the door. I shook my head as my cheeks flamed. She chuckled and looked around the room. It was blatantly obvious we had slept together in the middle of the bed.

She hummed to herself. "How was your night?" Her tone was knowing and smug.

I rolled my lips in and looked up to the ceiling. Her dimples pushed deeply into her cheeks. "I freaking knew it. Don't worry, your secret is safe with me. How are you feeling?" she whispered.

I couldn't stop the smile from taking over my face. "Amazing. He called me his girlfriend, and I guess I am officially a woman now."

Monroe grinned at me. "Are you happy?"

I nodded. "So happy. He was so sweet and attentive. He really likes me. He called me beautiful this morning. No one has ever called me that," I hissed.

She gave me a soft smile. "I'm glad. When are you going to tell Lily and Will?"

I shook my head. "We aren't. Not yet at least. We want to get to know each other because he's essentially been avoiding me for months. I learned more about him yesterday while he was talking to you than I had the entire time I've lived with him."

Monroe scowled at that. "You're asking for trouble keeping *another* secret from your family."

I shrugged. "It's fine. We aren't going to keep it a secret forever, just until we know we are good together and compatible.

The last thing I want is to openly date him and we end up breaking up and we still live together. Then everyone will know our business, and I'll probably have to move out because I'm the odd man out in the situation."

Monroe's lip curled. "You can't think so negatively. First of all, as long as everyone is mature, you'll be fine. Second of all, you know a lot about him. Just because you don't know his favorite color doesn't mean you don't already know and appreciate his personality. I fell in love with a complete stranger after only spending one night with him."

I twisted my lips to the side and sighed. "How was your night?"

She wagged her head back and forth. "Fine. We ate dinner and talked."

"Oh yeah, you had that thing you needed to talk to Lily about face to face. Did it go okay?"

"As good as it could go," she answered vaguely. The water shut off. I called out to Henry to let him know that Monroe was in our room. He yelled back with an appreciative, 'thanks for letting me know.'

I turned back to her. She looked tired and worried. "Are you sick or something? I mentioned to Will that you wanted to surprise Lily and that you needed to tell her something face to face. I didn't think it was serious, but he wasn't convinced. Should I be concerned?"

She blew out a harsh breath. "I *am* sick, but I'll be fine by mid-April."

I blanched and then my chin quivered. Her mom had died of breast cancer when she was 14. It was hereditary, but she had tested negative for the gene. She frowned at me and then her eyes widened. "Not like that, Ava. Calm down."

My eyes watered and my chin quivered as I nodded. Henry walked into the bedroom with a towel slung low on his hips as a tear slipped down my cheek.

"What's wrong?" He was immediately on guard. He turned to Monroe. "What did you say to her?"

Monroe held her hands up and then clapped one over her mouth before sprinting past Henry towards the bathroom. He walked up to me and cupped my cheek. He kissed the trail the tear left behind. "What's wrong?" he asked quietly as Monroe retched loudly.

My eyes widened as I slipped out of Henry's hands and into the bathroom. I held her hair as I rubbed her back.

When she was done, I passed her a glass of water from the sink. She swished her mouth and spit. "I'm pregnant. I'm not sick, sick. And I'm due in April," Monroe said.

Relief coursed through me and then confusion because Monroe was definitely single and hadn't dated anyone seriously in months.

"Ah shit," Henry said from the doorway. He had pulled on his jeans and a t-shirt. "Do you need us to get you anything?" he asked Monroe.

She shook her head. "No, I needed to tell Lily. I'm heading home to tell my dad next. He's supposed to be in New York for a few weeks."

I nodded. "Who's the dad?"

She shrugged. "One night stand, Jack the pirate astronaut." My brow pinched in confusion. She chuckled and shook her head. "We didn't exchange actual names or details about our lives."

"Oh... Are you freaked out?"

She shrugged. "I was. I'm not anymore. I have the means to be a single mom. I have several homes I can live in for free. I have a great job. Lily and my dad will support me however they can."

"I will too. I don't have summer plans. I can come out and help."

She smiled at me and pulled her knees to her chest. "See, I have a support system in place. I can do it on my own."

"Is that why you made the joke about condom expiration dates?"

Henry's brow went high as he looked between us and sighed. He walked away from the bathroom doorway, giving us some privacy. She nodded. "Yeah, turns out mine were out of date."

"Lesson learned, I guess."

Monroe snorted and nodded along. "Indeed. Anyway, I came in here to let you two know the plane is going to be ready to go in two hours."

Henry

"Please," Ava begged.

I grinned against her thighs. I had been edging her for the better part of two hours. She was tied to my bed, and I had no plans on letting her cum or untie her for another hour at least.

"Are you going to sneak out of my bed again?"

She was trembling, sweat dotted her brow. Her lips were swollen from the kissing I couldn't stop myself from doing. She shook her head. I leaned forward and kissed her clit. She shuddered as I rose to my knees.

We had been back from Waco for almost a full week. Sunday night was weird. She was impersonal towards me until Tama went to bed and then she pounced. I understood it, sort of. Will and Lily had stayed over for dinner. Matt had taken Nicole out for a date. We had all crowded around the dining table as Ava talked about her trip, running into Daphne, breaking her thumb, and hanging out with Monroe. I was a footnote in the story.

Will was surprised and annoyed when Ava talked about running into Daphne and then hiding from Lucy. I think I saw a flash of regret when she mentioned hiding in the bathroom at the medical office. I didn't know whether he was regretting not going or if he was regretting dating Lucy in the first place. Everything I had heard about her had been negative and my friend had been obsessed with her for years.

Ava slept in my bed Sunday night and every night since then, but she would wake up at 5am and sneak back into her room so Tama wouldn't know about us. Tama hadn't spent the night at our place a few of the nights. I tried to tell her that Tama wouldn't care and wouldn't mention anything to Lily or Will, but it didn't stop Ava's behavior.

It took Ava until Tuesday night before she asked me when we were going to have sex again. It was so adorable that she was anxious about it. I was patiently waiting for her to be ready. And then she asked me to teach her how to ride me. I have to admit, she was getting *really* good at it.

I told her to pretend to write all the letters in the alphabet in cursive with her hips and then whichever letter felt the best for her to repeat that over and over again.

She turned it into a game where I had to guess what she was writing to me. A game that I lost because she was so tight it was hard to concentrate on anything except the chokehold she had on me. It was amazing.

Today was the first time I had tied her to the bed. We spent our Saturday morning eating breakfast alone. Tama, who had already told me she was suspicious that Ava and I were together, had spent the night out again and wasn't going to make food so Ava exercised her breakfast skills.

Tama informed me that she had all day plans with Rhys and that she wouldn't be home until the volleyball game tonight, which was their first home game of the season. I didn't mention that Tama had been spending *a lot* of time with Rhys. I hoped he wasn't stringing her along like he had been doing for a full year. My friend was head over heels in love with the douche and in such blatant denial it drove me insane.

Ava and I went to the gym, ate lunch, and then as soon as I got her home, I rushed us into my bathroom to shower. That is where the edging had begun. She sucked me down her throat, which was a lovely surprise because I was expecting to hold out until we were able to cum together. But I am a weak man when it comes to the fact that my Babydoll lacked a gag reflex, a fun thing I had been experimenting with all week.

My eager kiss distracted her, and I slipped the handcuffs around her wrist after our shower. She wasn't indignant like I thought she would be. Lust filled her already dark eyes as I rubbed and played with every inch of skin on her body.

"I'm going to get some water. Do you want any?"

She nodded.

"What about food? Are you hungry?"

She shook her head. "I'm still full of lunch. Are you going to keep me tied up?"

I chuckled. "Of course, this is your punishment for sneaking out of my room every morning. Those actions simply won't do. Tama already suspects we are together, so until I get back the hours you stole from me by sneaking out, tied up is how you'll stay."

She chewed on her bottom lip. "What if I have to pee?" she whispered.

I grinned and leaned forward, kissing her sweet lips. "Then I'll let you up, but the moment you are done, you go right back into my bed."

She nodded. "Yes, sir."

A shiver ran up my spine. I fucking loved her acknowledgment that I was in charge. "I'll be right back," I murmured against her lips and rolled to my feet. I was tempted to walk out naked, but it was broad daylight, and I wouldn't put it past someone stopping in unannounced.

I gulped back some cold water and stood in front of the fridge in my sweatpants. I reached in and grabbed an apple to eat. Ava may have been full from lunch, but I was not. Swimming always made me ravenous. I took a bite of the apple and moved the few containers around looking for something quick to eat. Tama had made meatloaf this week and I loved taking the leftover pieces and creating a sandwich with it.

My front door swung open. I glanced in the direction of whoever was walking into my apartment without knocking.

Will grinned at me. "What are you making?"

"Meatloaf sandwich, want one?"

He nodded gratefully. "Yeah, thing is with you guys hosting most of the dinners, this is where the leftovers reside."

I pulled out an extra two pieces of bread while I warmed up the slices of meat. "Haven't seen you during daylight hours, what do I owe this pleasure?"

He rubbed his face. "I came to see if Ava wanted to hang out. She in her room?"

I shook my head and grinned at him. "She's tied up in my bed."

He scowled at me. "That shit is still not funny."

"I saw her getting ready to go to the gym earlier." It was also true; I did see her getting ready to go to the gym. I helped her pull her singlet up her body and sucked on her tits until they disappeared under the tight fabric.

He hummed. "How is she?"

I wagged my head like I was unsure. "Fine, I guess. She and Tama talk mostly about school together, so from what I overhear she's doing well."

I plated the two sandwiches and walked over to the couch where he was sitting. He grabbed his lunch as I sat in my gaming chair. Ava was going to be pissed that I left her tied up, but a punishment is a punishment. It was for the best. I highly doubted she'd be cool around only Will with no one to distract her.

"Is she dating anyone?" He said it with his mouth full. That alone told me he had no clue that Ava and I had been spending so much time together. He asked with too much ease.

Another noncommittal shrug. "I saw some guy ask for her number a few weeks ago. I don't know what came out of that, though." It was another honest answer that seemed to satisfy him.

He dug back into his sandwich and groaned. "I forget to eat lunch most days. Lily has been a godsend in reminding me to come up for air, but when that happens, I mostly end up fucking her for an hour straight."

I chuckled. "I'm glad you two figured your shit out, seriously. Watching you two dance around each other all last year was frustrating. I wanted to tell you both individually to grow a pair, but it wasn't my place."

He frowned at me. "I was that obvious?"

I grinned. "That and you had a few drunken confessions that I witnessed where you essentially told me and Matt that you thought Lily could be 'the one' but you fucked it up by talking about Lucy."

His lip curled. "I guess it's a good thing I've been too busy to get drunk. Though, with everything out in the open, I don't have anything else to confess." I finished my sandwich and placed my plate on the table.

"So, what about you? How's school? Seeing anyone new?"

"I'm fine. My dad is bugging me about interviewing with the local PD again. I guess the DA has established a possible lead that the attackers knew me through a third party. I tried to tell my dad I had no idea who those guys were, but he's badgering me. Even the DA has left me a few messages. I don't want to deal with that shit, you know? It already fucked with Matt's life. I was hospitalized. I know it traumatized the girls. I want it over."

He twisted his lips to the side and nodded. "I understand, but maybe talking to the DA will make it go away faster."

I grunted and decided to change the subject. "I guess. School's fine. Easy, but I'm not getting a degree to be challenged. I'm only getting it to access my trust fund. Though my algorithm is churning out decent yields with the stock market."

He gave me a questioning look. I had tried to explain to both Matt and Will my algorithm last year, but their eyes sort of glazed over so I had kept it vague. "Don't worry about it. I'd bore you with the details, like you'd put me to sleep if you talked to me about torts."

He chuckled. "What about any new girls? I saw Raven on campus the other day. You still talk to her?"

I lowered my voice. Hoping our conversation wasn't carrying straight to my girlfriend. "Not really. We broke up. I saw her a few weeks ago at a diner, she said hello, but nothing came out of it."

"Why did you break up, exactly? Because I know that you liked her and I know that Tama liked her." He had lowered his voice to match mine.

"You want the real answer or are you going to judge?"

He held up his hands. "No judgement."

"She wanted me to cut her. She got off on pain and it got to the point where I couldn't do for her what she wanted. I'm not into knife play; I'm not into pain. It highlighted a disconnect that I couldn't get past." *Because she wanted me to abuse her like her stepfather did.* Something I'd never do and believe strongly that she needs serious therapy, and her stepfather should be in jail.

His eyes were wide on me. He blinked a few times and swallowed. "I was not expecting you to say that. Yeah, I'd say that's quite a difference in expectations." He looked down at his watch. "If Ava isn't here, I'm going to take advantage of an empty apartment and nap. I haven't had one of those since the semester started. You're coming to the game tonight, right?"

I nodded. "Yeah, I love supporting the girls. The match in Waco was crazy."

He grinned. "We were watching here. I forgot to mention that we saw a glimpse of you and Ava in the stands with Monroe. It was a crazy match." He rolled to his feet. I waited for him to shut the door before I got up and placed our dishes in the sink.

Ava was not amused when I came back. "That wasn't funny."

I chuckled and helped her sit up. I delicately held the bottle of water to her lips and let her drink. She moved her face when she was done, spilling a little water down her chest. I licked it up. She groaned. "I can't believe you told Will I was tied to your bed."

I was smiling so hard my cheeks hurt. "It was the truth; he didn't believe me."

"What if he had?" she hissed.

I shrugged. "Then I could touch you whenever I wanted and you'd definitely not sneak out of my room while I am sound asleep."

She chewed on her bottom lip. "We'll tell him soon. I like having this secret, it's exciting."

I leaned forward and kissed her again. "I know, your pussy gets so wet when you hear someone outside my door. You don't want to get caught, but you want the thrill of possibly getting caught."

She nodded. "Exactly, although I will say I dried up pretty quickly listening to Will talk to you about your ex."

I chuckled, pulled her legs apart, and dipped my fingers into her. She gasped.

"Not that dry, Babydoll."

She bit her lip as I situated myself onto my stomach. "Don't be jealous of someone that's not in my life anymore." I swiped my tongue against her clit.

She whimpered. "I want to push your face into me, but I can't."

I grinned and nipped at her thigh. "I know. I like it. I can feel you trembling. I'll give you a choice. I can edge for another hour before I finally give us both what we want. Or I let you come and then I keep making you cum for the next hour."

"Please make me cum, sir."

Gripping her thighs, I spread her wide and tucked my hands under her butt to elevate her hips so I could eat whatever the fuck I wanted to. Her first orgasm came fast and hard after hours of depriving her. I had hardly gotten past my first knuckle, and she was exploding on my tongue.

Her body was twisted around as I hiked her hips up. Her hands were still cuffed, crossed at the elbows as she held onto my headboard. I dove my face back in. I licked from clit to ass. She shuddered but didn't stop me from sticking my tongue inside her rim. I flicked her clit with my finger and shoved my thumb into her channel.

She started bucking against my face as I ate her from behind. She wasn't as quiet as I wanted her to be, but we were alone in the apartment. The door was locked after Will left and Tama habitually slammed the front door to let me know she was home.

Ava was cursing and moaning nonsense as I pinched her clit and fucked her harder with my thumb. My tongue explored all of her. Her second orgasm doused my face in her juices. I rose to my knees and slapped her ass hard. She moaned.

"You have to be quiet, Babydoll." I delivered another smack. I watched her pussy flex and gape, waiting to be filled.

My sweatpants eased down to my knees, and I pressed into her. She buried her face into my pillow as I started to rapidly fuck her. Her gasps panted in quick succession. She was nodding to me and had turned her face to look back at me. She looked lust drunk and half delirious.

My hips snapped forward again. I wasn't going to last at this pace. I pushed in as far as I could and stopped. Her eyes had rolled back. I leaned forward and kissed her mouth. "Who's the only one that gets to fuck you?"

"You," she whimpered.

"Do I get to fuck all of you?"

She moaned and nodded a yes. I smiled against her mouth and pulled out.

"What are you doing?" she hissed.

My brows wagged at her, and I walked into my bathroom. I opened the little safe I kept under my sink. Will stole all my condoms once, so I had started storing those and other sex items in the safe. I hated the idea that he had gone into my space in the first place, but it pissed me off that he saw my small supply of toys I used.

"I'm going to fuck your ass, Babydoll, but I need to prep you."

I snagged a small butt plug and some lube. I didn't have time to thoroughly prepare her. When I had done this with prior subs I spent a full day of stretching with the three different plug options. But one thing I had learned about Ava was she had zero patience, and she had a decent pain tolerance.

She blinked innocently at me and nodded rapidly. I smirked at her and dripped lube between her cheeks and then along the toy.

"Take a deep breath."

She followed my instructions.

"Exhale." As she did, I slipped the toy into her ass. She whimpered. A little of the lube had slipped down into her already drenched channel. My mouth watered.

Ava gasped and bit into the pillow as I slipped inside her. She was so fucking tight with the toy taking up enough space for me to feel choked. I twisted the plug the tiniest bit and activated the vibrator. My eyes rolled to the back of my head as the vibrations hummed against my shaft. Everything felt so fucking good. I braced my hands on her hips and pulled her against me as I pushed hard into her.

"How do you feel?" I gritted out.

"Amazing," she breathed.

I chewed into my cheek. I had plans and I wasn't going to last to fulfill them if I didn't stop some of the stimulation. I turned the vibrator off. She mewled quietly as I pulled out. "I'd prep you more, but I can't wait. I'll go slow." I set the plug on my nightstand and generously covered my cock in lube.

My head pressed into her ass and paused. She gasped. Her chest was rising and falling hard as she bit into my pillow again. A puddle of drool marked where she had been. Very slowly, I sunk into her. If I thought her pussy was tight, nothing compared to this. Once I bottomed out, I waited.

"Let me know when you're ready." My control was going to snap if she wasn't ready soon.

She nodded. "Do it."

My hips eased back and in until I worked up to a frantic pace. My balls were bouncing against her pussy with every thrust. Her clit was slick against my fingertips. When she began to cum, she squeezed me so hard it milked my cum straight out. I shuddered and caught my breath at the intensity. I reached over to the plug. I timed my pull out with the insertion of the toy. She collapsed down when I wasn't holding her hips anymore. I twisted her around to be on her back again.

She looked drunk and high. "We aren't done, Babydoll." I walked into my bathroom and washed my dick off. I was going to fuck her one more time, but I wasn't going to risk her health by not cleaning up after anal.

"I need like fifteen minutes to rebound." I looked over to the clock on my computer.

"And it looks like we have to start getting ready for the match in thirty minutes. I expect you to cum two more times."

She shook her head. "I can't."

I chuckled. "You can and will." I got back between her thighs and delicately flicked her clit with my tongue. It didn't take long before she was a moaning, gasping mess. My fingers deeply stroked into her and rubbed her g-spot while I sucked her clit into my mouth. Her squirted orgasm was a delightful surprise.

"I'm so sorry, I didn't mean to," Ava said. Her cheeks were red in embarrassment.

I grabbed a discarded shirt and wiped my chin and neck. "Sorry for what?"

She squeezed her eyes tightly shut. "I peed on you."

I tipped my head back and laughed. "No, you didn't, Babydoll. Your clit is way too swollen to allow yourself to pee right now. Now, you did squirt on me, but trust me, I loved it."

She didn't look convinced. I leaned forward and kissed her slowly. "I'm going to fuck you again."

She looked wrecked. Her lashes were wet, cheeks red, lips swollen. Perfect. I pushed into her and reached between us to turn the vibrator back on. We were both going to need a little assistance to cum as fast as possible for me to make my goal.

Her back arched as her eyes rolled back. I bit her nipple as I rutted hard into her.

The vibrator heightened all the sensations for me. I licked my bottom lip back and forth and looked at her lust-drunk face. My lips glided to her other breast and sucked hard. She started squeezing me as the flutters started. I reached between us and rubbed her clit which had to be bordering on painful at this point, so I kept my pressure light. She yelped out an intense scream as she came again. My teeth gritted, and I followed suit.

My chest collapsed on hers as I caught my breath. I turned the plug off, but I didn't take it out. "You were being so good and quiet, Babydoll. Now I need to punish you."

She whimpered. "I can't cum again."

I chuckled and pushed myself up and looked down at her. "I know because we don't have time, but if we did, trust me, I'd make you cum another three times."

I pulled out of her and pushed her knees to her chest. "Keep your legs there."

She followed my instructions because she wanted to be a good girl. I went into my dresser and plucked out the pair of her white panties that I never returned from her first day in the apartment.

"Where did you get those?" Her stony expression was narrow and angry.

I grinned at her. "You left them in my room, Ava. I'd never make you wear something of someone else."

She chewed her lip. "Oh. I forgot I showered here and left my clothes. Hey, do you have my jean shorts too?"

Her denim landed next to her foot. It was too cool this evening for her to wear them, but there was no reason for me to hang on to them. I had all the intentions in the world to hide them in the back of her drawer in her room, so she thought she put them there, but I never had the time or remembered about it when I had the opportunity.

I pulled her legs away from her chest and slipped her panties up her legs. I snapped the waistband in place.

She squirmed. "They're going to get messy," she whined.

"I know. My cum is going to be slowly seeping out of you all night. Every time you feel a little drip you'll think about what we did all afternoon and what you did to deserve it."

Her hands fell to the pillow the moment the handcuffs released her. There was a small pink spot where the bones of her wrist jutted out. I kissed the spot.

"Sorry," I whispered.

She looked at what I worried about and shrugged. "It doesn't hurt." She chewed her lip, like she wanted to say something.

"What?"

"There is still something in my butt," she murmured.

"Yeah, and it's going to stay there all night, too. Does it hurt?" My lips rolled together to keep my smile at bay.

She shook her head. "No, I thought you forgot."

"Nope, it's a part of your reminder. It will help seal my cum in you longer, too." I shivered at the thought. I didn't think I had a breeding kink but the thought of my cum filling her up made me ready to go again, unfortunately we didn't have the time.

Her knees knocked together as I helped her to her feet. My jeans eased up my legs, and I grabbed my hoodie. Ava stood in the center of my room in nothing but a pair of white panties. She kept looking furtively out the door.

I bit back another grin. "No one is here, but I'll double check. Or do you want me to grab clothes for you?"

"Can you check to see if the coast is clear? We already had one scare with Will."

Tama's door was still barely open. It was what she did to signal she wasn't home. I pressed my palm to her door to make sure she wasn't sitting on her bed. Empty. The apartment door was still locked.

"All clear."

She rushed past me to get to her bedroom. I chuckled but I didn't give her a hard time because within three minutes of Ava disappearing in her room Tama came home.

Chapter 14

Ava

"So how's everything going with Rhys?"

Tama shrugged and wagged her head back and forth. "Fine. We went on a mock date together where he pretended, he didn't know me and critiqued my body language. It was enlightening."

My lip curled. "Critiqued how exactly?"

She shrugged. "He basically told me that my posture was military straight, but I was raised to have excellent posture. He said it made me look a little pretentious, but I could combat it with a smile."

"Ugh, don't tell me he told you to smile. I freaking hate it when guys tell me to smile. It makes me want to growl at them and throw them the bird."

She grinned at me. "No, it wasn't like that. It was about how a smile will put the guy at ease. I had no idea men were such sensitive creatures. Which I said to Rhys, and he seemed obstinate about it. I thought it was a sort of an emotional response to my simple observation, but what do I know? I'm a 21-year-old virgin that's never been kissed."

My eyes rolled. "First of all, you've only been around men for a year now. I've been around men my entire life and it took me until I was seventeen to have my first kiss. You aren't that far behind. And honestly, if getting your first kiss is making you nervous, rip the bandage off. Ask Rhys to kiss you for teaching purposes."

She twisted her lips to the side. "I was going to ask Henry, but obviously he's not a viable option anymore."

My heart started pounding as I rolled my lips in. "Why do you think that?"

It was her turn to roll her eyes. "I'm incredibly observant, Ava. You and Henry, both liked each other. It was a matter of time before you decided to do something about it. I had a feeling something happened on your trip to Waco, but you attempting to sneak out of his room every morning confirmed it."

My cheeks burned. I didn't know what to say because I didn't want to lie to her. And this was exactly what Henry had been telling me all week.

She smiled at me. "I'm not going to tell anyone. I'm sure you two are still trying to get to know each other, but you both have a crazy amount in common."

My brows pinched together. I didn't think that Henry and I had many commonalities.

Tama made a face. "You clearly haven't asked him about his childhood if you are making that face."

I chewed my cheek.

She shrugged. "It's fine. He keeps everything very close to the vest. It took him ten months and a road trip where he shared a bed or hotel room for almost two weeks for him to open up to me. I respect his stories as his to tell, but I encourage you to ask him about himself. He won't volunteer any information."

I swallowed thickly and nodded. I hadn't been that verbose in trying to find out stuff about him. We both recognized that we didn't know each other. I knew our personalities were compatible, but I hadn't delved into his past to see where we may share similar upbringings.

"How long do you think it will take them to realize that we are all the way back here?" Tama asked.

We were walking to the match following Matt, Henry, and Will. They were about a hundred feet in front of us, walking in a row, laughing. For Tama and I to keep up with their natural strides we would have to jog, and we had already bonded in our hatred of jogging and running.

"Not long, honestly, I'm surprised Henry hasn't noticed. He stayed close to me in Texas and every time we walk to the gym on the weekends he keeps my pace. I think it annoys him to walk so slowly, but I can't really help it."

Tama laughed. "It's his ADHD, slow walkers irritate him. He starts tapping his leg when he feels like he isn't moving fast enough."

It was another observation I hadn't made about my own boyfriend. He told me when I first moved in that he had ADHD and that's why he was using cannabis to help him sleep, but I hadn't asked further about his symptoms.

Henry looked over his shoulder and tapped Matt's arm when he saw we were so far behind. The boys all stopped and turned around.

"Ava Bear, double time. We are going to get shitty seats," Will yelled over to us.

I tossed up my middle finger. "I'm too exhausted to move any faster."

That and I had a freaking butt plug in, and I wasn't sure if running was a smart decision. The jig would definitely be up if that fell out of me while I was running towards my brother. Although my jeans were only tight around the thighs. I also didn't want to move around more than necessary because Henry was seeping out of me slowly, making a mess between my legs. I needed to go to the bathroom as soon as we got to the match.

Tama sighed. "What was having sex like?"

Air hissed through my teeth because I wasn't expecting her to ask that. "Uh, it hurt until it didn't. I think I'm lucky that Henry was my first because he did everything to make sure I was as comfortable as possible. I bled all night long. I wasn't expecting that, and my vag throbbed all the next day."

Tama's lips twisted to the side. "I've been thinking about getting rid of my hymen myself, you know, that way when the time comes there isn't any blood or embarrassing moments."

I frowned. "You don't want to tell the first guy you are with that it's your first time?"

She shook her head. "The only people that know about my virginity status are my roommates."

I glanced over at her. She was looking straight ahead.

"Rhys doesn't know?"

"He may suspect, but I've never told him. He does know that I've never had a boyfriend. I don't think he knows I've never been kissed either."

I hummed. "That means if you ask him to teach you how to kiss, he'll be suspicious."

She nodded. "It's a problem I can think of a solution for. Maybe I'll tell him I'm worried that I'm bad at it. I've been watching tutorials, so I've gotten some decent tips, so I won't be clueless."

"Do you want your first kiss to be special?"

"No, I honestly don't care who it's with."

"Okay. You can kiss me. I doubt if Henry will mind."

She poked her lip out. "Maybe later. I appreciate the offer. It's the first one I have ever had, but I'll use you as a solid backup plan. Rhys said he's setting me up with a blind date in a few weeks."

"Oh! That's exciting."

"What's exciting?" Will asked as we approached them.

"I have a blind date soon," Tama answered. She turned to me and grinned. "But if I don't get kissed then, then I'll take you up on being my first kiss."

"Whoa, Ava, seriously, you can't kiss your roommate," Will said.

Henry perked his brow at me and tilted his head the tiniest bit. I looked at my brother innocently.

"Will, once again, you don't get to dictate who I do anything with. If I want to kiss Tama so she can get over the anticipation of having her first kiss, then I'm going to do that."

Will groaned.

"And might I add, you kissed your roommate and so did Matt before you both were officially together," Tama said.

I grinned over to my friend. I appreciated her support more than I could express.

"Technically we were neighbors at the time," Matt said.

Henry sighed and looped his arm around Tama's shoulders. "So let me get this straight. You asked Ava before you asked me?" He shot a look over to me as my jaw clicked.

She giggled and was less subtle about looking at me. "Ava volunteered."

"Did she now?"

He wasn't impressed by the situation. I thought I was offering something innocent, but he seemed annoyed.

Tama shrugged. "You know how sweet she is. She figured if I ripped it off like a bandage it would make me less nervous for my date."

He drew in a slow breath from his nose as Will sighed loudly. "Listen, you both are worth more than wanting to 'rip it off like a Band-Aid'. You should expect the guy to take you on dates, spoil you, and prove that he's worthy of you," Will said.

Matt pointed at Will. "Yes."

I shot a look over to Henry who was chewing on his cheek. I wanted to tell him that I didn't need him to take me on fancy dates or whatever Will had implied.

"You'll honestly allow Ava to date without interfering?" Tama asked Will.

He curled his lip. "I didn't say that."

Tama rolled her eyes. "Make up your mind Will. You can't expect Ava to want to date someone out in the open when you are admitting to interfering. All you are establishing is Ava deciding that a secret relationship is going to be her only option."

For the love of God, Tama.

That was a little too on the nose.

Matt grabbed Will's shoulder and squeezed. "She's right. Knowing there were going to be consequences is what made me and Nicole keep our relationship quiet for months. It didn't stop us from having one. It made us be more careful and stressed us out."

Will squinted at me. "Are you dating someone in secret?"

I nodded innocently at him. "Of course, I am."

He rolled his eyes. "Fucking smart ass."

I shrugged. "I'm not going to ask permission to date anyone. You really need to accept that."

"I'm not saying you need to ask for permission. *They* do though."

My brows furrowed. "And what makes you think that?"

He turned and looked at me over his shoulder. "Because I need to protect you to make sure no one is trying to take advantage of you."

A low grunt vibrated my chest. "You sound a lot like my mom. Next thing out of your mouth might as well be 'he needs to be from a good family' or 'he's a gold digger'."

Will gaped at me. "That's the second time I've been compared to your mother. I don't appreciate it."

I shrugged. "And I don't appreciate you *acting* like you know what is best for me."

"But I know men and what they think."

"That is such a bullshit excuse. Honestly, say what you are thinking, you don't trust me. And why would you? I'm the stupid baby of the family. There's no way I can make the correct decision for myself, huh? You know I wanted to come to this school because you always treated me with respect, but I'm thinking I made a mistake."

Everyone in our little group was watching me and Will argue. Henry's eyes were bouncing cautiously between me and my brother.

Will looked gutted when he turned towards me. "I don't think that, at all. But I do feel responsible for you. I've always *been* responsible for you. When your mom would take Jacob and Daphne to Six Flags, or whatever other fun place, and wouldn't let you go because you were too small and made me stay home because she didn't want me to have an ounce of fun, I was responsible for you. The only reason why I went to Daphne's wedding was so I could protect you from your mom and

Daphne. And I will keep protecting you because you're my sister and I love you."

My ire died at that. My brother was never gushy with his emotions. I knew he loved me, but his declarations were limited. My throat knotted. It had always been the two of us when I was younger. Jacob didn't start noticing the injustice of everything until the past few years.

Jacob had always been the golden child and Daphne had always been the princess. He really saw it when my parents chose to move to Pasadena to be near his child versus allow me to finish my senior year. My happiness took a backseat to spending an hour a week with their grandchild. Even when I was younger, he noticed how Daphne treated me, but there was a blindness to how our mother treated me. Will always saw it, though.

Will looped his arm around my shoulder. "I don't want to fight about this. Let's go to the match and have a good time, yeah?"

Guilt that I hurt his feelings by comparing him to my mom and telling him it was a mistake to move here gripped me. I shouldn't have said it. His actions were not born from his desire to control my life like they were for my mother. They were about protecting me. He couldn't see his own bias, and it was an argument I wouldn't win today to make him see my point of view. I also didn't want to fight with him because he was one of two family members that would have my back and Jacob wasn't here.

Sitting next to Henry at the match didn't happen. Will put me on the end next to him. Henry tried to shoot me subtle smiles at the game, but with Will and Matt between us it was conspicuous. He spoke quietly to Tama between cheering for Nicole and Lily.

We were able to briefly sit next to each other at the pub we went to for dinner after the match, but it was short lived when a pretty girl stopped by our table and asked Henry if they could talk. He squeezed my knee under the table. "Sure, Raven."

My heart sank a little when he left with his ex-girlfriend. Someone that my brother and Tama both liked for him.

Henry

Raven's dark hair swished against her shoulders as I followed her out of the restaurant and into the parking lot. I didn't want Raven to see me with Ava and try to stalk her.

It was a tough decision to leave her at the table, but if I would have stayed, Raven would have invited herself to sit. She was keen-eyed enough to see the way I was around Ava. Tama had been pointing it out for weeks. I watched her, I couldn't keep my eyes off her. And now I've had her in my bed, I couldn't stop touching her.

"What's up?" I leaned against the wall.

She chewed her lip, looking innocent, but her eyes were too wild. "Who's the short girl you were sitting next to?"

I kept my face neutral. "Will's sister and my roommate."

She nodded. "What's her name?"

My brow perked up as I shook my head. "Not relevant. What do you want?"

"You." She gazed up at me through her lashes. She looked healthier than she had a few weeks ago. The sallow look from before was replaced with a light pink flush and her eyes looked less hollow.

"We discussed this."

She shook her head. "No, you talked, but I didn't agree with you. We are good together. I was happy when I was with you. You were happy with me."

My finger tapped against my thigh. Irritation bubbled forward for having to repeat myself. "I'm not happy about you pulling me from my friends to have the same argument again. I'm not happy that you stalked someone I was dating and drugged them. I'm not happy that you came here looking for me."

She furrowed her brow as she shook her head. "But you *would* be happy about all of that if you would listen to me. I waited until you were done eating so I wouldn't pull you away. I know how important food is to you. Also, I didn't stalk or drug Lydia Carmichael. If I had, wouldn't she have gone to the police? But she didn't because I didn't do that." She closer to me.

I was against the wall, so I didn't have anywhere else to go. She was in my personal bubble of space. My eyes narrowed on her. "I never said Lydia by name, but you knew exactly who I was talking about. And you completely missed the point. I'm not happy to see you, Raven. We broke up. We both moved on. The end."

She pouted. "I want to unbreak up."

I shook my head. "I don't want that. I am with someone new. I am very happy with her."

She scoffed. "I don't believe you. Where is she then?"

The challenge perked my brow. "Tied to my bed, waiting for me like the good girl she is. Not interrupting me with my friends and making demands of me or my time. You need to move on."

Her eyes glistened with tears. What I said was cruel. I used words to trigger her. She preened whenever I called her a good girl, and I knew she'd be devastated and jealous that someone was in my bed. But I had to pull the attention away from Ava since she had already asked about her.

She rolled her shoulders back. "I could join you two. I know you enjoyed your times when I brought my coworker over."

I tilted my head to her. "Move on."

She sucked in a breath, her eyes flitting over my shoulders before gazing up at me. "At least let me have a goodbye then."

My lip curled, not understanding what she wanted. We had broken up *months* ago. And then for the month following I put up with her bullshit. We had plenty of goodbyes.

Before I could react, she had clutched my face and was kissing me. I was stunned and pissed. It took me a moment to control my anger that was telling me to fling her off me.

I pried her hands off my face and gently pushed her away.

"Are we interrupting anything?" Will asked.

My heart dropped to my toes. I flicked my gaze behind me to see Ava's eyes. She looked blank as Tama looped her arm within my girl's and tugged her away.

"Don't touch me again. Move on. It's over," I said harshly. Raven sobbed a breath as I brushed past her. I knocked my shoulder into Will's.

"I love you. No one will love you like me," Raven yelled after me.

Her heels clicked towards us, but Will and Matt did me a solid. Matt's voice was placating, "Hey Raven, I don't think he wants to see you."

Lily and Nicole were following closely behind Tama and Ava. The four were talking about the match. I wondered if Tama started the conversation with something other than my drama. Will and Matt flanked both of my sides a few minutes later.

"You okay?" Matt asked.

I rolled my eyes and shrugged. "I'm fucking pissed she touched me. We've been broken up for seven months. I have no interest in getting back together with her, which I have told her several times." I was speaking loud enough for Ava to hear.

Lily turned around with a grin. "Henry has that dick game that makes the girls go crazy, apparently."

I snorted and watched a light flush paint both Ava and Tama's cheeks.

"Seriously?" Will hissed.

Lily cackled and nodded. "Sorry Peach, but his ex just made a spectacle. What else could be the reason?" Her logic made me smirk.

Will growled. "She's not mentally stable."

I rolled my eyes. Raven was proving to be a little mentally unstable, but I didn't diminish my bedroom abilities. I took great pride in taking care of anyone in my bed. Their pleasure and safety were my main priorities. I loved taking care of my girlfriends and learning what their bodies liked.

Lily giggled with a nod. "Right, Henry's dick drove her crazy."

Nicole laughed next to her when Will launched forward and picked Lily up in a fireman's hold and smacked her ass. "Less talk about other men's dicks, Sunshine."

Tama slowed down so I could walk with her. Ava walked ahead with Nicole.

"That looked really bad," Tama hissed.

I closed my eyes and nodded. "What's the damage?" I whispered back.

Tama shrugged. "She's upset. Apparently, you told her not to worry about someone not in your life. That kiss didn't look like it came from someone not in your life."

I rolled my lips in and bit down. My anger had abated to worry that Ava was upset with me. I needed to have a moment alone with her so I could explain and make her feel better about everything.

She didn't allow that to happen. Everyone hung out at my apartment until late. Ava went to bed long before Will and Matt left. They were playing a video game tournament that I took part in for a little bit. Ava had mostly stayed to herself. She joked with Lily and Tama on the couch but avoided my eyes. It didn't sit right with me.

Tama and I went to bed before the other two were finished with their game. They said they'd lock up when they were done. I waited impatiently for the sound of my front door closing before I got up from my desk. Ava didn't answer my knock. I tried the handle, but it was locked. My jaw clenched, and I went into the kitchen to grab a butter knife.

The bedroom locks in the apartment were ridiculously easy to pop open. Ava was sitting at her computer with her chin propped on her bent knee. She looked over her shoulder to me, posture stiff. She turned back to her work without saying anything.

Her bed bounced as I made myself comfortable. My back nestled against her pillows, and I rested my arms behind my head. I liked her room. It smelled like her. The faintest trace of a sweet lemon and vanilla filled my nose as I took a deep breath. Ava looked on to her computer. She wasn't working, she wasn't typing, moving the mouse around, or scrolling through the document on her screen.

"Come here, Babydoll."

She sucked in a breath and looked over her shoulder to me but didn't follow my instructions.

I sighed patiently. "Ava, I didn't ask Raven to come out tonight. I don't want to be with her, and I didn't ask her to kiss me. I'm sorry that her actions have upset you, and if you allowed me to touch you around Will I would have wound myself around you hours ago. You have nothing to worry about."

Her eyes flit to my face before looking over my head towards the wall. "She's really pretty."

I rolled my eyes. "Not compared to you."

She swallowed and turned back to her computer. "Do you two have a lot in common?"

My lip curled. "Not really."

She nodded slowly, shut her laptop, and walked over to her dresser to pull out her pajamas. "I'm going to take a shower. You can let yourself out." She walked into her bathroom.

I rolled to my feet and caught the door before she was able to lock me out. The bathrooms were small, but I was able to slip in behind the door while she undressed. My lids grew heavy when I saw my dried cum on her inner thighs. I rolled my lips in to keep from smiling when she bent over. I had forgotten she still had a plug in. The little jewel end was bright against her tan skin.

The vanity dug into my hip as I watched her get into the water. She scrubbed her thighs and then huffed loudly when she saw me watching her so intently. "Can you at least turn around?"

My lips rolled in, and I did as she asked. The mirror's reflection still provided me with the view of her squatting down and pulling the plug out. She shivered when she stood up and left it on the floor of the shower.

I turned around when she started to lather her hair and watched her clean the rest of her body off. My dick that was painfully hard, but she was pissed at me. It was not looking likely for me to get lucky tonight. It would be a miracle if she let me kiss her good night at this point.

I wrapped the towel around her shoulders and kissed her forehead. "I'm sorry. I'll leave you alone to process anything you need to process. I did want to ask you something, though."

She looked up to me with her clear brown eyes. I wanted to lean down and kiss her, but I didn't.

"I agree with what Matt and Will said earlier. You deserve someone who takes you on dates and so far, I haven't done that. I'd like to remedy that. I know that we have a little bit of an obstacle because of Will, but we can get creative."

She chewed on her bottom lip. "I don't need you to take me on dates."

I tilted my head. "You deserve it though. I overheard Will talking to Matt tonight. They are planning on taking Nicole and Lily to some fair tomorrow since it's one of the only weekends where Will feels a little caught up on work. We could go do something together, just the two of us."

"What do you have in mind?" She sounded cautious and guarded. Not that I could blame her.

"It's a surprise. Are you interested?"

She rubbed her lips together and nodded reluctantly. I leaned in and kissed her forehead. "Okay, good night, Babydoll. I'll see you in the morning."

<h1 style="text-align:center">Chapter 15</h1>

Ava

I woke up to a light triple tap on my door. It was Tama based on the knock. I quietly answered for her to come in. It was still too early for Henry to be awake. I had no doubt he stayed up late because I had too. He didn't sleep well most nights and had told me that sharing the bed with him was the perfect remedy to his insomnia.

Anger warred with my guilt for not cuddling with him like I wanted to, but I couldn't stop the memory of Raven kissing Henry repeating like an obtrusive reel in my head. Every time it did, my heart dropped and pounded. Blood rushed through my ears like I was experiencing it firsthand again. The ripple of self-doubt that was always on the edge of my thoughts turned into a wave of nausea in my stomach and my throat burned. It felt inevitable and I was helpless that eventually Henry would kiss another woman again. Because Daphne was right, a man like Henry couldn't be interested in me long term.

My blonde roommate popped her head in my room and slipped inside when she saw me under my covers.

She gave me a soft smile. "You okay?"

"Eh, slept like shit, but what else is new, right?"

I had opened to her about my anxiety and how most nights I had to self-medicate. She didn't judge me and because she was who she was, she promised to keep it between us. She wasn't entirely surprised and told me she was curious what I did every night around 2am because she had heard my door open and close around that time every day. She did admonish me for driving across state lines with that much cannabis in my car and was grateful that I didn't get pulled over. Lesson learned, I guess.

She stuck her bottom lip out and nodded. "Well, I'm here if you need to talk to anyone. I won't discuss the ins and outs of Henry's relationship with Raven, but trust me when I tell you, he is finished with that union. The end of it wasn't good for either of them."

I was intrigued and wanted to know more, but she had already drawn the line in the sand. She would keep what she had observed to herself. I wasn't privy to the details. Besides, if there was any person I would want to tell me, it was Henry. I wasn't ready to stomach hearing him talk about her, though. It was all too fresh.

Pulling myself into a seated position, I curled my knees under my chin. "She really loves him, though. I don't know the first thing about love and here is a girl that loves him so much she is willing to scream it on the streets."

Not only was she beautiful, but she *loved* Henry. Maybe it was closer to obsession, but she wasn't afraid to mince words. She was passionate about her feelings for him to stake a claim. She looked into my eyes right before she pulled Henry's face to hers. I tried to stay impassive because reacting strongly would have tipped Will off, but it was hard to not leap forward and yank her dark hair. I wanted to pull her off Henry and smack her for going after him. It was such a strong primal reaction that I was grateful that Tama looped her arm into mine and pulled me away. I don't know what she said to unstick my wooden legs because my own heartbeat was too loud in my ears.

Tama hummed and sat on the foot of my bed. "Is that what is bothering you?"

I chewed on my bottom lip and shrugged.

She raised a brow. "Didn't think so. So what if she claims to love him. What she did, ignoring what he wanted, that's not love, Ava. That's desperation. When you love someone, you listen to them, even if it hurts, you do what they need you to do. Henry told her that he needed her to leave him alone. She keeps ignoring it. Now, I have no experience with romantic love, but I have a lot of experience with parental love. And while my mom has done a lot of odd things, she recognized that what I needed versus what she wanted didn't align. She's still dealing with it, but she respects my wishes. Raven isn't respecting Henry right now. And I don't know if you've noticed, but Henry is *big* on respect. Her stunt completely closed the book of their relationship."

My molars chewed into my cheek. I didn't want to talk about it anymore. I had a million more questions for Henry when I was ready, but not now. My eyes still felt hot from lack of sleep and my body was sore from holding tension for so long throughout the night.

She gave me another soft smile. "So, what are your plans today?"

"I don't know. Henry said he wanted to take me on a proper date or something like that. I guess what Matt and Will were saying last night resonated with him."

She grinned at me. "He's a romantic at heart, I think. Are you anxious about going out in public with him?"

"Oddly, no. I'm an anxious person in general, but being with Henry makes me feel calm."

Tama nodded. "He has a calm demeanor about him. It's one of the reasons why I have gravitated towards him for so long. He's like a rock in a storm, immovable and steady."

A solid double rap on the door followed by my door swinging open.

"Morning," Henry said happily. "How'd my girls sleep last night?"

He didn't seem surprised in the least to see Tama on my bed talking to me.

She grinned at him. "I slept like a baby."

Henry smirked at her. "Wrapped like a burrito in the center of the bed?"

She scowled at him. "I don't see how that makes a difference. I didn't bedshare with anyone last night. I can steal all the covers and sleep diagonally across my bed if I want to."

He tittered a laugh and walked over to me. My body jostled as he pulled me into his chest. I allowed him to nestle my head against him. His lips brushed the top of my head, and he slung his arm around my shoulders.

"What are your plans today?" Henry asked Tama.

She sighed and shrugged. "I'm supposed to go on another mock date with Rhys. Last time was enlightening, but I really don't know how much more he can share with me."

Henry's lip curled a little. "Don't go then."

She twisted her lips to the side. "I appreciate his help though. Besides, maybe today I can tell him I am paranoid about my kissing skills and see if he's willing to practice with me."

Henry grunted. "If that's what you want to do, I'm not going to dissuade you. Also," he turned towards me and perked one eyebrow high, "don't think for one second I'm not going to talk to you about offering to kiss Tama, Babydoll. These lips are mine and I'm not sharing them."

My mouth dropped open the tiniest bit. There was a possessive edge that made me know that despite the teasing lilt, he meant what he said.

Tama let out a small nervous laugh. "It wasn't that serious Henry. She wasn't plotting to cheat on you; she was offering to help a friend in need. What if I lick his teeth? What if I bite his tongue? These are the questions that are plaguing me."

A low chuckle vibrated between us. "You aren't going to strongarm me again like you did with the blowjob lesson. I'll give you some tips, but you aren't kissing my girlfriend."

Tama's smile stretched wide. "I love that you called her that. I've never actually heard you say that term before, come to think of it."

I rolled my lips in to not ask the question that was burning on my tongue. He clearly never referred to Raven as his girlfriend, based on that comment. So, what did he call her?

Henry rolled his eyes. "Don't change the subject. Do you want my tips or not?"

She nodded.

"Perfect." He picked me up and awkwardly perched me on his lap, while still wrapped in my blanket. My arms were pinned between his chest and mine. He cupped my cheek. His eyes had a devilish glint in them.

"First things first, follow his lead until you feel more comfortable." He leaned in and slid his lips against mine quickly.

The sneaky bastard was using this as an excuse to kiss me. He knew he was still in the doghouse after yesterday.

"That is the standard kiss. You don't want to pucker your lips too much, but as you could see as soon as my lips touched Ava's, she moved hers to match mine."

Damnit, I had.

He leaned forward again. His hand was still on my cheek, but he slid his fingers back into my hair and brought my mouth closer to his. He tilted his head for a better angle and gently pressed his lips to mine before working my mouth open.

He pulled away and swiped my lip with his thumb. "That's stage two of a good kiss. You saw how she adjusted herself to me. I was also holding her to me. I love it when a girl lightly scratches my head while kissing me. Actually, in general, I love it. But when I'm kissing, it makes me pay less attention to my surroundings."

Tama adjusted how she was sitting, facing us fully and nodding along like she was taking mental notes. "Perfect. What next?" she asked with wide eyes.

"Next, I'm going to tease the seam of her lips with my tongue. I'm nonverbally asking if she wants to kiss me deeper. If she opens more, then I can *gently* dip my tongue into her mouth. I'll let it glide against her tongue and then I'll pull it back into mine. I don't want to choke her with it, nor do I want to leave it between her teeth for too long."

I mimed snapping my jaw shut. He chuckled.

"Got it." Tama motioned for us to continue.

Henry leaned forward again and kissed me. This was a little more aggressive then the first two. He licked the seam of my mouth as I adjusted my head to deepen the kiss. The slide of his tongue made me moan, and I rewarded him with my gentle flick. I worked my hands out from being pinned between us and gripped the nape of his neck, allowing my nails to lightly drag into his scalp. He groaned into my mouth as he pulled away.

My eyes fluttered open. Tama was still watching us with a wide-eyed grin. "That was hot. And you didn't bite each other, interesting." She stood up from the bed. "Okay, well, I'm pretty sure that's all that you can effectively teach me before I become a little voyeuristic on accident and your next lesson becomes intercourse."

It was my turn to laugh nervously because his kiss lit me up. I missed sleeping against his chest, and although I was still reeling from seeing Raven kiss him, his affection was winning me over.

Henry chuckled lightly and cleared his throat. "I'm taking Ava out for the day. We aren't going to be home until closer to six tonight. Matt and Will are planning on being back with the girls around seven after being at the fair all day. If they come home sooner, can you let me know?"

She nodded. "Of course. Where should I say you both are?"

He perked a brow over to me and sighed when I didn't add anything to have a ready-made alibi. "Tell Will I'm swimming and Ava mentioned going on a date."

I scoffed. "Don't do that. If he thinks I'm willy nilly going out on dates, he'll try to recruit you both to spy for him and I don't want to put either of you in more of a position to lie for me." I sighed.

"Tell him," I chewed my lip, "tell him that I saw a contemporary ballet company has a new show and I was checking it out."

Tama nodded, but Henry turned towards me. "Is there a show you are interested in?"

I strummed my lip a few times with my teeth and nodded. "Yeah. I saw an ad for the show a few weeks ago. It's down in Denver and going for another month."

He nodded at me. "Then that's where we are going next week."

He adjusted me to sit back on my bed and stood up. "Get dressed in comfortable clothes. We are going to be outside all day, so wear shoes you can walk around in."

He turned towards Tama. "Call me if you need anything. I mean it."

She nodded and walked back across the hall to her room. I kicked the covers off as Henry followed her out. I checked the weather and hummed to myself. It was supposed to be sunny with a high of 60, but a low of 40, so I was going to need to bring layers.

I slipped my jeans on and rifled through my clean laundry, that I hadn't folded yet, and pulled out a fitted tee. It was a little wrinkled, but I wasn't trying to impress Henry. It was him who needed to impress me. I finished getting ready for the day and met Henry in the kitchen. He was filling up a water bottle and passed me a coffee mug to go.

"It's a three-hour drive to where we are going, so we need to hit the road."

My brows pinched together, but I nodded. He leaned into me again and kissed me quickly. "I'm driving, so if you are tired, you can sleep on the way there."

My teeth gripped my lip. "What about you? Aren't you tired?"

He rolled his eyes up to the ceiling and shrugged. "Yes and no. I'm always a little tired, but I've gotten a lot of sleep this week, so last night was manageable."

"I didn't sleep well."

He gave me a sad smile. "I know, Babydoll."

He checked his watch and nodded to himself. "If we leave now, we will get there right when it opens. Let's go." He scooped up my keys and held the door open for me.

"You aren't concerned about anyone coming over for brunch?" I whispered in the hallway.

He shook his head. "Nope. Tama told them that she wasn't making breakfast today because she has plans with Rhys that start soon. If Will comes over and sees that you aren't here and he messages you, you can tell him you are out running errands. I know the guys are planning on leaving for the fair around noon, so after that we don't have to worry about it."

"But that's five hours from now," I hissed as he opened the passenger door for me."

He grinned broadly at me. "Yeah, and I lived with them for a year. I know for a fact that no one in Will's apartment is getting up before eleven. The girls had their match yesterday and both my cousin and Will have been working themselves to the bone. They aren't going to wake up early to make sure you are still in bed."

He leaned forward and gave me a quick kiss like he couldn't stop himself. It was risky because my car was parked in the front of the building, and I could see Will and Matt's office window.

My stomach growled as we got onto the highway. He grinned over to me. "We can do a drive thru in about ten minutes or there is a good diner in thirty, which do you want?"

I licked my lips. I hadn't asked yet where we were going because I didn't think it would make a difference. His grin told me he was clearly excited to surprise me with wherever our destination was. And the sooner we got there, the better. "Drive thru is fine."

He laced his fingers within mine and navigated us a few more exits before we got off again. I fed him his hash browns and egg sandwich while he drove. It made me laugh how wide he was opening his mouth for me to feed him. He kept grinning at me and poking my side when I would try to miss his mouth and smear a little food on his cheek. He was too quick for me though.

When we were fed and sated, my eyelids felt heavy. I rested my head against the window and fell asleep as we drove deeper into the mountains.

Henry

The parking lot glowed brightly as the sun rose in the sky. Ava was sound asleep and looking too beautiful and serene. I didn't want to wake her, but I also couldn't wait to show her where we were.

I unbuckled my seatbelt, leaned over to nuzzle into her neck, and kissed along her pulse point. She moaned in her sleep. I trailed my lips up to her ear. "Babydoll, we're here."

She sucked in a sharp breath and jerked away from the window, blinking at me a few times and then looked around the lot. It gave nothing away to where we were. "Where is 'here' exactly?"

I grinned at her. "I was waiting for you to ask. We are at Glenwood Caverns Adventure Park. I know it's not Six Flags, but it's the biggest theme park in the area."

Her lips parted in a breath as her brows pinched together. "I've never been to a theme park before," she whispered.

My lips tugged harder upwards. "I know. Come on, Babydoll. Let's go ride some rides, eat sugar, and mark this off your life's to-do list."

She looked a little teary as she nodded to me. She met me in front of her car and allowed me to braid our fingers together. Her eyes were wide as we walked through the front gates. She had never been on a roller coaster before. I had to explain to her that the little two-seater car wasn't the norm, and the coaster wasn't that robust. But for the first ride, it was perfect. I liked that she nestled between my thighs. She yelped and gripped my shins during the turns and dips.

Her smile was wide when we got off. "I feel shaky with adrenaline. And that's a small roller coaster?"

I chuckled. "I'll take you to California Adventure Park this summer. Or we can go to any theme park you want."

She flung her arms over my neck and tugged me to kiss her. Her eager tongue made me want to toss her over my shoulder and have my wicked way with her, but I wanted her to ride every ride that was available first.

We went on a cave tour. She clutched my hand and marveled with me as we explored with our little group. We rode a few more rides before we stopped for lunch. She was vibrating with happiness. "I can't believe I was deprived of this my whole life."

I knocked my hotdog into hers like I was toasting her. "To never allowing someone to take away our happiness again."

She wagged her brows at me and nodded. "To boyfriends who make me happy."

I smirked at her and gave her another quick kiss. I couldn't allow our lips to touch more than a quick peck, or I would lose it. We rode a real roller coaster next when I felt like she was ready to experience the real thrill of the loops. She clutched my hand and screamed at the top of her lungs during the initial drop. My cheeks hurt from smiling so hard.

We rode the swings and finished the day on the gondola ride. I kissed her hard as we rode high in the air. I wanted to go down on her and had she worn anything other than jeans, I would have because nothing beats a good view than a good view while getting eaten out. Though I doubt the camera in the corner of the gondola was there just for show.

"That was amazing, like, for real amazing. And you want to know a real kick in the teeth?" she asked while we were walking back to the car. It was still early, only 3:30, but we did have a three-hour drive home and we had already ridden every ride.

"What's that?"

She rolled her eyes over to me. "I've been this height since I was ten and I was tall enough to ride every single ride. Which means the excuse I was given when I was ten to twelve when my mom would take Daph and Jacob was a lie. I wasn't too small to go."

I chewed on my cheek and nodded. "That's shitty."

She let out a long sigh. "It is. But you know what?" I looked over to her with a perked brow. "Fuck my mom and fuck Daphne. If they don't want me exactly how I am then I don't want them either."

Pulling her against my chest, I kissed the top of her head. "Cutting out toxic people is tough. I'll support you however you need."

She nodded against me. "Thanks for today."

"Of course."

We settled back into her car. I laced our fingers back together and left our hands in her lap. She sighed and rolled her eyes over to me. "Tama told me we have a lot in common. Do you think that's true?"

My brow perked at her, and I kissed our intertwined hands. "I do."

Glancing over to her, she was rubbing her lips together. "Care to share our commonalities?"

My head tilted as I gathered my thoughts. "As I tell you each thing you're going to want my story behind it. There are some things I don't want to dwell on, so be patient with me." She nodded and squeezed my hand.

Stalling to figure out where to begin, I licked my bottom lip. "Well for starters, anxiety and ADHD are comorbid so they share a lot of behaviors and responses. For instance, we will both mentally go over and over situations or think about every detail of possible interactions."

She let out a soft laugh. "It's the worst. That's half of what keeps me up at night."

I nodded while looking out the windshield.

"We both self-medicate the same way," she said.

One brow raised. "True except I prefer my edibles to your vape. You're going to trash your lungs. I smoked for a while in secret after my mom moved to Paris and my swimming suffered." Though it had more to do with my depression than anything else, but I didn't want to talk about that.

She scowled at me. I shrugged. It was the truth, but I wasn't going to judge her for finding something that worked for her. But I would be negligent if I didn't try to make her see what the consequences of her actions may be. She was an amazing dancer, and I would hate her to hinder herself unintentionally.

We were quiet for a few minutes while I thought about how to start the next topic. I let out a deep breath and started.

"My dad was having an affair on my maman with my swimming coach when I was fourteen. I was having an innocent conversation about my practice. She had been away visiting her sister in Seattle, so we were catching up. I mentioned something about my dad going into my coach's office for like thirty minutes while everyone else was gone and I was swimming laps because I was slow off the block. She asked if my dad did that often and I admitted that it was every practice."

She sucked in a breath through her teeth and winced.

"Yeah, I had no idea what I was telling her. It was also the same day I had an edible, which is a whole other story. Regardless, my maman and I slept in a hotel that night and within a week we had moved into a rental house in the neighborhood below my dad's estate. Their divorce was messy. Security footage for the swim school was summoned as well as personal messages between my dad and my coach. He violated their prenup, so she got a lot, and my dad has treated me like a disappointment ever since."

An indignant breath huffed out. "He blamed you for his actions?"

"Yep." I licked my lips. "But before then, my parents fought a lot. I didn't know it wasn't normal because it was *my* normal. I don't know if you know this, but I have eight state titles for swimming. I was approached to try out for the National Team when I was seventeen, but by then I was burning out. And then my mom moved to Paris and my motivation to swim kind of went with her."

I looked over to her. "I don't want to talk about that particular detail, but I was pushed really hard by both my parents to swim. I love swimming, but I hated the pressure both my parents put me under. My dad didn't talk to me for a month when I didn't try out for the team. It was his dream for me, not mine. Honestly, I think at the time I blamed swimming for my dad's affair.

"It wasn't until a year ago that my mom told me my father had cheated on her when I was born and again when I was six. Before that point, I had the lingering thought if I hadn't been swimming my parents would still be together. It's a fucking stupid thought now, but it's the truth."

The sun was starting to set, the golden light made her brown eyes glow amber. I tore my gaze away from her before I became transfixed.

"After the divorce, my dad was more emotionally neglectful than before. When they were married, I was his second favorite person alive behind my maman. After the divorce, I was this punk kid with loose lips and a drug addiction."

She flinched.

"I don't have a current drug addiction. If I did, I'd still be hooked on the powerful painkillers I was on after my skull was cracked."

Her swallow was audible. I let out a shallow breath.

"I do have an addictive personality, though. It comes with the territory of having ADHD. My brain can't regulate dopamine, so when I get it from outside stimulants my brain craves it."

She twisted her lips to the side. "What are you addicted to?"

I hummed at her soft voice. She seemed hesitant to ask like she was afraid of the answer. My fingers squeezed hers. "Gambling to a certain degree, stock market trends, but both are tied directly into my algorithm. I'm not going to blow a ton of money on online poker. I did that when I was struggling with my mom leaving, and now I associate it with that time in my life.”

Traffic was slowing down in front of us as we started to drive down the mountain. I looked over to her. She was chewing her lip, her body was turned in my direction, but she wasn’t looking at me. She was looking to the side like she was in deep thought.

“Are you addicted to anything else?” She sucked in a breath and held it.

I treaded lightly. “Sex, food, especially your lemon bars.”

The breath from her lungs gushed out in a laugh.

“I’m serious. I cut a huge piece and hid it in the fridge. I ate off that for almost a week until it was gone.”

She smiled softly. “I can make you more.”

My grin took over my face. “I’d love that. They taste like my gran’s. She was my second favorite person to have ever lived behind my maman. She was so freaking awesome. She watched me a lot when I was younger and when the divorce turned nasty, she stayed with me and my maman even though she was my dad’s mom. She bought herself a hot pink mountain bike with fat tires and we went camping the weekend the divorce finalized. We stayed on this campsite that we found out later was popular with a nudist colony.”

Ava giggled. I grinned and looked back over to her. “I was fifteen and sharing a tent with gran when the other campers from this colony started this crazy sex ritual. It was mortifying. My gran laughed to herself and pulled out her phone. I have no idea why she had recordings of bears growling and wolves howling but she did. She played that soundtrack on high until the orgy stopped abruptly.”

I chuckled to myself. "She was so smug about it the next morning when we were biking back out." I sighed. "She passed away almost four years ago. I spiraled when that happened. My dad had divorced wife number two and wasn't mentally able to recognize I needed help. My maman was here for the funeral so she took me to spend a few months in Paris. I had already been kicked out of high school at that point and needed to finish my senior year at an alternative school. I took the first semester of my senior year remote from France before Maman and Dad decided I needed to head back to Colorado."

My brows wagged. "I guess catching your eighteen-year-old son in a menage a trois wasn't the French lesson she wanted me to learn."

Ava groaned and laughed. "How embarrassing."

"Not my favorite moment. She was horrified. She's not a prude, but her two-bedroom apartment felt a little too small after that. I was eager to get back to The States at that point, too. Don't get me wrong. I love visiting Paris, but I missed mountain biking and my friends. The time difference was tough for me to turn my assignments in on time and communicate with my teachers if I had a question."

The clicking of the turn signal broke the lull in conversation. "Have you been to Paris before?"

She shook her head. "No, my mom and Daphne have gone a few times to go on shopping sprees, but I haven't been invited."

I sighed heavily. "I'm taking you to Paris as soon as time permits. My maman will fucking love you."

"Do you speak French?"

"Of course. My maman spoke French and English to me as a baby. I'm fluent, but it's not perfect because there are certain words I don't know. What about you?"

She shook her head. "I don't speak French. I learned how to curse in Italian because my nonna had a temper against her neighbor that would climb onto her property and steal her lemons."

I chuckled and squeezed her hand. "Did you spend a lot of time in Italy?"

She shrugged. "A week every summer until I turned sixteen when she and my mom had a falling out. We aren't allowed to mention nonna around my mom anymore."

My lip curled. "Is she still alive?"

Ava nodded. "I email her once a week. She was only fifteen when she had my mom and my mom was 22 when she seduced my dad. My nonna is in her early sixties living her best life in Sorrento."

I gave her a half-smile. "It sounds like our trip to Paris needs to have a pitstop in Italy."

She grinned at me. "That would be awesome. I miss her. It's only been two years, but it feels like a lot longer than that."

I nodded. "What caused the fallout between your mom and her?"

"Unsolved mystery. My mom dropped me off at Nonna's house and took Daph to Paris. She came back six days later, and my bags were packed when I woke up." She sighed wistfully. "I love my nonna's home. She lives on the hillside with her little two-bedroom house overlooking the cliffs. Everything there smells like lemons. My mom hates it there. I think it's because it's modest. My nonna has a little pastry and gelato shop that she runs six hours a day, five days a week. It's another thing that is *beneath* my mom."

I hummed. "Was your mom born here?"

Ava nodded. "Yeah, my nonna fell in love with my nonno while she was visiting New York. He was roommates with her cousin." She flashed a grin at me. "Ironically. Anyway, they had a torrid affair while she was visiting and got knocked up. She didn't realize it until she was back home. He convinced her to come back to New York for the last three months of her pregnancy, so my mom has dual citizenship."

"What happened to your nonno?"

She blew out a breath. "He's still alive. My mom talks to him often enough, but he's a lot like my mom in personality. He's super charming when he wants to be, but as soon as you realize how he really is he doesn't attempt to be charming anymore."

Ahh, another narcissist.

"My nonna realized when my mom was ten that my nonno was cheating on her. She moved back to Sorrento with my mom and lived on her parents' estate. My mom moved to Texas where my nonno was living at the time when she was eighteen. She went to Baylor and met my dad when she became his secretary. Within six months she was pregnant."

My head shook as I absorbed her mom's history. "I can't believe she left Sorrento for Dallas."

Ava giggled. "I can. Sorrento is picturesque and amazing, but it's not full of rich businessmen offering my mom the ability to live without ever working again."

Her mom sounded like my dad's second wife. I could say she's like his third wife too, but I have only spent a total of three hours in Petra's presence, so I couldn't tell her motives.

"What about your mom's grandparents?"

I shrugged. "I didn't really know them. My mom didn't have a close relationship with them, but they are both gone now."

She nodded. "My dad's parents are still alive. They're in Texas, but they hate my mom, so we haven't seen them in a long time. According to Charlotte, they took her side in the divorce. Will sees them sometimes, but they never took an interest in Jacob, Daph, or me, which pissed Will off. My grandpa owns land with oil on it. It's what funded my dad's company's inception and apparently Will is the sole heir when they pass away. I guess my dad won't be written back into the will until he divorces my mom. Huh, I just realized something." She adjusted her weight to face me. "My dad gave Will an ultimatum at the wedding: break up with Lily or they weren't paying for law school."

My head whipped around. I had heard rumblings of some bullshit stunts his dad and stepmom had pulled with Lily, but I didn't hear the details. "What the fuck? Lily's amazing."

Ava nodded. "Yeah, anyway. I realized my dad gave Will a similar ultimatum his dad gave him. And now he's shocked there was fallout. Talk about history repeating itself. My dad only talks to his mom because of that."

"I think the one thing that keeps me from completely cutting my dad off is the fact that I want my trust fund. My mom keeps telling me that everyone is entitled to make mistakes because this is everyone's first time living this life, but there are some things that are a given you don't do."

Ava let out a deep sigh. The sun had almost completely set. "Do you have any big regrets?"

"Nope, even the dumbest shit I've done led to the next thing that made me who I am. For instance, my junior year I got talked into leading a prank against the seniors. I stole a few goats and let them loose on the newly turfed football field. I didn't realize it was astroturf, so not only did the goats ruin the field, but they got sick. Now I do feel bad about the goats, but they were fine after a few days. Anyway, I got kicked out of school which meant my dream of attending Harvard on a swimming scholarship was dead and buried. I had already been recruited and essentially told if I kept the status quo, I was in."

I could see her cringing out of the corner of my eye. I shrugged. "If I hadn't done that prank then I would be at Harvard instead of here and I feel pretty positive this is exactly where I should be." I squeezed her fingers and kissed her knuckles.

She shook her head. "Tama said you were crazy smart, I had no idea it was Ivy smart."

I chuckled. "Perfect score on my SATs my junior year. But that was before my mom moved. As soon as she left," I sucked in a breath, "I don't want to get into that, but it was hard, and I really didn't care about Harvard or swimming for the National Team."

I glanced over to her. She had her lips twisted to the side. "You were depressed?"

I nodded. "Understatement, but yeah."

She blew out a breath. "I had to be on antidepressants when I was fourteen, my freshman year. I've always been the youngest in my class. Anyway, Daphne and Lucy's bullying reached a fever pitch. Daphne had spread rumors about me in school. It was so stupid because she hadn't been in my high school for two years at that point, but she still knew some cheerleaders that were on her squad. She told everyone that I was a lesbian and a psychopath that would stand over her while she was sleeping with a knife in my hands. She and Lucy were at Baylor so not that far away from where I lived. They'd come home on the weekends and hide notes in my backpack.

"Daphne knew people at my dance school and poisoned the waters there too. She isolated me as much as she could. I tried to tell my dad what Lucy and Daphne were doing, but he said there was no way they meant to hurt me. I stopped going to him and vented to my mom. She told me to not bother my dad with it again and she'd take care of it."

She strummed her lips a few times. "I was really depressed. I had zero friends. Lucy was telling me to kill myself weekly. My mom was restricting my eating to around a thousand calories a day so I could keep weight for a ballet I was headlining. Will was already at Pineview, Jacob had just gotten engaged to Stephanie. The only person that I could talk to was Charlotte, but she was in the middle of a huge case." She sucked in a shuddering breath.

"Lucy left another note and talked to my ballet partner. She told him that I had a crush on him, but I was born a man, and she wanted to warn him. He told me what was said and that he didn't like me like that and had the ballet school switch my partner out. I had a panic attack and went to Charlotte's office. She was terrified for me. She called my dad because she was concerned, I was going to hurt myself. I was babbling and honestly, I was seriously considering it."

My throat knotted. Rage and sorrow for my beautiful girl was coloring my vision.

"Things calmed down after that. Mom was furious that I went to Charlotte and told Daphne and Lucy they couldn't talk to me unless she was in the room. It helped, but I don't think she would have said anything to either of them if I hadn't gone to Char. My mom knew what was going on for months. She found the notes they left in my backpack, and her response was for me to 'ignore them'. She *hates* Charlotte and I feel strongly that the main reason for moving to Pasadena was to get away from her. She used Taylor as a readymade excuse. She only spends about an hour a week with her granddaughter. While we were in Barbados, she probably only spent fifteen minutes alone with her."

I chewed on my cheek. I wanted to say so many things. I was furious that her sister was such an abusive fuckface and I never wanted Ava to talk to her again. I wanted to punch Lucy in the ovaries for being such a cunt, and I wanted to scream at her mom for being so neglectful.

Ava made a thoughtful noise in her throat. "I guess we do have a decent amount in common. At least as far as our upbringing and traumas are concerned."

Swallowing thickly, I nodded. "We do." I kissed her hand again and tried to concentrate on the drive.

Chapter 16

Henry

Addiction is a scary, all-consuming temptress. You have no idea the depths you are in until you can't imagine your day without it. It's easy to spin out of control in hopes of scoring your next high. Becoming addicted to a person… is more terrifying and thrilling.

It had been five days since we went to the amusement park and every day since my brain has been seeking the incredible high that only Ava gave me. Sleep doesn't exist unless she's in my bed. Jokes lose their humor unless she's laughing. Every thought goes back to Ava. Everything reminds me of her.

A guy in my data annotation class was loudly slurping his lemonade and shaking the ice the entire class. As opposed to wanting to smack the drink from his hand because his incessant noises were distracting, my brain went to Ava and how she smells like lemon cake. The thought made me smile so wide that lemonade guy's lip curled like I was a psycho.

No relationship I had ever been in felt like this. They have always been *different*. My subs praised me for my caring and loyalty, but there was always an imbalance. The relationships started and ended on my say. And when they ended, I was done. There were no longing or worried thoughts that made me second guess my decision. But with Ava, the thought of end ing our relationship made my stomach churn.

All other relationships I kept everything private and never paraded my subs around town letting everyone know my business. But with Ava, I wanted to show her off. The first time in my life, the imbalance had swung in the opposite direction.

Instead of her being my little secret, I was hers. I dominated her in private, and she loved every fucking minute of it, but she controlled our world outside the bedroom. The reason for secrecy came from her, not me. Maybe that was why I felt the overwhelming urge to let the world know Ava was mine.

It was a dangerous thought. I had never publicly claimed anyone and doing so was rife with complications. I would have to deal with Will. He would feel betrayed, but I was willing to handle that uncomfortable situation if it meant I could be with Ava openly.

My finger tapped against my thigh as I waited outside the office of Mallory Burton. She was the head of Performing Arts at Pineview. I was overstepping, but I was doing something for Ava. Something that she wasn't going to do for herself.

She had been fretting on what her major should be, and I had mentioned that there was a dance major. The glimmer of excitement in her eyes revealed that she didn't know that was an option. But she told me that auditioning wasn't something she was able to do and shut the conversation down. I wanted to push, but the expression on her face made me pause.

I had learned so much about her in such a short amount of time. She was still annoyed about the Raven situation, but I was close to being completely out of the doghouse. And I didn't want to start another fight. There was no way I wanted her to sleep in another bed, so being in this particular office was a risk.

"Henry Foust?" An older woman stood in front of me. She was waif-like with long white hair piled into an elegant bun at the top of her head. Her long arms waved for me to follow her to her office. Her gait was graceful from years of dance, straight posture with a purposeful stride until she pushed her office door open. It was as feminine as the concrete walls allowed it to be. She warmed the room up with a large wooden desk and a bouquet of flowers next to her computer.

"I was told you have questions about the dance major. Intrigue pushed this meeting through. You are top of your class in the computer science major. You've never taken a dance class, but you have eight state titles for swimming. So, I am dying to know what I can do for you?"

My cheeks warmed at the fact that she had looked into me. And now I was going to have to let her down gently. I cleared my throat.

"I'm here on behalf of my very shy friend. She is a phenom when it comes to ballet. She has danced from the age of four and starting at the age of ten to the age of seventeen she starred in every ballet her company put out."

Mallory tilted her head to me and sat down at the wingback chair that was upholstered in paisley fabric. I licked my lips as she assessed me.

"She is amazing, and I think that she would be a perfect candidate for the dance program here. She doesn't get stage-fright, per se, but she does get nervous about auditioning."

She steepled her long fingers together, her mouth was pulled into a small pucker as her eyes narrowed on me. A slow breath filled her lungs before turning back to her computer screen. "What is her name?"

"Ava Reiser, freshman, undecided major."

She nodded and began typing on her computer. She paused and squinted at the screen. "Where was her last company?" she asked without looking over to me.

I scratched my temple. "Dallas. Her parents moved to Pasadena last year, so she stopped dancing because she was too anxious to audition for a new company."

She sat back in her chair and clicked the mouse. A quiet recording of classical music playing from her side of the desk broke through the silence. She hummed lightly.

"What is her height?"

"About five feet."

She nodded. "She makes her partner look tall."

Her lips pursed again, as she scrutinized the screen. I listened until the music faded, and she clicked her mouse. She turned to me with a warm smile; it was calming because thus far she had been cold. "She's a beautiful dancer. Even with a year off I doubt her skills have regressed too terribly, but I'm not sure how I can help you."

My thumb tapped along my thigh again. The buzzing was back in my brain which was an awkward backdrop to the silent office in front of me.

My throat was dry, I tried swallowing before speaking again. "I want to know if she has a shot of joining the program. I don't want to get her hopes up if you don't think she does."

Her smile softened. "She's immensely talented, but I can't force her to join a program. She must show interest on her own."

I winced and nodded. "Is there any way you can talk to her, maybe?"

She shook her head. "I don't see a scenario where I could approach her. Does she take lessons off campus, perhaps I could show up there."

"No, she dances every day at the gym in a racquetball court."

She laughed lightly. "Oh dear, I have heard of this ballerina before. One of the male dancers in the program saw her dancing and told me all about her."

I wanted to ask which male dancer and go pay him a visit for watching my girl, but that would be counterproductive to what I was trying to do.

"Milo had only good things to say. Don't worry." She leaned forward with her forearms resting on the edge of her desk, hands clasped back together again. "And say I see her dancing in the ill-equipped racquetball court, do I tell her you sent me?"

I shook my head quickly. "I don't want her to know that I'm here. But she loves to dance. If you take the time to see her, you'll see the passion coming from her pores. She's a little jaded. It's not my story to share, but her mother put a lot of pressure on her when she was younger."

She let out a musical laugh. "Dance moms, there is a reason why the show was so successful. They are a different breed." She sighed and rifled through her desk and passed me a pamphlet on the dance program. "Here are the basics she'll need to know. My contact information is at the bottom. If you perhaps send me a few different times when Ava will be *performing*, I will do my best to be there myself."

Folding the brochure, I shoved it into my back pocket. "I really appreciate you meeting with me."

She hummed and tilted her head. "My dear friend coaches the swim team here if you ever want to try out. He was practically vibrating when I told him you had requested a meeting with me. I had to tell him our meeting is in another hour so he wouldn't be tempted to crash."

"Good to know." I tipped my head towards the door. She nodded as her way of allowing me to leave. I tightened my grip on my backpack as I made my way back across campus towards the gym where Ava was no doubt dancing and Nicole and Lily were working out with their team.

I yanked my jammers on as Will walked into the locker room. "Hey man, I figured you'd already be in the pool."

"Had a last-minute meeting with an advisor. What brings you to the gym during daylight hours?"

He rubbed his face and yawned. "I'm meeting Matty. He's worried he's getting soft from all the traveling and fast food. I'm trying to rearrange my homework schedule to allow time to work out every day when the girls are here."

I slicked my hair back and snatched my goggles from my bag. "Well, they'll be done in about forty-five minutes, so I better get to it." He waved me off as he pulled his hoodie over his head and tossed it in the locker he was using.

Ava was in her least favorite court today. It looked out onto the weight training benches, but it gave me the best view of her. I swam steadily while keeping an eye on my girl as she moved through her workout routine. Will and Matt were outside of her view as they shared a bench. Will saw her, but kept his distance to not disturb. At least he did until the last five minutes when she deviated from her standard moves to where she freestyled across the wooden floor.

He was in the middle of a set when Matt stood up straight and nodded towards the court. They both stood and watched as she leapt into a forward roll. I pulled myself from the water and dried off while I watched her transfixed. My phone dinged in my bag, flashing a message from my dad.

Dad: You have a meeting with the

*DA tomorrow morning. It's very
important that you show up. They
have proof that the attack wasn't
random.*

My stomach clenched. If the attack wasn't random, then I truly was to blame for my cousin's lost career. The thing was, I had no idea what link I had with the three men. I had seen their mug shots, read their names, nothing jogged the slightest of memories as to our common connection. It was a mystery that I wanted to solve for my own curiosity but wanted to remain unknown for my own guilt. It would gut me knowing I was the reason for Matt's arm being dislocated and broken. For putting the girls in danger, for traumatizing Nicole and Tama.

*Me: I got the email and the voice
message.*

*Dad: Good! Do you want me to
meet you there? I know you feel
guilty about everything. You have
no reason to, but I want to support
you regardless.*

Oh God, no.

He was the last person I wanted with me tomorrow. My dad's support came with limitations that I had learned at the age of fourteen. God forbid the common denominator is my weed dispensary. He would turn on me on a dime. It didn't matter that my edibles were legal and that I had a doctor's prescription for them. My father never warmed to the idea and if anything linked back to a behavior he found unfavorable, I would see the other side of his support.

Me: No. I'll get Matt to go with
me.

I scooped my bag up and made my way into the locker room as Will stepped into Ava's space. Which I had noticed, had more than only my girl in it. Grant was in there, too. At least Will was going to shoo him away. Me storming back across the gym was not going to be productive in keeping as Ava's dirty little secret.

Ava

"Let me guess. Another roommate?" Grant asked me as Will strode into the court. I rolled my lips in to hide my smile. Grant had popped in to say hello when Will followed in behind him.

"Sort of," I dragged the last word out. "Will is my brother, Will, Grant, Grant, Will." I waved my hands back and forth between the two men in my court. My eyes darted over to the pool wall that was one way glass, I had no doubt that Henry had caught at least a part of the exchange.

Grant held his hand out to shake my brother's hand. "Grant." Will gave him a tight smile and turned to me. "Is this the guy you had a date with last Sunday?"

Will and Lily had gotten back from the fair an hour before Henry and I got home from the amusement park. Will had asked Tama where I was and she panicked and said I was on a date. Will had been asking me all week to tell him who I had gone out with. Obviously, I had refused.

Grant shook his head and raised a brow to me. "No, but I'm gathering she declined my dinner offer for the other guy." He didn't look pissed, just amused. He turned back to Will. "Why do you look familiar?"

My brother rolled his shoulders back and held one finger up before turning back to me. "How many guys have asked you out, exactly?" I rolled my lips in as Grant snorted.

I shrugged. "A few. Now, don't be rude, tell Grant why you look familiar."

Will rolled his eyes. "I was the catcher for the baseball team last year."

"Oh shit, you were, weren't you. Grant Wooley, sophomore on the football team. Finneas Morrow is my roommate. He spoke highly of you and was excited that Matt Foust joined the coaching staff this year. It was fucked up what happened to him. Did they ever find the guys that mugged him?"

My stomach pitted. I knew all about the mugging, but I also knew that Henry hated talking about it. He felt guilty about what happened to his cousin.

Will rubbed the back of his neck and nodded. "Yeah, they were arrested, but I think two of them are out on bond. Anyway."

"My ears are burning." Matt walked into the court.

Grant's eyes rounded in shock. "Holy shit. I wasn't trying to talk about you. Morrow speaks so highly of you."

Matt chuckled and turned to me. "You didn't tell me that Morrow's roommate is the one that asked you out."

My cheeks were burning.

"To be fair, we didn't exchange that sort of information," Grant said.

Matt nodded and tilted his head towards me. "What's for dinner tonight?"

"Shit, you live with Matt Foust, too?" Grant whispered. I snorted and turned back to Matt. "It's Tama's night, but she mentioned something about pot roast."

"Tama Bulris?" Grant asked.

This had me whipping my head back to Grant as I nodded. "You know her?"

He shrugged. "Not really, Tama isn't a common name, but she's best friends with Rhys Goodman. He asked me if I wanted to go on a date with her."

"You should definitely do that," Henry said from the doorway. He walked over to give Matt a weird bro hug. He looked back over to Grant. "Tama's the best. She might be Rhys' best friend, but I'm hers and I think it's a great idea for you to take *Tama* out." He emphasized her name. It was subtle enough for me to catch it, but I doubted Will did.

Grant's eyes flicked back between Henry and me. I rolled my lips in and walked over to my bag.

"Uh, yeah, I guess I'll do that then," Grant said awkwardly. He swung his arms back and forth and then pointed to the exit. "I'm going to get back to my workout."

As soon as he left, I shook my head at the three neanderthals in front of me. "Really?" I asked Will. "You told me that you wouldn't interfere and the first scent that someone is interested in me you come in like that?"

Henry's eyes narrowed to me briefly before turning to the exit. "I'm going to head to the car."

Shit, that came out wrong. "Hold on. I'm coming with." I yanked my bag over my shoulder and pointed my finger at Will.

"I'm not interested in Grant, but that wasn't fucking cool," I hissed at him.

Henry was waiting for me on the other side of the glass door. Will and Matt followed me out and went back to their bench. Henry and I kept enough space between us to not be suspicious, but we were close enough that I could feel his body heat and tension in the air.

"Are you mad at me?" I whispered when we got outside and away from the windows of the gym. Henry shook his head and gripped my hand. He tugged me to the side of the building where no one could see us. My back was eased against the brick wall as Henry kissed me urgently. I wasn't sure if this was jealousy or something else, but it felt a little primal and desperate.

"Who do you belong with?" he whispered against my lips.

"You."

His lips captured mine again. His tongue lapped at mine, making me shiver as his fingers were lightly holding my throat. My pulse fluttered wildly under his thumb.

He pulled away again and kissed my jaw and neck. "We need to tell Will," he murmured against my ear.

My stomach whooshed as I shook my head. "Not yet. Everything is perfect right now, and I don't want to deal with his mood when we tell him."

Henry growled and bit my shoulder. "When are we telling him?"

I swallowed thickly and rolled my lip between my teeth. "I don't know. A few more weeks?"

His breath puffed against my neck as his hands slipped from my throat, down my arm until he clasped my fingers and tugged me back towards the path to the parking lot.

He was disappointed that I wasn't ready to come clean to Will, but it was confusing. Everything I had learned about Henry pointed to the fact that he was a very private person. It made no sense to me why he was having any issues keeping us a secret.

He dropped my hand when Nicole came into view in front of us. She was lagging behind Lily, and Tama was leaning against the car looking at her phone. I missed his warmth immediately on the mid-October day, but if Lily saw there would be questions. I would never want her to keep something from Will.

We chatted about our days on the short drive home. We all separated into our own apartments while we showered. Henry pulled me into his bathroom and held me up as he pounded into me. It was possessive and hot. My legs felt like jelly by the time he set me down. I caught my breath as I buried my face against his pecs. Water streamed down my back as Henry lathered my hair.

He was so good to me. Any time things got a little rough he would spend extra time being gentle and doting on me. I was falling in love with him but kept that to myself.

Henry pulled a pair of panties up my thighs. He had a decent amount of my clothing he kept in his room. Any time he got me naked, and my clothes ended on his floor he'd wash that laundry for me.

He kissed my stomach and chest as he stood up and grabbed a shirt for me to wear. I groaned as my phone buzzed.

Henry chuckled as he passed me my cell. He was still completely naked. His back muscles bulged as he pulled on a pair of basketball shorts and a hoodie. It took a lot of willpower to look away from him.

Mommy Dearest: Your dad and I are going to be in Dallas next weekend.

Daphne told me you had a boyfriend.
We expect to meet him at dinner.

My heart pounded as my hands shook. *Shit, shit, shit.* I had gotten complacent and forgotten about my duplicity. Which reminded me, I needed to post another picture of me on the Baylor campus soon.

"What's wrong?" Henry asked. I passed him my phone and groaned. He chuckled and rolled his eyes. "I'll book our tickets."

I whimpered. "Okay." I had to tell Will about how Daphne had treated me in order for him to not object to me and Henry flying to Dallas together again.

Tama was in the kitchen getting dinner ready. She gave me a knowing smile as the front door of our apartment swung open. Will walked in with Lily wrapped under his arm. His hair was wet from the shower. He nodded at me as I chewed on my lip.

"You still pissed at me?" He snagged a dinner roll from the basket.

I pressed my lips together. "I am, but that needs to take a back seat. So, listen, when I was at Baylor and I ran into Daphne she was being really awful."

He sucked in a breath as he shook his head. I winced and waved my hand. "It's fine because Henry was there and sort of implied that he was my boyfriend. She backed off pretty quickly, but as it turns out she mentioned to mom that I had a boyfriend, and she is expecting both of us for dinner next week."

Will's lip curled. "Tell your mom you and Henry broke up."

I let out a huff. "And let Daphne win? Hell to the no. As she was leaving, she told me that no one like Henry would be interested in me long term."

Will growled. "God, she's such a bitch." He blew out a breath as Lily cleared her throat.

"Is Henry okay with going?" she asked with a tilted head.

I shrugged. "I don't know. I was going to ask Tama to come this time too, hopefully she doesn't get sick, but I don't have Monroe's private jet at my disposal to invite everyone."

Lily nodded. "Do you want me to ask Henry if he's willing to go? I get the sense that you two still don't talk very often."

Yeah, I'm sure she thought that considering he ignored me completely when we were in her car; dinners we hardly spoke to each other; and every time someone popped in, we were seemingly in different rooms. They didn't know that a few times that she or Will had popped over, I was tied to his bed while he said I was studying at the library.

"Ask me what?" My secret boyfriend walked into the kitchen and snagged a cooked carrot from the platter. He breathed out the steam with wide eyes.

Tama giggled. "I just took it out of the oven, you goof."

"Ava may need you to go to Waco again," Will said.

Henry's brow perked as a knowing smile stretched across his face. He turned it from elation to sarcasm pretty quickly. "Does she now? Interested in breaking more fingers?"

I snorted a laugh and shook my head. "Hopefully, no. My parents want to have dinner with me next Saturday and they want to meet my boyfriend."

He chuckled. "Do you think they'll like me?"

Lily giggled. "Probably. Tell them who your dad is, and they'll love you. Their issues with me were because I wasn't Lucy. To my knowledge they don't have a love match picked out for Ava."

"Ahh, yes." He turned back to Will. His smirk was a little devilish. "What do you say, man, mind if Ava's my girlfriend?"

Will groaned. "I'd fucking hate that, even pretend it's making my skin itchy."

My hackles rose quickly. "Hey! Be nice to my boyfriend."

Will raised his hands. "Seriously Ava, I love Henry like a brother and you're my sister. It's like incest to me." My lip curled as I shook my head.

"Aww, thanks buddy, I love you too." Henry turned to me. "So, Ava, I've been dying to ask you. Do you prefer handcuffs or rope for when I tie you to my bed."

"Motherfucker, I swear to god, that shit is not funny," Will groaned. Lily sniggered as Nicole and Matt walked into the apartment. "Fuck, that smells good," Matt said.

"Handcuffs, especially since the ones in your room are padded."

"How the fuck do you know that?" Will asked.

I grinned. "The first day here I saw them."

Will's lip curled. "New topic, for the love of God, let's find a new topic."

"Oh Peach, calm down. Henry hardly talks to her, they're fucking with you," Lily whispered to him loud enough for me to hear.

It was awkward but thankfully someone knocked on the door. "I'll get it," I announced.

"It's probably Rhys," Tama called over her shoulder as she carved up the pot roast. I nodded. I was too short to check the peephole, so I swung the door open blind. My eyes bulged as my jaw fell open in shock.

"Dad?" I whispered. The voices and merriment ceased behind me like a record being ripped.

"Ava Bear, what are you doing here?" My dad asked as he scooped me up in a hug. I swallowed thickly.

"She wanted to surprise me this weekend," Will answered coolly. "The question is, what are *you* doing here?"

My dad's arm was still draped around my shoulder as he turned to Will. He sucked in a deep breath. "Listen, son, I've been trying to talk to you for a few months now. If I told you I was coming, you'd tell me no. I wanted to talk to you, and you left me with little choice."

He looked over Will's shoulder and nodded to Lily who was frozen in the living room, halfway between standing and sitting. Her eyes were wide as they flicked between my dad and me. My nerves made my knees shake. My cover was about to be blown wide open.

"Good to see you, Lily. I'd like to take you and Will out for dinner, but it smells like that's covered for the night. Can I interest you both in dinner tomorrow night?"

Lily nodded and then smiled brightly. "You should stay for dinner tonight. We were already hosting Ava, her boyfriend, and her roommate Tama, the more the merrier."

Oh shit, I forgot that Tama was my fake roommate at Baylor. Thank god for Lily and her fast thinking.

"I'd love to stay for dinner. I haven't had a home cooked meal since Ava moved to Texas." He squeezed my shoulder and walked further into the apartment. Henry's eyes bounced between all of us. Tama's hands shook as she wiped them on her apron.

"Dinner's ready," she squeaked. "A thank you for allowing us to stay this weekend."

My palms were sweating as my dad pulled Lily into an awkward hug. I went over to stand next to Henry. I sucked in a shaky breath. "Dad, this is my boyfriend, Henry."

My dad grinned and took Henry's hand in a solid handshake. He was standing next to Matt, which would have been fine, but they looked freaking identical. "I feel like I'm seeing double," my dad pointed out.

Henry chuckled and squeezed Matt's shoulder. Matt cleared his throat. "Yeah, Henry is my cousin," he said slowly.

My dad's brow pinched in confusion. "Matt's the reason why I met Ava," Henry said. "He told me that she was new to Baylor and to keep an eye out for her. I met her on her first night on campus and we hit it off. We drove up here so we could see both Matt and Will."

My stomach was clenched in nervous knots. My dad nodded his head, like that explanation made all the sense in the world. Sweat dripped down my back as Henry looped his arm around my shoulder and kissed the top of my head. Will's jaw clicked. I glared over to him and turned my face to nuzzle into Henry's chest. A low rumble of laughter came from him. Clearly, he was happy about this turn of events. Not only was he allowed to hang all over me now, but he was going away with me next weekend too.

"Let's eat," Lily announced. Tama's fingers were flying across her phone screen. She gave me a nervous smile and whispered something to Matt. He nodded and grabbed a plate. The apartment door swung open again as Rhys slipped in. "Sorry I'm late for dinner."

Henry grunted behind me. "Got caught up at the gym." He walked right over to me. "You must be Ava and Henry, Matt mentioned that we would have three people staying with us this weekend." He turned to Tama. "Tama, right?"

She gave him a nervous smile and nodded.

"Anyone ever tell you that you look like Anya Taylor-Joy?" His grin made it obvious that it was some sort of inside joke, but she truly did resemble the actress.

Her smile faltered into a sarcastic one. "I have actually. A handsome bartender told me last week. Anyway, I made a pot roast as a thank you for allowing us to stay here."

Rhys dramatically rubbed his stomach. "Smells awesome. Too bad Tonya is visiting her boyfriend this weekend." My brow pinched as Matt nodded.

Who the fuck is Tonya?

"Yeah, but she was nice enough to let Tama stay in her room."

Oh God, these lies were getting too much. I was touched that so many people were accepting what I was doing. It was like I was on a big improv set.

My dad filled his plate and looked around to where he should sit. Lily pointed to the dining room. We had already taken two chairs from Will's apartment to have six squished seats around the table for the nights when one of the couples was on a date.

I sat down next to my dad while Henry sat next to me. Will and Lily took their normal seats across from me and Tama took her seat at the head of the table. Rhys, Matt, and Nicole ate in the living room, their heads bent together in a silent conversation. Rhys chuckled a few times, clearly thinking this entire situation was funny.

Henry kept one arm draped around me all of dinner. Will kept giving him stink eye whenever he thought he could get away with it. My dad kept his head bent towards his plate.

"Tama, this is really good." He had finished his cooked carrots and potatoes. He swirled his dinner roll into the juices and nodded. "My mom used to make pot roast every Sunday," he said.

"How is grandma?" Will asked.

My dad wagged his head back and forth. "Fine. She's convincing Dad to redo their kitchen, but Dad doesn't want to hassle with contractors in their home for weeks at a time."

Will chuckled. "Grandpa is particular about who is allowed in his home."

I rolled my lips in as my eyes dropped to my plate. My shoulders rolled down. My grandpa was *very* particular. I had never been invited in fact. Will clocked my expression. "I didn't mean it like that, Ava."

I waved him off. "It's fine. Charlotte told him that he's missing out, and I have to agree."

"He *is* missing out, Babydoll." Henry kissed my cheek. Lily's eyes narrowed at the exchange as I nodded softly.

"How's this semester going for you, Lily?" my dad asked.

She blinked rapidly. "Oh, um, it's going well. I'm studying for the GRE so I can get my master's in business. Volleyball has been going well. We're undefeated and have a match at home tomorrow afternoon. If you are still in town, you should come."

My dad gave her a grateful nod. "I can do that. I'm flying out Sunday morning, and I'd like to spend as much time with all of you that you can afford." He patted my knee. "And I heard that next weekend I'm heading to Waco to spend some time with Ava." He looked over to Henry and then to me. "Mom doesn't know I'm here, if you can keep this visit under wraps, I'll keep your visit under wraps, too."

My brows shot up as I nodded. My mom held a tight leash when it came to my dad. As soon as his divorce was finalized, my mom latched on to him and wouldn't let him go anywhere without her knowledge."

"Where does she think you are?" Will asked.

My dad sighed and wiped his mouth with a napkin. "Manhattan with Jacob. He's finishing out the contract with Michael Young. I was initially going to go, but Jacob convinced me that he was basically going to play video games with Monroe for a few days while Stephanie and Taylor toured the city."

"Jacob's with my sister?" Lily asked.

My dad nodded. "I've been looped into a few meetings with Monroe. She has a solid head on her shoulders. I understand that both you and her are being primed to take over ML."

Lily nodded. "It's why I'm going for my MBA. Monroe has a degree in Finance and Business. Between my degree in communication and an MBA we should have the education portion covered well."

My dad looked back down to his plate. "How's law school going?"

Will cleared his throat. "It's a lot. The only time I can see anyone is at dinner. I'm at the halfway point in the semester so the professors have said if we haven't drowned yet we should survive the first year. I guess they purposely start fast and heavy to get people to drop out before add/drop."

My dad chuckled and pushed his empty plate away. "Thank you so much for dinner, Tama. It was delicious." He turned to Henry. "Tell me about yourself, son." Henry's fingers tightened on my shoulder for a moment before he relaxed again.

"I'm a junior and getting a degree in computer science. My dad is a property developer in Colorado Springs. He has neighborhoods from here down to Tempe where Matt's family lives. I'm an only child. My dad is on wife number three. I'm pretty sure he brought her from some Slavic country. My mom lives in Paris. She's a writer for a French television production company. She specializes in romantic comedies."

I rolled my lips in, doubtful my dad appreciated the Slavic wife comment, but he took it in stride. One thing about Henry was he was honest to a fault. Which was probably why he didn't like Will not knowing about us.

My dad nodded and turned back to me. "Your hair has gotten so long, kiddo. How are classes going for you? Have you thought of a major yet?"

I chewed my lip. "Classes are fine. I'm going through the required courses now, nothing crazy. I haven't declared a major and really don't know what I want to do."

My dad patted my knee again. "Don't stress. If it comes down to it, do something fun. You can always join the family business if you need a job."

When all the plates were empty my dad said, "Can I take Lily to get ice cream? I know I owe her an apology, and I would like to do so with a real conversation."

Will shook his head as Lily smiled. "I'd love that." She turned to Will. "Peach has some homework he needs to get to anyway, but I'm sure he won't mind if we bring some ice cream home."

My dad stood awkwardly at the front door. He gave me a hug and shook Henry's hand. As soon as he left with Lily on his heels I let out a breath, my shoulders rolling down as Nicole burst into a fit of giggles.

"That was tense," she hissed.

Henry chuckled, his arm still draped across my shoulders, pulling me into his chest.

"That shit was crazy. I don't know what's going on, but I could see how fucking nervous everyone was at the dining table," Rhys said.

Tama laughed and walked over to him. He pulled her into a hug and settled her on his lap. I saw Henry's lip curl as he turned back to me.

Will was watching us as he waved his hand between me and Henry. "Okay, okay, my dad is gone, let her go. You were way too fucking convincing, and I didn't like it."

Henry chuckled and kissed the top of my head before letting me go.

Will scoffed loudly. "You're fucking lucky I know better than to think you'd be interested in Ava, or I would have a big fucking problem with that. I know you're fucking with me."

My insides clenched at Will's words. He didn't mean it how I was taking it, but it fucking hurt regardless. It confirmed my bigger fears that I wasn't really the type of person that someone like Henry would want to be with long term. I bowed my head to look at my toes as Henry glared at him. He leaned forward and I grabbed his arm before he could say anything. Nothing good would come from Henry coming to my defense.

"I dunno, he seems *really* into her," Rhys said.

Tama elbowed him hard which caused him to smile wide and trap her arms together in a hug. "All I'm saying is Ava is beautiful. I don't think—"

Will pointed at him. "Not you too. My sister is off limits!"

I was mentally exhausted and feeling like shit after Will's comment. "It's fine," I whispered. I gave Will a sad smile. "I have a tension headache from the stress. I'm going to bed." I turned to Rhys. "Thanks for playing along...and the compliment."

I stepped into my room as my chin quivered. It was stupid to cry, but I couldn't stop the tears like I couldn't stop my self-doubt from clouding my thoughts.

A part of me wanted to tell Will that Henry *was* interested in me to see him eat crow. The realistic part of me decided that now wasn't the time. Maybe never because realistically could I keep Henry's attention for the long haul? Maybe it was for the best to let my relationship with Henry run its course without Will being wise to it. Henry and I were both mature enough to handle breaking up, but if Will knew… then Lily would know, then Matt and Nicole would know. I wouldn't be able to handle everyone's pity when he ripped my heart out for someone better suited to him.

Chapter 17

Henry

My body hurt as I pulled myself from the pool. I slept like shit after Ava refused to sleep in my bed. Well, refuse is the wrong word. She fell asleep in her own bed and as opposed to moving her, I tried to fit next to her. Her bed was small enough that I barely fit with her in the center of the bed and unaware of me trying to snuggle. I gave up at 5am and decided to get an early morning swim in before I went to the DA's office.

I was still pissed at Will for his shitty comment about Ava not being my type. I wanted to tell him that Ava was my literal dream girl, and he needed to apologize, but she stopped me before I could. At least their dad was still in town, it gave me an excuse to hang all over Ava at the game and then dinner which I *was* invited to. I also had already booked our flight to Dallas, so it was more time I was going to have with her one on one.

Some girl stopped me on my way out of the gym. She was in one of my classes, but I had no idea what her name was, but she knew mine. I feigned interest in the conversation until she asked me out. Then I let her down gently, explaining that I had a girlfriend. She seemed annoyed, but considering I couldn't remember her name even though she told me twice, in this conversation alone, she'd get over it.

No-name wouldn't take a hint as I inched towards the exit and put me behind schedule. I looped my leg over my bike and pedaled my ass off to get to the apartment.

The need to see Ava's smile before I went to the DA's office to relive a nightmare that I only had glimpses of drove me to ride faster. Ava wasn't up yet, which was bittersweet. She needed the sleep.

My shower was quick as I rushed to get ready. The front door of my apartment swung open as my hand hovered over Ava's doorknob. Matt's brow inched towards his hairline when he saw whose door I was at. I took a step back.

"I was going to see if I could borrow her car to drive to the DA's office."

Matt grinned and jingled his keys. "No worries, cuz, I'm going with. They attacked both of us and we both sustained serious injuries. Are you ready?"

My molars pinned my cheek at the reminder that my cousin was injured because of me. I may be a selfish bastard with some things, but I hated the idea that someone was hurt because of my actions.

Matt cleared his throat when we got on the highway. "So how long have you been fucking Ava?"

Air hissed from between my teeth as I winced. There was no point in lying to my cousin. I swallowed hard. "Since Dallas."

He nodded as he passed by a semi.

"What gave us away?"

He chuckled. "How you look at her. I've been suspicious for a few weeks, but how comfortable Ava was with you hanging all over her last night sealed it for me." He glanced over at me. "You really like her, huh?"

I licked my chapped lips and nodded. "I do. I told her I want to tell Will. I've wanted to tell Will since Dallas, but she doesn't want him to know yet. First, she told me that it had to do with the fact that we didn't know each other. But at this point we know basically everything about each other. She's my dream, and I don't want to rock the boat. I'm going at her pace, so whenever she's ready we'll tell Will." I closed one eye and tilted my head back to Matt. "I know he's your best friend, but please."

He held up his hand. "I'm not going to say a word, but I do think that you do need to tell him. Last night I was not the only person to notice and suspect there was more going on between you and Ava. Rhys clocked it immediately and told me all about how you held Ava's hand at that party you took the girls to. Nicole also asked me last night in bed if I thought there was something going on between the two of you. Apparently, you called Ava Babydoll, and she didn't get pissed which surprised Nic. And if Nicole clocked it, Lily did too."

"Fuck," I groaned.

Matt chuckled. "Don't worry, Nicole and Lily won't say a word, and I doubt Rhys will either. Whatever is going on between him and Tama will prohibit him from mentioning anything to Will again. He won't want to piss her off especially after he ate dinner with us. Which reminds me, you should probably expect him at more dinners."

My lip curled as I grunted. "I'm sure he's a good guy, but he's using Tama as his emotional fluffer and it's fucked up."

Matt chuckled and repeated 'emotional fluffer' under his breath. "Point is, it's better to tell Will then have him figure it out on his own."

"And I agree. Here's the fucked-up part though. I have told him, sort of. The other week he came by and asked where Ava was, and I told him she was tied to my bed."

My cousin's face screwed into a disgusted frown. I bit back a smile.

"Then later that day Will asked Ava if she was in a secret relationship and she said yes. We have told him; he's choosing not to believe us."

Matt rolled his eyes. "You know all those conversations had an edge of unseriousness to them. He's not going to clock the honesty, so yeah, he thought you were being sarcastic. Especially because you've made the tied up joke a few times now."

I shrugged. "It was a joke only once, but she was still in my bed when I made it."

Matt grunted as we pulled into the mundane looking office park. "Ready for this?"

"Nope because nothing that guy says to me is going to make me feel less guilty about fucking up your life."

My cousin scowled. "First of all, the DA is a woman. Second, you didn't fuck up my life. The three guys trying to murder you did. No matter what the DA tells us, you didn't ask for it. You didn't plan it; you aren't responsible for it. And if I'm being honest, I'm making the same salary I would have at some minor league team, I travel less, and I'm able to keep Nicole by my side. All in all, shit worked out, so don't think for one second I'm upset with you."

The pit in my stomach clenched, but the tightness in my throat eased a little at his words. I followed my cousin into the building. He gave our names, and we were taken directly to a conference room. There was a glass wall looking onto the hallway. A mousy middle-aged woman came in and gave us a tight smile. Her eyes were sharp as she introduced herself to us. "I'm Dorthy Waters, thank you for coming in today." She turned to me when we sat down.

"Henry, I want to get right into it. I know you are busy, and your father told me that you want to put this all behind you," she said. I nodded. She pulled out her briefcase and passed a few photos for us to look at. "Do you know Clyde Mays?"

Fuck. I nodded slowly. She gave me another tight smile. "How do you know Mr. Mays?"

I rubbed the back of my neck. "He's a bookie out of Las Vegas."

She nodded. "The assailants all used the same bookie, were you aware of that?"

I shook my head. "No, I only met Clyde this past summer, before then it was all done through his website, which is all legit and legal."

Dorthy nodded. "You aren't in trouble for gambling. All his interactions with you and the assailants seem to be legal. We are having a problem connecting why Mr. Mays may have spoken about you to your assailants. Do you have any idea why they may have intentionally sought you out?"

I chanced a glance over to my cousin. His knuckles were white as he balled his hands into fists. He sucked in a breath. "When they were beating my cousin, one of the guys asked him who was going to win the college world series." He shot a quick look at me before focusing back to Dorthy.

My gaze swung over to Matt. He was chewing on the inside of his cheek; it was his tell that he was nervous. Dorthy flipped through   her   paperwork. She sighed and hummed to herself. "Yes, I saw that in the interview you gave to the police." She turned back to me, but my gaze was focused on my cousin.

"You knew they targeted me?"

He licked his lips and shrugged. "I had a feeling."

Dorthy cleared her throat. I tipped my head towards the ceiling as the back of my eyes burned. I *was* responsible for the attack. "I successfully predicted the winners of every major sporting event from September last year until the attack. I used Clyde to make my bets. I don't know why he would have shared anything with anyone considering he got a cut for all my winnings."

Dorthy squinted at me. "You successfully predicted the outcome of every major sporting event last year?"

I nodded.

"How?"

"If I tell you, I do not want it submissible in court. I don't want the details of how I was able to do it summoned. It's proprietary information with a trademark that I have copyrights to it."

Matt whipped his head to me with a confused furrow to his brow. I rolled my eyes. I had told him about my algorithm multiple times.

"I created a program that annotates all stats available online and gathers additional information about the individual athletes like interviews given to determine their likelihood to succeed based on stats, mental preparedness, and conditions of wherever they are playing. It's taken a few years to fine tune it, but last year was successful. I compared the predictions to that of my cousin's." I thumbed over to Matt.

"He's into stats for baseball and football. I used his research as my control group to determine how successful my program was. It was very successful. I was worried about March Madness because it was predicting some significant upsets, but I stayed the course. I made close to $250k since September of last year. Though I stopped betting after the attack. I focused my program on something else.”

“Holy shit,” Matt murmured.

Dorthy sat back and rubbed her lip with her pointer finger. “Who all knew about this program?”

I scratched my chin. “Not Clyde, I’ll tell you that for sure. Not a lot of people. At the time, my roommates, my girlfriend, but honestly every time I explained it people’s eyes glazed over.”

Matt nodded. “This is true. I didn’t understand what he had been talking about until just now.” He turned to me, “Do I get a cut for being your control group?”

I chuckled and nodded. “Sure Matty, we can discuss that later.”

“Can you write down a list of everyone that knew about your program at the time of the attack?”

I shrugged. “Sure.” She passed me a piece of paper, and I jotted down the names: Matt Foust, Will Reiser, Lily Young, Tama Bulris, Nicole Winters, Lydia Carmichael, and Raven Larmier. I pushed the paper back towards Dorthy and let my hands rest in my lap. My thumb tapped against my thigh as she looked at the list. She squinted and rifled through her paperwork again.

“All of these people were present for the attack except Lydia and Raven, correct?” She was still shuffling papers around.

“Yeah, and they saved my life, so I doubt they did anything to put it in danger.”

Dorthy glanced up at me. “I wasn’t implying that. All of your roommates were marked off as suspects within a week of the investigation when we found zero ties between them and the assailants." She went back to her paperwork, licking her thumb as she fingered through the pages in front of her. She cleared her throat when she pulled out what she was looking for.

She studied the page and sucked in a breath. The recorder on the edge of the table was pushed to the center. She quickly explained that she wanted to record our conversation so she could take notes later.

"Do you feel like Lydia Carmichael or Raven Larmier would want to harm you?"

My eyes bulged as I shook my head.

"Uh no. Lydia wouldn't hurt a fly and Raven's lowkey obsessed with my cousin. She professed her love for him on the street a few weeks ago," Matt said.

Dorthy squinted. "Are you still currently with Raven?"

I shook my head. "No, we began our breakup in February, and it lasted until March. I didn't see her again until September."

Dorthy scrutinized me. "Who broke up with whom?"

"I broke it off with Raven."

"Why did the breakup last a month?"

I licked my lips and tipped my head back. "She didn't want to break up. She thought my reasoning for our parting was something she could change. After a few weeks I had a long conversation with her about coming to my place late at night drunk out of her mind. Every time she did, I would take care of her until she was sober again. She tried it while I had another woman, Lydia, over which prompted the more serious conversation about how we needed to go no-contact."

"Do you think she would ever hurt herself in order to gain your attention?"

I rolled my lips in and shrugged. "A few months ago, maybe. Not now."

She nodded. "Do you think she would hurt other people in order to gain your attention?"

I groaned and rolled my head back. "I suspect she drugged Lydia. I dated her after Raven. I can't prove anything, and Lydia has no memory of the night. All I know is she kissed Matt thinking it was me because she was so wasted. She went to the clinic and tested positive for Rohypnol the next day. Tama told me about seeing Raven at the same party, so it's a stretch to assume."

Dorthy nodded and tapped her lip.

"I can confirm she was wasted and kissed me. I don't know Lydia well, only in reputation but I know trashed when I saw it. She was hardly able to stand and keep her eyes open."

I was getting increasingly nervous about this interview, but I didn't want to think that Raven did anything to orchestrate my being hurt. Dorthy asked us a few more questions and told us we would be in touch. It was quiet for our ride home. All Matt kept telling me was nothing was my fault, and he praised me for the algorithm.

Ava

Something was wrong with Henry. He was worried about his interview with the DA, but Matt had insisted to everyone that it went well. Maybe I was being paranoid he was upset about me not sleeping in his bed, but something was off. He looked exhausted, and I felt partially responsible for it. He slept best with me and even though my dreams were of Henry holding me in my sleep, my bed was empty in the morning.

Maybe I was paranoid after hearing Will tell me that I wasn't Henry's type, but he seemed stiff and uncomfortable as he draped his arm around my shoulders. My dad was sitting next to us while we watched Nicole and Lily play.

He was cheering loudly for both girls. Tama sat next to Henry while Will and Matt sat behind us. The heat of Will's glare had me want to back away from Henry, but he pulled me closer to his chest and kissed the top of my head.

"Are you okay?" he murmured against my ear. My lips rolled as I looked over to him giving me a soft smile.

Will's head appeared between ours. "Thin ice, Hank," he hissed.

Henry chuckled and tugged me closer by palming my hip and sliding me against him. I shot a look over my shoulder to Will, who was paying more attention to us then the match.

My dad stood up and cheered. My head whipped around to the court. Henry answered my confused expression. "Lily spiked hard and scored." I nodded and joined my dad in standing and clapping. When we took our seats, I leaned over to my dad.

"How was ice cream?"

He smiled at me and nodded. "It was nice. I got to apologize, and we got to talk about her childhood. I know it doesn't erase what she was put through at Daphne's wedding, but I'm trying. And it shows a lot of character that she is allowing me the grace to make amends."

My smile had a hint of 'told-you-so'. "She's cool, isn't she?"

He chuckled and gripped my knee. "She is. I should have listened to you and Jacob over Daphne. You both had always been the more reasonable between the three of you. And I want to apologize to you. I've felt gutted to learn about Lucy's role in your teenage years. I know there were a few times where you mentioned something and when I asked your mother, she waved it off saying you were being sensitive. I should have paid better attention, and I want you to know that I've started talking to a therapist. The past can't be changed, but I can take responsibility for my actions here on out."

My brows were in my hairline. "Thanks for saying that." He squeezed my knee again and clapped at another point scored. "I get the sense that Will isn't totally on board with your new relationship."

I rolled my eyes and nodded. "You could say that. I know it comes from love, but he's getting dangerously close to overstepping."

My dad chuckled again and nodded. "He's being a big brother to you."

As promised my dad treated Will, Lily, Henry, and me to dinner. Will was still guarded, but Lily seemed as open and lovely as ever. Henry continued to shower me in small affections that made my stomach tingle and Will growl.

I excused myself to go to the bathroom between dinner and dessert and Lily came with me. She looked furtively over to me in the mirror as we washed our hands. She passed me a paper towel. "It's not fake, is it?"

I dried my hands and gave her a questioning look. "What's not fake?"

"You and Henry."

My stomach dropped as my heart started to pound. I didn't want to lie to Lily, but I wanted her to lie for me even less. "He's convinced you, huh?"

Lily scoffed and leaned her hip against the sink. "More than convinced. I've never seen him look at someone like he looks at you. I've practically lived with him for a year and seen him with enough women to know how he looks at you is different."

I rolled my lips in. "I doubt you've seen him in this situation. He really likes my cooking and doesn't want Dad to figure out that I live here."

Lily rolled her eyes. "I would believe that *if* he gazed at Tama like he's been looking at you. Listen, it's not only me. Nicole asked me about it while we were warming up. Apparently, Matt mentioned something to Nicole about being concerned you two were actually in a secret relationship. He said that he has *never* seen Henry act like how he has been with you."

My throat felt too thick to swallow. "What do you want me to say?"

Lily waved her hand at the door. "The truth would be nice."

My eyes flit to the corner of the bathroom. "We're together. I don't want Will to know yet because it's still new. We like each other and have a lot in common."

Lily whimpered. "Shit, I thought you were going to tell me I was crazy. Now I know something, and I can't tell Will."

My hands raised palm up. "You pushed. I tried misdirection, you pushed. And honestly, I know it may kill you to not tell Will, but I am begging you. I'm not asking you to lie to him, but I am asking you to keep my private life private."

She blew out a harsh breath and nodded. "When are you going to tell him?"

"A few more weeks, end of the semester maybe. I want to make sure that what I have with Henry will last. I won't lie and tell you that I think what we have is going to be long term. I want to get past some insecurities first before we go public."

Lily nodded while chewing her lip. "You don't have any reason to have any insecurities, Ava."

"Sure." My eyes rolled. "I have had two of my siblings tell me that there is no way Henry is interested in me, now or long term. For all I know his attraction to me *is* the fact that I'm forbidden fruit. As soon as it comes out, he might dump me, and I really don't want to find a new place to live."

A confused furrow pinched Lily's brow. "What are you talking about? What two siblings?"

I explained to her what Daphne and Will had said. Her expression became stony. "I'd love to say he didn't mean it like that, but I won't downplay how he hurt you. That was fucking shitty what he said, and I will call him out on it the next time I hear it."

I chewed my lip and pointed to the door. "We better get back to the table before Will comes looking for us."

"I'll see you next weekend, kiddo." My dad squeezed into me.

I volunteered to ride with him to the car rental return to spend a little more time with him. Henry followed behind in my car. I thought he was going to scoff, but he assured me he had something he needed to grab while in Denver, so it worked out.

"Yeah, it'll be warmer than here, that's for sure." According to Lily the air smelled like snow was coming and the huge gray storm clouds that blanketed the drive from Boulder to Denver tended to agree with the assessment.

"When are you driving back?"

"Tomorrow morning. The three of us are going to miss classes tomorrow and drive straight through. We were going to leave today, but I wanted to spend more time with you."

The lies were coming easier and easier. I was hoping he wasn't going to need me to recite anything. He hugged me again before he wheeled his bag to the check-in door. Henry was idling in the drop off lane, scrolling through his phone.

His smile was bright when I slipped into the passenger side, and he braided our fingers together. "I have a confession to make." My heart started to pound, unsure about what he was about to tell me.

"I bought us tickets to the ballet you wanted to see. The show starts in an hour and a half." My eyes bulged at him as I stared down at the sweatpants and hoodie I was wearing. He kissed my fist with a chuckle.

"I packed a small bag with a change of clothes."

I blinked at him. "That's the nicest thing anyone has ever done for me."

He shrugged. "Get used to it, Babydoll." The whistle blared from the traffic cop telling us to move on from our spot. "It's close to an hour drive to the performing arts center, so we need to head. We can eat something before we get there, but we need to go." My head nodded quickly as I pulled my seatbelt on.

It was gestures like this that made me think that I was more than forbidden fruit. It gave me stupid optimism that what we had wasn't a shot in the pan. But every time I let the flutter of hope take flight my brain heard Daphne's words and saw Raven's face. He may have liked me, but I was waiting for love to prove my doubts wrong.

Chapter 18

Ava

My limbs felt loose and happy as I settled into my favorite part of my workout routine. I was in my least favorite court, but Henry loved it when I was in it. He told me he had the best view of me dancing while he swam. And today I needed to blow off some steam before a weekend with my mom.

It had been four days since my dad left, and Henry surprised me with tickets to the ballet. Will wasn't as suspicious as I thought he would be. He knew that we drove Dad to the airport but didn't clock that it took us an additional four hours to get back. I guess it helped that Henry mentioned something about needing to pick up a few things in Denver, so it gave us a larger window of time to enjoy ourselves.

The ballet was an amazing contemporary performance that was a fresh take on Cinderella. The dress Henry had picked out for me was perfect for me to go from ballet to dinner without feeling overdressed. He had packed a nice outfit for himself as well, and we changed back into our sweats before we got back to the apartment.

Fortunately, Sunday night Lily had ordered pizza, so it wasn't noticeable that Henry and I barely ate any considering Will and Matt were insatiable. Lily kept throwing me knowing glances when we got back. Actually, everyone but Will seemed to know that Henry and I had spent the entire day together as a couple. Will chilled out immediately when Henry didn't sit next to me or drape his arm over my shoulder.

I rolled my neck and ankles around as I switched from my recorded routine to Sia's Elastic Heart and started dancing freestyle. I had been getting bolder with my leaps. I knew enough about tumbling when my mom made me take gymnastics from five to ten before fully concentrating on ballet.

My music moved through my limbs as the song reached its chorus. My pirouettes were strong and fast as I leapt out of it and slid across the floor on my knees. Will and Matt were nearby. They had changed their routine to workout at the gym in the afternoons like the rest of us.

I saw a few people sitting outside on the bench in front of the court. I didn't pay them any mind knowing it was most likely my brother making sure no one else hit on me while he was here.

I landed my aerial and went directly into a spin and worked down to my knees to allow the momentum to twirl me along the wood floor as the last note of the song faded out.

A light clapping from the now opened doorway pulled my attention away from the floor. An older woman with a white bun stood in the entry. She was tall and elegant, and without her speaking a word I knew she had danced ballet for much of her life. It was how she carried herself. I swallowed hard and stood up. Will was standing outside the door looking unsure. I gave him a soft smile as I approached the woman.

"My dear, you have true talent. I am Mallory Burton, head of the performing arts school here."

My hands trembled as I wiped the nervous sweat from my palm.

"Ava Reiser." I shook her hand. Her fingers were cold but strong.

"I have been hearing many stories of a lost ballerina dancing on a racquetball court for weeks and I had to see for myself."

My stomach knotted and floated at her words. Someone had seen me dance and was so impressed they asked Mallory Burton to come see me. "I didn't want to impose on the studio spaces," I said quietly.

Mallory gave me a knowing nod. "Tell me dear, what is your background? It is clear you have strong technical training."

I rubbed my lips together. "I've danced since I was four. I took lessons five days a week until I was seventeen. I have some stage experience, but that was in a small school in Dallas."

She rolled her shoulders back. "And why, pray tell, did you not audition to be a part of my dance program?"

My mouth went dry as I attempted to gulp through my nerves. "I didn't know dance was a major until recently, and I get really nervous auditioning."

She squinted at me. "With your talent, you shouldn't. What makes you nervous?"

I blew out a breath and shrugged. "Disappointing my mother. If she found out I auditioned for something and didn't get it," I shook my head, "it's not worth it."

She hummed sympathetically. "Well, good thing your mother isn't here, isn't it?"

My heart fluttered as I nodded. Mallory smiled at me. "There are two auditions needed in order to make it into the dance program. I'll consider this your first. If you are interested in majoring in dance, congratulations you've been invited to the final audition. It takes place the week of finals. It will determine whether you make it in the program and if so the level of scholarship you may be entitled to." She pulled out a pamphlet with a business card stapled to it.

"I do hope to see you at the audition, Ava. And by all means, email me if you would like to use a private studio space. We have some upstairs that are only available to people in the performing arts school or auditioning to become a part of it."

She floated out of the court with the elegance of a queen. I giggled to myself as I clutched the pamphlet.

"What's going on?" Will asked.

My cheeks hurt from smiling. "I was invited to audition to the school of performing arts by the head of the freaking school." Happy energy had my shoulders bouncing and knees vibrating.

"Whoa, really? Ava, that's incredible!" Will came up to me and pulled me off my feet. "How did she hear about you? Are you considering it? How's your mental health?"

I chuckled as he sat me down. "I guess a few patrons at the gym have seen me and mentioned that I like to dance so she came to see for herself. I'd be lying if I said I wasn't considering it. There is a dance major that I could do, which seems too good to be true. And my mental health is fine. I'm telling you; mom and Daphne were the ones that made me spiral."

He blew out a breath and nodded. "Are you ready for this weekend?"

I shrugged. "As ready as I can be. At least Dad will be there. He implied that he spoke to mom about the abuse that Daphne and Lucy put me through. So, I think he'll be sensitive to anything that mom or Daph says around me. Did he tell you he's been seeing a therapist?"

Will rolled his eyes as he shook his head. "No, he mentioned it to Lily while he was groveling and apologizing. I'm skeptical about this whole turnaround. I think it's suspicious timing that ML Properties is making a deal with Dad's company and now he wants to spend time with Lily. She said I needed to give Dad the benefit of the doubt, but after what he put Lily and I through." He sighed and shook his head. "It's still pretty fresh in my head and I'm not ready to forgive him."

I twisted my lips to the side. "I understand, but I'm going to take Lily's lead. If she is comfortable about everything then I will be too."

"Are we working out or what?" Matt asked from the doorway. Will flicked him the bird but turned back to me. "See you at dinner, then the match after, right?" I nodded. It was supposed to be Nicole's night for dinner, but she swapped with me. I had been slow cooking pasta fagioli all day with bread bowls rising and ready to be baked as soon as I got home. I also made Henry more lemon bars, but those were a surprise.

"Yeah, but I'm not going out after the match. I need to finish my laundry and pack for the weekend."

Will grunted. "You got all your hotel room stuff figured out?"

I looped my bag over my arm. "Yes, now go finish your workout."

I shooed him to the door and walked over to the locker room where Henry would be coming out soon. I was vibrating to tell him about the conversation I had with Mallory.

His wet hair dripped into the hood of his sweatshirt. He wagged his brows at me as he walked to my car that was parked in Lily's spot. Because they had a game they weren't working out. We swapped cars earlier so I could take Henry and Tama home.

"You look happy." Henry clutched my hand and walked towards the parking spot.

"I am. Did you see me talking to an older woman?"

He nodded and shot up an interested brow. I told him everything Mallory and I had discussed.

"That's great, Babydoll. Are you thinking about auditioning?"

I rolled my lips in and nodded. "I hate auditioning, but that has more to do with dealing with the rejection *and* my mom's disappointment. I get the sense that Mallory wants me in the program, or she wouldn't have invited me to audition. I think I'm basically going to dance to see what sort of scholarship I can qualify for. Which would be great to save some money for my dad. It'll also put me in a better situation in case my parents stop funding school for me."

He sucked in a breath. "Do you think they'll do that?"

I wagged my head. "Yeah, my mom is vindictive enough to. If I don't fall in line, there will be consequences, and me being here is *not* falling in line. If I can get a scholarship, maybe all I will have to worry about is a place to stay and food."

Henry hummed and kissed my cheek. "Well, if that's all that's standing in your way in order to get you to stay, then I've got good news."

I turned to him. He wagged his brows. "I paid for our apartment in full for the year and I have no problems whatsoever footing your food bill." I went to object, but he shook his head. "Babydoll, I eat all your food anyway. If you keep feeding me, I'll keep paying."

Tama came into view. She was talking to Rhys. He was bent low like he was having an intense conversation with her. His gaze met with Henry's, whose hand fisted briefly.

"Hey, love birds," he called to us.

I rolled my lips in. Tama smacked his stomach as he chuckled. "No worries, it's been explained to me. The whole situation is lowkey funny." He turned to Tama and hugged her tightly. "See you tomorrow, right?"

She blushed and nodded.

Henry

"Henry, dear, tell me about your family," Kim Reiser asked me as the waiter filled her third glass of wine for the evening.

We hadn't gotten our main courses yet, and Ava had never mentioned that her mother was a wino, but I wasn't trying to judge. Actually, I had judged her before I had officially met her. I already didn't like her for the horrible things that Ava shared with me, but I knew that me being obstinate would not help Ava in the long run.

"My parents are divorced. My mom lives in Paris as a television writer. My dad lives in Colorado Springs. He owns a property development company with neighborhoods from Cheyenne to Tempe."

Kim held her wine glass to her lips listening to me before taking a sip and setting her glass down.

"So how did you find yourself at Baylor?" Daphne asked.

I had been giving her the cold shoulder most of the evening. Her husband seemed cool, but Daphne seemed exactly how I thought she would be, spoiled and bitchy.

I gave Daphne a tight smile. "My dad was looking into breaking into the Waco market a few years ago. I traveled with him to see the area and liked what I saw." I was lying out of my ass. I didn't want to mention that I didn't particularly like Texas. It was October and still hot as fuck. I liked the snowy weather we had left behind. I liked snowboarding and watching the leaves change for the seasons. And I loved living in the mountains. So far everything was flat and boring in Texas.

"Did he find property suitable for his needs?" Jim asked.

I shook my head. "Still looking. He finished another neighborhood in Albuquerque. He wants to break into the California market, but another development firm has a bit of a monopoly right now." Which was true. I had heard him bitch about some company owned by his rival and old roommate from Columbia, enough times that there was serious validity to my comment.

"Which company in California?" Jim asked.

My shoulders lifted. "I don't know the official name of his company, but it's owned by Fred Whitaker."

Jim's brow rose high. "He's partnered with Mitchell Berry in a few developments in California. I believe our home in Pasadena was built by Whitaker's company because it's on a golf course and that's what he's been specializing in."

I nodded like I knew exactly what he was talking about. "My dad builds luxury homes, so it doesn't surprise me that some of the properties are golf courses."

Jim seemed satisfied with the answer. Daphne licked the front of her teeth as Kim took another sip of wine. Russel tipped back his scotch and wiped his lip with his thumb. Ava's hand gripped my thigh under the table. She was nervous about all my answers. We hadn't discussed what we were going to say, but I was sticking as close to the truth as possible.

"I'm confused how you two met. It's such an unlikely pairing," Daphne said.

If I didn't know what a cunt she was, I wouldn't have caught the sneer on her face. I gave her a charming smile and looped my arm around Ava's shoulder and kissed her cheek.

"We met at orientation. I thought she was gorgeous." I looked over to Kim. "It clearly runs in the family."

She rolled her shoulders back and preened, setting her wine glass down. Ava did favor her mother, but the biggest difference was Kim's smile wasn't genuine like Ava's was. Both Kim and Daphne looked like they smelled something foul when they attempted to smile. The filler and Botox was preventing normal facial movements.

"I struck up a conversation with her and we learned we had some friends in common. I had dinner with her and that's all it took."

I looked over to Ava as she pressed her lips together. I could see the blush surging up her cheeks. She was so fucking beautiful. I leaned over and kissed her cheek again.

"What are you majoring in?" Jim asked. He already knew, but I'm sure he understood it would seem suspicious if he didn't inquire about me.

"Computer science," I answered.

Jim hummed. "So, you don't want to join your father's business?"

I shook my head. "No. I've already started my own company with a program I wrote. My work has copyright, but essentially, it's an algorithm that makes accurate predictions from sporting events to the stock market."

Russel's brow rose dramatically as he shot a look over to Jim. I hadn't discussed what I wanted to do post-graduation. Jim blinked at me as Kim smiled over to Ava. "Look like you've snagged yourself a keeper."

Ava's shoulders stiffened as she let out a slow breath. "Henry is a wonderful man," she said diplomatically.

Daphne huffed and reached for her own glass of wine. "Don't put too much pressure on her, mother. This is Ava's first relationship with a man, I doubt it's going to last past the New Year."

Ava sucked in a breath through her teeth as I narrowed my eyes to Daphne.

"Is there a reason why you're making that assumption?" I challenged.

She gave me a cold smile. "My sister is young, with no experience. I'm sure someone like you will get tired of explaining everything to her. I'm being honest and don't want my mom to put undue pressure on my sister. She's *very* sensitive."

Ava didn't say anything, she continued to stare at the table. She was shutting down as Daphne's words washed over her. Her stare became more vacant as her shoulders stiffened, her posture was impossibly straight.

I hummed quietly and kissed her cheek. It was the only form of physical affection I felt was appropriate at dinner. At this point my lips should rest on her face from how often I was kissing her. Jim cleared his throat. His head was tilted as he looked over to his oldest daughter.

Daphne tipped her chin down as she looked at her wine glass before straightening her shoulders and staring back to Ava. "I'm only looking out for you, Ava Bear. It's your first relationship, and to be honest I figured it would have fizzled out by now. It's rare for someone to marry their first boyfriend."

Ava nodded but didn't look up. I had a feeling she was trying to make herself small because Daphne had hit a nerve.

"How are classes going for you, Ava?" Kim asked.

"They're going well," she murmured. She was acting like a shadow of herself, and I fucking hated it.

I leaned over to her. "I know you aren't okay, but I'm here. I'm not going anywhere. What Daphne said is bullshit," I whispered in her ear.

She swallowed as she gave me a grateful smile and leaned into me and kissed me quickly.

The rest of the dinner was much the same. Daphne made passive aggressive comments that made my girl curl into herself as Kim drank herself into a glazed-eye stupor. Russel seemed oblivious to everything around him and Jim kept trying to keep the conversations light.

"I'd love to see your dorm and meet your roommate." Daphne dipped her spoon into her dessert. Ava's whole body froze.

I rolled my eyes over to Daphne. "Unfortunately, Tama is out of town this weekend. She's visiting her mom in Hemet, and Ava doesn't like staying in her dorm alone. She's staying at my apartment until Tama gets back in town."

"Can't my sister answer her own questions."

Ava gulped her water and looked over to her sister. "I can. It's the anniversary of Tama's dad's death, she is spending time with her mom. We were going to be out late tonight, and I hate walking to my dorm at night. Henry has a nice apartment that he doesn't share with anyone, so I'm staying there."

I rented an apartment for the weekend, and it was a two bedroom. What I didn't want to happen was for us to be staying at the same hotel as the Reisers and have that complication to deal with. The apartment was decent, close to campus, and furnished. It also had a two-person shower in the main bathroom, so I was really looking forward to taking advantage of it once this godforsaken dinner was over.

"Oh, now I get it." Daphne leaned back. Russel ordered another scotch, ignoring his wife.

"What do you get?" Ava asked. She was starting to get some of her ire back.

"Why Henry is with you. You're easy and clearly do whatever he tells you to do."

"Daphne, that's enough." Jim looked over to us. I kept my body as relaxed as possible, but my blood was boiling.

Daphne turned to her father. "You don't think it's odd that Ava is punching so far above her weight? Either there is something wrong with Henry, which we can see there isn't. Or she is giving him something no other woman will because she's too desperate to say no."

"Daphne, a word outside," Kim said. Considering how much she had drunk you'd think she would have stumbled as she stood up, but she didn't. She strode out of the restaurant with Daphne on her heels, rolling her eyes.

"I am so sorry Ava. I don't know what's gotten into her," Jim hissed.

Russel leaned forward. He had a light mist of sweat dotting his forehead. "She's on her period," Russel said.

My jaw clicked at his naïve reasoning. Russel leaned back and stood up and stumbled. "I'm going to hit the head."

Jim closed his eyes and shook his head. "Are you okay?" he whispered to Ava.

She gave him a shaky nod. "I'm tired, and I hope you know that what she said isn't true about me and Henry."

He chuckled lightly and reached across the table and squeezed her hand. "I know, kid. I knew last weekend that this isn't some fling to either of you. By the way," Jim turned to me, "it was a smart move to keep the fact that your cousin lives with Will out of the conversation. I have learned a lot this week in couple's therapy and Will has been a major point of contention. I had no idea that she harbored so much animosity towards him until my therapist pointed it out the next day in my individual session."

This man has been living in the land of delusion.

I may have only heard from Ava and Will's point of view but hearing about the whole amusement park thing, made me understand that Kim didn't like Will and treated Ava unfairly. My guess was Kim turned on Ava as soon as she insisted that Kim put Ava up to hugging her dad in public. It would have been perceived as an act of war against her. It didn't matter that Ava was a fucking child who was being honest. She stepped out of line in her mother's brain.

I nodded at Jim. "No worries, I hope you understand that I really care about your daughter, and this isn't some shot in the pan relationship. I have no intention of ending it."

Jim smirked. "Ava is a special woman. I'm glad another person can see it."

He leaned back into his chair as Russel stumbled back and sat down roughly. "What's new with Midwest sales?" Jim asked him once he settled back in.

Russel nodded and yawned. "Good, not scoring a killer deal with ML Properties good, but we have surpassed our numbers from last year."

Jim seemed happy with that answer. "Everyone benefits from the ML deal, not only Jacob. If all goes well in San Diego, we have potential for more hotels and resorts in the near future."

Russel nodded. "Oh, I know, it all goes towards the profits that we all bonus off of."

Not what I would say to my boss, but what do I know? I've never had a boss and didn't intend to.

"Exactly," Jim said.

Kim and Daphne sat back down at the table. Daphne's lips were pulled into a pout and her arms were crossed over her chest.

"Ava Darling, Daphne and I are having a spa morning. We would love for you to join us. We could have some nice bonding time."

Daphne gave Ava a cruel smile and nodded. Ava looked up to me with her big brown eyes. We were supposed to fly back home tomorrow night.

I cleared my throat, but Ava spoke.

"Henry and I have late lunch plans tomorrow, so I don't know if I can make it."

Kim made a noise in her throat. "Your father and I have a flight tomorrow afternoon, so I was planning on going to the spa first thing in the morning in order to be back at the hotel by noon."

Ava rolled her lips between her teeth and bit down. All the color leached from her mouth as she thought about it. She didn't want to go, but there wasn't a valid excuse I could give her without looking like a possessive fucker and proving Daphne right. "That can work. What spa?" Ava said finally.

Kim cooed over to Daphne who looked like she had sucked on a lemon. "Spa Bella, 9am. I've booked the three of us for an hour and a half massage each. Jim and Russel have a tee time at the same time."

"Yes, we do. Henry, interested in hitting the links first thing in the morning?"

I fucking hated golf. It was boring as fuck, but it was a favorite past time of my dad and uncle. Every time we would visit my uncle and Matt we would go.

"I don't have my clubs with me."

"No worries, we can lend you some," Russel said. "I'm right-handed, Jim is left-handed. We've got you covered if you're a south paw."

I gritted my teeth and nodded. "Sounds fun."

Compared to Ava's morning, I had a fighting chance of it being decent. Jim seemed okay. Russel seemed drunk and oblivious. I could work with both, but I didn't want Ava to be near Daphne without my protection. I was going to worship her after spending the morning with her caustic sister.

"Oh, and before we forget," Kim said airily. "We are taking Ava's suggestion and taking a long vacation over the Thanksgiving holiday this year. We are heading to Bali for two weeks." She sighed. "A much-needed time to reconnect with my dear husband."

Ava nodded and grinned for the first time this entire evening. "Good for you, mom. You deserve it."

Jim furrowed his brows and leaned forward. "You aren't upset?"

"No, Henry and I were talking about spending the holiday together, so it makes my decision so much easier."

My smile didn't reach my eyes. Thanksgiving wasn't a fun holiday for me after my parent's divorce. I spent the last one in Paris after Matt's mom declined to host the dinner and deferred to my stepmom to cook the meal. I'm still not convinced Petra knows how to turn the oven on. I heard from my dad that they ended up catering it from a restaurant since it was just the two of them.

"Ava's welcome to have Thanksgiving with my family," Russel said. "Lucy will be there with Holden, I think. I don't know, they're relationship has been struggling since Barbados. I guess she's a cheater, who knew, right?" he slurred.

Daphne snapped her head over to her husband and gave him a look that said *shut up*. I wanted to laugh because Ava and I already knew the whole story from Holden, Will, and Lily. I wanted to reply that Lucy was a skank-ass bitch that was a hundred percent a cheater, but I couldn't.

Ava forced a smile. "I appreciate the offer. Your parents are so wonderful, but like I said, Henry wants me to meet his family."

Kim nodded and looked at me. "Wonderful, see Jim, I told you it wouldn't be a big deal."

He gave her a tight smile as he paid the bill. I wanted to get the fuck out of this restaurant and fuck my girlfriend until she stopped thinking about the shitty things her sister said or implied. I wanted to worship her and make her know that what we had wasn't a temporary fling.

Chapter 19

Ava

"There is something going on between you and Henry that I don't trust. I don't know whether you are paying him to be with you or what, but there is something up. There is no way he'd be with you on his own volition. You are a pathetic baby that no one likes. I'm going to figure out what you are using to blackmail him," Daphne hissed in my ear.

My eyes snapped open as I let out a huff of air. It was my sister's parting shot to what was a decent spa day. The three of us all had separate massage rooms booked so I didn't have to listen to Daph bitch and moan for an hour and a half. She scrutinized my body as we changed into robes.

"Perhaps Henry is gay because you have the body of a twelve-year-old boy." She had cornered me as soon as our mom stepped out of the locker room.

"He's very straight and loves that my body is natural. He can hardly get enough of me." I had said back, holding my head high, but on the inside, I was falling apart. She knew exactly what insecurities to push; she put them there. Sure, he told me that he liked my body, but it could simply be him being attracted to the forbidden fruit that I was.

"Are you okay?" Henry whispered.

It had been a few weeks since the trip to Waco and my sister's cruel words played in my brain every night while I attempted to sleep. I rolled onto my side to face Henry and nuzzled into his chest. "I am now. It was a nightmare."

Looping his arms around my back, he kissed the top of my head. So safe and secure. He had given me zero reasons to doubt our relationship, but my mind was sabotaging my thoughts. Daphne had burrowed into my brain and was wreaking havoc. I hated her, I wanted to prove her wrong. And I was terrified to voice my fears to Henry and give him the idea that Daphne was right.

"Do you want to talk about it?" he murmured against my hair. This was becoming a regular occurrence, waking up from a nightmare and Henry calming me down. Every night I refused to talk about it, making up some excuse that seemed believable enough.

"No, I don't remember it all. I'm anxious about the audition coming up."

His palm was gliding up and down my bare back. He hummed. "You are going to do great. I haven't seen you dance in a few weeks, but I'm sure it's better than ever."

I leaned forward and kissed his chest. I had taken Mallory up on her offer for me to use the actual dance studios. They were private with a decent speaker system as well as mirrors and a ballet barre across one wall so I could do proper stretches and check my form.

"I can also come up and watch you dance. I miss it. Don't get me wrong. I hated seeing meatheads walking into your space and hitting on you while you were in your splits, but I miss seeing you dance. You're so graceful and beautiful. There's so much passion and I can tell you love what you are doing."

My finger traced up the vein on his neck to his ear lobe. His eyes fluttered shut as I gently scratched against his scalp. He moaned lightly as his erection grew against my stomach. I took advantage and looped my leg over his hip. I didn't want to think about Daphne haunting me anymore and my best form of escape was Henry's body.

Pushing him onto his back, I grinded down on him for a few swipes until I had lubed his dick with my wetness. I had stopped attempting to sleep with clothes on when I shared the bed with Henry. He ran so hot that they made me sweat and they got in the way when we wanted a 3am quickie.

I slid down his shaft until I felt full. It had taken a while to get used to his size, but now I didn't feel complete until I felt the pinch of pain from him bottoming out. Air hissed between his teeth as I started moving my hips, writing him my secret message: Ava loves Henry.

There were zero doubts that was how I felt about him. I hadn't dared tell him. I wasn't sure if he felt the same way, and I had read way too many books to know the fatal flaw of saying it first.

Between my books and my mom, I had learned one fucked up lesson: A relationship works best when the man loves the woman more than she loves him. No matter how toxic and jaded that sounded, I couldn't help but believe it. So, I stayed quiet and wrote him my secret message with my hips over and over again because the V's hit a spot in me that made me gasp every single time.

Henry was licking his bottom lip and squeezing my ass. "Fuck, Babydoll, just like that."

One hand snaked to my chest as he plucked and played with my nipples. The other hand went to my clit and smoothed circles with his thumb. His nostrils flared, he was close. It turned me on knowing I had this effect on him. I loved when he allowed me the pleasure of taking charge. It didn't happen very often. He must have felt my need to be in control after my nightmare.

A whimper vibrated my throat as he thrust up into me. I tipped my head out in a silent cry. My thighs were trembling as my orgasm rushed through me.

"Fuck yes, squeeze me like that. Milk my cock," Henry gritted through his teeth.

I couldn't catch my breath as my body fluttered around him.

"I fucking love your pussy, Babydoll. God, fuck, you're still cumming. Fuck, fuck." He grunted and thrust hard into me.

My whole body was vibrating as I rode him through either the longest orgasm of my life or a second one that rolled through me after the first. His thighs tensed as he spilled into me, hot liquid gushed between us. The intensity of his body connecting to mine made my eyes roll back as I bit my lip.

I gasped out as my head drooped down. Henry caught his breath with a smile on his face. He was so fucking sexy with his lips parted, eyes closed, and head tipped back. I loved looking at his chest as he flexed while he was gripping my hips. Corded muscles that lead to his stacked six pack relaxed. His biceps bulged as he pulled me down to kiss him.

My tongue greedily swiped against his. I could still taste the mint from his toothpaste as he cupped the back of my head to keep me from pulling away. I moaned into his mouth. My love confession was fluttering around my brain, but I sealed the thought up. We still had not told Will about us. I was the only hold up in that situation.

After playing a round of golf with my dad, Henry renewed his efforts in trying to convince me to come clean. I already had too much on my plate with the audition coming up. I wanted to focus on that and then deal with Will after.

And then there was Thanksgiving to worry about. Will was spending the holiday with Lily, Monroe, Michael, and Charlotte. Apparently, his mom felt terrible about last year's Thanksgiving and had made sure she didn't have a case this year to focus on. Will invited me to join them at his mom's house and I was tempted, but I also needed to concentrate on my dance routine. And god forbid I ran into Daphne while in Dallas visiting Charlotte, it would give her more incentive to question my relationship.

Matt and Nicole were spending the holiday at her parent's house. They had invited Matt's parents to join them, and Tama was flying home for the week. Henry mentioned that his dad expected him home, but he declined. Last year he went to Paris but told me that the jetlag was crazy for him to get over. He was planning on spending his winter break with his mom this year, so he had more time to deal with the time differences. I was a little jealous, but I didn't voice it. He missed his mom, and I wanted him to spend as much time with her as he could.

Henry pulled his face away from mine. "Where did you go?"

I licked my lips, tasting him on them and felt my cheeks flush in embarrassment. I guess my kiss had gotten a little too lazy as I spiraled about the next few weeks. "Sorry, I'm stressed."

He hummed and moved us around, so I was on my back. He wagged his brows as he pulled out of me. I shivered at the loss of his warm body as he stood up from the bed. He came back a moment later with a washcloth. He cleaned me up and crawled next to me. "Do you want to talk about what is stressing you or do you want me to go down on you until you pass out?"

I giggled and pushed his shoulder. One brow rose high as he shook his head. "Babydoll, don't make me handcuff you to my bed and have my way with you."

I smirked at him. "You haven't done that in a while."

He hummed and rose on his knees. His chest rubbed against mine as he snatched the arm that pushed him before snapping the cuff around my wrist. "Is that why you pushed me? You wanted me to punish you?" He hissed as he pulled my other arm up. I licked my lips and nodded.

"Naughty girl. I hope you got enough sleep because I am happy to edge you the rest of the night."

We didn't have plans to worry about tomorrow. Lily and Nicole were in Tucson for their afternoon game. Matt was also in Tucson checking out some high school. Tama had plans tomorrow night, so she wasn't going to do anything early in the morning. And Will was studying for his exams before Thanksgiving. It was going to be me and Henry for most of the day. We could nap and explore each other as much as we wanted to.

My eyes rolled back again as Henry put his talented tongue to work. It was my favorite way to disassociate.

"I really think you should reconsider your Thanksgiving plans." Will muted the television.

The volleyball match was set to start soon. Henry had ordered Chinese food and was destroying the pork dumplings.

An irritated groan rolled down my throat. This was the fourth time Will had brought it up since he found out my parents were not participating in the holiday this year. "And I told you that I'll be fine. I'd love to see Char, but I can't risk running into Daphne while I'm in Dallas. I swear to you she has an Ava radar when it comes to me. And I made a big deal about meeting Henry's family so if she finds out that I am in Texas she'll assume we broke up."

Will groaned. "I don't see the big deal about her thinking you two broke up. It isn't realistic or sustainable. What happens a year from now? You still going to pretend to be in a relationship with Hank? What about when someone is interested in you? What if Hank wants to start an actual relationship, do you think she'll be okay with you cosplaying with him on your arm?"

My stomach pitted. I was being sensitive and twisting his meaning in my brain.

"The big deal is that Daphne was a horrific cunt and told me that she doesn't believe that Henry would *ever* actually be interested in me long term. I want her to eat her words."

Will huffed a breath as Henry cleared his throat.

"I'm ready to take this as far as Ava wants." He grinned. "Daphne is the biggest insufferable bitch I have ever met in my life. At this point, I'll marry Ava to make her back off."

Will's lip curled. My stomach fluttered and knotted at the same time. What Henry said was sweet, but his motive wasn't.

"I think that may take this ruse a smidge too far." Will shot a hard look at Henry who shrugged and dipped his last dumpling in his sauce.

"Yeah, if I marry Ava, it wouldn't be a ruse, huh?" Henry smirked and turned to me. "What do you say Ava, want to get hitched?"

I tossed my chopstick at him. "Not if you're only marrying me to prove my sister wrong."

He chuckled and placed his empty container on the table. He glanced over to me to gauge whether I was actually mad at him. He winced when he saw my annoyed expression.

"What are you going to do? Spend the holiday alone?" Will asked.

I chewed on my cheek and shrugged. "I made the entire dinner last year, so if I felt so inclined I could easily make my own meal. I don't mind being alone for a few days. Besides, I need to concentrate on something that I didn't want to mention to you, but now I feel like I should."

Will scowled over to me as Henry perked his brow in interest. The look of hopeful relief flitted across his face, and I realized he thought I was finally going to come clean. I cleared my throat and focused on my brother, feeling guilty about letting Henry down again.

"My audition for the dance major is during the week of finals. It will determine if I get into the program and if I do, if I qualify for a scholarship. I didn't want to make you worry because you think I am going to spiral. But I want to be prepared, and I can take the holiday as a perfect way for me to get my head in the game and come up with the routine that I am going to audition with.

"I want that scholarship. I was looking into it, and it is like any other athletic scholarship. They only give out one full ride per semester. The rest of the dancers can qualify for partial scholarships, but if I get a full ride then I won't have to worry about Mom and Dad pulling my financial plug. I can come completely clean with everyone about everything."

Henry's eyebrow perked again, reading my meaning as he relaxed back into his gaming chair. A small smile played across his lips as he turned his head to focus back on the television.

"Match is on," he rumbled.

Will unmuted the television but continued to talk to me. "Have you considered all the consequences to that?"

I rubbed my lips together and nodded. "It's a high chance that my mom will disown me, and Dad will follow suit. I couldn't care less about any fallout with Daphne because I'm sure at that point she will talk to me as often as she talks to you. Which for me would be a blessing. Jacob already knows everything, and I have a found family that I am more than happy with. A silver lining is that I could go see nonna without pissing mom off."

Will blew out a breath. "You know your mom will throw all your things away."

I nodded. "I took everything that meant anything to me when I moved here. I never intended to leave once I got here." Will's eyes bulged as Henry's head swung round to me. I chewed on my lip.

"You didn't think it was odd that I brought over a hundred books with me? I told Jacob as I was leaving that I wasn't coming back. He offered me his guest house for winter and summer break, but I'm thinking I will probably have to find some sort of a job for the summer to afford rent."

Will shook his head. "Don't worry about rent, Ava." He sighed and tipped his head back. "You know Kim will view this as an act of treason. She'll see it as you picking me over her."

I shrugged. "That's her toxic problem and if that was the real ultimatum I would pick you a hundred times before I picked my mom now that I've seen who she really is."

Will bit into his cheek. "That was the first time Dad ever visited me here. You understand that he had to visit me in the guise of being in Manhattan for work. He would sneak to my baseball games if we played Texas Tech or Baylor, but he never came here. After your betrayal she won't let him visit. Are you ready for that?"

My heart broke a little. My dad was far from perfect, but he was the only father I had ever known. And despite all his faults, loving his children wasn't one of them. He may have been upset with me when I was seven and a half for spoiling his double life, but when he got over it, he still supported me the only way he knew how.

I swallowed thickly. "I know."

"And what happens if you don't get a scholarship?"

I licked my lips and sighed. "My original plan would play out. Dad would pay for my first year before realizing where I've been living. Next year I may have to take the year off and save money. I can also reach out to Nonna and see if she's willing to cosign a student loan for me. I haven't thought through the logistics of next year. I'm focusing on what's right in front of me and that's working my ass off to get that scholarship."

"Lily Young is a senior at Pineview and has had a tremendous season this year," the announcer said. It drew my conversation with Will to a close as he turned his attention to see his girl clapping and yelling out encouragement to her teammates.

Henry

"Mr. Foust, this is Dorthy Waters, the DA in charge of your case. I need you to come in for another interview. We have found further evidence that you were intentionally targeted in the attack. It is imperative for your case that you come in to clarify a few details. I am available on Saturday Dec 5 at 9am. Enjoy your Thanksgiving and I will see you next Saturday."

I rolled my eyes and tossed my phone on my bed. I wanted to erase the voice message and pretend I never got it, but that wouldn't make my problems go away. My brain started to buzz. I had limited outlets for my restless energy. My dad had been hounding me all week about coming to his house for the big meal tonight. I didn't want to share Ava with my dad and Petra. We had the entire apartment to ourselves for the next four days as all the rest of our roommates went their separate ways for the holiday plans.

My fingers tapped my thigh as I looked around my messy room. Ava's and my clothes were scattered everywhere. I had been intending to clean since Monday and now I had too much energy to worry about laundry. Ava had gotten up way too fucking early to make us breakfast and prepare a small Thanksgiving dinner for the two of us. I had spent some time watching her dance in the kitchen with her headphones on. She didn't know that I often watched her dance as she made our dinners.

I groaned as another message from my dad popped up. I snatched my phone up and grit my teeth together.

Dad: I have half a mind to invite myself
over to your Thanksgiving dinner. Matt
shared with Gene that your girlfriend is
an incredible cook. I haven't seen you
since you were in the hospital. I only
want to see you, son.

The emotional manipulation was strong. Stalking out of my room, I abruptly. My girlfriend twirling around the kitchen while she stirred the boiling potatoes. Everything smelled incredible. She had fresh yeast rolls rising on the breakfast bar. The apartment smelled like the turkey she had been roasting all day. She had been bouncing back and forth between the two apartments using the other oven to bake an apple pie.

She spun around and startled when she saw me leaning against the wall watching her. My annoyance drained away at seeing her in my t-shirt, knee socks, and nothing else. She popped her headphones down. "What's up?"

Snagging some of the excess fabric of the shirt she was wearing, I tugged her towards me and captured her lips. She sighed against me and dropped down from her toes. Her smile was so sweet and tender.

A groan left my throat. "My dad wants to have dinner with us. I told him that you were making dinner so I couldn't come down and now he wants to come up."

Her mouth opened as she blinked rapidly at me. "Are you okay with that?"

My lip curled in a pout. "Honestly, I don't know. A year ago, I couldn't think of a worse way to spend my holiday than with my dad and his third wife. And I'm not thrilled about the prospect of that happening this year, but I'm not about to fly to Europe to avoid him."

Ava snickered. "Okay, well I am making enough for six because I knew you would want leftovers, so the more the merrier."

My nose wrinkled like a petulant child. "I was hoping you were going to tell me that meeting my dad was too much for you and not to invite him."

She giggled. "It's not too much for me. I have half a mind to take a picture of us at the table and post it so Daphne will see I actually met your dad."

My lip pushed out. "Fine, I'll tell him to come. But I am warning you, I am already twitching. The pool is closed, so I need to blow off steam."

She grinned at me and bit her lip. "I am on a strict dinner schedule. I don't have an hour to wear you out before we eat."

"I figured, and this energy would require at least two hours of your body in the bedroom." I sighed. "I'm going to grab my bike. Are you going to be okay for the next hour?"

She nodded and shooed me out of the kitchen.

> *Me: Ava made enough food. Dinner will be ready in two hours. Come if you want to.*

Dad: I'll leave in about fifteen minutes.
I should get there right before dinner.

My eyes squinted, not missing that he didn't say 'we' implying Petra would be coming as well. I pulled on warmer clothes and headed out. The parking lot and street were empty, but as I got farther into Boulder, I saw more cars parked outside of homes. There was hardly anyone driving around, which made me have free rein on the road.

My legs pumped up a large incline, feeling my heartbeat and my muscles burn. The buzzing in my brain dulled enough for me to enjoy the chilly air whipping through my hair. My nerves about the DA's message and my dad's impending arrival fell to the wayside as I enjoyed the brisk evening as the sun began to set.

My cheeks and nose were pink when I locked my bike up. My fingertips were a numb, but it was worth the exhaustion in my limbs. Ava didn't hear me come back in. She was still in my t-shirt, dancing around the kitchen like a little nymph.

She yelped out in surprise when I slid my freezing hands under the shirt and gripped her waist. Her eyes were wide as her chest heaved in the adrenaline rush, I caused. "You scared me half to death," she yipped out.

My cold face nuzzled against her neck. She squirmed in my hold until I lifted her up and set her on the only free space on the counter. Stepping into her parted thighs, I ran my nose up and down from her collar bone to ear lobe.

Her little nipples were pebbled as she ran her fingers through my windblown hair. She shivered against me. I leaned down and bit her nipple through the shirt and grinned at her as her thighs clamped around my waist.

My brows wagged. "While I love you wearing my shirt and nothing else, my dad will be here any minute, Babydoll."

Her head snapped to the clock as she shimmied off the counter. "The timer that's about to go off is for the dinner rolls in the other apartment. Pull them out of the oven, please," she called over her shoulder.

"So bossy," I yelled back.

I watched the countdown and tapped the timer off before I headed next door. My dad's fist was raised in the air as he was about to knock. We startled each other. I hadn't seen my dad in six months. He looked like he lost a few pounds, nothing dramatic. He had a few more gray hairs at his temple, but for the most part he looked the same. Petra was nowhere to be seen, but I decided not to mention anything.

My dad pulled me into a hug. It was awkward. He wasn't an overly affectionate person, but I reciprocated.

"Ava is getting dressed, and I need to grab something from the oven in the other apartment."

My dad nodded and followed me into Matt's place.

"How was the drive?"

He looked around my cousin's home. It was more brightly decorated, but had the stiff corporate furniture provided in the furnished apartment.

"No traffic."

The oven door snapped shut with the pan of rolls in my hand. The apartment smelled incredible. The apple pie was cooling on a rack next to the sweet potatoes souffle.

I glanced up to my dad. He was wringing his hands together. I had never seen him look nervous. My eyes narrowed. "What's going on?"

He huffed out a breath. "Petra and I have broken up."

I kept my face neutral as I nodded. It made sense why he didn't want to spend the holiday by himself. It made me feel like a shitty son for not knowing or inviting him. "Annulment or divorce?"

My dad was quiet as I pulled the rolls out of the pan. My previously frozen fingertips felt the singe of heat from the bread. "To be determined."

I nodded slowly. "Are you okay with it?"

He popped his neck to relieve some tension. "She wasn't faithful."

Oh, the irony.

He had cheated on his first two wives. I guess he didn't like the shoe on the other foot.

I didn't believe that they had a true love match anyway. What 27-year-old marries a 50-year-old for anything other than financial security? It's not a surprise their union lasted less than two years.

I never approved of her because she was only seven years older than me. Perhaps had they not only known each other longer than three months before the green card wedding, I would have made some effort in getting to know her. Or if they had anything in common, I would have spent more than a total of three hours with her. The limited time I had spent with her pointed to the fact that she was a gold digger looking for a sugar daddy. Now wasn't the time to gloat or mention it, though.

My chin tipped towards the potholders. "Can you help me carry the sweet potatoes next door?"

With the dinner rolls piled into the designated basket, I balanced the apple pie on top and led my dad back towards my apartment. It was the first time he had been in my place. Even when I was hospitalized, he only visited me in the ICU until I was discharged.

Ava was in a cute dress. She had vacuumed and tidied up while I was biking. She beamed at us as my dad followed in behind me. We set the food down as I introduced the two of them. I slipped my arm around her shoulder as they talked about the drive and the weather.

"I need to finish carving the turkey and dinner will be ready. Thanks for bringing the food over from next door."

"Can I get you anything to drink?"

"Water would be great."

It was a surprised, he was a scotch-when-stressed-out type of guy.

Squeezing Ava's hip, I scooted past her to grab my dad something to drink. My nose glided against her neck, and I kissed her quickly.

"Smells amazing, Babydoll."

The heat from her cheek against my lips made it difficult to pull away. My dad had retreated to the living room. I turned the television on and muted it so he could watch the bowl games.

We all sat down and ate dinner. My dad asked Ava a lot of questions about her childhood, her dad, his company, and finally ballet when she told him what she hoped her major would be. She held her own throughout his small interrogation.

Ava had brought our plates to the kitchen and was cutting into the apple pie when my dad turned to me.

"Did the DA get a hold of you?"

The good feeling I had from the dinner faded away with that question. I nodded. "Next Saturday at 9am."

He gave me a stoic nod. "Whatever their motive for attacking you, they will go to prison for it." The angry edge was all too familiar. I had heard it throughout my childhood. It was normally geared towards something I had done to disappoint him. My blood pressure spiked as my palms started to sweat.

"Even if it was my fault?" My own self-loathing, insecurity rearing its ugly face.

My dad narrowed his eyes on me. "How could it have been your fault?"

I shrugged. "The DA thinks she found someone that linked the attackers to me. She was asking some questions last month about someone we all knew and worked with."

He huffed out a breath. "What did you do?"

There it is. His good mood was spoiled as soon as he realized he was dining with me.

I rolled my lips in. "I honestly don't know. We share the same bookie."

An angry flush crawled up his neck. Ava cleared her throat as she came into the dining room with three plates balanced on her arms. She set the apple pie pieces in front of us and went back into the kitchen to grab some vanilla ice cream.

"What do you mean bookie?" His anger was under control, but barely.

I swallowed thickly. I don't know why I was telling him this. Maybe it was the hope that after a decent meal he wouldn't be too harsh on me. Maybe it was the fact that I wouldn't be able to hide the connection for too much longer.

"Tell him about your algorithm." Ava scooped herself some ice cream on her plate and mine. She motioned to my dad silently asking if he wanted his pie ala mode.

She seemed completely unperturbed. She read the tension in the room shift immediately and took charge. It was a skill she learned to make her childhood easier. It made me simultaneously annoyed with myself for putting her in the situation, angry at her mom and sister for forcing her to hone that survival skill, and relieved that she threw me a raft to keep myself from drowning.

When I didn't say anything right away, she took charge again. "It's amazing, really. He created a program that gathers all sorts of information to gauge a level of success. He used sporting events as a test subject to see if the AI engine was spitting out accurate predictions. Because Matt was already logging some statistics, he used his data as a control to confirm the predictions. He used a legal bookie to profit off his program. Once all the kinks were worked out, he plugged it into the stock market. It's impressive, you should be proud."

The way Ava explained my project made my stomach float and heart slam against my ribs. I fucking loved her. I wanted to yell it out loud, but I didn't want my dad privy to such a private moment. I had yet to fully understand the depth of my emotions towards her, but I fucking knew this was love, not an obsession, not an addiction, love.

My dad's gaze flitted between me and Ava. The angry red flush had toned down to a muted pink across his cheekbones. "Is that correct?"

I nodded. "It's more nuanced than that, but yeah, I saw an opportunity to profit while finishing the code. I successfully predicted every winner of every major sporting event last year until the attack. Most of the money I made I have poured into server space and memory storage because the data needed to understand the stock market really is robust. It's not only previous trends, but also political keywords, mental health of CEOs, whispers of class action lawsuits, viral social media trends, it's a lot to compute." Ava grinned at me and laced our fingers together on the table as she dug into her dessert.

My dad rubbed his jaw while he thought about what I was saying. "So, I don't need to worry about a gambling addiction?"

Ava giggled like a fucking schoolgirl and shook her head. "I think the only thing Henry is addicted to are my lemon bars." *And edibles, sex, swimming, and her, but who's really counting.*

The tension bracketing my dad's mouth loosened into a smile. "My mom used to make the best lemon bars."

And just like that, Ava charmed my dad, de-escalated a fight between us, and explained my life's work. I joked to Will about marrying Ava to stick it to Daphne, but Daphne was far far away from my motive to want to marry her. We were still way too young, but fuck if I was going to ever let her go.

Chapter 20

Henry

"Thank you so much for taking the time to see me today." Dorthy Waters sat down in the same conference room from a few weeks ago. There was no Matt today to help ease my nerves from the meeting. I had borrowed Ava's car to make the trip. Everyone else was either still sleeping or enjoying a lazy Saturday morning while I was stuck waiting for the other shoe to drop.

I nodded at her and wiped my sweating palms along my jeans. It was way too cold to be sweating. There were a few feet of snow on the ground, and another storm was predicted to blow through tonight. Ava had been fascinated with snow for the first few weeks, now she was over feeling cold all the time. We needed to go shopping for better winter shoes, but one thing at a time.

"I'm going to come right out and tell you what we have found," Dorthy said.

I braced myself, knowing whatever she was going to say was going to suck for my mental health.

"Raven Larmier is related to one of the assailants. She is the former stepsister of Alvin Washington. Their parents were married until about four years ago. They retained a close relationship until last year when they had a small falling out. I have asked Mr. Washington to explain what the falling out was about, but he has declined to say."

My blood was rushing through my ears making me only catch every other word.

Raven knew.

Dorthy continued as if she hadn't simply destroyed my brain. In no world would I think that Raven would intentionally hurt me. Herself, yep. Others, definitely. But not me.

"However, Dwayne Conyers was able to enlighten us in a bid to opt into a plea deal. Dwayne was the assailant who sustained a few broken bones. According to his intel he was only with Mr. Washington visiting for the weekend after his wife was away visiting family. He claims he was not a part of the planning and didn't intend to participate in the attack until he saw you fighting back. Seeing as how we do not have any eyewitness accounts to verify he didn't attack you before you attacked him, we are considering the plea deal. We can corroborate that his wife was visiting family in Macon, Georgia and text message conversations that he was invited to stay at Mr. Washington's residence." She looked up to me from her paperwork she was reading from.

A nip of pain lanced through my cheek as I bit harder.

"According to Mr. Conyers, Mr. Washington had been engaging in a sexual relationship with Ms. Larmier on and off for a few years. She broke it off with him to engage in a relationship with you. When you broke off the relationship she went back to Mr. Washington. Mr. Conyers conveyed a story shared by Mr. Washington that Ms. Larmier became increasingly inebriated and began to share your penchant to win big gambling events. Mr. Conyers shared that Mr. Washington wanted revenge on you 'stealing Raven away' and he also wanted to take advantage of your winning streak.

"Ms. Larmier was interviewed by Boulder PD last week in connection with your attack. According to the interview she had a feeling that her stepbrother may try to retaliate against you but asked him to 'avoid your face' if a fight came to blows. She relayed that she tried to talk Mr. Washington out of a fight and felt confident that he wouldn't attack you."

My shaking hands were tapping relentlessly along my thigh. I couldn't understand why Raven would do this. Sure, she was upset over the breakup, but the woman I had been in a relationship with would never have done this. She wouldn't hurt a fly before my relationship with her. The only pain she wanted was towards herself.

I was still reeling from the fact that she had stalked Lydia and drugged her, but I was also giving her the benefit of the doubt that it all was coincidental. Because if it were completely targeted and intentional it would mean that I was the reason for her changed personality. Her relationship with me had destroyed her enough to want her to destroy things around her. I ruined her, just like my dad had been telling me for years. I ruined a perfectly good person because I was reckless.

"We are not looking to press charges against Ms. Larmier, but I do need you to verify a few dates in the timeline of your relationship," Dorthy droned on.

I swallowed the thick knot in my throat. She passed me a few pieces of paper. One was a handwritten timeline of my entire relationship with Raven. The other pieces of paper were photographs of Raven with, who I assume was, her stepbrother. I tried to recall if she had ever mentioned that she had a stepbrother. It didn't ring a bell, but I did vaguely remember her mentioning her ex by name one time. She called him Vin, and I told her never to mention another man's name while she was tied to my bed.

I clasped my hands together after I passed the papers back over to Dorthy. Everything that had happened was my fault. If

I hadn't gloated about winning, Raven wouldn't have said a word. If I had treated the end of our relationship with a little more respect, maybe she wouldn't have gone directly into the arms of an abusive fuck. If I would have done anything differently, Matt wouldn't have lost his baseball career. But I didn't because I was tainted, wrong, and reckless.

I walked out of the office in a stupor. When I had begun my relationship with Raven there was so much sweet innocence about her. She was eager to please me because I praised her so much. She blossomed under my care, and I threw her aside.

I made her go crazy.

What if I did the same thing to Ava? What if my brain came up with some bullshit excuse to end things and the light, she illuminated dimmed? It would be my fault. It would be my doing, I would have stolen her light, her innocence. I would be the reason for anything bad happening to her. Just like my dad had been warning me for years.

The drive home was slow and quiet as I navigated the snowy streets. Ava's car had decent handling considering it was so small. I pushed my palms into my eyes after I parked. I felt restless, annoyed, angry. I wanted to crawl out of my skin and drown in chlorine.

Everything is my fault.

I rushed into my room to grab my gym bag. I had noticed right away that everything was too quiet in the apartment. There were breakfast rolls covered in the kitchen and if I didn't feel like my stomach was going to revolt, I would have eaten. Tama and Ava's doors were both propped open, indicating they were both gone. The only place Ava would have gone to would be the gym. I wanted to see her, verify that I wasn't going to ruin her, but I needed to get the itching sensations that were crawling up my arms and legs under control.

Snatching my bike, I went to swim laps until my limbs burned, and my lungs couldn't keep up anymore. I pulled my aching body up the pool wall and gasped for breath as I tried to drink water. What I needed to do is ask Raven if I ruined her. I needed to hear it from her mouth directly that I was the one that pushed the dominoes over.

Tracking her phone was too easy. I have no idea why she still had me as one of her FindMe friends considering I had disabled the function on my end. I frowned when I saw she was sitting outside the gym. Another surge of adrenaline coursed through me. Raven wasn't one to work out, so either she followed me here or she followed Ava. Either way, it wasn't good.

With my dry sweats and a beanie over my wet hair to keep it from freezing in the winter air, I marched out of the gym. She was sitting on a bench facing the gym doors. It was way too fucking cold out to be sitting on a bench.

She had her head bent down as she looked at her phone. I could see the puffs of air clouding her face. She looked up when I approached her, a smile stretched wide.

"Fancy seeing you here." She adjusted her bag to the concrete. She was dressed in thick layers; her nose and cheeks were both pink from the weather.

"What are you doing here?" My legs were burning from the punishment I had put myself through, but I didn't sit as she indicated for me to.

"Waiting for a ride."

"From whom?"

She smirked at me. "Don't be jealous. You want me back; all you need to do is ask."

I gritted my teeth and attempted to ignore her. "Vin coming to get you?"

Her eyes widened a fraction before she slowly shook her head. "No, he is busy today."

"But that's who you are with, right?"

Her jaw clenched as her eyes squinted. "Just because you threw me away doesn't mean someone else didn't want me."

My breath clouded my view of her. "Tell me one thing, Raven." I steeled myself before I blurted out my fears. "Was I so awful to you that you decided having me killed was the only way to move on?"

Air gushed from her lungs as she shook her head. "That's not what happened."

A humorless smile tipped my lips. "But you know exactly what happened, right?"

Her eyes watered as she nodded.

I huffed out another strangled breath. "Why?"

She flinched at my tone that sounded like a wounded animal more than anything. Her shoulders had rolled in on themselves. "I didn't want you to get hurt, Henry. Believe me when I say, what Vin did was not what I wanted."

My throat knotted. "I ruined you, didn't I? I threw you aside and you changed."

Her brows furrowed as she shook her head. "I'm not ruined. And if you want to make amends, we can be together. We were so good together."

I tipped my head back to control the thoughts swirling in my head. I snapped my attention back to her face. "I told you; I'm with someone. I don't see that changing any time soon."

She scoffed, stood up, and stopped in front of me. "We were good together. I was happy, you were happy. What Vin did was a misunderstanding. I'm sorry for that, I really am. But if it's the catalyst for us to be together then I don't regret it."

I staggered back. "I was in a fucking coma, Raven. My cousin lost his career. Tama was fucking traumatized. You don't regret your part in it all?"

She winced and then rolled her shoulders back. "Not if it means we get to be together."

My eyes narrowed into slits. "We are never getting back together. Leave me alone. Leave my girlfriend alone. Vanish from my life and I will do the same for you."

Her eyes welled again as she shook her head. "You don't mean that. You have a shiny new toy, but you'll get bored of her. What we had was real. It was soul-deep real."

Walking away was the mature option. I wanted to rage at her, diminish our relationship but I'd already damaged her enough. "Forget you ever knew me."

I unlocked my bike and headed home without looking towards Raven. She yelled some nonsense in my direction, but I felt too raw to understand the words she said. It was too much. My mind was a mess; thoughts were ripping through my brain at such a fast clip I couldn't hang on to a single one for long enough to consider what I was thinking.

Rushing up the steps to my apartment, I hoped Ava was home. I wanted to feel her against my chest and breathe in her lemony scent. I needed the calm she gave me.

She wasn't home yet. I settled for a shower, staying way too long in the hot water. My phone buzzed on the bathroom counter.

Ava: How did your interview go?

352

I wanted to be home when you
got there but I was feeling
inspired. I'll be home soon.

I could hear her message as if she spoke it directly in my ear. Even knowing she wanted to communicate with me made me feel better. I wasn't so damaged that she didn't want me. I hadn't ruined her to the point of crazy like I had Raven.

Me: Terrible. I'll tell you about it
when you get home. I went to
the gym to swim, but didn't see
you. Do you want me to drive
over to get you?

Ava: Terrible how? And honestly, if
it's not too much trouble it would be
amazing if you come get me. I'm
freezing and my shoes got wet walking
here.

Me: Give me five minutes. Stay
inside and keep a look out for me.

I pulled on fresh sweats and grabbed her keys. A feeling of calm washed over me with every foot closer I got to Ava. Raven was gone by the time I had gotten back. Ava floated towards me with a smile that pushed her flushed cheeks over the edge of her wrapped scarf that hid half of her face. I stepped out of the car and pulled her against my chest, snagged the scarf down, and tipped her face to mine so I could kiss her. Every swipe of her tongue against mine made me feel more at peace.

"Hi," she whispered against my lips. I grinned and tugged her to the car. She giggled as I kissed her again as she pulled her seatbelt on. "What has gotten into you?"

I perked a brow. "I need to disassociate, and it turns out my gorgeous girlfriend is my favorite way to do that."

She twisted her lips to the side. "You want to tell me about the interview on the way home and then tie me to your bed?"

She was so fucking perfect for me that she knew when I needed to have some semblance of control.

I gave her the brief rundown on what Dorthy Waters had shared. I didn't mention running into Raven afterward. I didn't see the point. Ava was so indignant about the whole thing.

"I can't believe anyone would want to hurt you. Ugh, god. Don't let me in the trial because I will stab everyone that had a hand at hurting you." It was so cute to see her anger. It was like a kitten hissing at a tiger.

Having Ava in my bed was the exact thing I needed. After an hour of teasing her, I took a small break to get a sip of water. We weren't going to be interrupted. Tama was out with Rhys. Will and Lily were probably fucking all day since her season was finally over. Matt and Nicole went to Breckenridge for a weekend getaway.

Gulping my water, I admired a sleeping Ava in my bed. The blankets were tucked neatly around her, but I could see her spread-eagle form beneath the down comforter. Her face was turned to the side; her hair was fanned behind her across my pillow. She looked like a fallen angel. My phone lit up with a message.

My eyes rolled. It was a social media message as opposed to a text. I had a feeling it was Raven attempting to get in contact with me since I had blocked her number after the last interaction with her after the pub parking lot kiss. Curiosity got to me when I saw it was a message from Daphne Nichols.

What does this psychopath want?

Daphne: You do not have me fooled for
one moment that you are with Ava for
real. I have been asking around the Baylor
campus and I have learned some interesting
things. For instance, there isn't an Ava Reiser
enrolled there. Curious. Then I investigated
you. Even more interesting was the fact that
you also aren't enrolled at Baylor. But you
know what is the most interesting? You are
both enrolled at Pineview University.

Oh fuck. Not the message I thought I was going to receive from her, that's for sure. What a toxic harpy to dig this much into her sister's life. She clearly was hellbent on ruining whatever made Ava happy.

Me: What do you want?

Daphne: It's simple. You will break off this
ridiculous ruse with my sister or I will tell
my parents where my sister actually is.

Me: This is ridiculous. She's crazy
about me. I'm crazy about her. I'm
not going to break up with her. Why
are you doing this?

Daphne: Because my sister is a liar and
I don't think she should get away with it.
Break it off or I tell my parents.

Me: It's about jealousy. No one

*likes a jealous bitch. You see your
sister is with someone that pays
attention and adores her and your
reaction is to want it gone. At least
when you pulled this shit with Will
I could see it as a misguided attempt
to get your friend and him back
together, but this? No, now I get it.
You can't stand to see either of them
happy. You're a miserable piece of
shit.*

*Daphne: Do you understand what will
happen to Ava if you don't comply?*

*Me: Fuck all the way off with your
threats. I'm not going to break it off
with her. Get off your high horse.
Leave her the fuck alone. Maybe if
you paid more attention to your
husband he wouldn't have to
drink so heavily to stand to be
around you.*

*Daphne: And you claimed to care about
her?*

*Daphne: I will ensure my parents cut her
off. Do you want that on your hands? All
you have to do is break it off. If you don't,
I'll tell them. I'll give you until the end of the
semester to make the right decision.*

*Me: So let me get this straight. You
want me to break up with your sister
or you will tell your parents. You need*

356

*serious fucking help. She hasn't done
a fucking thing to you to deserve this.
And what, you want me to punish her
on your behalf. Get fucked.*

*Me: What should I say? Ava, you are
too clingy and not good enough for
me. I want to see other people. No
that's what your ex says about you.*

*Me: I thought you were a cunt before
this, but seriously you are sick in
the head.*

*Daphne: Say whatever you need to say.
She deserves to know the truth, however
you feel.*

*Me: The truth? You've swallowed
all the crazy pills if you think me
lying to her and telling her I want
to break up would be anywhere near
what I want. The fucking truth is I
Love Ava. I want to be with her. And
after this I will do everything in my
power to ensure she never fucking
talks to you again.*

Me: Get fucked.

*Daphne: Wait until the end of the semester
so her grades don't suffer.*

My chest heaved as I blocked Daphne on ever being able to contact me again. She was fucking nuts and was actively looking for ways to hurt her sister. What a sick, twisted, bitch.

I took a few calming breaths. This was turning out to be a shitty day. I didn't want to burden Ava with this. She was way too stressed about the audition and her finals. Her knowing that her sister was trying to sabotage our relationship and was willing to tell her parents about her duplicity would push her over the edge. She had only recently started to sleep through the night again after the last visit to Dallas.

I had suspected Daphne had said something to her that was stressing her out, now it was confirmed. I wanted to crawl into Ava's head and pluck out her insecurities. I wanted to burrow myself into her marrow like she was in mine so she would know that I wasn't going anywhere.

Ava

I rolled quietly over to my side to observe Henry while he slept. He looked so at peace. It was such a stark difference to how he had been when I saw him arguing with Raven at the gym. I wasn't trying to snoop. I had taken a moment outside the studio to fill up my water bottle. The water fountain was right next to the window that overlooked the parking lot where I saw Henry talking to Raven.

Too frozen to move, I tried to read all the body language from so far away. It was clear he was pissed at her. I wasn't worried that they would see me spying because the glass was one-way. I tried to pry when I was done dancing. I was surprised that he shared with me what the DA had said about Raven's part in his attack.

It was a disappointment that he didn't mention arguing with her. I wished he had volunteered the information, but then I would have admitted to seeing them together. And I knew he was sensitive about me seeing him with her. Not that I didn't understand. No one wanted a repeat of the last time Raven darkened our doorstep.

So, I didn't push about him not mentioning that he confronted Raven. It bothered me, but I decided that if it was anything serious, he would have told me. I also didn't tell him that Raven was inside the gym lobby when he pulled up. I acted like I didn't recognize her as I strode past her and into Henry's waiting arms. Him kissing me so aggressively was a welcome surprise, one I wasn't keen to end. Call me petty, whatever. I wanted her to know that he was taken, and she needed to back off.

The overwhelming urge to wake Henry up and tell him that I loved him nearly paralyzed me. I stopped myself, justifying my decision to remain quiet until the end of the semester. I'd tell Will about me and Henry and allow the chips to fall. I would wait for him to catch up with me on how he felt, and I would relish in the feeling of safety and security of being in his bed every night.

I could wait another two weeks before nearly everything was out in the open. I could be patient. I didn't have winter break plans. According to Jacob, Mom and Dad enjoyed their Thanksgiving vacation and hadn't mentioned anything about Christmas. The last place I wanted to be for the holiday was with my mom. Daphne and Russel were planning on being at my parents' house for the holiday since they spent Thanksgiving with his family.

I would be happy to never see my sister again. I needed to think of a viable excuse to not go home. Or maybe I'd go stay with Jacob for the three-week vacation. Henry was flying to Paris to visit with his mom. He hadn't invited me, which was fine. Sort of. Okay, it hurt that he didn't invite me when a few weeks ago he was making plans for us to go to Paris and Sorrento.

I swallowed down the anxiety as to why he didn't ask me to meet his mother. Maybe Daphne was right after all. Henry and I were not going to last in the long term.

My fingernails dug into my palms, I hoped to pain away the intrusive thoughts. I hated that Daphne had sowed the seeds of doubt. She didn't know the first thing about my relationship with Henry and yet a part of my brain invited her toxic opinions in.

Think about something else.

I chanted in my head until that was all I was thinking about, something else. And it was then that I realized that I hadn't needed to smoke in months. Not since I started to share Henry's bed. He took the anxiety away. He calmed my brain down. He made me happy.

Focus on that.

My breathing evened out as I thought about how much Henry had impacted my life in such a short amount of time. He empowered me and worshipped me. He made me feel seen and heard. He made me feel loved and cared for. And I was pretty sure I was helping him too. Tama told me that she had never seen him so happy and well rested. We were good for each other. That meant something, right?

Chapter 21

Henry

"You have your final and then your audition, right?" I passed Ava a glass of orange juice. I had attempted to make her some toast, but I burned the fuck out of it. I needed to pay better attention if I ever wanted to feed myself food that wasn't prepared in the microwave.

Ava nodded her head nervously. Things had been a little weird since the DA interview and my altercation with Raven. Ava had been more reserved with me than before. She told me that she was stressed, and I didn't want to add to it. I also worried that Daphne was fucking with her since I had made it clear I wasn't the avenue for that nonsense.

I had asked her a week ago if Daphne had left her alone. She gave me a wide-eyed stare for a few moments too long before nodding and saying she hadn't spoken to Daphne since Dallas. The rest of my roommates were practically ghosts.

Tama was burning the candle at both ends. She was spending way too much time with Rhys while also keeping up with her 18 credit hours' worth of classes. She had been consistently taking 18 hours a semester and taking summer classes so she could 'catch up' to people her own age. I understood it, sort of, but I didn't think it made a lot of sense for her to take on so much. We were still young. So what if she graduated at 24 instead of 22, it's not the end of the world.

I only saw glimpses of Will at the gym and then at dinner. Otherwise, he was in the office in their apartment studying. The other girls were happy to stay by their men as they worked themselves to the bone. Matt had a decent reprieve from traveling but was spending a lot of time conditioning his pitchers. And Ava had been spending every spare moment in a dance studio.

I had watched her routine last week, and I had to stop myself from having an emotional reaction. She was such a beautiful dancer, and her choreography was stunning. I had no doubt she was going to kill it. She was a little worried about her math final, but I had helped her work through some of the problems she was nervous about.

"It's a closed audition, so you can't watch me. But I'll be home right after."

I grinned at her and leaned forward to kiss her mouth. "And we are telling Will today?"

It was the last day of her finals. I still had another one tomorrow, but after her audition she was officially finished with her first semester of college. She had already signed up for second semester classes. We synced our schedules as much as possible, so I was looking forward to having lazy mornings with her Tuesday and Thursday.

She chewed her lip and nodded. "I don't know what I'm going to say but let me take the lead. I think maybe ripping the bandage off at dinner would be good."

I smirked. "Because there will be more witnesses and people to stop him from beating me to a pulp?"

She giggled. "Something like that. I made his favorite dessert, chocolate chip cupcakes with peanut butter frosting to soften him up."

I grunted and kissed her again. "Are you sure you are ready?" I was the one that was pushing it, but I had backed off a lot since Thanksgiving because I didn't want to pressure her anymore. She had too much on her plate, and I was going to go at her pace.

Her brows puckered at my question, but her alarm went off before she answered. "That's my warning alarm. I need to go."

I walked her to the door, giving her one more kiss before she left. I didn't have to leave for another forty-five minutes. Her audition was almost two hours after her last final, but she said she needed to spend that time warming up and getting her head in the game. I took it to mean she didn't want me to distract her.

After my final, I biked over to the gym for a long swim. I was too keyed up about telling Will and nervous for Ava. I wanted her to do well. Her getting that scholarship meant that Daphne's threats were less than worthless. If Ava got a full ride and was cut off, I would pay for her housing and food. I would take care of her.

If she didn't get the scholarship… that was what I had been dedicating all my free time to. I had made a decent amount in the stock market. I was able to set money aside to pay for her second year. I still had a way to go for her third and fourth years, but by then I would be finished with school and have access to my trust fund. I'd pay for her schooling. I'd take care of her.

The gym was blissfully empty as I swam my laps, unfortunately they had started to prepare the pool for the winter break which meant way too much fucking chlorine. I powered through for an hour before my brain felt like it was splitting open from the chemical smell.

The pounding in my head made me squeeze one eye shut as I biked home. Walking as fast as my tired legs allowed towards my closet, I grabbed my supply of edibles. I hadn't been taking them as often because Ava helped me sleep at night. It was only when a migraine started to come on that I took one now.

I chewed through the entire gummy and turned the water on in my shower to clean off the strong chemicals that were etched into my skin. My migraine turned into a dull roar by the time I had turned my water off.

Ava was supposed to audition any second now. I grabbed my phone to message her but stopped at the unread text on my phone.

Unknown number: Are you going to break it off?

Fucking Daphne. I knew it was her based on the Dallas area code. What I didn't know was how she got my number. I rolled my head back, trying to relieve the tension that was building in my neck.

I pulled my clothes on, trying to tame down the anger that was billowing through my veins. I stepped out of my room and stood in the center of the living room. My hand was clutching my phone painfully tight. I needed to wish Ava luck. I needed to respond back to Daphne. I needed to calm the fuck down because my blood pressure was making my headache ratchet back up again.

Me: Go to fucking hell.

My apartment door swung open. I glanced up to see Will with Matt striding in right on his heels. I nodded at them and went to text Ava when Will snatched my phone from my hand and threw it hard against the wall.

"What the fuck?" My lip was curled in confusion for half a second before I clocked the fury on Will's face.

This is going to hurt.

Will pulled his arm back and punched me hard in the eye. I stumbled back a few steps. Blood leaked down my cheek.

"I deserved that."

"How fucking long have you been taking advantage of my sister?"

I glanced up to see my cousin holding Will back from punching me again. It was a solid thing to do because Will looked like he wanted to kill me.

"Ava and I have been dating since the end of September." I winced when blood dripped into my eye.

He split my brow open.

"Not anymore. You two are breaking up, today. She's too young for you. You're too *you* for her."

I snorted and went over to the kitchen to grab some paper towels to stem the blood that was gushing down my face. "I'm not breaking up with her," I said simply. I was surprised by the amount of blood pouring from the cut. The paper towel had already bled through.

"Yes, you the fuck are. Break up or I will tell my dad where Ava's been living," he threatened.

I scoffed. "Daphne already tried that threat. I thought you were better than your narcissistic sister, but I guess not." Will blanched, but I continued. "Listen, I know you are pissed. I know you don't think I am right for your sister. And I know that I deserved you sucker punching me in the face, which is why I didn't fight back. But I'm not breaking it off with her. And the fact you are threatening to tell your parents is such a low fucking blow. I'm surprised you went along with Daphne's plan. I didn't think you actually liked her."

"What the fuck are you talking about? I haven't spoken to Daphne since her wedding," Will seethed.

I looked over to him. Matt still had Will's arms pinned to his side. My eye was swelling shut, but from my limited point of view I could see genuine confusion.

"Huh, you're telling the truth. Well, Daphne has been threatening to tell her parents for weeks and said the only thing that will stop her from telling Kim where Ava has been living is if I broke up with her. Which is so fucking shitty because I'm in love with Ava. And I'm pretty sure she's in love with me, so for both of you to want to take that away from her is beyond selfish."

Will straightened his back and gaped at me. "You don't love her."

I rolled my good eye and winced when the pain shot through my swollen eye. "Yes, I do. What you saw in front of your dad was real. I care about her, I love her, and I have no intention of breaking it off with her. And if you want to be the one that tells her parents and *betrays* her like that." I shook my head, my vision swam. I was pretty sure he gave me another fucking concussion. "Then you aren't the man I thought you were."

I squinted at my friend. There were now two of them. I swayed a little on my feet and grabbed the counter for support. My migraine was pounding in an unforgiving rhythm against my brain.

"Don't turn this around on me. You both lied to me for months," Will said.

I smirked. "We didn't, actually. You didn't want to believe us."

Matt clicked his tongue at my argument. It was weak. He had already poked holes in it, but I couldn't stop myself from joking, even a little to rile Will up. Probably not the smartest move, but I wasn't thinking straight.

"You didn't exactly make it easy to tell you the truth, which by the way, she was planning on telling you tonight."

My eyes squeezed shut as a wave of nausea hit my stomach. "How'd you find out if Daphne didn't tell you?" I managed. I braced on the counter and slumped my face towards the cool surface.

"Whoa, cuz, are you okay?" Matt asked. "Oh fuck," he hissed as my arms gave out leaving me splayed out onto the counter. "Hey buddy, how many fingers am I holding up?"

I bleared my eyes open. "They're two of you Matty," I slurred.

My cousin growled. "I fucking told you to be careful. He's still healing from a concussion, and it looks like you gave him another one. Be pissed all you want, but this is done now. Their relationship is theirs to figure out," Matt said. Arms loop around my stomach and heaved me up.

"You said not to punch him in his vital organs because those were healing, and I *did* pull my punch. I expected him to dodge it a little."

"S'kay. I deserved it. Whotoldyou?" My slurring was getting worse.

"Anonymous text message with pictures of you and Ava kissing all over campus."

"Huh, not Daphne, then," I mumbled.

"Okay, buddy, let's get you to the training room. I'll call the head trainer and have her look at you. I think you need stitches above your eye, and you'll be on concussion watch tonight."

I hummed. "Ava will take care of me. My edible kicked in, the pain's not so bad."

Matt cursed, Will growled. My legs stumbled forward as the cool rush of winter air breezed against my face. It felt good against the open wound.

"Tell Ava good luck." I passed out in my cousin's truck.

Ava

I paced back and forth waiting for my turn to dance in front of Mallory. There were four judges total including her. The hallway had twenty different dancers in it when I arrived.

I shook my fingers out and reached for my phone in my bag. I half expected to find something from Henry wishing me luck. I blew out a breath when I saw there was nothing. It didn't mean anything. He had his own final and he was probably swimming. It wasn't a big deal. It didn't stop me from reaching out to him though.

> *Me: I'm so nervous. I think I'm going to throw up.*

I stared at my screen and willed him to answer back but he didn't. I put my phone away and resumed my pacing before stopping in front of my bag again and dropping down into a stretch. I figured if I were close enough to my tote, I would at least hear my phone buzz with his message of luck.

I went through my stretching sequence trying to calm my brain down, but my thoughts kept flitting back to my phone. I unzipped my bag and checked for any messages I may have missed. Still nothing. My nerves were fluttering along my stomach, making my hands shake.

It wasn't only the audition that had my stomach knotting. It was the fact that I had been seeing a lot of Raven over the past few weeks. Even as I was walking into the auditorium I could have sworn, I saw her watching me from the parking lot. Maybe I was being paranoid. Maybe it wasn't actually her and I was seeing things because I was so paranoid about her and Henry getting back together again.

After another few minutes of fretting, I snatched my phone back up.

> *Me: I know you are probably busy and this seems so needy but I would appreciate if you could wish me luck.*

I wished immediately that I could unsend it.

> *Me: Ignore me, I'm being crazy and dramatic and I hope you killed your final.*

I chewed my lip when he didn't refute my messages and whimpered to myself as I stowed my phone away. *Focus.* It was probably nothing. It was fine. He was busy. He wasn't with Raven. *Deep breath.*

"Ava Reiser," Mallory called from the auditorium doorway.

A gush of air released from my lungs, and I grabbed my bag from the floor. My phone began to vibrate as soon as my bag was against my hip. I wanted to check, but I knew it was Henry. He was probably wishing me luck, telling me I wasn't being crazy or dramatic, and explaining why he wasn't answering my messages for the past twenty minutes. The thought calmed my nerves.

I set my bag down on the steps leading up to the stage. I had already turned in my choreography and submitted the music I was going to dance to. I took my position at the center of the stage and waited for my music to play.

You know the moment you come out of a hyperfocus, and you look around yourself and think, man how did I get here? That was how I felt as the last chord of my song rang through the auditorium. Mallory and three others were on their feet clapping. My cheeks hurt from how hard I was smiling. I had crushed it. My performance was as flawless as I could have made it. Every tumble and jump landed correctly, I had kept my toes and fingers aligned with my limbs. And most importantly, I had felt the soul of the music.

"That was astounding my lost ballerina," Mallory called from her chair.

I stood up from my position and bowed to the judges before scooping up my bag and hurrying off stage. All the other dancers had left the same entrance I had gone in. Mallory stopped me to let me know when I should check my student email.

I pushed the exit doors open and reveled in the cool air against my heated cheeks. I had nailed it and that alone made me proud. I dropped my bag to the ground to rifle through it to get to my phone. I frowned at the sheer volume of missed messages. I had only been away from my phone for seven minutes. My brow pinched when I saw none were from Henry, all were from Daphne, my mom, and my dad.

Daphne: I tried to warn you that it wasn't going to last.

She attached a screenshot from her social media chat. I blinked rapidly trying to clear my eyes as I read through the messages. My heart started to pound wildly out of my chest.

Henry: This is ridiculous. She's crazy

Henry: It's about jealousy. No one likes a jealous bitch.

Daphne: And you claimed to care about her?

Henry: What should I say? Ava, you are too clingy and not good enough for me. I want to see other people.

Daphne: Say whatever you need to say. She deserves to know the truth, however you feel.

Daphne: Wait until the end of the semester so her grades don't suffer.

I let out a slow breath. That didn't make any sense. He doesn't feel like that, right? And why would he go to Daphne of all people? But the more I stared at the screenshot, the more I knew it was Henry's profile responding back.

Me: I don't believe you. He wouldn't

do that. He wouldn't say that.

*Daphne: Believe it. He wanted you out
of his life so badly, he told mom and dad
that you aren't at Baylor. They know
you lied and are at Pineview and
have been all semester.*

My lungs were sipping air in, not able to keep up with the influx of oxygen my brain desperately needed. That couldn't be true. Except I had so many messages from my parents. I sucked in a shuddering breath.

*Mommy Dearest: You ungrateful lying
brat. How dare you live a double life.
After all the shit your father put us
through you went and did the same
thing?*

*Mommy Dearest: We aren't funding
your lies. Consider yourself dead to
me and your father. There is no
excuse. I'm ashamed that I ever
had you.*

*Mommy Dearest: Don't think for one
second you are ever stepping foot in
my home again.*

And on and on the vitriol went. My fingers were shaking violently as I switched to Dad's messages.

*Dad: I don't understand why you
lied. Why didn't you tell me the truth?*

I thought you, of all my children, would have come to me. I can't believe you did this. You destroyed the trust we had in you. Your mother is furious.

Dad: I can't pay for you to go to school there. She's cancelling the credit card in your name next week.

Dad: Call me kiddo, let's try to talk this out. I'm still in the office so we can speak freely.

My legs felt numb as I walked to my car. I was using Lily's parking spot today as she didn't need to use it until tomorrow. I slumped into the driver's seat. It was still cold, but at least the bitter wind stopped whipping my hair around as soon as the door slammed shut. With shaking fingers, I dialed my dad's number.

"Ava." My name came out like an admonishment.

I was too overwhelmed to feel much. The fact that my parents knew where I was, was proof that Henry had told them. It was proof of what Daphne had told me.

"I wanted to be my own person," I whispered on the phone.

It was quiet enough on the other side of the line that I could hear my dad breathe. "I understand, kid, but there were so many lies. You could have told me. Why didn't you tell me?"

I sucked in a breath. "Because you always side with mom. You never believe me. You don't listen to me when I need someone to listen to. You listen to everything mom says. I can't live like that anymore."

My dad blew out a deep breath. "I know I made some mistakes with you kids, but honey, so many things could have gone wrong. I'm assuming you drove to Boulder by yourself. That's a long drive; anything could have happened."

I nodded at the windshield. "Yeah, Jacob was worried." I knew it was the wrong thing to say as soon as my dad sucked in a breath.

"Jacob knew?"

I squeezed my eyes shut. "He did."

My dad made a noise like a dying animal before huffing out another deep breath. "This is what you are going to do. You are going to go to the bursar's office. You are going to pay for next semester. Then you are going to come home so we can discuss this face to face with your mother."

My stomach dropped. "I can go to the bursar's office, but dad, mom told me that I'm dead to her. She told me specifically not to come home," I said quietly.

I don't know why I sounded so calm when my world was crashing down around me. I guess my anxiety was good for one thing. I had already imagined every worst-case scenario, and I never expected to have my dad's support. It was a win, all things considered.

"Oh honey, I'll talk to your mom," he said quietly. "I'm still really upset with you, but it's mostly because I've been replaying all the things that could have gone wrong. And why did I get charged $6000 for Baylor and I got a doctor's bill from you breaking your thumb. How did you pull all that off?"

I blew a raspberry out and told him everything. He was quiet as I word-vomited the whole trip to Dallas. I left out the racy bits about my relationship with Henry. I didn't mention Henry at all because that relationship was over. He wanted me to disappear from his life so badly that he told my parents. He knew there was a high likelihood of me being cut off, he did it anyway.

I looked at the clock and winced. "Dad, the bursar's office closes in thirty minutes."

"Okay, honey. Lay low for a few days. Maybe stay in Boulder for the holiday. Or you know, I heard you and Monroe are close. Maybe head to Manhattan. I don't want you to be alone." He was taking the same tone he took with me when he found out I was depressed. I'm sure he was worried I was going to self-harm. I wasn't, I didn't feel enough to care about that.

My phone dropped into my lap as I cupped my face. After a few minutes of collecting myself, I stepped out of my car and walked as quickly as my numb legs could carry me to the bursar's office. There wasn't a line. And they were more than happy to take my dad's money.

It wasn't until I got back to my car that the pang of loss hit. The only person I wanted to talk to was Henry, and it was clear he was planning on ending it.

I walked slowly up the steps to my apartment. Will startled me by sitting in the living room. The anger on his face meant that he knew. I don't know how he knew, but he did.

"You have something you want to tell me?" He looked like he was trying to compose himself, but the tension was radiating off him.

I chewed on my cheek for a moment before I figured, what the hell, everything else is out in the open. "Henry and I were dating. We started at the end of September. I didn't tell you because you'd be a little bitch about it. It doesn't matter though because I'm ending it."

Will squinted at me and cracked his neck to relieve some of the tension.

"So anyway, if that's all, I need to pack. I'm done for the semester. I've had a shit day, and I don't want to be around anyone right now."

"I don't understand. Are you breaking things off because of me?"

I rolled my eyes at him. "Nope, he betrayed me. I don't want to talk about it. Please leave."

He stood up but didn't make a move for the door. "You heading home for winter break?"

Pain lanced through me. I didn't have a home anymore. I nodded anyway. "Something like that."

Will blew out a breath. "I only wanted to protect you," he said quietly.

I blinked at him, numbness taking over again. "I'll see you at the end of break." I turned away from him and marched into my bedroom.

I yanked down my luggage and started packing. I didn't know where I was going. Some place a little warmer than here, maybe. Manhattan had its merits because Monroe was there, but Lily was probably going to join her, which meant Will would too. And no matter how much I loved my brother, I didn't want to be in the same state as him.

The front door to my apartment opened and closed. I held my breath, listening for any footsteps heading towards my room, but there was nothing. I closed my eyes and sat on my bed.

I told Will I was going to end things with Henry, but that was mostly so he didn't have to end things with me. At least I could control the narrative of saying it was a mutual decision to end whatever we had. I needed to get away for a few weeks. Distance would clear my head. Next semester I'd deal with the consequences of living with an ex-boyfriend. I was mature enough to handle it.

As far as my world falling apart, at least I still had my dad. He couldn't be out in the open about his support of me, but he'd be there if I needed him. My mom was stubborn enough to hold steady on her desire to cut me out of her life. How she went no-contact with my nonna was proof of that.

Now there's an idea.

With a new purpose I packed clothes for cool weather versus the freezing bullshit I was dealing with. I grabbed my passport and when I made my way back to my car, I called the one person I had been missing for two years.

"Ava Bella?"

"Hey Nonna, are you up for some company?"

Chapter 22

Henry

It was somber when Matt and I made it back to the apartment. I was worried as fuck about Ava. I hadn't heard about how her audition turned out and every time I asked Matt, he told me that no one was answering their phones.

My head was pounding, but fortunately I wasn't concussed. Will split my eyebrow, requiring five stitches, and my blood sugar was low from having a small breakfast, missing lunch, and then swimming for an hour straight. I was also a little dehydrated, but it could have been worse. All things considered I had Matt on my side, and he told me that he'd make sure Will backs off. He was pretty pissed about the sucker punch at first, but he chilled out after it was determined to not be a concussion.

I stormed through my living room and went straight for Ava's room.

"Babydoll?" I called out when I didn't see her immediately. I checked her bathroom and closet and then looped back out of her room to check mine. It was also bereft of her. Tama cleared her throat from the doorway.

"How's the head?"

"I'll live, where's my girlfriend?"

Tama looked to the side and winced. "According to Will, she left to go home."

The air was sucked from my lungs. I knew for a fucking fact she wasn't planning on going home. I shook my head. "She wouldn't do that."

Tama chewed on the corner of her lips. "She told Will she was going to break up with you today."

And the hits keep coming.

I shook my head again. "Not possible. There's no reason for us to break up. Why did she say she was breaking up with me?"

Lily sighed in the doorway. "She told Will that you betrayed her, I've been texting her, but she isn't answering. Will said she was heading home. She packed her bag and left."

My brow furrowed, my brain wasn't computing. "I didn't betray her. The only thing I didn't do was wish her good luck but that's because Will demolished my phone against the wall."

Lily winced. "I'll keep trying to text her, but she isn't answering. Will's on the phone with Jacob. Apparently, her parents found out about where she's been living."

"Fucking Daphne. She found out and told her parents. She wanted me to break it off with Ava, but I refused."

Lily's lip curled. "Why would she care?"

I threw my hands in the air as my cousin's head appeared over Lily.

"I guess it's a fucking party in here. Everyone out." I waved my hands to corral everyone away from my space. I followed Tama out of my room and slumped into my gaming chair. Will wasn't looking at me, but at least he didn't look too pissed any more.

"To answer your question." I turned to Lily. "Daphne doesn't want Ava to be happy. She's been gaslighting her for years. She wants Ava miserable, and she saw that I was making her happy. She attempted to blackmail me, and it didn't work. She found out a few weeks ago that Ava was here with me."

Will cursed under his breath and snatched his phone up. I heard bits and pieces of his conversation with his brother Jacob. I squinted at Will. "Are you sure Daphne isn't the one that told you about me and Ava."

Will shook his head. "Unless she's been on campus for the past few weeks, no. All the pictures have snow in the background."

I tipped my head back. "What's the phone number you got those pictures from?"

Will pulled his phone out and a few moments later he recited a familiar number to me.

"That's Raven's," Tama whispered.

I stared at my shoes. "She wanted you to break us up. God, what a fucking psychopath. Not only did she partially orchestrate the attack, now this," I muttered.

"Wait, what?" Matt yelled.

I shared my conversation with the DA and then my own conversation I had with Raven right after.

Matt groaned and turned back to me. "It doesn't make any of it your fault. You have to believe that. Raven was sick before you and she was sick after you. And her stepbrother is clearly unwell."

None of this conversation was making me feel an ounce of relief. I wanted to know where my girl was because she was going through some shit and I wanted to support her. I wanted her to know that I didn't betray her, that it was Daphne, but I had no fucking phone.

"Can someone take me to the airport?" I interrupted Matt who explained to the apartment about my algorithm.

Lily's brow furrowed. "Don't you have a final tomorrow?"

"I couldn't care less about my fucking final. My girlfriend is alone after her family found out about her living here. Guaranteed her mom disowned her. I have my doubts that she is heading home. I need to find her. She thinks I betrayed her. I didn't. I need to see her and explain to her what a crazy bitch her sister is. So, who is taking me to the airport?"

Matt tipped his head back. "I'll take you tomorrow after your final. We don't know where she is going. If she isn't heading to her parents' house, where would she go?" he asked the room.

"Jacob's?" Lily asked.

Will shook his head. "She didn't call him to tell him she was heading there. Jacob told me that when dad spoke to her, he told her to go visit Monroe and lay low until her mom calms down."

Lily pulled her phone out and called her sister. I recognized Monroe's voice, but she sounded tired. Not that big of a surprise considering she was fairly pregnant.

"I haven't heard from her. I can give her a call when we get off the phone," she said. Lily ended her conversation quickly.

"That doesn't mean she didn't go to New York. She didn't tell anyone she was heading to San Diego when she surprised me earlier this year. She could call Monroe when she gets there." I shook my head. I didn't believe that for a second.

I dropped my face into my palms and winced when my fingers touched the stitches. "If no one is taking me to the fucking airport can someone at least take me to a store so I can get a new phone?"

Matt stood up. "Let's go."

I followed him as the rest of my roommates stayed put. "Let me know as soon as anyone hears from Ava." My cousin followed me out of the apartment.

I slept like shit. None of the countless messages I sent Ava were delivered. When neither Monroe nor Jacob confirmed that Ava made it to their homes, I started to panic. I had no idea whether I failed or passed my final. It didn't matter to me. I could have gotten a zero and I still would have passed the class.

Lily was waiting for me when I got home. "Where is she?"

She rolled her lips in for a moment. "I still don't know. She text messaged me an hour ago and said she was safe with someone who would never hurt her. She also sent me a screenshot from her conversation with Daphne."

She winced. "Did you ask Daphne what you should say to break things off with Ava?"

My whole face twisted in confusion. "No, let me see the message."

She hesitated for a moment. "It's a screen grab from her social media messages." I rocked back on my heels and pulled my new phone out of my pocket. It took me a moment to log into my account and pull the conversation I had with Daphne weeks ago. I shoved my phone at Lily.

She huffed a breath after a moment and shoved both phones into my hands. I compared the conversations. "She edited this. She fucking cut out huge swaths of the conversation to fit what she wanted to say."

Lily stood up and paced the living room with me. "I knew Daphne was the worst, but I thought it was reserved for me. This is disgusting, manipulative. Has she been like this Ava's whole life?"

I licked the front of my teeth, seething at Lily's assessment and nodded. "It's a safe bet."

I sat roughly down on my couch. "I need you to figure out where she is."

Lily nodded. "Jacob and Monroe are working on it. We'll find her. Have you talked to your mom?"

I shook my head. I was flying to Paris to spend the break with my maman. "I'll talk to her as soon as I know where Ava is. I'll change my flight around. I need to get to her. first"

Lily gave me a sad smile. "Will told me that you love her."

I nodded. "I do. I'm pissed as fuck she believed her fucking sister who has done nothing but lie to her for her entire life, but I get it."

Will burst through the door. He felt bad that he didn't stop Ava when she was here. He didn't know about what Daphne had lied about, and he regretted not trying to talk her through everything.

"How was the final, Peach?" Lily asked.

"Fine, just got off the phone with Jacob. Ava's in Italy. Her mom disowned her, dad is trying to talk Kim out of it, but he's been talking to Jacob about everything. My brother has been slowly trying to get information out of Ava. She's been pretty tight lipped about it because that's how she gets when she wants to be alone. She mentioned something about lemon trees, and he was almost positive he heard his nonna in the background. He called his nonna and confirmed."

Relief pulled through me at the knowledge that she *was* safe. She did go home. She went to the one place she had been wanting to go for years.

I nodded. "I'm packing my bags now." I stood up.

Lily moved away from the couch to greet Will. "I had my dad send his pilot here so when we found out where she was, we could go straight there."

I was so grateful for Lily for thinking ahead. "Thanks. I'll be ready to go in thirty minutes. Is the plane at Boulder Municipal?"

She nodded. "I'd like to go too," Will said.

I rolled my eyes. "I'm not breaking up with her. I'm not going to put up with you interfering. You're my friend, but she is the love of my life, so you need to deal with that."

Will held his hands up and nodded. "That's fair. I need to apologize to Ava. If I hadn't made it so difficult for her to come clean to me, we could have avoided half of this shit."

At least he's taking some responsibility.

"We leave in thirty," I repeated. Lily and Will shuffled out of the apartment as I ripped into my own bedroom. Clothes were tossed into my bag. I had partially packed for Paris, and I still intended to spend some of my break there, Ava was going to be with me. I snagged warmer clothes for her to use as well.

I sent my mom a quick message and headed to get my girl.

Ava

"Bella, I'm home," my nonna called from her front door.

I was laying in the grass in her backyard under her lemon tree. The weather was in the low sixties, warmer than Boulder, but too cold to swim in the navy waters that licked up the cliffs outside my nonna's home.

"I'm out here." I had been gone for two days. My flight to Naples was long and I'm sure I scared the middle-aged man that shared the row with me.

Since I only had a few more uses of my dad's credit card, I splurged on a first-class ticket. I spent the entire flight going between catatonic and crying silently. I numbly ate my food and as soon as I attempted to sleep the tears would fall.

I had done exactly what I told everyone I wouldn't do: I ran away. I didn't let anyone know where I was going, and while I felt bad about it, I was still trying to keep my lines of communication open.

Monroe and Jacob had called me a few times. I had messaged Lily back knowing she would get the messages to Will, Tama, and whoever else wanted to know that I was safe. Dad had sent me a few messages, mostly making sure I was okay after the fall out of everything. I heard from everyone in my life but Henry. I had blocked his number before I took off. I'd unblock him in a few weeks when I wasn't so emotionally raw.

My nonna was waiting at the airport when I landed. She scooped me into her arms and swayed me back and forth. Her citrusy scent and warm skin wrapped around me, making me feel at home.

I was practically her twin. She was my height and aging slowly and gracefully, making me appreciate the genes I inherited from her. I kept my sad tears at bay and shed a few happy ones at seeing my nonna after two years.

"Bella, what do you want for dinner?" She had spent the morning at her bakery. It was the riposo of the day, so her shop was scheduled to close, but she wasn't heading back for dessert patrons.

A lemon fell and thumped next to my head causing me to squeak and sit up. Nonna was smiling at me from her patio door of her bright turquoise house. "I made pizza dough. It's proofing now."

My nonna had a wood burning fireplace in her small backyard that was perfect for pizzas. The fireplace, like her home, was centuries old, and made the best pizza. "I forget you're American with your pizza addiction. Yes, Bella, we will eat pizza tonight. I have friends coming over. Do we have enough dough for five?"

I nodded. "You taught me to make enough food just in case. I was going to freeze the unused dough for later this vacation."

She grinned at me. "Tomorrow let's dine out. My friend has invited us to his restaurant to celebrate my Ava Bella coming home to me."

My heart warmed.

"Come inside, drink wine with me and help me bake a lemon cake." She turned back into her kitchen.

I grinned to myself. My whole world may be in upheaval, but at least I had my nonna. At least I had wine and cake and sunny days under a lemon tree to look forward to for the next three weeks.

Nonna was pouring me a glass of white wine as I made my way into her kitchen. She wagged her brows at me. "I've been looking forward to the day where you and I could drink wine and talk about life." She nudged my glass in my direction and pulled out the ingredients to make a cake.

"So, tell me, Bella, now that I have given you a day to settle in, what happened? I am so very pleased to see you, but I know what being here means. Your mother is like her father through and through, so I knew her promise that I would never see my grandchildren again was serious."

I twisted my lips to the side before I took a healthy sip of wine. "I'll tell you what happened to me if you tell me what happened to you," I countered. Nonna gave me a soft smile. She began sifting the flour with a thoughtful look on her face.

"Your mother and I didn't agree on something. She reacted strongly."

"I know, but what did you disagree about?"

She sighed and rubbed the tip of her nose with her wrist. I reached over and scratched the itch she was attempting to quell. "Grazie, Bella."

She looked up to me from her impossibly long lashes that never needed an ounce of mascara to enhance. "I offered to have you live with me. Your sister was a monster to you. You had just been weaned off your anti-depressants, and I heard Daphne saying terrible things to you. The whole time your mother and Daphne were in Paris I fretted about how I was going to broach the subject.

"They came back earlier than I anticipated. Daphne went right for your room while you were sleeping, even though she had no intentions of spending the night. I asked her to leave you to sleep. I followed them to their hotel to talk to your mother stating that I felt that you would be happier here with me. I may have implied that Daphne was not mentally stable." Her eyes flitted back down to the flour she had finished sifting.

She pulled some eggs from the basket on her counter. Her neighbor provided eggs in exchange for cake once a week.

My stomach twisted at the thought that my nonna lost her relationship with her daughter and grandchildren to protect me. I let out a shuddering breath. "She isn't mentally stable."

Nonna's brow rose high in a knowing way. "Is she the reason why you are here?"

I chewed on my lip and shrugged. "Yes and no." And then I started from the beginning and told her everything, even the parts that I skipped out on with my dad. From the move to Boulder to my duplicity in Dallas, falling in love with Henry, starting ballet again, and Daphne's warning that he was going to break up with me.

She grunted every time I repeated things that Daphne had said over the past few months. "Tell me more about Henry." She sat down after placing the cake in the oven.

I blew out a breath. "He's far too good for me and I think he was starting to realize it."

She hummed softly and drank her wine slowly. "Bella, you must know that no one is too good for you. And I have my doubts that Henry was planning on breaking up with you. Do you really believe a man that listened to you, gave you experiences that you will cherish, would reach out to your sister, to get advice on how to break things off with you?"

My molars pulsed into my cheek. "I saw the messages he sent her."

She rolled her eyes. "In this day in age a photo isn't enough proof. Daphne's degree was in digital art, is it not?"

I nodded. She waved her hands at me. "Wake up, Bella, she could have easily manipulated the images she sent you."

I shook my head. "But he told my parents where I was living."

She scoffed again. "I love your innocence and the way you believe the best in everyone. It is what makes you so beautiful and precious to me, but in this instance, I need you to consider that Daphne lied about that too."

"Then how did my parents find out?"

She waved a dismissive hand towards my phone and filled up my glass of wine. "The same way she found your boyfriend on social media. Ask yourself this, Bella, if Henry wanted you gone, then why was he encouraging you to audition and apply for the scholarship. You told me that Daphne asked to see your dorm, do you think it is possible she already thought you didn't live in Waco? I may be old and out of touch with all the technologies, but I know how people like Daphne work. It's the same way your mother and Nonno does. The world revolves around them and anyone not inline will be destroyed or dismissed." She tipped back her wine and laced her fingers in her lap.

"Ava Bella, I may not have met Henry, but the man you have described appears to be a man that loves you. So, tell me, between your sister and Henry, who is the more trustworthy? If you were in a coma, between the two, who would you want to make decisions on your behalf?"

My lip curled. "Daphne would pull the plug the first opportunity she had."

"There you go, Bella. I am not saying that Henry and you will last forever, but what I am saying is, Daphne lied to hurt you because she knew you were happy. Is that believable?"

The knot in my throat felt too thick to swallow let alone talk, so I nodded. She hummed to herself and sighed. "I'm sorry for what your mother said to you. I know firsthand how much that hurts."

I nodded again. "My dad is trying to talk to her."

She gave me a sad smile. "Your father is an interesting man. I have not spent too much time with him, but if he's anything like Jacob then he is a good person… deep down."

I snorted. My nonna never warmed to my dad because of the whole double life thing. "Maybe since I have broken the Nonna seal, Jacob will bring Stephanie and Taylor to visit you."

She smiled at me again. "I would love that. Maybe now I can finally meet Will. You've spoken so highly of him for years, but

I dared not invite him in worry of incurring your mother's wrath."

My stomach knotted again at the mention of Will. "He's mad at me for lying to him about being in a relationship with his friend."

Nonna rolled her eyes. "He'll get over it. He adores you, Bella. If Henry makes you happy, he will learn for it to make him happy."

I made a face.

"Or perhaps he'll ignore it is happening and save the peace."

I chuckled. "That sounds more like him."

She leaned forward and pushed a lock of hair away from my eyes. "Why don't you take a shower and get ready for our guests, Bella. They'll be here in about two hours. I'm going to nap when I take the cake out of the oven."

I nodded and sipped the rest of my wine back. "I'll stop by the store to pick up more cheese and toppings."

Nonna stood up and placed our empty glasses in the sink. "Shops will be closed for another hour. Shower, relax. Life will resume at 5pm."

My nonna's shower was dated with herbal plants in the stall that draped over the taps. I lathered my hair with the shampoo made by one of her neighbors. I wondered who we were hosting. My nonna regularly had guests for dinner. She met a lot of people through her bakery and always had friends coming into town.

My hair was getting too long to finger comb, dipping well below my shoulder. I rang the excess water out and selected a dress that was supposed to hit the knee, but on me hit mid shin. A light sweater kept my shoulders warm. I went outside to make sure we had enough wood for the pizza oven and picked a few ripe lemons for the curd that was going to be the filling between the layers of the cake we were making. Nonna was still napping so I made a frosting and curd, once those were setting and the shops opened back up from their riposo I headed towards the store.

I borrowed Nonna's bike that had a cute basket attached between the handlebars and glided down the hill.

Henry would love these hills.

My heart clenched at the thought of him. I had left him with zero note, making him fend off Will on his own. If everything Nonna said was true and Daphne did orchestrate my rift with Henry, then I was going to have to grovel when I got back to Boulder.

I filled the basket with pizza toppings that would make Nonna scoff, but I wanted to bring a little bit of American tastes for our Italian guests. Nonna had dressed in white jeans and a pink top. Her feet were bare as she started to assemble the layer cake together. Her long dark hair was down, cascading over her back like chocolate satin.

"Grazie Bella for making the icing and filling. It was perfect. Whoever taught you how to cook should have their own patisserie," she said cheekily. I grinned at her and started rolling out the pizza dough. The tomatoes for the sauce were simmering, and I chopped the ingredients for the toppings.

"Pineapple on pizza, Bella." She gently whipped my butt with her tea towel. "You might as well wear an American flag; it would be less obvious that my Italian Bella was raised in the States."

I giggled. Someone knocked on the door. "Bella, can you get that for me? I have icing on my fingers. Bring our guests to the backyard so we can start the oven." I wiped my hands and headed to the front door. "Ask what kind of wine they want," my nonna called from the kitchen.

I pulled the large wooden door open and smiled broadly like a welcoming host. The setting sun blinded me as I blinked up at the silhouettes of the three people standing at the door. Before I could see or greet our guests I was pulled off of my feet into strong arms against a chest, my head cradled. The air stopped in my lungs when I recognized Henry's heady scent.

"Babydoll," Henry breathed in my ear.

It had only been two days since I had last seen him, but it felt like a lifetime had passed. My eyes pricked as he peppered my face and neck with kisses.

"Put her down, Hank," Will grunted.

"Not until she knows Daphne lied, and I have no intentions of letting her end this," Henry murmured. I doubted it was loud enough for Will to hear. My heart was beating in a frantic rhythm, too happy and overwhelmed to be calm at Henry's words.

"You must be Will, you look so much like my Jacob," Nonna said behind me. Lily softly introduced herself.

"And you must be Henry," Nonna said a little louder. Henry kissed my jaw again before he set me down.

"I have heard so much about you." Henry reached his hand out to shake my nonna's hand. She batted it away and gripped his face to kiss both of his cheeks. "Likewise."

"Come, let's go to the backyard and make dinner. Ava Bella has prepared pizza dough and ingredients. Who is ready for food?"

Henry and Will raised their hands. Nonna beamed at both and looped one arm in Will's and the other in Lily's. "Come, let's give these two another moment to say hello."

As soon as they were out of sight, Henry gripped my cheeks again and kissed my mouth. His tongue gently swiped against my bottom lip as he tilted my head to get a better angle. He kissed me until my lungs burned. The kiss slowly ended in a series of pecks, and he leaned his forehead against mine. I panted into his mouth, catching my breath.

"Don't leave me again," he whispered. "You promised to never run away again. Promise me again and mean it this time because I've been going crazy for the past 45 hours."

"I can't promise I won't run away, but I promise I won't leave you behind." I chewed on my lip and slowly reached up to trace the red puckered skin of his eyebrow. A few butterfly bandages were layered on top of black stitches. He had a purple bruise to the side of his brow making his hunter green eyes more noticeable. I winced and dropped my hand. I had no doubt his busted brow and bruising were compliments of Will.

He smiled softly at me and kissed me again. "We will talk more about what happened later, but first I'm fucking starving."

I giggled against his lips. "We made lemon cake. The filling is the same filling in your favorite lemon bars."

He groaned and gripped my hand, tugging me towards the backyard where everyone else disappeared. "Come on Babydoll, I'm not ready to let you out of my sight yet."

Chapter 23

Henry

"Wake up, Babydoll, it's Christmas." The golden sunlight filtered into her bedroom at her Nonna's house. Her gorgeous brown eyes fluttered open as a sweet smile took over her face. She moaned and turned into my chest. "It's too early."

I surrounded her body with my arms and pulled her into me, kissing the top of her head. "Everyone will be here in an hour," I murmured against her ear. She whimpered.

We found out after we had landed that Monroe had borrowed another company jet to head to wherever Lily was spending her holiday, stating that she was over the ice-rain that had plagued Manhattan all winter so far. Their dad, Michael, was supposed to land today and spend the rest of the month at his resort a few miles away. Charlotte came a few days after Will arrived. She loved Ava like she was her own and wanted to spend more time with Will.

After Ava's brother Jacob found out that Will, Charlotte, Ava, Lily, and Monroe were all in Sorento he got a hella case of FOMO.

He packed up Stephanie and Taylor and headed to Italy to spend the holiday with his Nonna. Will had implied it was causing quite an issue in Pasadena when Kim found out, but Jacob was unapologetic about the whole thing. He'd been drinking his weight in limoncello with Ava and Nonna was hanging in there shot for shot.

Nonna was as cool as Ava had described and literally the best cook I had ever met in my life. She was like an aged-up version of Ava, and I was a lucky man to see how gorgeous she was going to continue to be in the future.

I had eaten my fill in every amazing dessert Nonna had in her cute patisserie. Her little cliffside bungalow was warm and bright, and I had never seen Ava so at ease in the entire time I had known her.

Between waking up with Ava wrapped around me, all the secrets out in the open, the warm weather, and my own mom deciding that an Italian Christmas was exactly what she wanted, this was easily the best holiday break I had ever had.

My mom had gotten in town two days after I had arrived and she loved Ava instantly. She agreed to stay through Christmas and then the three of us were going to spend New Years in Paris. Ava was so excited. I had already created an itinerary that Ava was going to love, showing her all the main sites and then a little of my favorite places to be in the City of Love.

Will was a little sour, but as soon as Jacob showed up, he had calmed down. It was like he could take off his big-brother-hat because the biggest brother was there to take over. Jacob was easy-going and cool. He found out that I was a bit of a gamer and had spent a few days trying to convince Nonna to let him install his X-box that he had brought. She was having none of it, which was for the best because there wasn't enough space in the living room for everyone to comfortably fit. Most of the time spent with all the guests were in her backyard that overlooked the cliffs, shaded by the lemon tree, drinking wine and talking about life.

We had spent a few evenings in Monroe's suite playing Fifa. I was warned that she was good, but I wasn't expecting *that* good. It was quite a combination of seeing a pregnant woman divulge into a cursing heathen as she kicked our asses over and over again. Then as soon as the game was over, she would perk up from her slumped posture and gracefully stand, cupping her belly and talk to Lily about school like she hadn't called us titty baby motherfuckers.

I tightened my arms around Ava again as she kissed my chest. Her thigh, that was between mine, shifted, lightly grazing my dick which was quick to salute the morning. She straddled my hips and braced herself against my chest. I perked my brow at her as she slicked my cock with her arousal.

Goosebumps followed my hand as I snaked my palm between her perfect tits and gently lifted the little tank top over her head. Out of respect to her nonna, Ava slept with a midriff tank that didn't hide one little pucker of her nipples, but it was there in case Nonna looked into the room. She hadn't and I doubted she would.

I licked my bottom lip back and forth as she shifted her hips and sank down on me. My eyes rolled back when she squeezed me as I bottomed out. And then she started to move her hips. She was writing me a message, but it was so hard to concentrate on what she was saying, fortunately it was the same message she always wrote.

I bit my lip trying to figure out what she was saying. The first word was Ava. My eyes flew open when I put it together. I gripped her hips to slow her down. Her riding me like it was her favorite thing to do was one thing, her telling me she loved me… *fuck.* I was going to blow my load, and I needed a moment to process her very deliberate message that she had been telling me for months.

Her brows puckered as I stopped her from moving with a biting grip and a lift. She leaned further forward, her hair creating a curtain around us. I looked into her eyes.

"You love me?"

A beautiful blush crawled across her chest up to her face as she pulled her cheek between her teeth. Her pouty lips were parted as she took in a sharp breath. Glassy eyes blinked the moisture away as she nodded once.

My palm cradled the back of her head as I brought her lips to mine in a crushing kiss. Our bodies flipped around, and I nestled myself into the cradle of her thighs and slowly pushed back in. I kissed her jaw, neck, chest, before I made my way back to her mouth. She ran her fingers through my hair and gently scratched my scalp, causing goosebumps to rise up my neck. My thrusts were slow, steady, driving us both crazy, but I wanted to make love to this fucking woman, so that was what I was going to do.

"Ava." She began to flutter around me. Her chest was arched, mouth parted in a silent cry.

"Eyes on me, Babydoll." Her pupils were blown wide as she looked up to me from her lashes.

"Tell me you love me."

She whimpered, catching her breath, before whispering, "I love you, Hen."

A satisfied shiver raced up my spine as I took her mouth again. When I finally came back up for air I whispered back, "I love you too."

She squeezed me impossibly hard which caused me to rut forcefully into her, chasing my orgasm that was tingling my body and making my mind go blank.

"Fuck, I love you." I spilled into her. My chest collapsed onto hers while I caught my breath. She peppered my neck and shoulder with kisses whispering her own love affirmations in my ear.

I don't know what I did to deserve this woman, but I was never letting her go.

Ava

"Mon Canard, Ma Lutine, I brought fresh croissants and coffee from around the corner. Wake up, my loves, it's a beautiful day," Juliette called from the hallway.

We had been in Paris for a few days. Saying goodbye to Nonna was hard, but I had the relief of knowing I could visit her whenever I wanted. She seemed satisfied with the offer from Henry for us to spend a few weeks with her over the summer, so it made my farewell less bittersweet.

Jacob, Stephanie, and Taylor were planning on spending New Years with Nonna, Charlotte, Will, Lily, Monroe, and Michael. And I would feel a little left out, but I was too excited to see and spend time with Juliette in Paris. The few days we had spent together in Sorento were so great.

Juliette was everything I wished for in a mother. I saw the tenderness that Henry tried to hide from the world come out with how she treated him. She was lovely and cool, smart, but not pretentious.

It was Henry's turn to whine in my ear as he felt forced to get out of bed. Not that I blamed him. I loved his bedroom at his mom's apartment. It had an amazing view of the Eiffel Tower in the distance and the bustling street below.

The bed was large, warm, and cozy. The little fireplace still had glowing embers from the night before. I sunk further into his embrace. I wondered what we were going to do this afternoon. It was New Years Eve, so we were heading to spend the holiday at the tower like true tourists. Juliette had scoffed and rolled her eyes, but she then gave us tips on which streets to avoid. She had warned us that most places were going to close around midday, so it was possible that today we were going to walk around the snowy streets and absorb the atmosphere.

He had already taken me to Notre Dame, the Louvre, and the Eiffel tower. He had also indulged me in a bike tour of the Seine, taking me to his favorite parks to chill out, and the sweetest little bakery that had the best chocolate croissants I had ever eaten. He wanted to take me shopping and to the Palace of Versailles, but that was going to have to wait until January 2 when everything was fully open.

I squeezed into Henry's ribs, and he delicately ran his fingers up and down my spine. "What does mon canard mean?" I asked after a beat of silence.

He chuckled lightly. "My duck."

I grinned into his chest. Of course that's what she called him. It was fascinating and sexy to listen to him speak French so fluently. Juliette spoke French half the time, English the other half, and Henry would answer in whichever language she spoke first. Sometimes the conversations would start in French and Juliette would switch to English as if remembering that I had no clue what was being said in front of me.

I rolled out of bed and pulled on a pair of sweatpants and Henry's hoodie. Juliette was sipping her coffee while reading a book in a cute little nook that overlooked the street below. She had fresh flowers in the kitchen and living room. There was a light blanket of fresh snow covering the streets and rooftops.

She grinned at me over the rim of her mug. She was so beautiful. Her blonde hair was long and tucked behind her ears, her black turtleneck looked chic tucked into her wide-leg black pants. Her shoes were discarded by the door; her bare toes were tucked under her knee. She was like an ad for cool-French-girl vibes. I would have found her intimidating if I hadn't gotten to know her over the past week.

She complimented my nonna and me for what seemed like hours every time she ate food we had made. Then as we flew to Paris, she shared cute Henry stories about how wild he was in his youth. Now, I knew she wasn't intimidating, she was effortlessly cool.

"How are you this morning, Ma Lutine?"

The first time she had called me that Henry was quick to laugh and say, "She is a little pixie, isn't she?" Juliette wasn't trying to admonish me for my height; she was too warm and kind to bully me.

I stretched my arms over my head and yawned. "I'm well, the bedroom is so comfy."

Juliette perked a brow; it was the same thing Henry did which made me smile. Henry didn't look like his mother, but she was evident in his facial expressions and demeanor.

"Mon Canard used to snuggle with me all the time. When he was seven, he would crawl into my lap before bed and ask me to hold him and scratch his back. Not much has changed, oui?"

I nodded. "Not much has changed."

She hummed into her mug of coffee and took another sip before setting it next to her discarded book. "You are good for him. I am happy you found each other."

My chest fluttered as I nodded quickly. It was an acceptance I was not expecting. All my life I had been wanting a mom to tell me that I was good enough. A weight had been lifted at hearing those words.

She gave me another assessing smile. "You keep him calm, happy. He was always my happy handful when he was younger. In his teens a little less happy but I took it as teenager angst, after I moved." She stopped and sighed. A pucker had formed between her brows. "Had I known accepting my job here would have derailed him, I wouldn't have done it."

I twisted my lips to the side as she quickly swiped below her eye.

"He doesn't blame you or regret anything. He told me about losing Harvard and that it worked out because he met me. Don't get me wrong, I understand your point of view, but I understand his too. He's happy, he's smart, and I know he'll be successful."

His bedroom door closed with a snick, effectively ending the conversation, but Juliette seemed a little lighter after, like all she needed was a small affirmation that she didn't mess Henry up.

One arm wrapped around my waist while my phone was dropped into my hand.

"Morning, Maman." He snuggled into my neck as Juliette spoke in French. He answered back which made goosebumps bloom.

I'm pretty sure I was developing a foreign language kink. Especially with Henry's husky sleep-ridden voice speaking French while nuzzling my shoulder.

"Your phone chimed with an email," he murmured against my neck. I had only set up one email address alert and it was for Mallory. I scrambled to access my email.

Dear Ava Reiser,

Congratulations and welcome to the Dance program within the Russett Bailey School of Performing Arts. We thoroughly enjoyed your audition and would like to also congratulate you on winning the Russett Bailey Athletic scholarship for the School of Performing Arts.

The Russett Bailey Athletic Scholarship is awarded to one student athlete a semester and pays the next school year in full. Please read the enclosed attachment for the rules of the scholarship.

We look forward to seeing you for the spring semester!

Mallory Burton
Head of the Russett Bailey School of Performing Arts

"I did it." I collapsed backwards into Henry's chest. My eyes welled with tears. He kissed the top of my head, having read the email over my shoulder. "I knew you would."

"What is happening?" Juliette asked.

"Ava was accepted into the program she wanted and was awarded a scholarship which is great because of all the things going on with her mom."

Apparently, Henry's mom was more than aware of our relationship and all the things I had attempted to keep from my family this semester. She was indignant about my mother's reaction but didn't comment much further than "selfish mother."

Juliette rose gracefully from her chair and wrapped me in a hug. She swayed me side to side. "This is wonderful, we will celebrate when the shops open back up, oui?" She kissed both my cheeks and let me go. Henry was quick to wrap me back in his arms.

"I'm so fucking proud of you," Henry whispered in my ear. My body was vibrating with pure joy. A few months ago, everything was uncertain, and my life felt hollow. Now I had a boyfriend I loved, an apartment in a city that I adored, a major that I was passionate about, and a found family with friends who liked me for me. I knew moving to Will's school was going to be an adventure, I had no idea it was going to change my life for the better.

Epilogue

Henry

Four and a Half Years Later

"**B**abydoll, I know it's a private jet, but we still have to keep our flight plans as close to the schedule as possible," I called through the bungalow door of the private villa we were staying at in Barbados. We had spent an awesome week celebrating Monroe's wedding in the Caribbean, but we had a flight to Paris we had to catch within the next two hours. Ava was still lounging in bed with a pillow over her face.

I'd blame myself because I wore her out, but I got as much sleep as she did, and I had been awake for an hour already. The past week had been an indulgence of late nights, sex, rum, and spending time with our close friends and family. It was a stress-free week that Ava had earned and needed. She had graduated a year ago and ever since she had been traveling as a ballerina, dancing with some of the biggest companies in the world.

Four years ago, she had asked me to film her dance so she could see where she could improve. I had already figured out the social media algorithms to make things go viral and I was testing it out with a video of her dancing. Every video I uploaded went mega-viral landing Ava with a massive following and people clamoring to see her dance in person.

She wasn't a conventional prima ballerina, but she was adored and loved around the world. She brought so much attention to the Russett Bailey School of the Performing Arts that they awarded her with a standard scholarship that she didn't have to audition for every year, making her schooling completely free. Which ended up being for the best because Ava became no-contact with her mom and sister after everything happened.

She still spoke with her dad, but it was strained for her sophomore year as he had to hide his financial support of his daughter. I guess it was an eye-opener about what a toxic cunt Kim was because he divorced her eventually. I didn't know the whole story because Ava didn't want to know. She found she was the happiest when she didn't have to think about Kim or Daphne, so I never pushed to find out the details of the demise of that particular marriage.

She had finished a two-month stay at the American Ballet Theatre in New York where we lived in Monroe's building. She let us stay in Lily's old apartment. Now we were headed to Paris for another two-month stint at the Paris Opera Ballet. My mom was thrilled that we were staying with her for the duration of the ballet Ava was starring in.

After Paris, we were taking the month of October off and relaxing with Nonna in Sorrento before she was contracted to play Clara in the Nutcracker for the The Royal Ballet in London. Come January she was taking another break and was still deciding between San Francisco and Melbourne as her next contract.

As for me, I was my own boss, so I could work whenever, wherever I wanted. I made all my money from the stock market and had been offered dozens of times to sell my algorithm to investment firms, but I refused. I understood that giving access to my work to a larger client base than one would mess up the results and effectively manipulate the market too much, making my algorithm useless.

"Ten more minutes," Ava whimpered from the bed. I sighed and gathered up the last of her clothes that were tossed aside in a bid to get naked as quickly as possible last night. I normally wouldn't care about us leaving on time, but I had a surprise that required us to keep our schedule.

"If you get up now, I will stamp your mile-high pass again *and* massage your legs for an hour."

She barely moved the pillow from her face and squinted at me. "And my feet."

I shivered and resisted the urge to curl my lip. You know what they don't tell you about ballerinas? They have horrifically abused toes.

"Your arches and heels only." I loved every inch of my girl, but her toes were destroyed and made me wince every time I saw them.

She grinned and kicked the covers off. I rolled my lips in at the sight of my perfect girl completely naked, tan lines so dark it looked like she was wearing a cream bathing suit. "Fine, you've got yourself a deal."

We finally made our way to the private hangar where the three ML properties planes were still parked. Lily and Will were heading back to their home in California in a few days with their adorable daughter Elise.

They were spending quality time with their niblings and siblings. All the babies at the wedding had made the topic of children come up a few times between me and my girl. We both agreed that we had plenty of time and that Ava's career took precedence over whatever procreation we wanted to do. She said she only had a few more years left in her legs and toes before she was going to want to 'retire' and open her own school. *That's* when she wanted to have 'fifteen baby Henrys'. I don't think I could handle my duplicate, but I'd be content with one more Ava.

"Fancy." Ava sighed as the flight attendant passed her a glass of champagne. We didn't always fly private. This plane I shared with Matt and my dad after I invited them to be investors in my little company. Matty owned 5% and my dad 10%. They both made enough that they could retire, but Matty loved his job with the Angels way too much to ever seriously consider it. And my dad was married to his job. It was better than his normal mail-order bride bullshit, at least his job wouldn't cheat on him and vice versa.

"We are in vacation mode, Babydoll. Let's live it up." I took my seat next to her and gulped back my own glass of champagne to ease some of the nerves that were starting to flutter in my stomach. I had big plans today and I wanted everything to go perfectly.

My legs felt like jelly by the time we finally landed. Henry made good on all his flight promises. I did feel a little bad because I was positive that the flight attendant heard us the second time which Henry promised to punish me for later. It *may* have been why I was a little more vocal than normal because I *liked* his punishments.

A private car was waiting to whisk us away to our next destination. I was jetlagged and exhausted, but Henry's excitement for the day kept me awake. I don't know where he stored all the energy because even though we screwed around three times on the plane and he only got three hours of sleep, he was still tapping his thigh with his fingers.

The sun was beginning to set which was fine by me because that meant that I was going to be able to sleep soon. I squinted at Henry when the car went a different way than we normally went when we visited his mom.

He clasped my hand as the car drove through Paris and then beyond. A grin spread across my face when I started seeing signs for Disneyland.

He had made good on that promise too. He had taken me to every major amusement park in the States and apparently, he was going to knock some of the Disney's off the bucket list this trip too.

When the driver pulled up the front gates Henry squeezed my hand. "I rented the park for the next two hours. It should be enough time to ride every ride."

My shoulders bounced in excitement. When he took me to Disneyland four years ago, he lamented on how ridiculous some of the lines were and that one of these days he was going to rent the entire park so we could enjoy everything at our own leisure. After that he had opted for VIP tickets every time, but this was next level crazy.

Everything was still lit up and beautiful, ride attendants were friendly and eager for us to ride as many times as we wished. We stopped in front of the castle and asked for our picture to be taken. I waited for Henry to loop his arm around my waist like he always did when we took pictures. When he didn't, I turned around to see what was taking so long.

My brow furrowed as my mouth parted in surprise. Henry was on one knee holding a diamond ring between his fingers. I was too shocked to hear what he was saying, but I knew what he was doing. I nodded rapidly, letting a few tears fall as he slipped the ring onto my finger.

I'm sure the photographer was capturing every moment of it, which was great because my mind was working like it was stop motion. One second Henry was on his knee, the next I'm in his arms and he's swinging me around before he's cupping my cheeks and kissing the breath from me.

I couldn't have asked for a more perfect proposal from the most perfect man. He made me the happiest I had ever been and now that joy would last a lifetime.

The End

I hope you have enjoyed Ava and Henry's story! Keep reading for a sneak peek into Tama and Rhys's story, The No Girlfriend Rule

The No Girlfriend Rule

Chapter 1

Rhys

I spotted her at the party before I had fully walked into the front door. I didn't see her the entire summer, which sucked. I missed her even though we talked multiple times a week. We shared the same online summer course and would compare notes via email. The first two weeks of the semester had been too busy to hang out, but that ended tonight.

Tama's smile spread across her beautiful face as she delicately tossed the ping pong ball across the table, sinking it with ease into the cup. The past year of being friends with Tama had been great.

She wasn't jealous of other women that would approach me while I hung out with her. She was funny as fuck with a dry sense of humor and a sneaky sarcasm that made you question whether she was joking or naïve. It was a toss up half the time.

She was homeschooled and didn't leave her small community until she was twenty when she started at Pineview. I had no idea when I met her that she was technically a freshman, but she was two years older than most incoming first years.

Her mom guilted her into staying in their little town until her uncle finally convinced her mom to let her leave the nest.

410

Because of her nontraditional schooling, she didn't always understand pop culture references, but she was always eager to learn.

She was compassionate and supportive of my baseball aspirations. She went to every home game and streamed most of my away games. It always gave me a thrill when I would get a message from her after an away game letting me know she was cheering me on from afar. She was the best friend I had ever had.

I have been a little problematic about sharing her with the rest of the male population. I loved hugging her. Her skin was always silky smooth and warm. And she gave the best hugs. Every party we would meet up at I would wrap her in my arms. I wasn't consciously cockblocking her, but when my teammates Reiser and Foust pointed it out I decided I needed to chill out.

Will Reiser and Matt Foust lived next door to Tama, so they knew her almost as well as I knew her. The only person that could rival me in their friendship with my girl was Henry, Matt's cousin. Henry Foust lived next door to Tama last year and much to my dismay was now her actual roommate after Will and Matt coupled-up with Tama's roommates.

I groaned when I saw Henry standing next to Tama. I didn't hate him, per se, but I didn't like him either. She was the nicest person I had ever met, and Henry was a dick. I wasn't jealous of their friendship, but I didn't want him to corrupt her either.

When I had a bad day, she was the first person that would try to cheer me up. When I was sick, she made me homemade soup and nursed me back to health. She never asked anything from me. And never once did I get the vibe that she was sexually interested in me, so it kept that temptation at bay. So far my experiment on whether men and women could be friends despite attraction seemed to be working out for me. While I was very attracted to her, my desire to keep her friendship at all costs overrode every twitch of my dick that I had for her.

I watched her float another ball into her opponent's cup. She was weirdly good at all drinking games. Beer Pong, she ran the table; flip cup was too easy for her; cage match, put her opponents to shame. She even kicked me and my roommates' asses in poker last year. The irony was she wasn't competitive. She didn't play sports growing up. As far as I know the only sporting events she watched were to cheer on someone she personally knew. There's also the fact that she was extremely unathletic.

She and I had walked from campus to my house on a few occasions, and she would huff and puff attempting to keep up with my longer strides. At one point I was worried she was going to have an asthma attack. I had to give her a piggie back ride to my house. She refused to walk in the snow, said it hurt her lungs to attempt to keep up with me. Not that I minded one damn bit. Having her wrap her legs around my waist was like having a warm, giggling backpack on.

I made a few strides over to the beer pong table. "There's my girl." I pulled Tama away from Henry's side and wrapped her in my arms. My fingers stroked the warm smooth skin of her back that was exposed when I lifted her off her feet in a bear hug.

Henry scowled in my direction before his expression lifted into a chilly smile that didn't reach his eyes. I grinned over to him.

"Henry," I said with the same cool tone he gave me time and time again. My smile was forced. I didn't want to fight with Henry or even show Tama there was tension between the two of us. I didn't want her to ever feel like she needed to choose between us.

"Rhys, how was your summer?" Henry asked me. He looked like he was also trying to be on his best behavior.

"Fine. I missed my best friend." And to drive the point home I buried my nose into Tama's neck. She always smelled so fucking good. Uniquely her like someone baked an apple pie while jasmine bloomed in the summertime. Sweet but earthy. I inhaled deeply. My fingers flexed around her waist. Like I predicted a year ago, my thumbs touched across her stomach and my middle fingers touched across her back.

She squealed as I accidentally tickled her and elbowed me playfully when I set her down. I had forgotten she was so ticklish.

"Don't try to distract me. Henry and I are trying to run the table."

She was well on her way to winning. Their opponents were losing badly. I tipped my chin up at Bennet who was playing against my girl. He tossed the ping pong ball and overshot the table. I wasn't surprised that he missed considering his eyes hadn't left Tama's tits. Which I deduced were real, and she was genetically blessed. I never asked but after a thousand hugs and a few sleepovers, I knew.

I wrapped my arms around her waist and pulled her against my chest. It was a claiming move that I had promised myself I would chill with, but Bennet's blatant staring was annoying me. I rested my chin against her shoulder. "I can't believe I didn't get to see you all summer. Tell me about your road trip you've been mentioning for weeks."

Tama wiggled her ass against my thighs. She wasn't trying to rub against me. It was what she did when she was loosening up to make her shot. The ball sailed into her target before she answered me. "It was an epic road trip with Henry. We hit up a bunch of national parks and Vegas."

Henry rolled his lips in to hide a smile. Annoyance rippled through me. She had always maintained that they were just friends, but a fucking road trip with only the two of them was some intimate shit. My jaw clicked as I schooled my reaction.

"That sounds like fun. Why wasn't I invited, again?" I was going for playful, but I was annoyed as fuck. My eyes flicked back over to Henry who was looking around, not paying the slightest attention to Tama. His eyes raked the party as his mouth grew into a tight line.

"Well, for one, we left when you still had two finals to take. Second, it was supposed to be an all-girls trip with Nicole and Lily, but I can never say no to Hen."

My jaw relaxed. It wasn't some romantic getaway where he was trying to stake his claim.

Henry's eyes continued to rove over the crowd before he excused himself to get a drink. I pulled my body around to Tama's side, keeping her close with an arm looped around her shoulder.

"Well, I fucking missed you."

She turned to me as I gave her my best impression of puppy eyes. She rolled hers and elbowed my ribs. "You're so dramatic."

I grinned down at her as Henry came back. He passed her a beer and whispered something in her ear. She glanced over her shoulder before squinting at him and nodding.

"Be right back. Henry, Rhys, play nice." She turned away from the table before lightly tossing the ball into Bennet's last cup. It sank in dead center, and the crowd surrounding the table erupted in cheers.

"Fuck, she's awesome." I whispered, but Henry was close enough to hear me. He agreed with me before his eyes tracked to where Tama was ascending the steps to the bedrooms.

A swirl of anxiety made my stomach clench. If she was going upstairs, then it was to check out if there was a free bedroom. Since I knew she wasn't checking for my benefit, it meant she was checking for Henry's. The last person I wanted her in a relationship with was Henry. He would definitely try to limit my friendship with her.

I gripped the stack of used cups and reset the triangle as calmly as possible. "What's going on with the two of you?"

Henry's lip curled in disgust as he shook his head. His reaction calmed me down. It was not how I would have reacted.

"She's my roommate and friend. What's going on with the two of you?"

This fucking question again. I had to justify my friendship to my former and current teammates as well as my roommates on more than one occasion.

Nate Winthrop, aka Whinny, and Nathan Thomas had been my teammates and roommates for a few years. They knew Tama and asked me several times last year. I don't know why it was unfathomable that we were just friends, but it was always met with skeptical looks.

I braced. "She's my friend too."

Henry was looking worriedly over his shoulder and back to the stairs. Which made me second guess his lip curl from earlier. "So there's nothing romantic going on between the two of you?"

He rolled his eyes. The lip curl was back. He shook his head. "No, there isn't. If you want something to happen between the two of you, you better piss or get off the pot. You're stringing her along, and it's fucking shitty."

I saw red at the insinuation. We were friends. I was so fucking sick and tired of everyone assuming I was the one that didn't want her. If anything it was the other way around. Given the chance to have no-strings-attached sex with Tama knowing it wouldn't affect our friendship, I would every day that ends in Y.

I swallowed down the bitter pill and held my hands up. "I'm not stringing her along. She's my friend, nothing more. Actually, I told her I was going to help her find someone suitable for her this year."

We talked about it after class. She mentioned how both her roommates last year are now in relationships, and it made her want to see what the big deal was. It was a surprise to me. I had assumed she was like me with her drive to succeed.

She took a heavy school load, didn't take a break even in the summer, opting for online courses. I figured she saw relationships as distractions she didn't want to deal with.

He made another shitty comment like he didn't believe me. Thankfully Tama came back before the conversation could escalate to throwing fists. Henry's jaw tightened as he had another whispered conversation with Tama and then turned on his heel to storm upstairs.

Tama turned her warm brown eyes to me and squinted. "Why do you look annoyed?"

I shrugged and took a gulp from her beer and passed it back to her. She rolled her eyes and sipped after me.

"Your friend doesn't like me."

She smirked and shook her head. She lightly tossed the ball, and it landed dead center again in the middle of the triangle of cups. "My friend is recovering from a concussion. He's probably grumpy because he has a headache."

My stomach twisted. Henry had been attacked in an alley last semester. His cousin Matt and Will, my former teammates, intercepted to keep the guys from killing Henry. Matt's arm was too fucked up to draft which was a bummer for him. But now he's an assistant coach and the scout for our baseball team so not all was lost. Henry was hospitalized and placed in a medically induced coma for a few days. Tama was a wreck about it.

The night of his attack she ended up sleeping in my bed. She was too emotional and worried to be by herself. Her cop uncle kept her up to date on the case, so she knew while Henry was still in the hospital that he was targeted and attacked with the intent of causing serious harm. I held her until she fell asleep three nights in a row before she felt ready to sleep in her own bed again.

Guilt niggled at me. Tama's eyes moved to look beyond my shoulder. Her jaw loosened as her eyes widened. I glanced behind me to see Henry marching towards us with a cute brunette clutching his hand. She was as small as Tama and had the type of pretty face that made you certain someone had already claimed her. My brow perked at the way Henry's fingers had laced into the brunettes.

I tried to get a gauge on the situation. Introductions were made as I assessed Ava (the brunette) and Henry. I came to the easy conclusion that Ava was Henry's. She may not have known it, but it was blatantly obvious that he wanted her and he wasn't going to let anyone else near her. It was how he kept her close, constantly touching her. He arranged how she was standing so his body blocked her from the rest of the party. It was possessive.

I chuckled to myself. Fifteen minutes ago I was positive that Henry wanted to fuck Tama, and now after seeing him with Ava,

I understood. He saw Tama as more of a sister. I didn't have to worry about him trying to keep her away from me.

The four of us played together for the rest of the night before Henry decided it was time to go. I wanted Tama to come home with me and spend the night. I didn't expect anything sexual to happen, but I missed her. We had a lot of catching up to do and my favorite way to fall asleep was talking to her.

I begrudgingly hugged my friend goodbye, asking her to call me when she got home. I left shortly after them. Or at least I tried to. I was stopped by a few girls that called out my name and wanted my dick. Any other night I would have been more than ready to oblige, but I was too tired to take them up on their offers for a threesome.

It was my senior year. My last season to buckle down and prove to the baseball world that I was ready to play professionally. It meant I needed to stop fucking around. Even the ending of my friends with benefits situation was more dramatic than I cared for. I wasn't going to go on a sex ban, per se, but I was going to be a hell of a lot more selective this year. One thing I noticed last year was even the most 'low drama' girl had issues with my friendship with Tama. They'd be dismissive of her, rude, or act like jealous children. I had no patience for that shit this year.

"Call me," Lydia mouthed to me as I was leaving.

Not fucking likely. Been there, done that. Too much drama. First she was shitty to Tama, which I ignored for far too long. Then she flaunted Henry around me to make me jealous. She told me that she didn't want anything serious, that we were like-minded. And I believed her until she started showing up to my place unannounced. She complained about my lack of availability. I had baseball practice and workouts. Then she friended my mom on social media.

Maybe Henry did me a favor.

I made the two-block walk to my place. Whinny (Nate) was drunk as fuck in the kitchen with a girl making a mess. It looked like she was trying to make fried rice if the spilled eggs and rice kernels all over the counter were any indication.

Whinny gave me a lazy grin and saluted me as I took the steps to my room. Nathan's door was propped open. He was at his desk, headphones on. It looked like he was finishing his homework.

I kicked off my shoes as I walked into my room and pulled my shirt overhead. I paused as the chest of my shirt went over my nose. Tama's apple jasmine scent had etched into the cotton. I hummed to myself as I sniffed it again and tossed my shirt into the corner. I walked into my attached bathroom. I won a bet between my roommates and was given the bedroom with an ensuite; a perk I had no interest in ever giving up.

My shower was quick as I washed the stench of the party off of me. My phone pinged with a text as I wrapped the towel around my waist. I grinned at Tama's name.

Tama

I debated on whether or not to send Rhys a message that I had gotten home. I had noticed a fair amount of looks his way throughout the night. My friend was a hot commodity, and the clamoring female population did *not* like that I was in their way. It was the second reason why I wasn't always comfortable with his affections. The first being, it's confusing. I knew he wasn't interested in me *like that*. But his body language with me told a different story.

It made me public enemy number one in the eyes of all the Rhys Goodman fans. I had endured enough sneers in my direction to last a lifetime all from being his friend. But he was worth the momentary discomfort of seeing his fan's hateful side.

He was… the best. Mostly. Behind Henry, he was the best. I guess he was the second best, but I didn't have any romantic feelings towards Henry, so maybe they were in two very different categories.

I typed out a message and then erased it. It was likely he was in the process of hooking up with one of his many fans. I knew the moment I left the hyenas would swarm and he would be busy with choosing who was going to see his penis.

I tried to not be jealous of the lucky girl. He had made it clear he didn't want that with me. He had too many opportunities to seal the deal and never did. And I was happy to be his friend. It was rewarding. He was kind and funny. There was a tenderness about him that he didn't let a lot of people see. I may not have been around a lot of men in my life, but I recognized Rhys' tendency to soften when it was just the two of us.

I grew up in a retirement community and my mother homeschooled me. My first experience when people my own age was after I turned twenty. My mom and I lived where she worked as the activity director and taught a sewing and knitting class to the senior citizens of Hemet's Friendly Village Retirement Community. The youngest male I interacted with was my Uncle Beckett, and he was still twenty-five years older than me. He's my dad's brother. He became the male figure in my life when my dad died.

My dad was a teacher and protected his classroom before launching himself on a shooter. He was the only one who perished, and he died a hero. I was four so my memories of him are murky at best.

After his death, my mom snapped, and my safety became her number one priority. No public school for me, and since I lived in a retirement center no young people to interact with until I left for college at twenty. Without Uncle Beckett's support I wouldn't have been able to move away from home. Beckett and my mom married over the summer.

They admitted to me that they had been romantically involved for the better part of ten years. First it was about grieving together after losing my dad, Beckett's brother. Then it turned into real romantic feelings that they fought out of guilt. Next was the realization that they couldn't fight it anymore. And finally coming clean to me that they loved each other and wanted to get married.

He had already spent the night most nights so not much had changed in that regard. And had my mom not skimmed over the sex education chapters of my homeschooling (and threatened my neighbors not to teach me about sex) I would have been able to put together on my own that they were having sex nightly; however, I didn't know what sex was until last year when my roommates and Will explained the birds and bees to me.

We watched porn and Will showed me his penis. None of it was sexual for me at the time. I was too embarrassed to have been so naïve, so it wasn't erotic.

I went down a rabbit hole on attraction after that night. Up to that point in my life I hadn't experienced true attraction. Don't get me wrong, Will, Matt, and Henry are attractive men, but I never felt that stomach-tightening tingle. Then I met Rhys, and it was unexpected and confusing.

By the time I got home from my class, my thighs were damp to the point where I worried I started my period. Which would have been unfortunate as the only times I wore underwear was when I was on my period. It was a practice my mother had taught me. Good vaginal health meant fresh air and natural fibers when under garments were necessary.

I was certain the sticky residue that coated my thighs was blood. Nope it was arousal, straight up chemical reactions to procreate. It was fascinating. Since that moment only a few men had pulled that reaction out of me. I chalked it up to pheromones and my body's ability to sense the right amount of testosterone. At the end of the day, that is all that sexual attraction is, chemical reactions to stimuli. My stimuli came in the form of a certain 6'3 first baseman with brown hair, blue eyes, and a square jawline that made him look like a young Henry Cavil.

I whimpered at my phone. Rhys asked me to call him when I got home. I couldn't bring myself to do that. If he answered and I heard a girl in the background my heart would crack a little more at the knowledge that he didn't want me like that. Or worse, he didn't answer at all because he was too distracted by whatever the girl was giving him.

I tossed my phone on the bed and took a quick shower. My apartment was built for roommates. Every bedroom had its own private bathroom. They were small, but efficient. And after the horror stories my roommates Lily and Nicole had shared about getting athlete's foot from the communal shower, I was grateful to not have to share my space.

My phone sat innocently on my bed before I scooped it up. If I didn't send Rhys some sort of message he might worry, and I didn't want him to do that.

Me: I'm home. Sorry I didn't text sooner. I needed to shower.

There. That was short and to the point. If he didn't respond, no big deal. It was late. The party I had left was loud and crowded. He probably wouldn't even feel his phone buzz in his pocket.

My phone vibrated in my hand. I bit into my smiling lips as Rhys's handsome face flashed across my screen. He was FaceTiming me. I took a deep breath and settled against my pillows.

"Hey," he said with sleepy eyes and a smiling face before his brows pinched. "Are you naked?"

I glanced down and cringed. "Not really. I'm in a towel." I squinted at him. "But you aren't wearing much more."

He chuckled, his bare chest flexed. "That's fair." He hummed and then turned on his side, propping his phone on his nightstand, freeing his hands. I did the same thing. We video chatted most nights.

"Do you want to put your pajamas on?"

I looked back down at my towel. "Give me a minute. Tell me about your day while I get dressed." He chuckled as I stood up. I listened to his deep voice rumble.

I heard a little clatter as I dropped my towel and figured it was Ava in her room. I rifled through my drawer as Rhys' voice cracked and got deeper. I giggled to myself. *He must be very tired if he was losing his voice.* I bent over and pulled my wet hair into a knot.

"Uh Tama?" Rhys said after a quiet moment. His voice sounded strained.

"I'm still here."

My long hair was heavy and stubborn as I twisted it around itself and looked at my bare toes while still bent over.

I wonder if Ava would get pedicures with me.

I slipped the t-shirt that Rhys had let me borrow over my head.

"Yeah, I know," he drew out the last word before sucking his breath in through his teeth. "I think your phone fell over. I can see you."

I whipped my head into the collar of the shirt and swung my body around. Sure enough my phone had dropped from my nightstand and into my shoe. It was standing up and filming me from the floor. It took a moment of stunned silence for me to gather what happened. My cheeks heated as I yanked the hem of the shirt over my chest and covered my bare body. I had no doubt he had an uninterrupted view of my naked self.

"Oh my god, Rhys. I am so sorry. It was an accident."

His pupils nearly took over the light blue of his eyes. He shook his head and cleared his throat. "No need to apologize for an accident. I didn't want you to... uhhh...." He swallowed thickly. "Think I was watching you without your consent."

My brows pinched together. I could feel my embarrassment from the tips of my ears to my toes. No one had ever seen me naked as an adult before. I covered my face with both of my hands. *Oh god, I had bent over.* He probably had a straight view right into my vagina as I pulled my hair into a bun. *At least Lily had insisted on those brazilian waxes.*

424

I whimpered into my palms.

"It's not a big deal, Tama. It's not like you were trying to seduce me. And it's not like I haven't seen a naked woman before."

I peeked at him from my fingers. His pupils were still huge as he licked his bottom lip over and over again. "If it's any consolation prize your tits are perfect. Way perkier than I thought they would be braless. Also do you always sleep without panties? Wait, don't answer that."

He sounded flustered so I dropped my hands and took a deep breath. "Thank you for the compliment, and no I don't sleep with panties. I rarely wear them."

Rhys' eyes widened as his lips parted in a quick intake of air. Then he puffed his cheeks out. "We have to change the subject," he said abruptly. I rolled my eyes to the ceiling and agreed.

"I think Henry has a crush on Ava."

My assessment did the trick to get my mind off the fact that I had not only flashed my friend. I'm pretty sure he saw my insides when I bent over.

I crawled under my quilt and nestled around until my covers surrounded me. Henry called me a cover hog. Rhys didn't share the sentiment. Every time I woke up next to him, he was sharing as many covers as I had.

Henry and I had shared a few beds during our roadtrip over the summer. One thing I had learned about Henry was that he ran hot and turned the AC way down in all the hotels we had stayed in. That meant that I bundled to survive. He referred to me as a human burrito.

Our conversation flowed away from Henry and Ava and into how hard we thought Advanced Human Anatomy was going to be. His voice became deeper and more rumbly until he fell asleep. I liked looking at him while he slept. His face was relaxed and handsome. There was a sweet innocence about him that didn't show when he was awake.

I let myself stare at him for another minute before I disconnected our call. This is what we did most nights when we were both available to talk.

I flipped on my back and sighed, embarrassment heating my cheeks again. *I can't believe he saw me naked.* I felt confident it was a moment that would haunt me the rest of my life.

Acknowledgement

A million thanks to everyone that has read this book. I hope that you enjoyed it as much as I enjoyed writing it. Please leave a review and share. Reviews are the lifeblood of an author.

About The Author

DB Jacobson

DB Jacobson is an American romance author. Her favorite writing companions are her dogs. She loves writing in the romance genre, but has branched into women's detective, romantic comedies, and sci-fi romance. She was born in the South and currently lives in Southern California. She often uses her experiences within those distinctly different cultures to guide her characters.

To get into touch with DB check out her website at www.dbjacobson.com

TikTok: DBJacobsonwrites
Meta: DBJacobsonwrites

Books In This Series

Pineview University

What are the Odds

Matt is a senior with big league hopes. The only distraction he is willing to take on is finding her. A year ago, he ran into the perfect woman at a party. The problem? She was there was a total cheating jerk. He spends a year looking for her only to discover that she is in the math class he is a TA   for.

Nicole is a sophomore that wants to focus on school because she spent her freshman year getting her heart broken by unfaithful jocks. Going into her second school year she is resolute in refusing to date another jock again. It's only a little complicated that the one jock she is willing to   break   her   rule   for   is   her   TA.

Stressful, right? It doesn't help that some jerk keep stealing her
parking   spot   and   making   her   life   a   living   hell.

What are the odds is a steamy college romance. Tropes: enemies   to   lovers,   second   chance,   baseball,   forced proximity.

The Girlfriend Contract

Will just graduated school and has to attend his half-sister's wedding in Barbados. It doesn't help that Will does not get along with the bride or her mother. To make matters worse the maid of honor is 'the one that got away' and she is attending with her new boyfriend that Will suspects was the reason for their breakup.

Lily is Will's neighbor and friend. In a moment of weakness, she agreed to go to the wedding with Will. She knows all about Will's toxic ex, step-mother, and half-sister, so she's going and pretending to be Will's doting girlfriend.

The problem? Oh, just that she has a massive crush on Will and has for months. She just hopes she can get through the wedding with her heart intact.

The Girlfriend Contract is a young adult steamy romance. Tropes: fake relationship, vacation fling, forced proximity, one bed, friends to lovers.

Best Laid Plans

Henry is the reclusive dom who is recovering from a violent attack that ended his cousin's career before it even started. He's been busy trying to cope with the guilt of the attack and healing from a concussion. The last thing he wants to do is do anything that would jeopardize his friendships with the very people that saved his life.

Ava is Will's half-sister and just wants to escape the abusive shadow of her mother and sister. She lies to her parents about what school she is attending just so she can live her own life and be closer to Will.

Being only eighteen and doing everything on her own means she didn't know she needed to sign up for student housing. Luckily Will and Lily would never allow Ava to be homeless so they set her up with a place to stay.

The problem? Her roommate is Henry and he is without a doubt the most gorgeous man she has ever met. It make matters worse she's 'off limits' but that doesn't stop her from crushing on her brother's friend.

The Best Laid Plans is a steamy college romance. Tropes: brother's friend, roommates, forced proximity, dom/sub, first time.

Books By This Author

The Missing Girls

A human trafficking ring is terrorizing the young women of LA. In the meantime, Caroline gets roped into helping a new friend find a missing person, who just might be the key to figuring out the trafficking ring.

Catching the Killer

A serial killer is on the loose in Southern California. Caroline works tirelessly to figure out who is guilty, so another woman does not fall victim to the SSS. While balancing her usual life with her nighttime investigations, her mysterious friend, Beck, keeps showing up when she least expects it. There is nothing like being attracted to a mystery man knowing there is no way for reciprocation.

Broad Day Gone

If a guy you were interested in a guy and they said you can't be with him until you knew who he was, you would invest the time to figure out who he is, right? Caroline finds herself compelled to take a deep dive into the mysterious

Beck's background. She wants to figure out why he is so prone to believe he is not someone that can be loved

Running by Flight

Reeling from a break-up, Caroline is deep in a reckless well of depression. She is no longer careful with her investigations, putting herself in a perilous situation with a known rapist. After barely escaping, she is forced to face the one person that she is not ready to face. She is not ready for closure from her heartache, so she leaves before any confrontation could begin. There is nothing like a chase around the world and a good cold case of a missing woman to get Caroline back into the groove of life.

Dancing by Gaslight

Just when Caroline thinks she can put the whole human trafficking ring behind her, she gets roped right back into it. She gets tapped by an agency wanting to use her skills and her position as a board member from her bequeathed shares of KE. While investigating in Japan, she quickly learns what exactly Beck was doing during their six-month break-up and finds that something may still be going on with a gorgeous director of KE. Nothing like the crumbling of a personal life to complicate a professional one.

Chasing the Huntsmen

Grappling with the fall-out from the human trafficking ring, Caroline is trying desperately hard to rescue the women that were stolen and sold. After a particularly difficult extraction, she is forced to take a break from the gloom and doom of the victim's eyes. Just when she thinks she will be able to move past the depression that is looming over her head, a loved one is taken in an orchestrated scavenger hunt. Caroline is compelled to follow the clues, while being haunted by her past.

Dealing with the Devils

After running away from her life so she can find her center again, she returns home to realize that Beck is gone. She makes deals with two devils to find where Beck has hidden himself in the world. From the jungles to Colombia to the museums of Prague, she works tirelessly to get back to Beck. It gets complicated when she meets a man that is the spitting image of her late husband, John. Which would you choose: a man that ran away from you or a man that reminded you of the first love of your life?

To Have, Hold, Hide

Caroline and Beck are finally together again. Life is going great! Caroline and Beck are both expanding their businesses. Everyone is getting along in Caroline's large family, life couldn't be better. Beck even surprises her with her dream wedding and dream honeymoon. But just like any dream, when it's time to wake up, reality isn't always kind. She is confronted with an enemy she has wronged. She has to choose between staying with Beck and letting him know about what really happened in Prague. The decision is made when Roman is threatened, leaving Beck again without a trace.

Burning the Lead

Recovering from being brainwashed in the Russian reprograming camp, Caroline wants to get back to life as usual. An old friend needs her skills looking into a cold case of a missing child. It doesn't take long before she has dug a little too deep and finds herself in the crosshairs of hitman eager to finish a job he started a decade ago.